BIRD ON THE WING

A Tallyforth Mystery

Bob Bibby

PIERREPOINT

PRESS

First published in Great Britain by Pierrepoint Press 1999.
Copyright © Bob Bibby

Lyrics from *The Mighty Atlantic* and *Meadhan Oidche Air An Acairseid* written by C. & R. Macdonald, by kind permission of Chrysalis Music Publishing Ltd [© 1995]. Lyrics from *Crazy Love, Friday's Child* and *Bright Side of the Road* written by Van Morrison, by kind permission of Warner Chappell Music Ltd, Carlin Music Corp., and Exile Publishing Ltd./Universal Music Publishing Ltd [© 1979] respectively.

Cover design by Barry Perks Graphic Design

A CIP record for this book is available from the British Library.

ISBN 0 953319 61 X

Typeset, printed and bound in Great Britain by York Publishing Services Ltd., 64 Hallfield Road, Layerthorpe, York.

To Joanne and Alison and all our
Western Isles ancestors.

With special thanks to
Cailean Maclean

Speed bonnie boat like a bird on the wing
"Onward" the sailors cry;
Carry the lad that's born to be King,
Over the sea to Skye

ONE

Hebridean Bird-watching Cruise - escape the rat race and relax with us on our bonnie boat, as we speed slowly along the beautiful coast of Western Scotland. See majestic Golden and Sea Eagles. Enjoy the sight of oystercatchers, razorbills, cormorants, fulmars, kittiwakes. Watch the sun set on the isles. Experienced skipper and wife offer holiday of a lifetime to discriminating guests. Reply to Box 2367.

After the year he'd had, Tallyforth had needed a holiday that took him away from everything.

First of all, there'd been that business with his daughter, who had decided against all advice to take a job offer in Zambia through V.S.O. He'd argued with her, of course, pointing out to her that she was only half way through her university course and was throwing away a chance he wished he had had at her age but as usual she had stuck to her guns and insisted she knew what she was doing, knew the risks, knew how to look after herself, knew it would be good for her. And in the end, there was nothing he could say or do to dissuade her and two months ago, in June, she had left.

Since then there had been two letters and one phone-call, all confirming, in her view at any rate, the wisdom of her decision. Yes, she was safe and sound. Yes, she was healthy and well. Yes, she was keeping a diary and a photographic record of her time in Zambia, so that everyone could see what she had experienced. No, there was no warfare near where she was. Yes, there was a lot of disease, including Aids, but much of it was down to poor nutrition and even poorer education. And in any case she had had all the necessary vaccinations before she left England. No, it was unlikely

1

that she would be home for Christmas - the contract was for a full year and she wanted to see it through completely. Wasn't that the whole point of V.S.O.? To be a part of a community and to help it by being part of it, living with its people and sharing their life? Not to come flying home to western luxuries when the going got tough?

All this in response to his questions over the phone and in the letters he had sent back to her. He had tried, but failed, to come to terms with her absence. He had reasoned to himself that when he was her age - twenty - he had already served two years in the police force and witnessed enough of the evils of human beings. He had reminded himself of the first dead body he had seen when he was just nineteen and was called to a road accident, where the squashed and bloody corpse of an eight-year-old boy lay halfway across a zebra crossing - the victim of a hit-and-run driver who, it transpired when he was eventually caught two hours later, had no insurance and no driving licence and was still drunk. He had recalled the numerous domestic incidents in the high-rise flats which had been part of his beat in those early years - incidents which had normally resulted in violence of one sort or another and had led to one or other of the wrangling partners having to be taken off to hospital to have the resulting bloody wounds stitched. He still was able to visualise the battered features of the seventy-five-year-old man in the terraced house who had been robbed of two pounds by a couple of teenagers desperate for drugs money.

But it had been no use. Although he could rationalise thus, he could not rid himself of that paternal longing to protect his young. So he had learned to live with the constant anxiety that the next communication would be a telegram announcing that his daughter had been murdered by guerrillas.

Then, there was the situation with George Elliott, or Detective Sergeant Georgina Elliott as she was properly known. They had worked well together for some time but then things had begun to get too personal. It had really started at the Van Morrison concert at the N.E.C. in Birmingham in the summer of 1996, although he had to admit their relationship had been growing closer over quite some time. He had believed, foolishly he now realised, that this was no more than the natural closeness of two people who

2

professionally shared so much. They had become a good team, he knew. They worked well together. They each brought different skills to their work - she with her methodical approach and careful attention to detail, he with his greater reliance on intuition and on breathing in the air around a crime to enable him to see the fuller picture.

But then, when his daughter - now in Zambia - had turned down his offer of a ticket to the Van Morrison concert for her birthday, on a whim he had asked George Elliott if she would like the spare ticket and she had accepted. And that's where it had all started.

At first Tallyforth had been flattered. He had been on his own for several years now, throwing himself into his work more and more. From time to time it had crossed his mind that he might like to try again to form some sort of lasting relationship but he was by nature a loner and the hours he worked didn't make it easy to maintain any relationship. But with George it seemed so easy. At first, that is. Their working hours inevitably were virtually identical. They both enjoyed eating out, taking the opportunity whenever they were on a case to explore the local eateries. In many ways their professional relationship was already symbiotic and, he had to admit to himself, it had crossed his mind before now that there might be possibilities between them. So, when on that first night, as they strolled arm-in-arm through the N.E.C. car-park back towards his Range Rover, she had asked him why he was so locked up emotionally, he had been at first surprised, then flustered, and finally relieved. He had been denying himself for too long.

So, it had started and so it had continued for the next twelve months. But then there had come a time when he had had to call a halt. Even now, if challenged, Tallyforth couldn't say why but something inside him, some wriggling bit of uncertainty and discomfort, had made him pull back. He had said it was affecting their work, though he knew it wasn't.

'No regrets,' he had said to her, at the end.

'Don't bloody Edith Piaf me!' she had snapped back.

'George, I only meant....'

'Yes, I've heard it before,' she had said, still angry. 'You shouldn't have started this, you know.'

'But it was you...'

3

'You invited me to that bloody concert!'

'But you knew why,' he had tried to reason. 'Only because my daughter...'

'You and your bloody daughter!'

And she had stalked off. They had avoided each other for a week. And when they had finally met up again, interestingly she hadn't disagreed with the separation. Perhaps, he mused, she had been feeling the same uncertainty and discomfort. At any rate, things between them had cooled. She had taken some long overdue leave and gone to visit an aged relative in Ireland, while he had got on with work in the Mercian Police Force's headquarters in Birmingham.

The final straw had been Chief Superintendent Albert 'Nobby' Clarke summoning him to his office one day and telling him that he was proposing to second him to the Home Office for six months to work on a new crime force that the recently-elected Labour government was putting together. All this talk of zero tolerance of crime from the new Home Secretary had caused Tallyforth to grin wryly, when he'd seen the reports on the TV news programmes. He'd been a copper too long to believe that crime could ever be stopped. The roots of evil were too deep in some people, he knew. They would never be eradicated by mealy-mouthed, well-meaning politicians. And the thought of having to spend six months in London, desk-bound, arguing with civil servants and the like! Tallyforth had recoiled from 'Nobby' Clarke's proposal.

'You've been looking peaky lately, Tallyforth,' Clarke had said, as he sat magisterially in his clean-cut uniform behind his all-too-neat desk. 'You need a change of scenery. You're my most experienced Detective Chief Inspector and the new government claim that they don't just want to hear what the Met. people have to say about policing. It'll do you good and it will be good for the Mercian Force's voice to be heard.'

'Sir,' Tallyforth had replied, 'that's not what I'm good at and you know it. I'm a detective and I solve crimes, particularly nasty ones like murders. That's what I am and that's what I do. Don't send me off to London to waste my time listening to nonsense. I'd be worse than useless in that sort of environment. And you know it.'

Tallyforth and 'Nobby' Clarke had never really got on, even

though they had both been working in the Mercian Force for many years and had risen through the ranks simultaneously. Neither was the other's idea of what a good copper should be. Clarke believed in order and systems and efficiency, while Tallyforth believed in intuition, in following loose ends, in trusting his instincts whatever problems that got him into. But both had cause to be grateful to the other - Clarke because of Tallyforth's clear-up rate and Tallyforth because Clarke covered for him with the Chief Constable.

So Tallyforth suspected there had been some office tittle-tattle about Elliott and himself and that Clarke had been reacting in the time-honoured way - seeking to resolve the problem by removing the offending article, in this case Tallyforth, from the environment for a period.

But he had been determined to resist.

'Sir, I'd like to request a month's extended leave,' Tallyforth had said. 'I'm due that much at least from the hours I've been working this last six months.'

Chief Superintendent Albert 'Nobby' Clarke had looked at Tallyforth through his cold, steely eyes. There had been a pause.

'Right, Chief Inspector,' he had replied at last, stretching his hand out on the desk in front of him. 'You can have your month's leave and I'll find someone else to go to London. But, mark my words, you need to get away from the Midlands. Don't sit around at home moping. Get away, as far away as you can. Do something completely different. I don't want a burnt-out copper in my force. And that's what you're heading towards being.'

Tallyforth had taken a sharp intake of breath on hearing this. Was he really in such a poor condition? Burn-out? At his age?

So he had driven in the Range Rover back to his flat, where he'd found the previous Sunday's newspapers and searched through the holiday pages of *The Sunday Times* for something that might appeal to him, something that might take him away from Birmingham, and something completely different to anything he'd ever done.

That was how he came to be where he now was - driving through Glencoe, with its deep resonances of Scottish history, on the way to the Isle of Skye and the village of Portree where he was due to meet up with Willie MacPherson, the skipper of *The Flodigarry*, and his wife Mary. It was with them and their bird-watching cruise around the Hebrides that Tallyforth hoped to get away from his troubles.

He was also due to meet up with his only other travelling companion, Cassie Dillon.

The phone call had come from Willie MacPherson himself, within a very few days of Tallyforth sending his reply to the box number. Willie MacPherson had explained about the nature of the cruise, about his membership of the Royal Society for the Protection of Birds, about the cost of the trip, about the intended route and what they hoped to see on the way. He had then asked Tallyforth if he had ever sailed before.

'No, I'm afraid not,' Tallyforth had replied. 'Does that disqualify me? Your advert made no mention of wanting people with sailing experience.'

'Oh, no, no,' had come the reassuring answer. 'It was just I wanted to know. You know, the sea can be a wee bit rough at times and if you've never been on a boat, you might find it a bit difficult.'

'Put it like this,' Tallyforth had then said. 'If you're talking about stomach churning, I think my job has inoculated me against that.'

And he had then explained briefly the nature of his work.

'Aye, well maybe you're right,' Willie MacPherson had said in his light Scottish lilt. 'But I needed to warn you. The long-term forecast for the summer is good anyway, so we'll hope that means calm seas.'

There had been further conversation over the phone but Tallyforth had already, he knew, made his mind up that this was what he wanted. He wasn't going to wait for any of the other box numbers to respond. Willie MacPherson's bird-watching cruise suited him down to the ground. He had liked the sound of the man, those gently-spoken Scottish vowels, the calmness that lay behind them. He had agreed to send a cheque in the following day's post and confirmed that he would be driving up to meet the MacPhersons and board their boat on the first Sunday in August.

'Just one other thing,' he had asked finally. 'How many other people will there be on this cruise?'

'Oh, just the one,' Willie MacPherson had said. 'We've only a wee boat. I mean, it's a classy wee boat, it has all the latest equipment and it's very comfy. But we pride ourselves on giving a personal service to our guests and that's why we only take two at a time. That way there's plenty of room on board and plenty of opportunity for us all to get to know each other really well. It's much more satisfying we've found. The lassie who's coming at the same time as you comes from down your way. She lives in Tamworth - that's by you, isn't it? Her name's Cassie Dillon.'

The Tamworth connection was odd, thought Tallyforth. He had been there the previous summer on the Hubert Stanton murder case. But he had been given Cassie Dillon's phone number and Willie MacPherson had suggested that he might like to make contact with her before the cruise, maybe they could travel up to Scotland together.

And he had phoned her, almost to his own surprise. In the end, after mulling over the matter for a couple of days, curiosity had got the better of him. Her voice had sounded quite strong over the phone. She had been equally resistant to calling him, she had explained after they had exchanged the usual pleasantries, despite Willy MacPherson's suggestion. She had thought, as he himself had done, that it would be rather a provocative thing to do. After all they were only going on a cruise holiday together, overseen by Willie and his wife Mary. Tallyforth had agreed.

'The only reason I rang,' he had said, 'was because I thought you might appreciate a lift to Scotland in my car.'

'That's very kind of you,' she had replied, 'but I have actually planned to go up a week earlier. I have a friend in Oban who I haven't seen for a while. We were at university together. He teaches up there. I said I'd stay with him for a while before the cruise.'

In a way Tallyforth had been glad. He hadn't wanted even the remotest possibility of some relationship developing between them. He had supposed, in a way, that was why he had decided to ring - in order to make clear his intentions. But she had cleverly forestalled him with this revelation about a male friend she was going to stay with.

'Look,' he had said, 'I didn't realise when I booked on to this cruise that there would only be two paying customers aboard. Since

7

you're so close to Birmingham, what do you say to us meeting and getting acquainted a little before we go?'

There had been a pause, as she had weighed up this suggestion.

'What did you have in mind?' she had asked hesitantly.

'Do you like Chinese food?'

'I'm a vegetarian,' she had said.

'Indian? French? Thai? Greek?'

In the end, she had agreed to meet him for lunch at the Café Rouge in the new canalside development opposite the Symphony Hall. He had sensed that, though she was clearly an independent-minded woman, she also was not a risk-taker. She had needed to reassure herself about him as much as he had needed to reassure himself about her. Two weeks on a boat with someone you disliked was not a prospect either of them had felt drawn towards.

He had assumed she would be younger than she actually was. No reason, just the tone of her voice. He had put her down as being in her mid-thirties. He had also built up a picture of her, solely from the fact that she was a vegetarian and an independent spirit taking a holiday on her own, as probably being rather plain, maybe dressed in dull browns or greens, probably never been married, possibly worked in the social services.

So he had been surprised at the figure that approached him, as he sat at the table with his glass of red wine and *The Times* front page spread out in front of him - their pre-arranged signal for recognition. She was much closer to his own age, probably in her early forties he surmised. And she was dressed immaculately in a short black dress and a white jacket, which showed off her trim figure well. There was a pretty rainbow brooch on one lapel of her jacket. Her dark hair was neatly cut and she wore full make-up. Hardly the dunnish figure of his imagination!

'Hi, I'm Cassie,' she had said, a quick smile playing across her face, as she had come to a halt in front of his table and held out her hand.

He had stood awkwardly, automatically patting his hair, and took the slim fingers in his.

'Good to meet you,' he had said, as they had both then sat down. 'What would you like to drink?'

'Red wine suits me fine,' she had replied. 'Nice place. Never been here before. Don't have much cause to come to Birmingham. Used to be an awful place. Changed a lot, hasn't it? I like what they've done with the canal basin.'

While she spoke, Tallyforth had tried to catch a waitress's attention at the same time as listening to her.

'Yes,' he had muttered. 'I'm very fond of Birmingham. Are you from Tamworth originally? Oh, excuse me.'

A waitress had finally seen him and had come to the table to take his order. She nodded her head as she wrote down his order for a glass of red wine.

'No,' she had said, giving him another of those quick smiles. 'I'm from London. But I went to university in Edinburgh. Then I lived in Canada for twelve years. I've been in Tamworth for the past six years. It's where I work.'

'What do you do?' Tallyforth had asked, genuinely curious now. He could see where the independent streak came from.

'Social Services,' she had said, and he had allowed himself a fraction of a smile for at least guessing that bit right. 'Counselling manager. We give guidance and support to victims of abuse. What do you do?'

Tallyforth had looked up at her and sighed. Even in that short space of time, he had felt himself being attracted to her. Whether it was the coolness of her hand, the quickness of her smile, the rich brown of her eyes, the sound of her voice, or the way she punctuated her words, he had not been able to tell. But he had known that her reaction to his occupation might be problematic.

'I'm a copper,' he had said. 'A detective. I catch criminals, usually violent ones, often ones who've committed murder.'

There had been a pause, as he had expected. Then she had smiled back at him, but this time holding the smile and looking straight into his eyes.

'Then we have a lot in common,' she had said. 'We both work in society's fringes, we both deal with violence, we both see the results of evil.'

He had met her gaze unflinchingly and prepared to say something but the waitress had chosen that moment to return with Cassie Dillon's glass of red wine and to take their order for food.

'What would you like?' he had asked. Then, realising that she had only just started to read the menu and in order to give her time, he had ordered a dish of chicken breasts in redcurrant sauce for himself.

'I'll have the feta cheese and black olive salad,' she had said, closing the menu and handing it to the waitress. And she had smiled at him again.

'So,' she had begun again, 'what made you reply to Willie MacPherson's advert? You a sailor?'

'No!' he grimaced. 'Never done anything like it in my life. But I am a bit of a twitcher. Nothing serious, mind you. But I've got very interested in raptors over the years. There's nothing like the sight of a buzzard riding the updraught or a peregrine falcon swooping on its prey at the speed of light. It's a bit like police work. I like to think of myself as swooping on murderers once I know I've got them. But I've never seen a golden eagle and there's a lot of them in Scotland now. Are you interested in birds?'

'A little,' she had said. 'But I just fancied something completely different. And I love Scotland.'

By the time their meals had arrived, Tallyforth had known that he was becoming attracted to this woman. All his preconceptions about people who worked in the Social Services had been challenged and he had heard himself admitting that some of those he had been responsible for arresting and who had subsequently received life sentences for murder might well have suffered themselves in their childhoods from abusive relationships. The holiday in the Hebrides had begun to look more and more appealing.

They had stayed in the Café Rouge till almost three o'clock, talking their lives out. Tallyforth had told her about some of the more challenging murder mysteries he'd had to solve, particularly the one he'd been involved in the previous summer in Tamworth involving some of the staff of Æthelfleda High School suspected of being implicated in the death of their school inspector, Hubert Stanton. She hadn't known any of the characters involved, although she had remembered reading about the case, but she had told him that, surprisingly, a number of her clients were schoolteachers, usually women who were victims of physical abuse from their husbands. And then he had told her about how his own marriage had come apart, not because of violence but because of the hours he had had to work and his inability to provide a social life for his wife. He told her about his children and the continuing guilt he felt about leaving them when they were so young. And she had told him of her marriage, about her time in Canada with her husband, and then her divorce when she found that he was being unfaithful to her. They had never had children, she had said, because he hadn't wanted to be tied down and she had gone along with that but had come to regret it later.

It had been like meeting up with an old friend, someone he hadn't seen for years, he had thought to himself as he drove home after they had finally parted. She had planned to drive to Oban the following week to stay with her friend James Orr, who taught music in the Oban Academy. So they had agreed that they would meet up in Portree on Sunday week, ready to begin their cruise around the Hebridean Isles with Willie and Mary MacPherson in their boat *The Flodigarry*.

Tallyforth had been sure that she was looking forward to it as much as he was.

TWO

The first Sunday in August had arrived.

Tallyforth had driven from Kyle of Lochalsh that afternoon to complete his journey to Portree. He had crossed the new Skye Bridge, which he had recently read had become an object of much ridicule in Scotland as a whole, because its huge six-hundred-metre-long construction was felt to be completely out of place in the beautiful setting of the north-west Scottish coastline, and of much concern to the people of Skye because of the high costs of its toll for crossing, now that the ferry had been decommissioned. As he had driven across he had noticed half-torn posters for S.K.A.T. on the bridge and had wondered what S.K.A.T. stood for - presumably something to do with Skye Bridge protesters. For a moment, his almost-instinctive desire to find out what was going on had given him pause, but then he had reminded himself that he was here for a rest and for a holiday. Detective work, of any sort, was banned for the next two weeks.

The final stages of his journey had taken him along the coast road where the majestic soaring hillsides of the Red Cuillins, with their scree and grass slopes, followed him to the west and the distant peaks of the Black Cuillins beyond were visible. A grey heron had been startled by the revving of the Range Rover's engine, as he had changed gear, and risen majestically from the shore-line near Sconser. Two oystercatchers had remained in its place, scurrying along the shoreline about their business. Huge herring-gulls had swooped constantly ahead of his windscreen, filling the air with their distinctive screech, heard even above the tape of Van Morrison's *Avalon Sunset* album which Tallyforth was playing. As he had driven from Sconser towards Sligachan, following the estuary's line, he had noticed the purple heather that carpeted the lower heights of the Cuillins.

Though it had been warm the previous day, for most of his journey that Sunday it had been quite overcast, with white fluffy clouds over the hills. As he had entered the village of Portree itself, it had still been cloudy with some light drizzle but late afternoon, around about five o'clock, the sun had appeared, heralding a lovely evening with an azure blue sky.

He was in a room at the Royal Hotel, where Willie MacPherson had arranged for him to shower and change before dinner, as was the custom for their cruise, he had explained in his letter. As he looked from the window of his room in the town's oldest hotel down to the picturesque harbour where small boats bobbed in the blue waters, Tallyforth wondered which was *The Flodigarry*, the boat that was to be his home for the next two weeks. His gaze moved up and took in the steep, impassable slopes of the hillsides that bounded the natural harbour - to his right the craggy rock face behind and beyond the row of houses along the pier with their blue, pink and yellow washes, to his left an equally-steep gradient covered in green ferns and wiry shrubs.

Nothing to build on there, he thought to himself. No way out up those slopes for anyone who got trapped in the bay.

His thoughts turned to the tale he had read in the hotel's brochure, which had accompanied Willie MacPherson's letter. In it he had read that the hotel stood on the site of what had once been MacNab's Inn, where Bonnie Prince Charlie had bade his final farewell to Flora MacDonald. He ought to know the significance of this, he had thought as he had read that piece of information, but he didn't. Nor was he really that clear about the significance of Bonnie Prince Charlie and his place in the Scottish psyche. In fact, Tallyforth's ignorance of Scotland and its history was similar to that of most English people.

Tallyforth sat down on the edge of the bed and glanced at *The Sunday Times* he had bought in Lochalsh. The front page carried the news of the new Labour government's first major public relations gaffe - the story of the Foreign Secretary leaving his wife in order to live with his House of Commons secretary. It was curious, Tallyforth reflected, that the new government was so keen

13

on devolution for Scotland when some of its chief ministers were themselves Scots, who were now ruling England.

'Aye, there you are,' smiled Willie MacPherson, as Tallyforth approached the bar of the Royal Hotel's lounge. 'You have to be from the police with feet like that.'

Tallyforth looked down at his shoes, then back at his interlocutor, whose voice he recognised from their phone call. While Tallyforth was dressed casually, in a blue denim shirt and grey slacks, Willie MacPherson was dressed more formally in kilt and black jacket. His craggy face and twinkling smile epitomised Tallyforth's expectations of what a Scotsman should look like. Tallyforth guessed he was younger than himself, maybe in his late thirties, he surmised.

'Nice to meet you, Mr MacPherson,' he began, holding out his hand.

'Call me Willie. We're going to be together for the next couple of weeks, so we'd best not have any ceremony,' said Willie MacPherson, shaking the proffered hand vigorously. 'Welcome to Bonnie Skye! What you drinking?'

Tallyforth noticed that Willie MacPherson had a glass of whisky in his free hand.

'Is that the local poison?' he asked, nodding at the whisky glass.

'Aye, it's Talisker,' came the reply. 'It's on offer this week, because of the Games. But you'll be needing a chaser with it, for it's awful sharp, okay? Cameron's?'

Tallyforth nodded. He had seen Scots in Birmingham bars with their whisky chasers, dour men with ruddy Celtic faces and small round noses, who had settled in Birmingham because of the post-war boom in the car industry and had never found their way back home. Except through the memories brought on by their whisky chasers.

Willie MacPherson turned away from Tallyforth and leaned across the bar, seeking the young barman's attention in the crowded room.

Tallyforth looked around him to see where Cassie Dillon was. Willie MacPherson had explained that the purpose of having the first evening at the Royal Hotel was so that they could all get to know each other properly before they set sail the following day. It was part of the cruise, he had said, claiming it had been a tradition among Scottish trawlermen to celebrate together before a trip to sea because of the uncertainties that any trip to sea entailed. He had been reassuring that there were no such uncertainties about the Hebridean cruise Tallyforth and Cassie Dillon were to undertake, because *The Flodigarry* had all the latest navigational equipment and he personally knew every rocky outcrop, every bay, every sandbank, every channel in the Outer and Inner Hebrides, having sailed these islands since he was twenty years of age.

There was no sign of Cassie Dillon but someone was waving in his direction from the other side of the room. He quickly glanced either side of him but it did seem to be him that the woman was waving at. He peered through the smoke-filled room and could see that she was a middle-aged woman, also dressed in kilt and black jacket. Was this the skipper's wife, Mary? he wondered.

'My Mary is over there,' said Willie MacPherson, turning round to Tallyforth, having got the barman's attention. 'Over you go. I'll bring the drinks in a minute.'

Tallyforth did as he was told.

'I'm Mary MacPherson,' said the woman who had been waving cheerily at him as he sat down opposite her. 'I'm Willie's wife. Did you have a good journey? The weather wasn't very fine this morning for you, was it? Have you met our other guest? She comes from somewhere near you, doesn't she? Did Willie say you were planning to travel up here together?'

Tallyforth opened his mouth several times to reply but could not find a space to intervene, so he gave up until she had finished her barrage of questions. Instead, he took in her well-built figure that filled the kilt and white blouse she wore; he noted the weather-beaten face which had clearly spent much time exposed to the elements; he listened to the lilt of her voice, with its Norse inflections still evident centuries after the Vikings had first settled in these westernmost isles of Scotland. She looked to be slightly older than her husband.

'To tell you the truth,' he began, as she finished her burst of questioning, 'Cassie Dillon and I have met, yes. But we didn't travel up together because she was staying with a friend in Oban for a while before coming on up here.'

'And did you get on okay?' Mary MacPherson asked. 'You're going to have to spend a lot of time together in the next couple of weeks, so it's best that you can at least tolerate each other. We've had a couple of wee incidents in the past when folk didn't get on with each other. That's one of the reasons we always start with this dinner on the first night. It's very important that we all get on with each other. The sea can be a friend but it can also be a brute, even at this time of year. It's no place for folk who cannot get on with each other.'

Mary MacPherson stared meaningfully across at Tallyforth, who took her gaze and returned it. He could see the iron behind those smiling eyes.

'You've no need to worry on that score,' he replied. 'Cassie and I got on just fine. D'you know if she's here yet? I was looking for her.'

Before she could reply, the kilted figure of Willie MacPherson had appeared standing beside them, his hands clasped delicately around several glasses.

'There's a wee whisky for you, Mary,' he said, placing the first glass in front of his wife. 'And here's your tot with a pint of Cameron's.'

Willie MacPherson sat down next to his wife, straightening his kilt over his knees, raised his pint glass of orange juice to his lips and sipped.

'Has the missus been telling you about our American visitors?' he asked Tallyforth.

Tallyforth looked up from his drink.

'No,' he answered. 'Why?'

'That lot over there.'

Willie MacPherson pointed to the other side of the room where a group of four well-built men, dressed in tee-shirts and track-suit bottoms, sat.

'They're here for the Games on Wednesday,' Willie MacPherson continued. 'Big lads, eh? They'll be here for the throwing events. There's always some strangers here for that. We had a Swede here last year, but he didn't have the technique of the Scots laddies. He was big and strong, alright, but he just couldn't throw the heavy weight over the bar properly. And you should have seen him try to toss the caber! Hadn't a clue!'

'They say these Americans have been in training, though,' interjected Mary MacPherson, leaning forward towards Tallyforth. 'They're supposed to be professionals. Or as near as maybe.'

'Who told you that, woman?' Willie MacPherson turned to face his wife, a look of disbelief on his wrinkled face.

'Dugald,' she said firmly.

'Ach, just 'cos Dugald MacLeod runs this hotel, he thinks he knows everything that's going on in Portree."

'They're staying in the village, Willie,' she riposted, digging him in the ribs as she spoke. 'They've been here a couple of nights already. He's seen them up on the games field practising. And he's heard them talking at the bar.'

'Is this the Highland Games you're talking about,' enquired Tallyforth, cutting across this family bickering. 'I'd like to see that. When is it?'

Willie MacPherson turned away from his wife, snorted briefly, then answered.

'You'll not get the chance, I'm afraid. We set sail on the morrow and we'll not be back in Portree for twelve days. The Games are on Wednesday of this week and we'll be out beyond Lewis by then.'

'That's a shame,' mused Tallyforth. 'It would have been quite an experience."

'What would have been quite an experience?'

Tallyforth spun round in his seat, as he recognised the new voice in their conversation. Cassie Dillon stood behind him, dressed in black trousers and a cream blouse with a red silk scarf tied loosely around her neck, smiling at the three of them and with her right hand lightly touching Tallyforth's shoulder.

'Willie and Mary were just telling me about the Skye Highland Games,' he began. 'It's this Wednesday apparently and we won't be able to see it. Willie, Mary, this is Cassie Dillon.'

'I didn't think it was the Queen Mother!' retorted Willie MacPherson, holding out his hand as he stood up to greet her. 'What'll you be drinking, lassie?'

Tallyforth noticed a momentary freezing in her demeanour as

she reacted to the term of address but then she took Willie's hand and shook it warmly, repeating the action with Mary MacPherson.

'I'll have a Talisker, please,' she said, 'but without the chaser, thanks. I'll leave that to you big boys.'

And she sat down next to Tallyforth, smiling at him.

'What time are we eating?' she asked. 'I'm famished.'

'We're booked for eight,' said Mary MacPherson, then shouted to her husband as he made his way to the bar for the extra drink. 'Willie, get the menu for us, will you?'

'Thanks,' said Cassie Dillon.

'Did you have a good journey?' asked Mary.

'Yes, but I've only come up from Oban. I was staying with a friend of mine from university. He teaches there.'

'Maybe he'd know Donald McMillan. He's a teacher at Oban Academy. His brother's a solicitor in Portree.'

'Not a name he's mentioned,' answered Cassie Dillon. 'But then that doesn't mean anything. James may know him. I'll ask him when I speak to him next.'

But before they could converse any more, Willie MacPherson was back at the table, carrying a small scotch, which he passed to Cassie Dillon.

'Come on, all of you,' he said, grinning at them. 'Dugald says we can go through to the dining room now.'

They stood and followed his retreating back.

Sitting in the dining room of the Royal Hotel at a window table which looked out to the Portree harbour and the bay beyond were three men. They looked up briefly as Cassie Dillon, Tallyforth and the two MacPhersons entered, nodding recognition to the latter.

'Aye, aye, Mary. How're you, Willie?' said the oldest of the three.

'Fine, fine,' replied Willie MacPherson on their joint behalf. 'We're off on cruise tomorrow. These are our guests.'

The three men nodded to Tallyforth and to Cassie Dillon, then they turned back to their conversation which was focused on a newspaper spread out in front of them on the table, where the remains of their meal had been pushed aside.

'So where exactly does the government stand on this?' asked one of the trio, a short balding man with a ginger beard, who wore a tweed jacket over a bright green shirt and a yellow tartan tie. 'They've been in power three months now and still we don't know what they intend to do.'

'Aye, well, Hamish,' said the elderly member of the group, whose mane of white hair touched the top of his black jacket at the back of the neck and whose craggy features spoke of a life of considerable experience, 'you have to mind that they've other things to do apart from sorting out the Skye Bridge mess.'

'But it was in their manifesto, father,' spluttered the first speaker in protest. 'They have to do something. It was Labour M.P.s who marched with us and carried placards demanding action to remove the tolls on the bridge. Surely the Scottish Office can simply repeal the law immediately.'

At this point the third member of the group, a debonair-looking man with neat blond hair, parted in the middle, and wearing black trousers and a black shirt, open at the neck to reveal a gold pendant on a chain, spoke for the first time. He was younger than the other two men.

'It's not so simple, Hamish,' he began, pointing at the newspaper in front of them. 'You can see here in the *Free Press* that they have to get parliament to repeal primary legislation so that it becomes a civil rather than a criminal offence to refuse to pay your toll on the Bridge. And the Secretary of State has promised to reduce the cost of the toll to one pound twenty-five.'

'But, Iain, that's not enough,' interjected Hamish MacLeod, the manager of the Portree post office and one of the leaders of the Skye and Lochalsh Against Tolls action group. 'You've been with us throughout this campaign and we've been grateful for your legal advice. If it hadn't been for you, we wouldn't have been able to fight all those non-payment cases in court and the Procurator Fiscal wouldn't have got so much egg on his face. Can't you see that it's not enough to get the toll fee reduced? We have to get it abolished completely.'

'Aye, Hamish is right,' cut in Dugald MacLeod, father of Hamish MacLeod and manager of the Royal Hotel. He sat back in his seat, lifting his glass of whisky to his lips. 'We didn't ask for the bridge to be built and we shouldn't have to pay to use our own roads. Can you not push harder, man? It's affecting the tourist trade as well, you know. Bookings are way down so far this year. Aye, I know that they'll be fine this week for the Games, specially with all the old pipers back, but the season's longer than that.'

Iain McMillan, junior partner in MacDonald and McMillan Solicitors, also sat back, tugging lightly at the chain around his neck.

'And another thing, Iain,' said Hamish MacLeod jabbing his finger in the direction of the solicitor. 'We need to get all these charges against people who have refused to pay their toll dropped completely. It's no use saying that they won't have a criminal record if it becomes a civil offence. It shouldn't be an offence at all! You know that. The Secretary of State knows that. The whole of Scotland knows that. The law needs to be completely rescinded, all those who've been fined need to have their money returned and those still waiting to be tried need their summonses torn up. Why can't you get that to happen, Iain?'

Iain McMillan sighed. He was used to Hamish's angry outbursts. They had been useful for getting people active to fight the tolls on the new Skye Bridge in the first place but they were increasingly problematic when he turned up in court to support some non-payer. It was amazing that he had not yet been summonsed for contempt of court, given the frequency of his angry interjections during hearings. Only the sympathetic forbearance of the Sheriffs he had appeared before had kept him out of more serious trouble.

'Look, Hamish,' he began again, after waiting for the anger to dissipate a little. 'We have to take one step at a time. It's a completely new situation now with a new government. The Secretary of State has said that he's looking into the matter and that he will ask parliament to amend the law and that's a start. I think we have to put more political pressure on now. Remember that there's the devolution referendum just round the corner. The government will want the islands on its side. Maybe there's some horse-trading that can be done.'

Hamish MacLeod raised his right hand to point a finger demonstratively at Iain McMillan again, then lowered it as a young waitress in her black dress and white pinafore came to their table to clear it.

'Thank you, Annie,' said Dugald MacLeod, turning to the

waitress. 'Tell your mother I'll be needing the both of you on Tuesday and Wednesday, because of the Games, will you, lassie?'

He smiled at her as she blushingly carried the gravy-stained plates back towards the kitchens. She had only been working in the hotel dining room for a week, as a part-time job between her school sixth form years. Her mother had worked part-time behind the bar at the Royal for many years.

Hamish MacLeod began again.

'Iain, it's clear this Labour government is no better than the last lot. They've already broken their promise over repealing the toll, so how can we trust them by entering into some negotiation with them over devolution? I think we should up the action. I think we should go for another mass protest on the bridge, like last February.'

'You mean another sit-down on the bridge, Hamish?' asked his father.

'Yes,' came the reply. 'And soon, while the devolution issue is still hot. I'm going to call a special meeting of S.K.A.T. this Friday night. Will you be there, Iain? Can we count on you?'

Iain McMillan drained the contents of his gin and tonic, pulled the collar of his shirt up around his neck, and looked at his watch.

'Of course I will, Hamish,' he said, 'but I want an open debate. Don't go railroading your plans through, like you usually do. We need to hear everyone's point of view before we decide on action.'

'Aye, and just remember that next weekend could be just as busy as this one,' reminded Dugald MacLeod. 'It would be very nice to get the tourists on our side but we have to get them on to the isle first, you know!'

'I know, I know,' said Hamish in an exasperated tone.

Iain McMillan stood to leave, brushing a stray crumb from his trousers and smoothing his blond hair with the palm of his hand.

'It's getting on for nine o'clock,' he said. 'I have to go. I'll see you, Hamish. Thanks for dinner, Dugald.'

Dugald MacLeod nodded.

'You'll not forget your mint!' he called after the retreating figure.

A dapper young man, wearing a mauve turtle-neck jumper, looked up briefly from the notebook he was scribbling in at the adjoining table. His eyes followed Iain McMillan's smartly-dressed frame, then quickly flashed back to the two MacLeods, before settling back on his notebook.

They dined well. Willie MacPherson had stressed that the price of the meal was part of the price of the trip and reiterated how important a tradition he and Mary believed it to be to have a good feast before a voyage.

So, as a starter, Cassie Dillon had chosen garlic mushrooms, while Tallyforth had gone for the crofter's skillet, which turned out to be haggis cooked with onions and mushrooms and finished with a whisky and cream sauce. The MacPhersons had both had the smoked fish platter.

Assured by Mary MacPherson that it was locally-caught and cured, they all went for the grilled peppered lemon sole for their main course, served with mange tout, baby sweetcorn and potato wedges. Cassie Dillon had explained that, though she was a vegetarian, that merely meant she didn't eat meat or meat products but she enjoyed fish.

'So you're a fair-weather vegetarian, then?' Tallyforth had challenged her, only half in jest.

'No,' she had patiently explained. 'What I object to is the cruelty with which animals are bred and killed for human consumption. Animals are warm-blooded like us. They are part of the animal kingdom like us. I believe that killing and eating an animal is the equivalent of killing and eating a fellow human being. Fish, on the other hand, are cold-blooded. They are a different form of life. I see no difficulty.'

Tallyforth stopped himself snorting with disbelief and decided to hold his tongue. It was the sort of argument he could easily let himself get sucked into, he knew well enough by now. And he would have enjoyed it. But he was attracted to this Cassie Dillon. He didn't want to get into arguments with her. He wanted her to think well of him. He wanted her to.........Well, he knew from the way his heart had fluttered when she had first entered the bar of the Royal Hotel and placed her hand on his shoulder that he wanted her more than he had wanted any other woman for a long time. Too long, in fact.

But he had to play it coolly. He didn't yet know how she felt.

'I'm glad you can eat fish,' said Mary MacPherson, as the waitress

Annie placed the lemon sole in front of them. 'For we've plenty of that on board for the cruise. But you'll have to excuse the rest of us if you smell meat cooking. Willie's very partial to a bacon sandwich at any time of day or night and I think the Chief Inspector's fond of his food, am I right?'

Tallyforth grinned and nodded simultaneously.

'I was forgetting that you have a regular acquaintance with dead bodies,' Cassie Dillon teased him. 'Doesn't that ever put you off eating altogether?'

'It's not the same thing,' he replied. 'You become hardened to it, I suppose.'

'You mean you lose your feelings?' she teased again, looking up at him from under her dark eyelashes in a provocative manner and smiling.

'N-no,' he stuttered. What was going on here, he wondered to himself. Was she deliberately making a play at him on their first night? And if she was, how would that affect the rest of the cruise?

Mary MacPherson too had noticed the coquettish glance. She kicked her husband under the table, to bring his attention back to their guests, for he was watching Hamish and Dugald MacLeod still deep in conversation at the other end of the dining room. Probably busy with that stupid S.K.A.T. business, he thought. Them and their protests - killing off the tourist trade, they were!

'Did you know that Bonnie Prince Charlie said his last farewell to Flora McDonald in this very hotel?' said Mary. 'You're sitting in a very famous place.'

'I read that in the entrance hall,' responded Tallyforth. 'But I wasn't quite sure of the significance of it.'

'Tell them, Willie,' said Mary MacPherson with a grim smile. 'Tell your guests about the Forty-five.'

Willie MacPherson cut a large slice of his sole and chewed it ruminatively for a few moments, as he prepared for his story.

'You'll know that Scotland was ruled by the English King George at the time, though he was no more English than I am. He was a German and he hardly spoke a word of English. Bonnie Prince Charlie, who lived in exile in France, took on the mantle of his father who had failed three times to win back his throne in Scotland. The Prince got the support of the French king, Louis the Fifteenth, who gave him a fleet of ships and seven thousand troops but a storm destroyed most of the ships as they waited to leave Calais and Louis backed out of the deal. So the young prince sold his jewels and bought two armed vessels himself and set sail for Scotland. One ship was stopped by the English navy on the way but the Prince put his first foot on Scottish soil in Eriskay on 23rd July 1745.'

'Go on, Willie,' interjected his wife. 'Just give them the bare bones. They don't need chapter and verse.'

'Aye, well,' he said, putting his knife and fork down on his plate. 'Charles Edward Stuart marched through Scotland, winning the support of the Scottish clans who saw in him their opportunity to reclaim the land they believed was theirs. He raised his flag first at Glenfinnan, then marched on Edinburgh and then to Prestonpans. But the weather defeated him as he marched on London and his troops turned back from the bitter winter weather. That was his fatal mistake, because from then on he was pursued by the redcoat army led by the brutal Duke of Cumberland and finally overwhelmed at Culloden in April 1746. After the battle, the redcoats went round the battlefield killing every wounded Highlander and every prisoner. The Prince fled from the scene but there was a price on his head and he had to rely on his remaining followers in the Isles to smuggle him out of the country and over the sea to France.'

Willie MacPherson paused and took a sip of water.

'And how does Flora MacDonald fit into all his?' asked Tallyforth.

'I was coming to that,' said Willie MacPherson, resuming his story. 'During his travels, the Bonnie Prince was disguised as a maid accompanying Flora MacDonald on a visit to her mother in Armadale on Skye, sailing across the sea from Uist. It wasn't an easy journey, for they were fired on by the redcoats from the shore but eventually they made it. But the adventure wasn't over yet. When she reached her mother's house, she found that the local redcoat commander was dining there. He asked her a lot of awkward questions but she answered them fine, for she was a very clever woman. Then later she accompanied the Prince to Portree where a boat was waiting to take him to Raasay. The legend says that in his farewell to Flora the Prince promised to see her again at the Court of St. James in England. But, of course, they never met again.'

'Remind me what happened to Bonnie Prince Charlie,' prompted Cassie Dillon, smiling warmly in Willie MacPherson's direction.

'He had a number of adventures around the Isles before he finally escaped to France in September 1746, with some of his loyal Jacobites. And he never set foot in Scotland again. We've been under the boot of the English since then.'

'I suppose you'll be keen on the new government's devolution plans then?' queried Cassie Dillon, taking her last mouthful of fish.

'That's another story,' laughed Mary. 'Now, what are you having for sweets?'

It was after eleven o'clock when they finally left the Royal Hotel and carefully went down the Quay Brae to the pier and along Quay Street, past the coloured house fronts to the pier end, where the MacPhersons' dinghy was tied up awaiting them. They had drunk a lot and the MacPhersons had warned them that they would need to be up early and out with the morning tide. Willie rowed them out in the dinghy to where *The Flodigarry* was moored. There Tallyforth and Cassie MacPherson were shown to their cabins at opposite ends of the boat.

'See you in the morning,' she had said to Tallyforth, releasing the hand that she had been holding since he'd offered it as they climbed aboard *The Flodigarry* . 'It's been a lovely start to the holiday. I'm really looking forward to it, aren't you?'

'Absolutely,' he had said. 'This was the best decision I've made for a long time.'

'Sleep tight,' she said and leaned forward to kiss him on the cheek, before turning briskly away from him and slipping down the metal steps to her cabin.

Tallyforth took a deep breath and looked up at the starry sky.

A deep happiness suffused his body.

THREE

He was woken suddenly. Someone was shaking him roughly.

As he rubbed his eyes, he became aware that the person shaking him was Willie MacPherson, who stood over him, dressed in a navy blue sweater and denim jeans. The urgency with which he was being shaken was matched by the anxiety in Willie MacPherson's eyes.

'You've to come quickly, Mr Tallyforth,' Willie MacPherson said, his voice trembling. 'There's been a terrible accident. You have to come now.'

Tallyforth sat up in his bunk and looked up through the hatch. Day had broken and he could see the early morning sun glistening on the glass.

'What time is it?' he asked, as he swung his legs over the side of the bunk and reached for his trousers.

'Come on, man,' Willie MacPherson harried him. 'There's not the time for pleasantries. It's urgent. There's been an accident.'

Tallyforth looked at his watch before pulling on a green tee-shirt. He saw it was six fifteen.

'Is this the time you plan to start the trip?' he asked.

'Mr Tallyforth, this isn't a joke,' replied Willie MacPherson. 'Something awful's happened.'

Tallyforth, now fully awake and dressed, looked at the frightened eyes of *The Flodigarry's* skipper and realised that something very serious was wrong.

Willie MacPherson turned to lead the way out of the cabin and Tallyforth followed.

It was Cassie Dillon.

She lay prostrate on her bunk in the aft cabin, her body naked apart from a red silk scarf that was tied around her neck. Mary MacPherson sat on the bunk beside her, tears streaming from her eyes, clasping Cassie Dillon's still left hand.

'What.....?' Tallyforth tried to make some words come out of his mouth but it was as if his heart was beating in the middle of his throat and would not allow them passage.

'She's dead, Mr Tallyforth,' said the weeping Mary MacPherson, holding up the lifeless hand as if to demonstrate. 'Dead. Oh my, what's going on here? The poor wee lassie!'

Willie MacPherson put a protective arm around her shoulder.

'The missus came over thirty minutes since to wake the lassie up with a cup of tea,' he explained. 'She knocked on the cabin door and, when there was no reply, she went in. And this is what she found. The lassie's dead, Mr Tallyforth. I didn't know what to do, but Mary said you might. Nothing like this has ever happened to us before.'

Tallyforth, struggling to hold back his own tears, leaned over to look into the lifeless hazel eyes of the woman whom he had begun to fall in love with and who was to have been his companion on this wonderful Hebridean bird-watching cruise. He pulled the silk scarf lightly away from her neck and saw the ugly bruises underneath it.

'She's been strangled,' he said, as he straightened up and a tear glistened at the corner of his right eye. 'Willie, you'll need to fetch the police straightaway. Is the police station close?'

'Aye, it's in Somerled Square,' Willie MacPherson replied, already half way up the steps. 'I'm on my way, Chief Inspector.'

'I'll away and get you a drink,' said Mary MacPherson, getting up from the bunk and releasing Cassie Dillon's hand. 'You'll be needing something strong to see you through this.'

And she too ascended from the cabin.

Tallyforth's trained policeman's eyes looked around him in the small cabin. There were no obvious signs of a disturbance. The clothes that Cassie Dillon had worn the previous evening were neatly folded by the bunk, her underwear on top of the black trousers and cream blouse. It did not appear to have been forcibly removed. Her sleeping bag had been unzipped wide open but

Tallyforth himself had been warm in the night. Quite possibly she had unzipped it herself. He had no idea whether she normally slept naked or not. How could he have? he thought, and then felt again emotion rising through his body, but this time it was sheer and insistent anger. Someone had murdered his Cassie and, if he had that murderer in front of him at that moment, he would have forgotten all his police training, all his detective skills, all his belief in the justice of the law, and he would have become a killer too.

He took a step back and waited for the anger to diminish.

Steady, he told himself. That's no way to deal with the situation. You need to stand back, you need to remember your profession, you need to use your training, now as never before. A woman has been murdered, a woman whom you thought you were falling in love with, a woman you had only met twice but who had stirred emotions in you that you never thought to have stirred again. But she's now dead, strangled with her own silk scarf, by the look of things. You have to find out who did this. And why. And quick. But you won't do it in the state of mind you're in now. Steady.

He glanced around the cabin again. On a small teak table-top beside the bunk were some papers, a couple of books and a Sony Walkman headset. Tallyforth glanced at the two books and saw that they were paperback detective stories. Not quite what he had expected of her. He took up the Walkman, opened it and extracted the tape, which had no markings on it to indicate what it was. Probably some music she liked, he thought to himself. He pocketed the tape, planning to listen to it later. Maybe it was all he'd have to remember her by. Then he noticed that the papers were actually a map folded coarsely. He picked it up and opened it out. It was a map of the west coast of Scotland, including the Inner and Outer Hebrides. A number of small crosses had been drawn in pencil at various spots on the map. He supposed that they might have been places where *The Flodigarry* was likely to moor. He remembered that Willie MacPherson had told him their intended route and she would have been told the same.

This is silly! he suddenly thought to himself, throwing the map back on to the table. She's dead! Cassie's dead!

He allowed his eyes to settle on her naked body. For some minutes he gazed at her, lying there. Then he leaned forward and kissed her cold lips. Then his lips moved down to kiss her firm but cold nipples.

And he knelt down beside the bunk, taking the lifeless hand recently released by Mary MacPherson, and let the tears fall at last.

'Chief Inspector Tallyforth, I'm sorry to intrude on your grief.'

Her voice startled him. He looked over his shoulder at the dark-uniformed figure which was coming down the steps and into the cabin.

'I'm Inspector Fraser, senior officer at the Portree police station,' she said, standing now in front of him. 'Willie MacPherson has told me there's been an accident. I take it the lady is definitely dead?'

Tallyforth nodded. He took in the tall, slim figure of the newcomer, who he guessed would be a woman in her early thirties. Her voice was clear and the accent noticeably anglicised, though there was a hint of Scots.

'Do we have any idea how she died?'

Tallyforth pointed to the silk scarf.

'She was strangled with that,' he said, standing up now. 'Somebody came in here in the night and strangled her. I'd say it was somebody she knew, because there are no signs of a struggle and there doesn't look to have been anything taken, though I haven't checked. My guess is that she was drugged by whoever it was came in here and then murdered.'

'Thank you, Chief Inspector,' came the cold voice of Inspector Maggie Fraser, whose ice-blue eyes challenged his. 'You know the rules, sir. This death in suspicious circumstances has happened on my patch so I have to take control now. I've already sent for forensic, though it will take some time as they have to come from the mainland.'

'Just as well they built that bridge then,' Tallyforth said ironically.

'As you say, sir,' she continued. 'Now, if you wouldn't mind, I shall have to ask you to leave the scene. Perhaps we could go somewhere else and you could tell me all you know about the victim. I've a uniformed bobby with me who'll stay here to ensure nothing's disturbed. I assume you haven't touched anything, sir?'

'Don't be preposterous, inspector!' he suddenly blurted out. 'Of course, I've touched things. I'm a detective. It's what I do for a living. And murder's my speciality!'

'Not on my patch, sir,' came the cold voice. 'If you wouldn't mind.'

'You mean you're going to stop me from investigating the murder of someone whom I was going to share a two-week cruise with, someone who I dined with last night, someone who I .....'

His voice tailed off. He was going to say 'loved', but how could he? He hadn't even told Cassie that. He had hardly begun to admit it to himself. But that's what it was.

'Sir?' she queried, her right eyebrow arched.

'Nothing', he muttered. 'But I demand the right to join your team on this case. I'll speak to my Chief Super and get him to fix it if need be.'

'You must do as you think fit, sir,' she replied. 'But for the moment this is a suspicious death on my territory and you are a material witness.'

'Witness!' Tallyforth yelped. 'How do you mean?'

'By your own admission you were with the victim last night. And Willie MacPherson has told me that he left the two of you on deck together after you came back from the Royal Hotel and that was the last time he saw the deceased.'

'But don't be silly, woman!' he expostulated. 'Are you trying to say that I then took her down here and strangled her? Is that what you're saying?'

'No, sir, that's not what I'm saying,' came the reply. 'But what I am saying is that you are likely to have been one of the last persons to see her alive and that makes you a material witness. So you can't be involved in the investigation.'

She was calmly insistent and pierced him with her gaze.

'This is preposterous, Fraser,' Tallyforth stormed. 'I'm going to phone my Chief Super.'

And he made for the steps.

'Of course, sir,' said Inspector Maggie Fraser, smiling frostily at him. 'And I'll speak to my Chief Constable. Now, shall we go on deck?'

They were sitting in the galley of *The Flodigarry*, Willie and Mary MacPherson facing Inspector Maggie Fraser, each with a mug of tea in front of them.

'So, now that Chief Inspector Tallyforth has left us,' the latter began, 'perhaps you can tell me all you know about the deceased. Which of you exactly was it that found her?'

Mary MacPherson dabbed at her eyes with a tissue.

'Me, Inspector,' she said softly, her eyes cast down to her mug of tea. 'I went to wake her up at six with a cup of tea. And there she was!'

She cried gently to herself.

'Just tell me exactly what you did. You went to her cabin and......'

'I knocked on the door, like I always do, but she didn't answer, so I opened the door a wee crack to see if she was awake and that's when I saw her.'

'So she was lying naked on her bunk then?'

'Aye.'

'Would someone normally sleep naked in a bunk on your boat?'

'Well, not normally, but she would have worked out that no-one could see her and the only way into her cabin is through the wheelhouse and down those steps, so she'd have heard anyone coming. You see, the aft cabin is separate from the other cabins.'

'And why did you think she was dead?'

'I didn't. Not at first. I thought she was just in a deep sleep, so I went and shook her shoulder gently.'

'So you moved her?'

'No, I hardly touched her. But I felt she was cold. So I reached for her hand and I could tell there was no pulse. And I called Willie then.'

Inspector Maggie Fraser turned to Willie MacPherson, who had sat silently through this conversation.

'And you then appeared on the scene?'

'Aye, I did that,' he said. 'I've never been so shocked in my life, when I saw the body. Mary told me there was no pulse and I tried again at her wrist but there wasn't a thing. I tried to give her mouth to mouth, because you have to have a first-aid certificate these days to run the business we do, but it didn't work. She was well dead by then.'

'Did you move her?'

'No. Well, only as much as I had to in order to give her the mouth to mouth,' Willie MacPherson answered, with a worried expression.

'And what did you do then?'

'I went for the Chief Inspector, Mr Tallyforth,' he said anxiously. 'I thought he would know what to do. He's a detective, you know.'

'Aye, I know,' Inspector Maggie Fraser rasped, lapsing momentarily into her original Scots tongue. 'Tell me all you knew about Ms. Dillon. Had she told you a lot about herself?'

Mary MacPherson dried her eyes on her sleeve and took a strong slurp of her tea.

'We don't know an awful lot,' she answered. 'We put an advert in *The Sunday Times* at the start of May for customers to go on bird-watching cruises in *The Flodigarry*. We've been running wee cruises around the Hebrides for years but I thought we should try to be a bit more specialised this year, so we went for the bird-watching. Willie's always been interested and knowledgeable on the bird-life so we thought it would be a good idea.'

'That's right,' cut in Willie. 'I've been involved with the re-introduction of the sea-eagles on to Rum a few years since. And I know where the one pair of them has nested on Skye, though it's secret from most folk.'

'And how many trips have you taken?' asked Maggie Fraser, making it obvious that she was not interested in his bird-watching proclivities.

'We started at the beginning of May, so this would have been the sixth,' answered Willie.

'And no trouble before today?'

'No, none at all,' said Mary MacPherson.

'And what about Ms. Dillon? You were about to tell me.'

Mary MacPherson glanced sideways at her husband, who raised one eye-brow briefly.

'All we know is that she comes from Tamworth in England,' she said. 'She told us she was a social worker there - something to do with counselling, though I didn't properly understand all that. And she'd never been a sailor but she was quite interested in bird-life, from when she'd lived in Canada.'

'Did she say when that was?'

'No, I don't think so.'

'Anything else?'

'Only that she'd been staying with a friend of hers, a schoolteacher, in Oban for the past week,' said Willie MacPherson, recalling a conversation he had had with his wife about their two guests as they prepared for bed the previous evening. 'I remember Mary telling me that last night.'

'Anything else?'

Mary MacPherson again looked sideways at her husband but this time he did not return her look.

'Aye, she was fair making eyes at Mr Tallyforth,' said Mary MacPherson, her tone becoming much sharper now. 'All through the meal last night in the Royal she was flirting with him and the daft gawk was falling for it. You'd have thought, with him being a policeman and all, that he'd have seen right through her. But not him!'

'Now, now, Mary,' said Willie, butting in. 'You've no right to be saying that.'

'I'm sorry,' she said, dropping her voice again. 'I know it's wrong to speak ill of the dead. I know that. But she was, Willie, she was flirting with him!'

Willie MacPherson shrugged his shoulders as if to say that it was nothing to do with him.

'Men!' Mary MacPherson spat out. 'I bet you was taken in yourself, you great pillock! She wasn't making eyes at you, you know. It was that Tallyforth she was after!'

Maggie Fraser changed tack.

'So what time was it that you last saw her yesterday evening?'

'It would have been about eleven thirty,' said Willie MacPherson. 'Mary and I came below deck. Mr Tallyforth and the lassie stayed up on deck for a minute or two after us.'

'So Chief Inspector Tallyforth would have been the last to see her?'

'Aye, I suppose so,' said Willie.

'And did you hear anything in the night?' Maggie Fraser asked.

'No,' said Willie, shifting uncomfortably.

'And you didn't get up in the night?'

'No,' he replied firmly but with an anxious look.

'Are you sure?' she pressed, looking keenly at him.

'I can vouch for Willie,' said Mary defensively. 'He was snoring all night. I'd have heard him if he'd got up.'

There was a pause. Inspector Maggie Fraser continued staring at Willie for several seconds.

'Was there anyone else on the pier when you came back to the boat last night? Anyone acting suspiciously?'

'No, Inspector,' said Mary. 'There was just those Americans who are here for the games, they were sitting on the pier wall eating fish and chips when we passed. But there was no-one else about.'

Inspector Maggie Fraser drained her mug of tea and put the notebook in which she had been writing back into her tunic pocket.

'Well, if you think of anything else,' she said, 'let me know. I have to speak further with your other guest, Chief Inspector Tallyforth.'

In the small post office, which is situated on the narrow Quay Brae that leads up from the pier to the main town, Hamish MacLeod was serving. A small queue, comprising four people, waited to be served despite the fact that it was only just after nine in the morning and the shop had only just opened.

Hamish MacLeod at work was not the same as Hamish MacLeod at rest. At work, behind the counter of the post office, serving the community whose members relied on his services so much for their pensions and benefits, Hamish was the soul of discretion - modest, self-effacing, quietly-spoken, and a person of infinite patience. That may not have been the true Hamish MacLeod but it was the demeanour he had learned to adopt from years of serving in the post office, whose complexities were beyond the understanding of most people but were comprehensible to and therefore translatable by Hamish. This meant that he was relied upon; this meant that his word - at least in the matter of all things postal - was gospel; this meant, in short, that Hamish had power. And, having that power, he did not need to adopt the sort of aggressive tone and manner that the powerless sometimes adopt. Which helped to explain why Hamish was so aggressive in his attitude to the tolls on the Skye Bridge, against which he, like so many other of his fellow islanders on Skye, felt powerless.

'Would you be Hamish MacLeod?'

34

Hamish looked up from behind his counter where he was completing an entry relating to his last customer.

The man who smilingly faced him seemed somehow familiar, though he couldn't place him. He certainly wasn't a Portree man and his accent was very English. The man wore a thin mustard-yellow turtle-neck shirt. He was clean-shaven, almost cherubic in his features, his dark hair pulled tightly back from his forehead into a short ponytail. Rayban sun-glasses sat on the top of his head, attached to a dayglo green cord which dangled around the back of his neck.

'Who'd be wanting to know?' asked Hamish suspiciously, scratching his beard and eyeing the man who faced him through the glass partition. He'd heard of the various tricks got up to by their enemies in the Skye Bridge Corporation, or the Anglo-Canadian Bank, as they had now found out the real developers to be.

'I was given your name,' said the man at the other side of the counter behind the glass. 'By a friend.'

'Oh, yes!' growled Hamish MacLeod, even more suspicious now. 'And who would that be then?'

The man in the yellow shirt, whom Hamish put in his mid-thirties despite the cherubic face, smiled winningly through the glass at him.

'Let's just say it's someone who knows your work.'

'My work!' Hamish spluttered. 'Here? In the Oifis a Phuist? What are you talking about, man?'

The man smiled back at him again.

'Our deeds determine us, Hamish,' he said.

'What?'

'Or, as the bible has it, "By their fruits you shall know them",' the young man smiled again, seeing the confusion he was causing. 'I mean your work for the community, Hamish, your fight against the tolls of the new Skye Bridge, which I traversed for the first time yester morning and which I have to say provides a splendid view.'

'Splendid view, my arse!' said Hamish, then, realising that he was at his place of work and that this behaviour was completely out of character therein, he blushed bright red and touched the

35

knot of his yellow tartan tie.

'Quite!' said his interlocutor.

'Look, I don't know who you are or what your name is,' said Hamish fiercely under his breath, 'but I have a post office to run. I don't have time to discuss other matters with strangers.'

Beads of sweat appeared on his bald head and ran down to the fringe of ginger hair around his ears.

'No, of course not, Hamish,' laughed the other man. 'Oh, could you just let me have a book of stamps? Yes, first class. I never buy anything else! Do you think you might feel up to telling a curious English person all about your little SKATTY project some time? I'll be in the lounge at the Royal Hotel at lunch time. Would you care to join me? I might have something of interest for you.'

Hamish MacLeod looked again at the smiling face before him. Who was this person? he thought. What does he want with me? How does he know about me?

'Maybe,' he muttered.' I'll see if I can make it.'

As he said it, Hamish MacLeod was aware that he did not mean to turn up. He thought he was merely getting rid of this troublesome customer. And sure enough, as if on cue, the man in the yellow shirt span round and left the post office.

But, as the morning wore on, Hamish became more and more curious about this odd encounter. By midday that curiosity had finally got the better of him and he had decided that he had to go to the Royal Hotel and meet this stranger when he closed the post office for the lunch period at one o'clock.

'Look, I'm telling you that the woman I was going on this cruise with was murdered,' Tallyforth yelled into the telephone that he was carrying around with him as he paced up and down in the lobby of the Royal Hotel. 'Yes, murdered! This morning! And this Inspector Fraser is trying to keep me off the case by claiming that I'm a material witness!'

He listened to the calming voice from the other end of the line for a few seconds, then interrupted.

'Sir, this Inspector Fraser is just out of police college, I can tell. She's doing everything by the rule book because that's what she's been taught to do. I bet she's never seen a dead body before, let alone solved a murder. The nearest anybody gets to crime up here is protesting about the bloody tolls on the new Skye Bridge!'

He paused again to take in what Chief Superintendent Albert 'Nobby' Clarke was saying to him.

'Look, sir, I know I'm supposed to be on holiday. Yes, I know I requested leave in order to get away from it all. I know all that, sir, but there's been a murder. And it's of someone that I had got to know a little in a situation where I was actually present. I can't just walk away from it all.'

There was a further pause.

'Sir, I'm requesting that you insist I be involved in this murder enquiry.'

Pause. This time at both ends of the line.

'Sir, you can square this with the Chief Constable later. And he can square it with the Chief Constable of the Highlands Force. But don't cut me out of this, sir!'

A longer pause.

Then there was a reply, long, slow and detailed. Tallyforth's face drained of all its colour as he listened to it.

'Sir, are you ordering me back to Birmingham?' he said between clenched teeth. 'Because, if you are, I would remind you that I am still officially on leave. And I intend to complete that period of leave. You can refuse me permission to involve myself in the detection of whoever murdered Cassie Dillon, but you can't stop me having my leave here in Skye. Goodbye, sir!'

He slammed the phone into its cradle and put it noisily back on the reception desk.

'If they think they can keep me out of this, they've got another think coming,' he muttered to the lobby area, which was empty apart from the girl Annie who was doing temporary reception duty.

Tallyforth thrust his hand into his pocket and found the tape he had liberated from Cassie Dillon's Walkman. His face suddenly lit up.

'You wouldn't have one of those headset things, would you?' he asked Annie, striding across to the reception desk to do so. 'One of those Walkman things? I'm sure you have. All young people have them, don't they?'

'I've not got it with me, sir,' she replied. 'But it's only in the kitchen. If you wait a minute, I'll fetch it for you.'

And, before he could say any more, she was off to the kitchen, returning a few seconds later with the necessary article, which she presented to him.

'How does it work?' he demanded.

Patiently she showed him how to insert the tape, to fast forward or to reverse, and how to eject.

He followed her movements carefully and, when she had finished, inserted the tape he had taken from Cassie Dillon's machine, placed the headphones over his ears, and stood in the lobby listening.

'I don't recognise this,' he said after a couple of minutes. 'Van Morrison's my style. This is...I don't know how to describe it. Would you recognise it?'

He handed the machinery back to Annie, who in turn listened for a short while.

'That's Donnie,' she squealed, as she quickly recognised the rendition. 'Donnie Munro. He's from Portree. He was at the same high school I go to.'

Tallyforth was none the wiser.

'Who's Donnie Munro?' he asked innocently. 'Is he some local folk singer?'

Annie looked at him in disbelief.

'You don't know who Donnie Munro is!' she exclaimed. 'He's the singer with Runrig! They're Scotland's greatest band! Surely you've heard of them?'

Tallyforth shook his head.

'Sorry,' he said. 'New to me. Have they been going for long?'

She gave him another old-fashioned look.

'They've been playing for over twenty years,' she said. 'That tape is *Mara*. The one you were listening to is called *The Mighty Atlantic*. Surely you've heard their version of *Rhythm of my Heart*? And *Loch Lomond*?'

'Afraid not,' he said, shaking his head. 'Are they just as well known in England?'

'I guess so,' Annie said, 'though I don't really know. They certainly play gigs there. Donnie's leaving, you know.'

He was only mildly interested.

'Why's that?'

'He's going into politics. He stood in the election in May. Said he wanted to scrap the tolls on the Bridge. Did very well. They're going to have to find another singer.'

'Pity,' he said, though he didn't really have any view on the matter. 'Still, thanks for your help anyway.'

She passed the tape back to him and watched him as he strode across to the window and stared out at the clear blue sky, where the mid-morning sun was beating down.

'The map,' he was muttering to himself. 'I must get the map. I've got the tape. Now I must get the map.'

He watched a lone herring gull glide across the skyline, then dive suddenly towards the harbour, its white plumage reflecting the sun's rays.

FOUR

'Where is she then?' Tallyforth demanded of the elderly policeman behind the desk in the Portree police station. 'I have to see her immediately.'

'Who would you be seeking, sir?'

'Inspector Fraser, of course,' Tallyforth snapped.

'I'm afraid that isn't possible, sir,' came the reply, spoken in a slow voice. 'Inspector Fraser isn't available at the present. Who'd be asking for her?'

Tallyforth looked at the policeman facing him and paused. He recognised the type - solid, reliable, never seeking promotion, well-respected in his community but with no drive. Still, he might be worth getting to know.

'Sorry, Sergeant,' he said, in a milder tone, leaning one elbow on the counter between them and speaking in an almost conspiratorial tone. 'Drive you a bit hard, does she? Bit of a tyrant, eh?'

'Who'd you say you were, sir?' Sergeant Donald MacKenzie wrinkled his nose, which had the effect of causing his eyes almost to close. He was puzzled at this unexpected familiarity that was being shown.

'I'm in the same business as you,' said Tallyforth. 'In England. Work from Birmingham. Mercian Force.'

'Oh aye?' Donald MacKenzie was still quizzical. 'What you doing up here then?'

Tallyforth leaned even closer.

'I'm on holiday,' he said. 'Or I was. Till a few hours ago.'

'Sir?'

'D'you like having a woman as a boss?' asked Tallyforth, resuming his previous tack.

Donald MacKenzie stiffened.

'Inspector Fraser was put in charge of this police station in June and I do what she tells me to do. What's your name again, sir?'

'Detective Chief Inspector Tallyforth,' came the reply and Tallyforth flashed his police I.D. card. 'And yours? I wouldn't want to mention the wrong person to Inspector Fraser.'

Donald MacKenzie looked worried but told him, unsure whether he should be showing respect to a superior officer from another force or loyalty to Inspector Fraser.

'So, Donald, you're not keen on working for a woman? Never had to do it before, am I right?'

'Aye, that's right, sir,' came the reply. Donald MacKenzie had worked in the Western Isles all his police career, firstly in Stornoway where he originally hailed from, then for some years in Mull, and for the last fifteen years in Portree. Here he had become a stalwart of the local community, being one of the founder members of the Isle of Skye Pipe Band and in recent years one of the judges of the piping competitions at the annual Highland Games. 'Life hasn't exactly been the same since Inspector Fraser arrived from Edinburgh.'

'And that was in June, you said?' continued Tallyforth.

'Aye, that's right,' said Donald MacKenzie. 'Inspector MacLean retired in the spring and they sent us Inspector Fraser.'

Tallyforth could tell from Donald MacKenzie's sighing, head-shaking, and from his sagging shoulders that there was more to this than simply not liking to work for a woman.

'So, what's the problem, Donald?' he pressed.

'I'm not sure I should be telling you all this, sir.'

'Trust me, Donald.'

'Well, it's not just that I've never worked for a woman before in the police,' he began. 'I knew that it would be hard to do that but I've done my best and I don't think that she'd have that much to complain about, even though she may not like my style. I mean, she thinks I'm too familiar with the local folk and that's not good for police work.'

'And is that true, Donald?'

'I didn't think it was a problem,' he said hesitantly. 'Until we had the bridge.'

'Yes?'

'Well, we've never had major crime on Skye, you know. It's a small community and everyone knows everyone else's business. Aye, we have people who break the law but it's never anything that we cannot deal with. The worst we ever had in my time in Portree was a spate of burglaries five years since but that turned out to be some lads from Glasgow who thought they were on to some easy pickings. Till we caught them red-handed trying to prise open the till at the Community Centre in the dead of night. But, since the bridge opened, it hasn't been easy because we've had to police the toll. And that means we've had to face some of our friends who've been protesting about it.'

'And I'll bet that's cause a bit of bad feeling,' said Tallyforth.

'Aye, well it wasn't easy,' said Donald MacKenzie, 'but we managed it fine at first. Hamish MacLeod from the post office and I have known each other for years, for we used to pipe together. He's not a criminal. He's been one of the leading lights in S.K.A.T. - that's what they call themselves, the anti-toll folk. And people like Hamish knew we were only doing what we had to do and they didn't hold it against us. Until June, that is, when Inspector Fraser arrived and decided that we were being too soft.'

'What happened then?'

'We'd never used force to move the folk on when they were protesting. We used to just stand and watch and make sure that the protests were peaceful. Then, when they'd made their point, we all went home. That way we could all continue to live together. But Inspector Fraser said we'd to take a stronger line so, when the next protest came in July, we had to physically move some of them away from the tolls. And that wasn't popular.'

'So that's caused some friction?'

'Aye, it's not so easy to go out for a drink these days,' Donald MacKenzie said, shaking his head. 'She may be a good copper, but she's not so good at understanding this community.'

'So where is she now, Donald?'

'She's down at the harbour. There's been a death on one of the boats and she's there with one of the young bobbies. I don't know much more than that.'

'So you don't know who's died?'

42

'Just that it was a woman,' Donald MacKenzie answered. 'The inspector rushed in here about ten o'clock, just after I'd come on duty, went to her office with some bits and pieces in her hand, then rushed out again without them. All she told me was there'd been an incident and that a woman was dead on one of the boats. That was all.'

'Donald,' said Tallyforth, picking his words carefully, 'I know about the dead woman. I was on the boat with Inspector Fraser. If I'm not mistaken, one of the things she brought back to her office from the boat was a map of the isles and I really need to see that map. Would you go and see if it's there?'

Sergeant Donald MacKenzie looked very uncomfortable with this request.

'I'm not sure that the Inspector would want me to let you have it,' he said.

'I just want a look at it, Donald,' said Tallyforth. 'That's all. You can tell the Inspector when she gets back. It'll be no problem, I assure you.'

'Well, if it's just a look, maybe it'd be alright. Just wait a minute, will you?'

And Donald MacKenzie left his desk to look for the requested article, returning a moment later with the folded map, which he placed on the desk in front of Tallyforth, at the same time opening it up so that it could be seen fully.

'You'd better not touch it, sir,' he said. 'You know, fingerprints.'

Tallyforth half-smiled.

'I am aware of that, Sergeant. But thanks.'

And Tallyforth spent the next few minutes scrutinising the map closely, particularly the points where the pencilled crosses had been drawn. He made a mental note of each one, filing the geographical location and name of each in his head.

Willie and Mary MacPherson sat in the office of Iain McMillan in Wentworth Street. Facing them, behind his desk which was piled high with papers and files, sat Iain McMillan himself, no longer dressed in the casual apparel of the previous evening but wearing a sharp, double-breasted suit of light grey and a cream shirt with plain red tie. His blond hair was neatly parted and fell down equally on either side of his forehead. He wore a pair of gold-rimmed half-spectacles, over which he looked at them. His small office, situated above a gift shop, had three large black filing cabinets in it and a book case filled with legal reference books. On one wall hung a Paul Klee print.

'So why are you telling me all about this?' he asked, leaning back and swivelling in his chair, a silver pen in his right hand . 'There's been a death on your boat, a woman who was to be your passenger on a two-week cruise of the Hebrides. And the other passenger, who's a detective, has told you that she's been strangled with a silk scarf. And you think Inspector Fraser suspects you. What did she say to make you think that?'

Willie MacPherson looked at his wife and she looked back at him reproachfully.

'Well, Mr McMillan, we don't think she suspects either of us just now,' Mary MacPherson began.' But, you see, when she gets on to the police computer, she will, believe me, she will.'

Iain McMillan smiled thinly at them. He had never had much to do with the MacPhersons. Neither Mary nor her husband had been embroiled in the S.K.A.T. campaign, which was how he himself had come into contact with so many of the islanders. Iain McMillan had only been in Portree a couple of years, having joined the practice which old Alex MacDonald had run there for nearly half a century. It was Alex who had suggested to him that he offer free legal advice to the S.K.A.T. campaign - 'It'll be a way of getting accepted,' he'd opined - and it had certainly done that. And 'getting accepted' was shorthand for 'getting business', he had come to realise very quickly. For, as well as being embroiled in the saga of the court cases and appeals over the non-payment of tolls on the bridge, he had found that more and more of the islanders were wending their way to his door with their routine legal problems and concerns. So, business was booming, although as yet he himself wasn't feeling the financial benefits of this, since he had had to take out a large loan to borrow the money he needed to buy into the partnership with old Alex MacDonald.

'You've had a parking ticket?' he quizzed, with a light laugh. 'Or maybe you've been caught smuggling cocaine into Portree?'

But Mary MacPherson was not laughing. Nor was her husband,

who sat gloomily next to her, looking down at his feet. and saying nothing.

'I'm afraid it's more serious than that, Mr McMillan,' she said. 'Something much more serious.'

Iain McMillan frowned, pushed a stray blond lock away from his forehead, and leaned forward with his pen poised to write down whatever it was she was about to tell him.

'Aye, my Willie has a criminal record,' she said. 'He's done time, Mr McMillan. He was in Barlinnie for three months.'

Iain McMillan gulped. He looked at the mild-mannered figure of *The Flodigarry's* skipper who sat hunched before him. Barlinnie, he knew, was a high-security prison for offenders considered a threat to the public.

'What for?' he asked. 'When? Was it a long time ago? Recently?'

She sighed and shifted her weight to the right of her chair.

'Willie was eighteen. He'd left his family in Broadford to go and find work in Glasgow. And he'd found work in the Clyde shipyards, like many a Skye lad before him, though there's none go that way now the yard's nearly gone. Anyway, I'll not bore you with the details but you can probably guess them for yourself. Willie's a young man on his own in Glasgow, earning good money, looking to enjoy himself. And one Saturday night he's had too much to drink and he gets into a fight - he cannot remember to this day what the fight was about - but the man he's fighting goes down and catches his head on a lamppost. By the time they get him to the hospital, it's too late. He's had a brain haemorrhage and they put him on a life-support machine. He never regains consciousness and two weeks later they turn off the life-support, because there's no hope. And Willie's charged with murder.'

Iain McMillan could feel his heart fluttering.

'But surely that would be culpable homicide,' he protested. 'Didn't his defence argue for that?'

'Aye,' she sighed. 'In the end that's what they found him guilty of. And then, after he'd been inside for three months, his solicitor got an anonymous note which said that the dead man had a history of heart trouble and his doctor had only given him three months to live. Odd they never found that at the autopsy. Anyway, they went to appeal and eventually it was heard and Willie was released.

But he never got a pardon, so he'll still be on their records as a killer.'

Iain McMillan let out a whistle.

'Is that why you've not been involved in the bridge protests?' he asked.

'Aye, partly,' Mary MacPherson said. 'I took Willie on when he came back to Skye after his time inside. He was a damaged man and his own family didn't want anything to do with him. I was working at my uncle's in Uig, in the chandlers. I loved being about boats and my uncle had taken me on and trained me in the business. And he used to let me go with him in his own boat in the summer when he used to make a few bob taking tourists out for a day's fishing. Willie turned up at the door one day and I took pity on the poor soul. I persuaded my uncle to let Willie come and help us. Eventually we wed and got our own boat. But I made Willie promise never to get into a situation where he might want to use his fists again and to keep off the drink. So I kept him out of trouble. He cannot help it, you see, Mr McMillan. He was born with a quick temper, that's all. But he didn't kill that lassie on the boat last night. I know, because I was with him all night. He snores very heavy and I'd have known if he'd got up from my side. Anyway, what reason would he have, Mr McMillan?'

'I really don't know, Mrs MacPherson,' stammered the solicitor. 'But why are you telling me all this?'

'Because I think that Inspector Fraser, when she finds Willie's record, will be arresting him on suspicion, Mr McMillan,' she replied, leaning forward to emphasise her point. 'And we want to know if you'll represent him if that happens. What d'you say?'

Iain McMillan struggled with a set of conflicting emotions inside himself before he replied.

'Yes,' he said finally and forced a mile. 'I'd be delighted to.'

It was late morning and the sun was beating down from high above in a brilliant blue sky with not a cloud in sight.

A small knot of German students sat around the War Memorial next to the bus station in Somerled Square in the middle of Portree, their nylon rucksacks behind them and being used to lean against. The heat had forced them to discard their fleeces and they sat and absorbed the sun in their tee-shirts. In another corner of the square, the four brawny Americans that had been pointed out to Tallyforth on the previous evening - the Highland Games competitors - were dribbling a basketball around each other, dressed in black vests with red piping round the armholes and white track-suit bottoms, with similar piping down the seams.

Tallyforth was sitting on a bench in the square, drawing from memory on to a sheet of paper the pattern of islands and, in particular, the places which had been marked with a cross on the map which Inspector Maggie Fraser had taken from Cassie Dillon's cabin and which he had recently persuaded Sergeant Donald MacKenzie to show him. The names by each cross were etched clearly in his mind but he only had limited cartographical skills, so he was aware that his map would only bear a fleeting resemblance to an actual map. Nevertheless it would do. And he felt it was vital that he got this information down before his attention was distracted by anything else.

Consequently, he did not notice the thin young man with a pony-tail, wearing Rayban sunglasses, who passed in front of him, between the German students and the bench Tallyforth was sitting on. And he certainly didn't notice the thin smile on the man's face as he passed - a smile that was directed at Tallyforth, a smile that initially registered the surprise of recognition then a smile that became smugly self-satisfied as its owner decided against acknowledging recognition. The smiling figure gathered pace as he moved past Tallyforth and headed in the direction of the harbour.

When he had finished drawing his map, Tallyforth sat back and opened his face to the blazing sun, at the same time stretching out his arms along the back of the wooden bench. Above him, he could see a posse of seagulls circling, their outstretched wings gliding through the heat-sodden air. And, as he let the sun's heat seep slowly through his body, he pondered on Cassie Dillon's death.

It was now almost six hours since Willie MacPherson had roused him from his sleep to confront him with Cassie's dead body. The bitter wrath that had seized him at that time, to be replaced almost as quickly with equally bitter sorrow, had all been replaced by a cold and steely determination to find her killer. The voices of his

47

training and the voices of his experience as a detective had resumed their control of him. Though he was still angry, though he still was aware of what he had lost, though he still remembered that last - and first - look he had had at her naked body, though he could still taste her cold nipples in his mouth, he had channelled those thoughts into a focused resolve. And, if Inspector Maggie Fraser and Chief Superintendent 'Nobby' Clarke would not let him be officially involved in the investigation, he would do things unofficially and in his own way.

There was something very odd about this murder, he surmised. Cassie Dillon, as far as he knew, had never been to Skye before in her life. She had come there purely to go on the bird-watching cruise of the Hebrides, as he himself had done. So, the only people who knew she was on the island and about to go on this cruise were Tallyforth himself and the two MacPhersons. From what she had told him - and he had had no reason to disbelieve her - she had no close family, her ex-husband was still in Canada and they had been divorced for several years, and they had no children. Her parents, so she had said , were dead and she had been an only child. She might have told friends or neighbours in Tamworth where she was going, maybe even leaving a contact address such as the Royal Hotel, but that seemed an unlikely source for investigation. There was the friend she had stayed with in Oban - the teacher, who she'd known since university. What was his name again? Donald McMillan? No, that was the name of the teacher that Mary MacPherson had mentioned, brother of the local solicitor. He couldn't remember whether she had actually mentioned a name at all. No! Wait a minute! She had called him 'James' the evening before. And he searched again in his memories. Yes! he remembered now. James Orr. She had used his full name in the Café Rouge. That seemed like an eternity ago now, he thought.

And the anger re-entered his soul. Tallyforth gritted his teeth to keep it in check.

Maybe James Orr would be a starting point? Or maybe he should do some further work on these crosses on the map?

He must get a decent map from somewhere and transfer the locations from his hastily-drawn version to that proper map. Maybe that would begin to shed some light.

Tallyforth stood, folding his paper into quarters before stuffing it into his pocket. He looked around him, noticing for the first time the German students, who had now recovered some of their composure after their hot journey and were conversing with each other in loud voices, at the same time passing round bread and slices of bratwurst and cans of Heineken lager. He also saw the four Americans, who had now given up their basketball and were variously fastening up or slinging over their shoulders their huge sports bags.

He remembered that they had passed the Americans as they walked back to the boat along the pier the previous night. Maybe they were worth talking to? But no, Inspector Fraser would have been told about them. She would no doubt give them a grilling!

Tallyforth hitched up the waistband of his trousers and turned on to Wentworth Street to find a shop that sold a map of the Hebrides.

It was lunchtime in the Royal Hotel and the dining room was unusually full. A number of recently-arrived guests had swelled the regular lunch crowd. Most of these new guests were couples, most were elderly - in their sixties or seventies, though all were remarkably healthy-looking - and they all seemed to know each other. So, although they generally sat in twos or fours at table, it was not uncommon for conversations to be taking place across tables or across the room. Conversations were not untypically about each other's health, about each other's families, about each other's friends, especially any that were missing. Conversation also touched on the Skye Bridge, though this wasn't a major focus, and briefly on the hopes for a Scottish parliament.

A stranger might have surmised that these elderly couples only met like this once a year and such a surmise would have been correct, for the men present were all former champion pipers who returned annually to Portree to assist in the judging of the piping competitions at the Highland Games, due to occur on the Wednesday of that week.

One particular stranger, one who had indeed surmised all of the above, sat at a corner table, smiling gently to himself. He was the man in the mustard-yellow turtle-neck with the short ponytail who had confronted Hamish MacLeod early that morning and he was the same man who had spotted Tallyforth busy drawing his map in Somerled Square a short while previously. On the table in front of him was a glass of chilled white wine, which his left hand clasped lightly.

Suddenly Hamish MacLeod himself appeared in the doorway to the dining room, glancing round and nodding at several of the couples in recognition, for Hamish himself of course had had a canny reputation as a piper in his younger days. But it was not the old pipers that Hamish was seeking to renew acquaintance with today; it was the smiling man at the corner table.

'Good of you to come, Mr MacLeod,' said the stranger. 'I hope this is not inconveniencing you too much.'

Hamish MacLeod glowered back at him and pulled a chair out from beneath the table.

'No, we always shut for an hour at lunchtime,' he said, sitting down heavily and pouring himself a glass of water from the jug on the table. 'Now who are you? And what do you want with me?'

The pony-tailed man smiled again.

'Just call me Smith,' he replied. 'John Smith.'

'That's not your real name then?' queried Hamish, raising a ginger eyebrow. 'Where are you from?'

'Why, England, of course,' came the reply, and he sipped at his glass of wine.

'No, man,' said Hamish MacLeod exasperatedly. 'I mean, who do you work for? What are you doing here? Who told you about me?'

'So many questions, so many questions, Mr MacLeod.' John Smith held up his hands in mock horror. 'Or may I call you Hamish? You see, we have a lot in common, you and I. It would be nice if we could get on.'

'Well? What about some answers then?'

John Smith sighed and took another sip of wine.

'Such a shame!' he said. 'Why are people so mistrustful? All I want is to be your friend, Hamish, and you keep asking me all these questions.'

'Look, man, I'm giving up my lunch hour to talk to some stranger and all I'm hearing is blether,' said Hamish angrily. 'Now, either state your business at once or I'm off.'

'What we call our despair is often only the painful eagerness of unfed hope,' John Smith said mysteriously. 'You're angry with me, Hamish, because half of you believes that I may have something to offer which might be of benefit, while the other half of you wants nothing to do with an Englishman. Am I right?'

'I've had enough of this,' said Hamish, pushing back his chair and making to stand up. 'John Smith, or whatever your name is, you're just wasting my time.'

John Smith put up the palm of his left hand to stop him.

'Please, Hamish, listen to me for five minutes. If you don't want to hear any more then, you're free to go. And I shall not bother you any more.'

Hamish MacLeod grudgingly inched his chair back under the table.

'Go on,' he said. 'Five minutes. No more.'

'Thank you.' John Smith sipped his wine delicately again then leaned both his elbows on the table and put his hands together in front of his nose as if in prayer. 'Hamish, I work for the government. I'm in the Home Office and my normal work is in London but, since the election, I've been on secondment to the Scottish Office to help oversee the devolution plans. Since the end of May, I've been based in Edinburgh but actually I have been travelling the length and breadth of Scotland. My job is to ascertain the mood of the nation in its various manifestations. In order to do that, wherever I go throughout this country, I am given briefing papers by the civil servants in the Scottish Office about the movers and shakers in that particular territory. You would be surprised, my dear Hamish, how much information the government holds on its people.'

Hamish MacLeod, who had been taking in the first part of John Smith's explanation quite calmly, allowed a reaction to this last bit to show in the agitation in his manner.

'Yes, Hamish,' continued John Smith dryly, 'you would be very surprised. However, I am not here to bore you with unnecessary detail about the shenanigans of some of Bonnie Scotland's better known citizens. I am here because your name was very prominent among those I was advised I should talk to about reaction in the

Isles to the proposals for devolution.'

'Why me?' Hamish MacLeod asked in genuine surprise. 'I've lived in Portree all my life, nowhere else. I cannot speak for the rest of Skye, never mind the Isles.'

'My dear Hamish,' came the smooth reply, 'you have been chosen because, as the master of the Portree post office, you are a servant of the crown, a servant, moreover, who must speak to virtually every adult resident of Portree and the surrounding villages when they call to conduct their business. From this alone you would be in possession, inevitably, of an informed view of how these residents are viewing the government's proposals. You are also a judge at the Skye Highland Games piping competitions, along with a number of our fellow guests, as I assume.'

He wafted his hand briefly to indicate the rest of the dining room.

'I believe you won the coveted Dunvegan Medal yourself back in the nineteen seventies,' continued John Smith. 'After you came back from Glasgow University. That too gives you a unique insight into the views of the elders of this society, the people who strive to preserve the traditions of their forefathers and keep the Gaelic flame alive. But that's not all! Oh no, dear Hamish, you are also a very important member of S.K.A.T., the Skye and Kyle Against Tolls group, who gave the last government such a torrid time over their mishandling of the Skye Bridge exercise.'

'The present lot's not much better,' interjected Hamish angrily.

'Quite! But we will talk of that later. Remember, however, that S.K.A.T. provides you with another constituency, another source of views. But there is one other important fact about you, Hamish, and that is that you are a member of the Scottish National Party and have been all your adult life. In fact, I believe you considered standing for parliament in the last election, is that not so? But in the end you felt that you needed to put all your energies into the toll business.'

Hamish MacLeod looked at him in astonishment. He was totally amazed that these different facets of his life were so well known to this stranger, this smooth-faced, smooth-talking stranger with the thin fingers who sat opposite him and whom he had never met until a few hours previously, and then only through the glass partition that was the post office counter.

'Mr Smith, you know an awful lot about me but I know next to nothing about you,' he said. 'What is it you're wanting from me?'

John Smith took his hands from the prayer position and took another sip of his wine.

'No hurry, Hamish, no hurry at all. I want you to think about what I have said and then I want you to try to put together some thoughts on how you see the people of the Isles voting in the devolution referendum. No-one will hold you responsible if you're wrong, but the government does need to take a view as to where it might best need to focus its energies in order to ensure that the referendum produces the right result, if you know what I mean. You will probably feel the need to sound out some of those contacts you have, maybe talk to some of your friends, maybe do a bit of phoning round. You know the sort of thing. One point, however, is most important. I must ask you to do all this secretly. You are not, under any circumstances to reveal the fact of who I am or what I have asked you to do.'

Hamish MacLeod snorted.

'And why should I do anything for you, mister?' he queried.

'Because you are a loyal servant of the crown,' John Smith responded. 'But also because I have information that you will find particularly interesting.'

'About the bridge? About the toll? Has the minister decided to scrap it after all?'

'Dear, dear, Hamish, you do have a one track mind. No, this is not directly about the bridge, though the bridge will no doubt play its part. No, this is something much more far-reaching.'

'What?'

'It's about oil,' he said. 'It's about the biggest oil exploration ever, that will make the North Sea operation seem minute by comparison. It's about the Atlantic Frontier. When that gets operational, it could see an explosion of wealth in the Western Isles. Do you want to know more? Will you help me?'

FIVE

She had finally caught up with him, but only after sending Sergeant MacKenzie to hunt him down. He'd been found pacing up and down the pier and had apparently not been willing to come initially. He had allowed himself to be persuaded after agreeing with MacKenzie that it was probably better for both of them if no mention was made of the fact that he, MacKenzie, had let him, Tallyforth, look at the map Inspector Fraser had brought back from *The Flodigarry*. For, Donald MacKenzie had reasoned with Tallyforth, if she were to find out his interest in the map, it might lead her to suspect that the Chief Inspector was intent on pursuing his enquiries independently. And he, Donald MacKenzie, was fully aware by now, from the angry comments of Inspector Fraser, that Tallyforth had been barred by his own Chief Superintendent from getting involved because he was a material witness to the woman's death, which was looking more and more like murder. It would therefore be best, he had argued, if they kept the whole business about the map to themselves for the moment. And Tallyforth, as he listened, came to appreciate the wiliness of Sergeant Donald MacKenzie, who wasn't the slow-witted bobby he'd taken him for at first. It suited him to let the inspector believe he was not on the case, so he had accompanied the sergeant to the police station.

Though it was mid-afternoon, Inspector Maggie Fraser still looked as smart as she had looked first thing that morning - no creases apparent in her blouse, her brown hair pulled neatly back into a bun, her make-up freshly applied.

'Chief Inspector, I'm very sorry about this,' she began, after ushering Tallyforth into her office and offering him coffee, which he refused. 'We didn't get off to a very good start this morning. I apologise. I'm sure you'll appreciate that this is the most serious case I've had to deal with since I came here in June and I have to play things by the book. I'm aware that I've yet to win over some of the local police, Sergeant MacKenzie in particular, so I have to be sure that everything I do is done properly and according to police procedures.'

Tallyforth, sensing that there was a more emollient manner to her than earlier in the day, nodded acknowledgement but said nothing.

'You'll also be aware, I'm sure,' she continued, 'that your Chief Superintendent Clarke has been in touch with my Chief Constable to insist that you be kept out of this investigation. And that was not at my instigation, I assure you, though it does match with what I believe to be correct procedure.'

Still Tallyforth said nothing, though she noticed that he was listening to her carefully.

'So,' she tried again, 'shall we begin at the beginning? Would you like to tell me all you know about the deceased and your relationship with her?'

Tallyforth felt the blood rising inside him. What relationship? They had only met twice! How dare she? What was she suggesting? What had she found out? Was she deliberately trying to goad him? But, almost as soon as these thoughts had flashed through his brain, others followed - others which reminded him of her slender fingers in his, her lips kissing his cheek, her deep hazel eyes. And he remembered how his heart had been stirred by Cassie Dillon.

So, although the inspector may have been trying to goad him by asking a leading question [and he recognised the technique!], she had hit on a kernel of truth that he would not have really wanted to reveal.

'Inspector, I met Cassie Dillon for the first time just over a week ago,' he answered at last, measuring his words carefully. 'We had both, it turns out, replied to an advertisement in *The Sunday Times* placed by the MacPhersons for a bird-watching cruise of the Hebrides in their boat. The coincidence of both of us living in the Midlands led to us enjoying a meal together in Birmingham, at which we shared a little of ourselves as a preliminary to coming to Portree for the cruise I've just mentioned.'

'So did you meet again before coming to Portree?' she asked.

'No, inspector,' he said firmly, crossing his legs. 'I'm surprised you haven't already discovered from the MacPhersons that Cassie Dillon has been staying in Oban for the past week with an old friend of hers from university. Consequently, even if we had wished to meet again, it would not have been possible since she already made that arrangement before we met.'

Maggie Fraser looked up from the notes she was scribbling. She reached for a cigarette from the open packet of Benson and Hedges on her desk and then threw the packet across the desk in Tallyforth's direction.

'Smoke?'

'Never touch them,' he said briskly, pushing the packet back in her direction.

She clicked on her lighter and drew in the smoke, before releasing it slowly through her pursed lips.

'You wouldn't happen to know the name of this friend, would you, Chief Inspector?'

'Yes, it was Orr. James Orr. He teaches music at Oban Academy she said,' Tallyforth informed her. 'I think you need to talk to him, Inspector. I don't know of anyone else that might have known of her whereabouts. She has no family, or so she told me. And, if I'm right that it was someone who knew her who murdered her, then I think James Orr needs questioning about his movements in the last couple of days.'

He coughed as the smoke from her cigarette reached him.

'We don't know she was murdered, Chief Inspector,' she reminded him. 'I haven't had the report from forensic yet.'

'You have some other view of how she came to be lying dead in a cabin in a boat in Portree harbour with heavy bruising around her neck?' he asked, pulling a face of disbelief at her.

'I told you, Chief Inspector Tallyforth,' she said, her voice now back to its steely tone, 'I do things by the book. At the moment, all I know is that we have a dead woman on our hands, who was very much alive last night. Her body has now been taken away to the mortuary and I'm expecting to hear some preliminary results this afternoon.'

'Ha!' exhaled Tallyforth.

'You were the last person to see her last night, I believe,' she continued. 'What time would that have been?'

'About eleven thirty.'

'And what would you say was her mood at that time?'

Tallyforth looked keenly at her, noticing how she looked down at her writing whenever she asked a particularly pointed question. How could he describe Cassie's mood? It had seemed to him that she had been as full of happiness as he himself had been. She had been laughing and smiling all evening, as he had been. They had listened with amusement to the MacPhersons' tales about their cruises and about the foibles of some of their passengers. He hadn't been deluding himself, had he? She really had seemed extraordinarily happy when she had stood on tiptoe and kissed him on the cheek before going down to her cabin.

'She seemed fine,' he answered, aware of how tame a response this was. 'We'd had a good meal and a few drinks and the MacPhersons had kept us well entertained all evening with their stories.'

'And I assume you can account for your movements during the night?' she asked, again staring at her notes.

Tallyforth snorted.

'I'm surprised you haven't checked *The Flodigarry*,' he said, his voice full of disdain. 'If you had, like a good copper, you'd have realised that the only way I could have got out of the forepeak cabin I was sleeping in was through the main cabin that the MacPhersons were in. Not much chance of that without disturbing them.'

She wanted to ask about the naked body but couldn't find a way of doing so which wouldn't suggest that she thought he had been with her in the night. But, if what he said was correct, then there was no way that he could have been, without the MacPhersons knowing. She could feel herself blushing slightly at the train of her thoughts.

'Sorry, sir,' she said, slightly embarrassed now. 'I had to ask. You know, standard procedure.'

'Fraser,' Tallyforth said, rising from his seat, 'I've no idea whether you have it in you to be a good copper or not. You may have got promotion early in your career and you may know police

57

procedures inside out. But, unless you learn to go with your instincts at times, you'll never be a good copper. And now, if you'll excuse me, Fraser, I am going to do what everyone from your Chief Constable and my Chief Superintendent downwards wants me to do. I'm going to have a holiday.'

She opened her mouth to speak but thought better of it. There really was nothing more she needed from him at the moment.

'You'll not be far away?' she asked of his retreating back.' If I need to speak to you again? When I've got the forensic report?'

He paused in his exit, turning his head round to her.

'You can contact me via the Royal Hotel.'

The Flodigarry was a two-masted thirty-eight-foot ocean-going ketch with a central cockpit, which had a blue trim in contrast to the otherwise white boat. Its sloping gunwales led to a blunt stem with a traditional rake, which sparkled as the sun's rays reflected off it. Its sails were, of course, furled as it gently swayed on the calm and deep bluey-green sea of Portree harbour.

Tallyforth stood at the end of the pier gazing at the ketch, which was moored some twenty yards away from him. He noted for the first time what a fine-looking boat it was and, though not a sailor himself, he could imagine it in full sail riding at speed through the ocean.

An idea had been forming in his mind. Ever since the tape of the Scottish group Runrig singing *Mighty Atlantic* had triggered something in his head, he had begun to think that the solution to the riddle of Cassie Dillon's death lay further afield than Portree or even Skye, maybe even further afield than Scotland. It was that song which had brought to mind the map he had found by her bunk side and which, foolishly but unsurprisingly given the state of shock he was in, he had left there and which Inspector Maggie Fraser had taken possession of. When he had looked at Cassie Dillon's map in the police station, thanks to the connivance of Sergeant MacKenzie whose fortuitously-discovered dislike of his superior had led him to act in a surprisingly helpful way, Tallyforth had again had the sensation that there was some significance to those crosses. That was why he had been so wholly engaged in the redrawing of that map in Somerled Square earlier that day. And that was why he had now purchased a fuller map of the islands and marked precisely the places where the crosses had been on Cassie Dillon's map.

An idea had been forming in his mind, which had actually been helped by 'Nobby' Clarke's refusal to let him get involved in the murder inquiry and by Inspector Fraser's insistence on doing things according to strict police procedure. For, he now realised, the fact that they were keeping him out of the action actually gave him greater freedom of movement. And now he fully intended to exploit that freedom.

An idea had been forming in his mind and for the first time that day Tallyforth could feel the tingle of expectation running up his spine. This was what he was good at, this was what made him tick, this was why he was the way he was.

An idea had been forming in his mind. There was only one thing to do and that was to visit the sites of these crosses and look for some significance in them, maybe something that linked them to the tape-recording, for he had long ago come to the conclusion that nothing is coincidental in a murder inquiry. There were always linkages between the most unusual factors. And the linkage between Runrig's *Mighty Atlantic* and these sites around the islands seemed a stronger possibility than he had often found. He had also bought himself a cheap headset on which he could listen to the whole album, for maybe there were further clues to be found therein.

Suddenly he caught sight of Willie MacPherson's head appearing in the cockpit of *The Flodigarry* as he climbed up from the galley below. Tallyforth waved an arm at him vigorously.

'Willie!' he called. 'Willie! Can we talk?'

Willie MacPherson heard him and looked up from what he was doing. He saw Tallyforth on the pier waving in his direction and called down below to his wife.

'Aye, hold on,' he relied. 'I'll come over for you.'

And Willie MacPherson lowered himself into the small dinghy that was tied up to the side of *The Flodigarry* and, after unfastening it, rowed gently across to the steps at the bottom of the pier, where he secured it and climbed up to where Tallyforth waited.

'Very sad business this morning,' Tallyforth began. 'Cassie Dillon's death. It was a dreadful shock.'

'Aye, it was that,' said Willie, scratching his chin which was still unshaven. 'The missus and I don't know what to do about it all. The inspector's asked us a lot of questions but she hasn't said whether we've to wait here or what we're to do.'

'I think the inspector's handling this in her own way,' explained Tallyforth. 'I've not long spoken to her and I think we can leave everything to her for now. She's still waiting for the forensic report to help determine the manner and time of death. But what are your plans?'

Willie MacPherson looked sheepishly at him.

'Mr Tallyforth, I have to tell you something. It's not something I'm very proud about.'

Tallyforth stiffened.

'Go on, then,' he said.

'Mr Tallyforth, I once killed a man.'

And Willie MacPherson told the story that his wife had told the solicitor Iain McMillan earlier in the day, missing out none of the graphic detail but stressing that it had all been a long time ago, that it had happened when he was 'in drink', and that he was now a reformed character. He ended by emphasising that he had not been responsible for 'that poor wee lassie's' death and he hoped that the Chief Inspector believed him.

Tallyforth listened carefully. This was a development he hadn't expected. The one assumption he had thought was safe to make was that Cassie Dillon's killer had not been one of her dinner companions of the night before, not one of her fellow-sailors on the Hebridean bird-watching cruise. He knew he himself hadn't done it, and he could not see any reason why these two good Scots folk, the skipper and his wife, should have done it. What would have been their motive? And what would have been the point, even if they had a motive, of killing her when she was a guest on their boat?

But Willie's confession stunned him. Not because he believed it likely that Willie MacPherson was her murderer but because he knew that Inspector Maggie Fraser would sooner or later find out about his criminal record and, with her obsessive insistence on following correct procedure, would be placing him under suspicion and no doubt subjecting him to much more thorough investigation than he had so far undergone.

'Willie, I need your help and, from what you've just told me, you need my help just as much.'

And Tallyforth explained about the map that had been beside Cassie Dillon's bunk and showed the reconstructed version he had with him, pointing out each of the sites that had been marked with a cross on the original map and that he was confident he had remembered accurately. He also explained that he was fairly sure there was some connection between these sites, the tape-recording he had found in her headset and Cassie's murder. He was sure, he added, that she had been murdered.

'And it's in your interests to help me find a solution, Willie,' he ended, 'because, at the moment, in the light of what you've told me, I'd say you are going to be chief suspect in Inspector Fraser's mind by tomorrow morning at the latest. Are you game?'

'What you're asking me to do is to take you round these sites on the map? Just to look at them? Is that right?' Willie asked.

'That's right,' answered Tallyforth. 'Mind, I'll be relying on your local knowledge to tell me about them, because I don't know what I'm looking for yet. Anything you can tell me about them when we get there may help - any background information, any stories, any history, anything at all. I presume you know where each of these places is?'

'Aye, I do that,' replied Willie MacPherson. 'Though some of them are very wee spots and I've never actually been to some of those. But, if you think this'll help us find who killed the lassie, you're on.'

'Good,' said Tallyforth, clapping him on the back. 'Come on then, let's get going.'

'One thing,' said Willie, pausing at the top of the steps down to the dinghy. 'What about that Inspector Fraser? What if she's looking for us?'

'Don't worry,' grinned Tallyforth. 'I've left a forwarding address at the Royal Hotel!'

It was very late in the afternoon of what had been a very hot day. The sun's heat still beat down on Somerled Square on those, whether young travellers or elderly residents of the island, who were waiting for a bus, on those visitors who sat on benches writing postcards or passing on information to each other about their days or simply gasped in the unexpected warmth, and on the shopkeepers who had just closed up for the day and were heading for their favourite hostelry for a refreshing glass of something cooling.

Maggie Fraser was still working. Long after her duty hours had finished, she sat in her office smoking, reading the scribbled notes she had made, occasionally standing and pacing around her office as she sought inspiration. A full ash-tray sat on her desk, its ash trickling over the scattered papers. The blinds had been pulled down long since to keep out the sun's blistering heat and she had kept her oscillating fan on throughout the day while she had been there. She was in a dilemma and she knew it. She had no real experience of a case as serious as this. She'd seen her share of drug busts and violent crime during her time working in Edinburgh but she had no hands-on experience of solving a murder case. She knew the procedures, she knew she had followed them correctly, but she also knew that, by following those procedures to the letter, she had eliminated the possibility of Detective Chief Inspector Tallyforth of the Mercian Force giving her his help in this case. She didn't know his record - how could she? - but she was fairly confident that he would certainly have been involved in more murder enquiries and investigations than she had. And she, because of her intractability, had pushed him away, had refused his help, even worse had treated him as a suspect by her attitude if not by her words.

She looked at her watch, got up and walked to the door. Opening it, she called for Sergeant MacKenzie.

'Ma'am?' he said, looking up from his desk.

'Anything from forensic yet?'

'Nothing as yet, ma'am,' came the reply.

'Just give them another ring for me, will you, Sergeant?' she said, sighing with exasperation. 'They promised me a preliminary view this afternoon.'

'Yes, ma'am. Straightaway.'

And he dialled out.

Surprisingly, he was put straight through to the forensic

laboratory. He held the phone out for her to take it, motioning her to do so quickly.

'Hello! Yes, this is Inspector Fraser. Yes, I'm in charge of the investigation. Yes, I was the officer who first saw the body this morning.'

There was a lengthy pause as she listened to what was being said, occasionally nodding her head as if to indicate understanding. Donald MacKenzie watched her from behind his desk, his face expressionless but his mind trying to guess the substance of what she was being told.

'Thank you very much,' she said at length. 'You'll fax me a full report in the morning? Good. Thanks again. Goodbye.'

She passed the phone back to Donald MacKenzie, who replaced it in its cradle on his desk.

'It was murder then,' she said, leaning back against the wall. 'She was asphyxiated while she slept with the silk scarf that was round her neck. No traces of any drugs in her bloodstream but a heavy concentration of alcohol. She must have been out like a light. No signs of any forced sexual interference. I guess I'll have to talk to them all again, especially the MacPhersons, though I can't imagine they would have done it.'

She paused and took the cigarette that he was offering.

'I've not much heart for this, Sergeant,' she said, sucking in the smoke. 'I thought I could handle all this on my own but I can see now that all I was doing was trying to convince you and the men that I could cut the mustard. And I've failed to convince you, haven't I? You just think I'm some cleverclogs who's swanned their way from university through police college and on to rapid promotion without doing the spadework to know how to be a good copper. Well, maybe you're right. Maybe I'm not up to it. Anyway, I'm sure by tomorrow that someone from the mainland will be across the bridge to show me how to do it. Meanwhile, I've blown the one good opportunity I did have by telling Chief Inspector Tallyforth that he couldn't be involved!'

Donald MacKenzie listened to this impassioned disavowal and watched her as her face crumpled in a way he had not seen before.

'Ma'am,' he volunteered, 'you shouldn't blame yourself for all that. You were only doing what was right.'

'Maybe,' she sniffed. 'But Tallyforth was right. To be a good copper isn't just about doing what's right, it's also about doing what's necessary to make something right. And I've failed in that respect.'

'Ma'am,' Donald MacKenzie interrupted again. 'If it's any comfort to you, I'd have probably done the same as you.'

She gave him a half-smile.

'Thanks, Donald,' she said and straightened her clothing and pushed back the two or three stray hairs that had fallen across her face. 'Don't suppose there's anything from the computer about James Orr or the MacPhersons, is there?'

'There's a folder on your desk,' he said. 'I put it there a while back, while you were at the ladies.'

'You what? You mean there is something? Why didn't you tell me?'

She rushed back into her office, picked up the green folder, and brought it back to the doorway.

'One of the lads brought it from the other office and asked me to give it you. Said it was from the computer but I didn't know it was connected to this case. You didn't tell me you were waiting for something.'

But she wasn't listening by now. She was engrossed in reading the computer print-out that detailed Willie MacPherson's criminal past.

'Sergeant,' she said triumphantly. 'Forget everything I said just now. I think I may be on the way to a solution. Willie MacPherson was imprisoned for killing somebody when he was younger. Did you know that?'

'It must have been before I came to Skye,' he answered.

'Well, it's true,' she said brusquely. 'And that has to put him in the frame for now, doesn't it? Where are the MacPhersons staying?'

He looked through the papers on his desk.

'The only record we have is that they're on their boat,' he answered, looking up and reading from a scrap. 'They live in Uig but I doubt if they'll have gone home with all the fuss.'

'What about Tallyforth? I'd like to show him I can do this job.'

'I heard him say he could be contacted at the Royal Hotel,' said Donald MacKenzie. 'That's what he told you.'

'Oh, yes,' she said, nodding her head. 'I remember now. Come on then, Sergeant. Let's see if we can find him and then we'll go and confront Mr Willie MacPherson.'

The Camanachd Bar in Somerled Square, adjacent to the police station, was the favourite early evening watering hole of Iain McMillan, whose office was in nearby Wentworth Street, and Hamish MacLeod, who preferred to do his early-evening drinking away from his father's gaze in the Royal Hotel. The dark bar, where billowing clouds of white cigarette and pipe smoke drifted, was a sharp contrast to the brightness outside.

'Iain,' Hamish began, placing the gin and tonic before his friend and taking a sip from his pint of heavy, 'I'm going to raise the devolution issue at Friday's meeting. I think we ought to discuss the possibility of using it to put pressure on the government. What do you think?'

He loosened his yellow tartan tie at the neck and unfastened the top button of his shirt.

'You'll have to be very careful,' Iain McMillan said, 'for you'll be cutting across political party lines. The success of S.K.A.T. has been that people have felt this was a single issue on which they could unite. Nobody's been bothered about your Scottish National affiliation just as you haven't bothered about whether anyone else was Liberal or Labour or even Tory.'

'We didn't have many of them!' retorted Hamish. 'Surprise! Surprise! It was them who probably had their fingers in the till somewhere along the line. Remember all that stuff you found out about the way the tendering for the bridge had been done in the first place? It was the Scottish Tories who were responsible for that, wasn't it? It's not surprising that their local members kept away from S.K.A.T.'

Iain McMillan looked noticeably uncomfortable when Hamish MacLeod reminded him of this.

'Yes, you're right,' he said, emptying the remains of his tonic bottle into his glass. 'But the effect of the election result is to redraw the battle-lines. You know the Labour people here aren't so keen on upsetting the new government as they were the old one. And the Scottish Nationalists want a different form of devolution to the one that this government's going to offer them - they want a separate state, don't they?'

'Eventually, yes, of course,' replied Hamish, scratching his ginger beard.

'Well, then, do you not see that raising the devolution business at the S.K.A.T. meeting could be counter-productive. We don't want the meeting to turn into a political wrangle, do we?'

'Iain, I think it's time that people stood up to be counted,' said Hamish, taking a long draught of his beer. 'There's too many who think it's been just a game. I think we should raise the possibility of independence for the Western Isles, not just for a subject Scottish Parliament who'll do what their English masters tell them. We've a long tradition of resistance in the Isles and the campaign over the bridge tolls has reinforced that and reminded folk we're not to be messed with. Culloden didn't finish us, nor the Clearances.'

Iain McMillan again shifted uncomfortably.

'I know all that, Hamish,' he said. 'I know my history too, even though I'm not from Skye. But that kind of chauvinism has just no place in the modern world.'

'Look what's happening all across Europe,' said Hamish, enthusing about his subject now. 'Small independent states are becoming the norm. Look at what's happening to the U.S.S.R. Look at Bosnia. Everybody's doing it.'

'But we couldn't support an independent economy in the Western Isles!'

'Oh, couldn't we?' said Hamish, tapping the side of his nose. 'Have you not heard of the Atlantic Shelf? The oil exploration going on there?'

'But that's years off!' protested Iain McMillan, looking uneasily around him.

'Don't be so sure,' said Hamish, grinning. 'I think there's things we're not yet being told about going on out there in the Atlantic Ocean. Mark my words, Iain, this could be the start of something colossal!'

'The bastard! The complete bastard!' Maggie Fraser spluttered.

She was holding a piece of paper which she had been given in the Royal Hotel. On it was a message from Tallyforth, saying that he had gone on a 'wee cruise' with his friends the MacPhersons in their boat *The Flodigarry* and he would be in touch when he returned.

She had read the message, then run down Quay Brae and along Quay Street to the end of the pier to see if it was true or if it was some monumental practical joke that he was playing on her.

But it was true, she saw, as she stood there helplessly holding the offending piece of paper and staring hopelessly at the space in the harbour where not long ago *The Flodigarry* had been moored. Sergeant Donald MacKenzie, slightly out of breath from having followed her down to the pier's end, stood at her side.

'But where's he gone?' she asked of no-one in particular. 'The bastard!'

Donald MacKenzie coughed.

'There's something I have to tell you, ma'am,' he said sheepishly.

'What is it, Sergeant? I hope it's got something to do with this case.'

He coughed again, clearing his throat.

'I think you'll find it has, ma'am,' he said. 'You see, the chief inspector came looking for you this morning when you were down here. When I told him you weren't there, he asked if he could have a look at a map which he said you'd brought back from the boat earlier on. Well, I hadn't any idea at the time that you weren't working together, so I let him have a look at it. He seemed very interested in the wee markings on the map. Maybe they'll give you some idea of where he's gone.'

She turned on him, a look of fierce anger in her eyes.

'I was right, wasn't I?' she seethed. 'Right all along. I knew I couldn't rely on any of you lot to do proper police work. You've let your brains get soft living here all this time. And to think I was beginning to regret not involving you! Come on, Sergeant! We need to get to that map and see where he's heading. Then maybe we'll get a helicopter out looking for them.'

And she marched off back up the pier, followed by the chastened Donald MacKenzie.

It was a glorious evening. The sun was slowly going down but its golden rays still spread across the early evening sky as *The Flodigarry* made its stately way northwards through the Sound of Raasay. The sea cliffs on northern Skye were rich with sea campion and rose-root; on the flatter surfaces above them queen of the meadow and foxgloves filled the grasslands; and higher still the mountainsides leading up to the Old Man of Storr were patched with white and purple heather.

Tallyforth sat on the raised deck behind the doghouse, with his back turned to Willie MacPherson who was steering the boat. Mary MacPherson was below deck preparing something for them to eat. Tallyforth wore navy shorts, a white tee-shirt and dark glasses. On his nose was a blob of sun-cream, for he had suffered burning there before. Over his ears were the headphones attached to the small tape-recorder he had bought in Portree. His curly grey hair swept back by the wind from the sails, he sat and listened to the music of Runrig's *Mara* album, keeping time lightly with his hand on his right knee.

As they left the Old Man of Storr and The Quiraing well behind them and started to turn west around the top of Skye, Willie MacPherson leaned over and touched his shoulder. Tallyforth switched off the tape and removed the headphones from his ears.

'We're coming near to Flora MacDonald's monument,' said Willie. 'It'll be up there on the port side. Keep your eyes open. I'll tell you when I can see it. She was buried there in Kilmuir churchyard in 1790. Legend has it that it was the largest ever funeral in all of Skye. The procession was supposed to have been two miles long with nearly three thousand folk from all over the Highlands come to pay their last respects. Here, use these.'

Tallyforth reached for the binoculars that Willie held out to him, took them and focused in the direction indicated.

Suddenly he froze.

'Is that a sea-eagle, Willie?'

'Where?'

'Just there, way up high. Look at the speed! Or maybe it's a golden eagle?'

Willie MacPherson reached for another pair of binoculars and scanned the sky where Tallyforth was pointing.

'Aye,' he said, when he had at last caught the bird in his sights, 'that's the erne. That'll be one of that pair that's nesting north of

Portree. You can tell them from the golden eagle because of their white tails and their wings are almost rectangular. Can you see?'

'Brilliant,' said Tallyforth, letting out his breath which he had been holding in his tenseness. 'Brilliant!'

Willie MacPherson put down his binoculars and steadied the boat.

'We'll not be much longer now, Mr Tallyforth,' he said. 'Uig's just a bit away, maybe forty-five minutes. They'll not think to come looking for us at our house tonight. And tomorrow we can look for these places you're interested in. Is that okay?'

'Aye, aye, skipper,' Tallyforth laughed and replaced the headphones over his ears.

SIX

The man who called himself John Smith had risen early on the Tuesday in order to ride to Uig to catch the early morning Caledonian MacBrayne ferry to Tarbert and then drive on to Stornoway on the next leg of his opinion-finding mission. A stranger to the Hebrides himself, he had enjoyed the ride across Skye through the varied but rugged scenery on the road across from Portree. The latter place had been bustling with activity in the early morning sunlight, for the piping competitions were due to begin at ten o'clock, with simultaneous competitions for the Dunvegan Medal in the Community Centre and for the 6/8 March and the Jig in the Royal Hotel. He had noticed several of the competitors for these events, men in full Scottish dress with their clan kilts and green or black jackets, walking briskly through the town on their way to the selected venue, bagpipes held beneath their arms. He had also been aware of the distant strains of the pipes, as some of the competitors, arriving early, had begun to warm up for the competition, clearing their lungs, getting a good blow on, practising tricky bits of melody.

With some regret he had left all that behind him and, astride his red Harley Davidson 750 Bonneville with its chrome carburettors and customised leather seat, he had sped across the heather-strewn moors in the direction of Uig, arriving there in plenty of time for the ferry. He knew that he would be back in Portree the following day for the Highland Games, when there were more piping competitions and he would get a further chance, he hoped, to talk to Hamish MacLeod. As he rode, he had felt the wind around his ears but he could also feel the sun warm on his face, even at that time of day.

Riding the Harley was the one extravagance that 'John Smith' allowed himself. He had bought the bike from a dealer in the U.S.A. and had it shipped across to England at great expense. But the Bonneville was a special bike and he had coveted it for a long time. His work as a civil servant in the Home Office, and now temporarily in the Scottish Office, meant that he had to live within the behavioural expectations of his superiors and, as an ambitious person, he was prepared to do this. Recruited immediately after completing his studies at Swansea University, where he had gained a first-class degree, he had risen through the ranks very quickly because of his undoubted ability but also because of his willingness to fit in with the *mores* of the civil service. Hence, his secondment to the Scottish Office and the roving brief he had been given to ascertain the mood of the Scottish people in the run-up to the referendum on devolution of power to Scotland by way of the proposed Scottish Parliament.

John Smith's real name was Steve Anthony. It was the unexpected sight of Detective Chief Inspector Tallyforth sitting on the bench in Somerled Square in the middle of Portree the previous day that had caused him to adopt a *nom de plume* when he had talked to Hamish MacLeod. It had been his intention, indeed it had been an instruction, that he should travel around Scotland freely without drawing too much attention to himself. He had felt that he could do that using his own name where necessary since he had no intention of being specific about his work and therefore it seemed unlikely that anyone would wish to trace him to the Scottish Office, particularly since he was swearing his contacts to secrecy. But the sight of Tallyforth had changed all that.

They had only met once, and that had been quite some years ago, but he was aware that Tallyforth had taken an instant dislike to him. Steve Anthony was an old friend of George Elliott, Tallyforth's detective sergeant. They had been at Swansea together and had remained close in the subsequent years, a friendship that had been mutually supportive. George Elliott had never married, though she had had two long-term relationships and other briefer liaisons. Steve Anthony was gay and had never formed a permanent relationship, though in his case it was more through choice because he was naturally promiscuous and enjoyed the thrill of the chase as much as the success of conquest. Their friendship was unthreatened by either of their sexual proclivities, in fact was positively enhanced by them, because it enabled them to discuss their most intimate secrets with each other in complete confidence. Steve Anthony was also able, through his work in the Home Office and his access to classified information, to assist George Elliott from time to time in criminal investigations.

It was this latter that Tallyforth disliked. He had the view that solving crimes, particularly nasty ones like murders, could only be done by using skilful police detection. Which meant only by him! So he was averse to the titbits that George Elliott occasionally produced from her 'unattributable source' at the Home Office, although she had noticed that, after he had sounded off about 'that little creep', meaning Steve Anthony, he had not refused to use the information provided! Indeed, there had even been the odd occasion when he had requested some snippet of information himself via this source!

But the real problem between Tallyforth and Steve Anthony was that the Chief Inspector was homophobic. They had met once, when George Elliott had invited him out for a meal at a Greek restaurant in Birmingham, where she introduced him to her friend from university. At that time, Steve Anthony had his hair in tight curls and he affected a slight lisp. Tallyforth had taken an instant dislike to him. At work the following day he had explained to George Elliott how uncomfortable he had felt all evening. When she had laughed at him and called him old-fashioned, that had confirmed his prejudice in him even more and so they had never met up again.

Until yesterday, when Steve Anthony had passed Tallyforth busy with his map-drawing in Somerled Square. For Steve, it had been a momentary shock to see him there, for, since the cooling off between Tallyforth and George Elliott, he had inevitably not heard about the chief inspector's movements. So the coincidence of seeing him again, on the Isle of Skye of all places, was surprising to say the least. And Steve Anthony, in that flash of a moment in which decisions are often made, knew that he was in a precarious position. From being an unknown visitor one minute to being a known one, even though for the moment he would only be known to one person, was a situation he did not want. So he had been glad that Tallyforth had been so engrossed and had not seen him and it had been at that moment that he had decided to adopt the 'John Smith' moniker as a further protection to his anonymity.

He reflected on all this as he rode into Uig past the Uig Hotel and the tower opposite, which is known as Captain Fraser's folly, and towards the pier where traffic was assembling for the ferry crossing to Tarbert on the Isle of Harris.

He had become aware as he rode over that a strap on one of his bike's panniers had broken and, as he purchased his ticket, he noticed that there was a chandler's on the quayside and wondered whether he might get a replacement strap or a repair done. He parked his motorbike in the appropriate place, fastened his helmet to the bike and went into the chandlery.

'How can we help you?' asked a rather wizened old lady, dressed in black, from behind the counter. She was surrounded by piles of waterproof clothing and ropes of every width and length.

'Is there the slightest possibility,' he began, 'that you might be able to repair this strap? Or replace it? It's such a nuisance to have it flapping behind me.'

She looked up at the figure before her, clad in black motor-cycle leathers and with his dark hair lying evenly around his face, and raised her eyes.

'Are you English?' she asked.

'Of course!' Steve Anthony replied. 'Why do you ask? Don't you sell things to English people?'

'Aye,' she said, taking the strap from him and turning it over in her hand. 'I thought you was maybe German.'

He smiled at her.

'Is that worse?' he asked. 'Or would that be better?'

She did not reply but continued her scrutiny of the strap.

'You'll be going on the ferry, I dare say?' she said.

'Yes, I have just purchased my ticket,' he answered.

'You wouldn't be from the police, would you?' she asked suddenly.

'Good gracious, no!' he said, holding up his hands. 'Whatever gave you that idea?'

'You sure?' she pressed. 'You don't look like the police, I grant you, but you never can tell what's going on in England nowadays.

There's some very queer things going on.'

'Charming!' he said dryly. 'But why would you think I was from the police?'

She looked askance at him.

'My niece and her husband have a man from the police with them just now,' she said. 'They sailed back from Portree to Uig last night and I spoke to Mary on the phone. She said there'd been some lassie killed in Portree and they had a detective with them who needed to see some places out in the Minch. The police don't know much about the woman.'

'The happiest women, like the happiest nations, have no history,' he said.

She looked at him again, uncomprehending.

'Aye, well. Mary said that I wasn't to say anything if any other police came snooping around because it was secret work. Sounded very queer to me!'

Steve Anthony listened carefully, as she told him what she knew about the dead woman and the English detective. This must be Tallyforth, he reasoned. George Elliott had told him often enough what a maverick he was and how he broke all the normal rules of police procedure. So, that was what Tallyforth had been doing in Portree! Investigating a murder! But why was he here in Scotland? Didn't the Scottish police force conduct investigations themselves? And where was Tallyforth now?

'Do your niece and her husband live here in Uig?' he asked, controlling himself carefully. He did not want to indicate that he knew anything about what was going on.

'Aye, that they do,' she answered, 'but you'll not find them at home now. I don't care if you are from the police, they were off on the early morning tide. They'll be half-way to wherever they were going by now. So you're just wasting your time, mister.'

So, if it was Tallyforth, and it did seem likely, he was out at sea with these two people. He decided to pretend no interest.

'And my strap?' he queried.

'You'll be needing a new one,' she said, handing him back the broken one. 'I've something similar in stock.'

She moved to a shelf at the back of the shop and returned with a duplicate of the broken strap.

'It'll cost you five pounds seventy.'

Steve Anthony paid, left the chandler's and returned to his bike, which was surrounded by a small crowd of youngsters admiring it.

They had left Uig at the crack of dawn, having downed cups of tea and the day's first bacon sandwiches prepared by Mary MacPherson in their cottage just out of the small town on the road to Duntulm. Quickly leaving the horseshoe bay of Uig with its wooded glens, Willie set *The Flodigarry* out to sea into The Little Minch, rounding Vaternish Point then heading south west towards Benbecula. The wind was just enough to fill the sails and they made steady headway. Once they sighted land across the Minch, which was the eastern shoreline of North Uist, Willie handed the wheel to his wife and sat down beside Tallyforth at the rear of the doghouse.

Tallyforth was poring over the map that he had marked with the crosses he had remembered from Cassie Dillon's map.

'Can you see any significance in these crosses?' he asked the skipper. 'Any common feature? Anything that might link them in some way?'

Willie MacPherson shook his head.

'I've already told you that they don't all correspond to the route we had planned to take you both on,' he replied, reaching for one side of the map to steady it in the breeze. 'Wherever the lassie got those places from, it wasn't from me, I'm telling you. The only thing I can think is that it's something to do with Bonnie Prince Charlie, though just what I haven't the faintest idea.'

Tallyforth looked up sharply at him.

'Go on,' he said. 'tell me what you're thinking.'

Willie pulled the map closer to himself and began to point at each of the crosses in turn.

'Well,' he started,' the Prince was definitely in Benbecula, for I know he was taken to Rossinish after Culloden by Donald MacLeod, who minded him while he was in the outer isles. It was from there that he went, disguised as a spinning maid by the name of Betty Burke, with Flora MacDonald to Skye. You remember I was telling you about that last night?'

Tallyforth nodded. Maybe something was beginning to take shape here, he thought.

'Well, that's maybe a connection but, you see, where you've drawn the mark is at Petersport, not at Rossinish which is north of Nunton. You sure you haven't marked it wrong?'

'Pretty sure, yes,' said Tallyforth, staring closely at the map. 'I may be a fraction out in terms of precise measurement but I'm sure the cross was on the eastern side of the island. Tell me about Petersport. Is it used by boats?'

'No, hardly ever. The pier was built there in the last century before they'd built the causeways that join the isles and they even built a road to the pier that joined up with the main road. But it's not the easiest of places to sail into, because the waters around the east of Benbecula are very dangerous, so it's never really used now. Just the odd fisherman maybe. That's all.'

'You can see the isle for yourself if you take the glasses,' interrupted Mary MacPherson who had heard their conversation, and she raised one hand from the wheel to point to the starboard side.

Tallyforth lifted the binoculars to his eyes and looked in the direction that Mary was pointing. It was hard to see very much because Benbecula is very flat and has as many lochs as it does areas of land along its eastern coast, so that it is difficult in certain lights to distinguish the points where land and sea meet. However, he could just make out the black stone of the pier of Petersport jutting out and the narrow tarmaced road behind it heading inland.

'Did you say the road joined up with the main road?' he asked, trying to focus the binoculars even more sharply. 'Where would that lead to?'

'If you go south, you'll come to the causeway across the water to South Uist and the road eventually takes you to Lochboisdale at the southern tip of the island,' said Mary MacPherson.

'And what's there?' asked Tallyforth.

Willie MacPherson looked at his watch.

'The CalMac ferry goes from there to Barra and then back to Oban,' he said. 'You may just catch sight of it later steaming across the water.'

'What about going north?' asked Tallyforth.

'If you go north from the Petersport road, you'll come to

Gramisdale, where the road to the airfield is,' answered Mary.

'What airfield's that?'

'The Air Force built it during the war, after the army base was put on Balivanich. There's regular flights from Glasgow and from Stornoway.'

'How regular?'

'I don't know all that,' replied Willie tetchily. 'I'm a sailor, not an airline pilot.'

Tallyforth scratched his head in thought, at the same time folding the map. Was there any significance in all this, he wondered. Bonnie Prince Charlie? An unused port? A road that led to an airfield one way and a ferry terminal the other?

At around the time when Steve Anthony was boarding the ferry to Tarbert from Uig and Detective Chief Inspector Tallyforth was sailing in *The Flodigarry* past the shores of Benbecula with the MacPhersons, Inspector Maggie Fraser was failing to get helicopter assistance to help her track down the missing threesome. And, not only was she being refused helicopter assistance, she was being told to take no further steps in the murder inquiry until a senior officer, Chief Inspector Gordon from Inverness, arrived in Portree to take charge. When she asked the reasons for these two actions, she was told that the police helicopters were all out in the Cairngorms looking for lost climbers and walkers and that Chief Inspector Gordon had decided to take over the case now that it clearly was one of murder, as confirmed by forensic, and not one of accidental death, as she had at first surmised in her initial report.

Maggie Fraser was very, very angry. So angry that she had summoned Sergeant Donald MacKenzie to her office in order to sound off about the injustice of all this, forgetting the fact that the previous evening she had berated him for his inadequacies.

'This will teach me to play things by the book, eh, Sergeant?' she began through gritted teeth, holding a cigarette in the fingers of her right hand. 'Bugger police procedure! Bugger Chief Inspector Gordon! Bugger the system! This was my inquiry and now it's being taken away from me, because of the system. What did I do wrong? I've kept them informed right from the start. I told them I didn't need assistance. I told them that we needed to wait for forensic before we began the inquiry. I told them we could keep the lid on everything here. And I thought they were listening! God! What a fool!'

'Yes, ma'am,' said Donald MacKenzie, shuffling uncomfortably on the balls of his feet as he stood in front of her. 'Would you like a cup of something?'

She glared up at him.

'I need a cup of something, Sergeant,' she said, drawing on her cigarette, 'but something stronger than you're offering.'

'I could put a drop of rum in your tea, ma'am,' he offered. 'Sailors swear by it.'

'I'll bet they do,' she said grimly. 'Go on, then, but better not make it too strong. I don't want to be out on my feet when Chief Inspector Gordon arrives.'

Donald MacKenzie left her office and went to the small kitchen area opposite, where he made two mugs of tea and poured a nip of rum into both.

When he returned, she was pacing the office, blowing clouds of smoke around her.

'Thanks,' she said, taking the steaming mug and sipping from it, at the same time stubbing her cigarette end in an ash-tray. Her face creased as she felt the strong liquor bite the back of her throat. 'Mm, that's better. What time would you estimate Chief Inspector Gordon will get here?'

Donald MacKenzie looked up from his own mug.

'Well, it was only half an hour ago that you were told he was leaving,' he said, calculating mentally. 'Now he must be coming by car so that would take him maybe two hours to Kyle and then another hour up to here. So you could be looking at one o'clockish.'

She looked thoughtfully at her mug, then put it down on her desk, reached for another cigarette and lit it.

Donald MacKenzie supped his rum-laced tea and watched her. He had never seen her like this before, never been allowed to see her like this before, never been consulted as an equal about any decision. Since she had arrived as station commander back in June, she had always been at pains to remain aloof, to give the impression that she was in command and would brook no questioning of her decisions, and to keep her thought processes to herself. Now, for the first time, she was being forced by the pressure of external events to react more like a fellow-officer.

Donald MacKenzie watched and waited.

'Sergeant,' she said at last, 'I'm not going to wait for Chief Inspector Gordon. As far as I'm concerned, I'm in charge of this inquiry until he arrives here. Which means that there are several things we can do immediately. Do I have your support or not?'

He nodded acquiescence. He knew that, whatever happened subsequently, they were in this together now and that was better than how things had been this past two months.

'Aye, ma'am,' he said. 'What's the plan then?'

She smiled at him, exhaling smoke through her nostrils

'The plan, Sergeant, is this. We have three possible leads and very little time to pursue them, so I'm going to make some time. First of all, there's Tallyforth and MacPherson. Now I don't believe for a minute that Chief Inspector Tallyforth murdered that woman, although I do think there's some things about his relationship with her which he's not telling me. However, I'm not so sure about MacPherson. If he's killed somebody before, he has the capacity to kill again. What do you know about him?'

'Willie MacPherson and his wife have been running cruises for tourists out of Portree ever since I moved here. As far as I'm aware there's never been any bother involving either of them. They have a little house in Uig but they're not great social folk. They keep themselves to themselves and never bother anybody.'

'Were they involved in the bridge business?' she quizzed, aware that his local knowledge far exceeded hers.

'No, never,' he explained. 'They don't care for that sort of thing. They're just quiet law-abiding folk, who make a living out of tourism, like many folk here do nowadays.'

'Even so,' she said, inhaling from her cigarette again, 'MacPherson once killed. We need to find them. If those marks on that map mean anything, they're probably heading for one or other of those now. I'm going to put out a message to all the local police stations they might go anywhere near and ask them to keep an eye open for them. You never know where they might land. Where's that map?'

She reached for the map under the papers on her desk and

opened it up. They looked at it together, with Donald MacKenzie tracing the likely route from Portree with his finger.

'So, Sergeant, we need to get an alert out to the stations in Uig, Tarbert, Lochmaddy, Lochboisdale, Benbecula, Barra, Arisaig and Mallaig,' she said, as she followed the movement of his finger. 'You see to that, will you?'

'Yes, ma'am.'

She stubbed out her cigarette, stood up again and looked at him.

'Now there's two other leads,' she began. 'There's the four Americans that were seen on the pier late last night when Tallyforth and his friends were going aboard the boat. I don't think it's likely they were involved but they may have seen something or somebody. It's worth checking. Will you do that too, Sergeant?'

'Yes, ma'am.'

'Good, that's that then,' she said, briskly straightening papers on her desk and emptying the ash-tray into a rubbish bin. 'I feel better now that we've taken control again. And, when Chief Inspector Gordon arrives, I hope you'll keep him appropriately informed.'

He reached for her now-empty mug.

'And where will you be going, ma'am?' he asked, aware there was a third line of inquiry that she had not yet revealed to him.

'I am going, Sergeant, to visit this mysterious James Orr in Oban, the person that the murdered woman was staying with until two days ago, ' she said, smiling pointedly at him. 'That also means that I won't be back until this evening. So I shall miss Chief Inspector Gordon sadly. Please convey my apologies.'

She swept past him, pulling her peaked cap over her hair.

'What shall I tell him, ma'am? About where you are?'

'As far as I'm concerned,' she said, 'you can tell him to suck his own cock! Though I'm sure you'll find a much more delicate way of phrasing it, Donald. Good-day to you!'

They were sailing east of Bruernish Point and past the small island of Barra. A flock of black guillemots skimmed the waves to their port side, heading in the direction of western Skye. Willie MacPherson was telling Tallyforth about *Whisky Galore*.

'The writer Compton MacKenzie lived on the isle and he knew

all about the ship with a cargo of whisky that sank off Eriskay in nineteen forty-one, so he made it into a story and they filmed it here on the isle. It was very popular at the time and they occasionally show it on TV on Sunday afternoons,' he said. 'Have you seen it?'

Tallyforth shook his head. They had been out at sea for some hours now and, although the sun was as hot as ever, a few clouds had appeared and the breeze had picked up a little, so he was wearing his navy blue fleece. His hands were thrust into its pockets.

'What about Charlie?' he asked. 'Was he here?'

Willie shook his head.

'Not as far as I know,' he answered. 'D'you know, Mary?'

She shook her head from where she sat in the cockpit, plotting the next leg of their journey on the charts.

'I know he was in Eriskay,' she said. 'That's where he landed when he first came from France. But I don't think Charlie was on Barra.'

Tallyforth pondered this news.

'What else is there on Barra?' he asked.

'Well, Barra was the home of the MacNeils who were supposed to be the terrors of the Western Isles because of their warrior reputation,' replied Willie MacPherson. 'The story goes that the greatest of their chiefs used to employ a bard who, when the chief had eaten, would go up to the hills and shout 'The MacNeil has supped. Now the princes of the world may eat.' That's the MacNeil castle over there.'

He pointed to the castle with its square keep and curtain wall that sat on a rocky islet just off the main harbour of Castlebay.

'The twenty first chief sold it in the nineteenth century and many of the MacNeils set sail for a better life in America. The forty-fifth chief, who was an architect, came back from America in the nineteen thirties and bought back the castle. He got it restored and arranged for water to be piped in from Castlebay and the telephone cable laid. There's now a clan gathering every ten years.'

'Aye, the gathering's this week!' said Mary MacPherson, looking up. 'My auntie in Uig was telling me that there was a big yacht stopped off there a few days ago, full of Americans, who were sailing down from the Orkneys to the gathering. She said some of them were from the oil rigs. They were all MacNeils, with their families, you know. The Yanks are awful keen on their roots. And there were many families from the Isles that left for America after the Highland Clearances.'

Tallyforth pondered again. Was this why Cassie Dillon had marked Barra? But why would she want anything to do with the MacNeil clan gathering? Surely it was of little interest or relevance to her. Or maybe she had some connection with the MacNeil clan? He remembered that her husband had been a Canadian but he had never asked whether her surname was her own or whether she had kept her husband's.

'We'll just take you a wee bit west so you can see Vatersay Bay,' said Mary MacPherson, turning the wheel in the direction stated. 'Willie thinks that your cross is maybe nearer to there than to Castlebay itself.'

'What's on Vatersay?' Tallyforth asked.

'Well, as you'll see shortly, there's a long sandy beach on this side of the island. There's a new causeway was built in 1990 that links Vatersay with Barra.'

Why a sandy beach rather than a proper harbour with a pier? It didn't make sense. Maybe he hadn't remembered the positions of the crosses as precisely as he'd thought.

'And there's two ferries go from Castlebay,' chipped in Willie from the wheel. 'There's one to Mallaig and one to Oban. And there's daily flights from Glasgow and from Stornoway.'

Tallyforth's ears pricked up.

'Where's the runway?'

'It's in the north of Barra on what they call Cockle Strand. It's a long beach and the planes have to be sure that the tide's well out before they land! The locals collect cockles on the beach and they're always looking out for the planes landing. They say it's the only runway in the United Kingdom that's washed by the sea. Compton Mackenzie's old house is there. It's a white bungalow that looks over the beach and the runway. His grave's there as well, in the local cemetery. Some folk call the island Barradise!'

Tallyforth scratched his head again. No Bonnie Prince Charlie connection this time but easy access to ferries and planes, just as at Petersport on Benbecula. Was that the connection?

He opened up the map again to look at the next destination.

SEVEN

James Orr was a man in his early forties, whose hair had largely receded though this fact was being hidden from view by the low parting on the left which produced a long wave of lank blond hair that swept across his forehead. He was wearing a brown tweed jacket with leather elbow patches and a pair of green canvas trousers. He was surprised, as he opened the door of his semi-detached house on the outskirts of Oban, to see the tall, uniformed policewoman standing there.

'James Orr?' she inquired. 'Am I at the right address?'

'Yes, that's correct,' he replied, somewhat bewildered.

'You teach at the Oban Academy?' she continued.

'Yes, that's correct. Why? What's happened?'

She smiled grimly at him.

'I'm Inspector Fraser of the Highlands Force. Can I come in, sir?' she asked. 'I'd like a few words with you.'

James Orr, clearly flustered, opened the door more widely and ushered her in. As he did so, the length of hair fell over his face and he swiftly swept it back with his hand - a movement that was clearly well practised.

'Yes, of course,' he said. 'What's the problem? How can I help?'

'I won't take much of your time, sir,' she said, preceding him along the hallway. 'In here, is it?'

'Yes please go in. Take a seat. Can I get you anything? A drink? Tea? Coffee?'

'Tea would be fine,' she said, as she went into the back lounge. 'Milk and no sugar, thanks.'

James Orr hurried into the kitchen and switched on the kettle. Then, fetching two cups and placing a tea-bag in each, he poured the boiling water in and added a splash of milk.

Inspector Maggie Fraser sat down in a wooden-armed armchair and looked around the room. Photographs of weddings. None of children. Pictures of highland cattle. A curling calendar. A shelf with books. A music system and a television.

'Here you are, Inspector,' he said, as he returned and placed the cup in front of her on a small wooden table covered with a linen cloth. 'Now, what's all this about?'

'Mr Orr, you are a friend of a Cassie Dillon, I believe?' she began again.

'Yes, that's correct,' he said, balancing his cup carefully as he sat down in a deep armchair.

'How long have you known her?'

'We were at university together,' he replied. 'Many years ago now. At Edinburgh. We lost touch for a while when she was in Canada. Close touch I mean. You know, just Christmas cards. Then, after she got divorced and came back to England, she got in touch with me again.'

'How long ago was that, sir?'

'Oh, let me see, that would be about five or six years ago now, I suppose,' he said, pressing the strand of blond hair back in place again. 'Why?'

She ignored his question.

'You live alone, sir?' she continued.

'Yes.'

'May I ask the nature of your relationship with Ms. Dillon?' she asked.

'We are very good friends,' he replied. 'We always were, when we were at university. And, since we met up again, we've resumed that friendship.'

'She's an attractive woman.'

'Yes, she is,' he answered, then realised where the questioning was leading. 'No, Inspector, we are just very good friends. Nothing more.'

'You sure of that, sir?' she pressed.

'Absolutely!' he assured her.

'Yet she stayed with you for the past week. Is that right?'

'Yes,' he answered. 'How do you know this? Is she in some sort of trouble?'

Maggie Fraser was watching him carefully.

'I'm afraid Cassie Dillon is dead, sir,' she said slowly, letting the news sink in. 'We believe she was murdered in Portree harbour on Sunday night while she was asleep.'

The strand of hair fell across James Orr's face and this time he made no attempt to move it.

'Cassie? Dead?' he whispered, wringing his hands involuntarily. 'I can't believe it. Who would do such a thing?'

'At the moment we have no idea, sir, although we are pursuing certain enquiries. We thought you might be able to help us.'

'Me? But how?' he looked up at her and swept his hair back again. 'Of course. Anything I can do.'

'Would you tell me what your movements were on Sunday evening, sir?' she asked.

'Of course. I went to the cinema....But you don't think...?'

'What did you see?'

'Why, it was *The Colour Purple*. It's one of my favourite films. They brought it back for a special showing. But you don't think I was involved, don't you?'

'Sir, we have to investigate every possible lead. Your name was mentioned by the couple who own the boat on which Ms. Dillon was found murdered. She was due to go on a Hebridean cruise with them and she had told them that she'd stayed with you before going up to Portree. I found your address from the education authorities. Would anyone have been with you at the cinema or seen you there?'

James Orr blushed.

'I was with someone, yes,' he mumbled.

'And would that person be prepared to vouch for you?'

'If it was absolutely necessary, yes,' he said, looking her in the eye. 'But only if it's absolutely necessary. It's someone I work with. She's married. It would be difficult.'

She looked at him. She had wondered if he was gay. Now she wondered if he was telling the truth.

'It is necessary, sir, I'm afraid,' she said, 'if we are to eliminate you from our enquiries. And was this person with you all evening?'

He stared down at the floor, sighed, then looked her in the eye again.

'Yes, Inspector,' he said, firmly now, 'And all night too. She stayed here. Her husband had taken the children to stay with friends. It seemed too good a chance to miss.'

She frowned.

'I will need her details, sir,' she reminded him. 'Do you know of anyone who might have had a reason to want Ms. Dillon dead?'

'I'm afraid not, Inspector. As I said, Cassie is a good friend of mine. We speak on the phone once, maybe twice, a month. I've been to stay with her in Tamworth. She's been to stay with me here. We have a number of common interests, but that's all.'

'Such as?' she queried. So far she had found out very little about the dead woman.

'Cassie became very interested in environmental issues when she was in Canada. I suppose it was the destruction of all those forests that started it. That and the business about whales and dolphins. And I've always been a conservationist, right from when I was at university. She knew that and that was one of the reasons she got back in touch when she came back from Canada. Oh, and we both support the same football team?'

'Which is?'

'Hamilton Academicals,' he chuckled. 'It was the name we liked. It started at university. We used to go and watch them whenever we could.'

'Is that all?' she asked.

'I'm afraid so,' he said. 'Poor Cassie. I can't believe all this. She was so looking forward to her cruise, you know. She mentioned this policeman that was going to be the other passenger.'

'Yes, Detective Chief Inspector Tallyforth,' she said wryly. 'What did she say about him?'

'Only that they had met up one lunchtime just before she came to stay with me. Said she was attracted to him and was looking forward to getting to know him better. She's been on her own for some years now. She felt it was time she moved on. And she thought that, maybe, you know....'

James Orr's voice tailed off, as he realised he was still talking about her as if she were alive.

So, she thought, there had been more going on than she had been told by Tallyforth. That didn't put him in the frame necessarily, but it did throw up one or two interesting possibilities. If there had been anything going on between Cassie Dillon and Tallyforth, maybe he had managed to find his way to her cabin without disturbing the MacPhersons.

She closed her eyes momentarily in order to visualise the cabins on *The Flodigarry*. Yes, that was it! There was a hatch above the bunk on which Tallyforth had been sleeping and it was big enough for someone to squeeze through. So, he could have climbed out, gone to her cabin and then climbed back in without alerting the MacPhersons. That might explain the naked body!

'Can I call Lindsay and warn her?' James Orr interrupted her thoughts.

'Who?' she asked. 'Oh, is that....?'

'Yes,' he said. 'You will be careful, Inspector.'

'The soul of discretion, Mr Orr.'

Maggie Fraser stood up and replaced her cap. There was a gleam in her eye. She wasn't bothered any longer about James Orr and his sordid little affair, though she would just check out his alibi before she returned to Skye. But Tallyforth was a different matter! She was bothered about him!

The journey was taking longer than Tallyforth had anticipated. Mary MacPherson had explained that with the breeze as gentle as it was they could not make as good speed as they had originally estimated. So Tallyforth had decided to change the route slightly and to miss out going past Balephetrish beach on the Isle of Tiree, which was the site of the next cross on his map. Willie had told him that there was no known connection between Tiree and Bonnie Prince Charlie but that there was an airstrip and, of course, the CalMac ferry to Oban.

They had been out at sea for many hours now and had just left the Isle of Muck on their port side. Beyond Muck lay Rum, whose looming shape had been clearly visible on the horizon as they approached Muck. In any other circumstances, Tallyforth would have liked to spend time on Rum because that was where the sea-eagle had been reintroduced to Scotland from Norway and where there were now reputedly fifty to sixty breeding pairs in secret locations in the hills. Willie had told him about his involvement with the project, working with the Royal Society for the Protection of Birds warden, and how they had to be constantly on guard against egg-thieves, who would go to uncanny lengths to raid the nests.

The next cross on the map was against Ockle Point on the Ardnamurchan peninsula and it was this on which they were now closing as they entered the Sound of Arisaig.

'Aye, the Prince was in Ardnamurchan,' Willie MacPherson was telling him. 'When he first came over from France, his ship anchored just south of Arisaig and he and his men first stayed in a house in Borrowdale. That's from where he sent his messages to the Highland Chiefs, asking them to join him. The minister on Ardnamurchan found out from one of his parishioners and preached a sermon saying he knew the Pretender was in his parish and he sent word to the Sheriff in Inverary. So you could say that the Forty-five Rising began in Ardnamurchan and the action to crush it started there as well.'

Tallyforth was scanning the horizon as he listened to Willie's historical guide.

'What else is there about Ardnamurchan?' he asked.

'Well, one of the greatest Gaelic poets lived there,' came Willie's reply. 'Alasdair Mac Mhaighstir Alasdair, lived there in the eighteenth century and started a school for the local children. He was a cousin of Flora MacDonald, you know. And he prepared the first Gaelic-English dictionary.'

Tallyforth listened again and wondered if all Scots were related to each other.

'What about transport? How do you get to Ockle Point?'

'There's a narrow road that runs over the hills from Salen and then you can drive up through Lochailort and Glenfinnan to Fort William, or you can take the Corran ferry and get on the road going north to Fort William and south to Glasgow. Or, if you wanted the long way round, you could go to Kilchoan and catch the ferry to Tobermory on Mull and then another ferry to Oban from Craignure.'

'Airstrip?'

'No, nothing like that. Your nearest airport is Glasgow.'

'How far?'

'I'd say about four hours,' said Willie MacPherson. 'Maybe a wee bit less. If the traffic's not too bad.'

Tallyforth was watching the shoreline as they approached Ockle Bay. It didn't look very hospitable but there were several inlets, he could see, which looked navigable.

'Could you sail into Ockle Bay?'

'Aye,' said Mary MacPherson. 'But I wouldn't try it, for it's very shallow when you get near the sands. There was a minke whale got washed up there a couple of years ago and they couldn't get it back out to sea. It died there.'

Tallyforth looked up at her but there was no expression on her face as she steered the boat away from Ockle and on to a northerly tack.

There was still plenty of heat in the sun, though it was late afternoon. One more port of call, he thought, then back towards Portree. He wondered what Inspector Fraser had been up to and how she had reacted to his going missing. He smiled to himself. It still wasn't making a lot of sense, this journey to the sites identified by Cassie Dillon. There did seem to be some connection with the travels of Bonnie Prince Charlie but not in every case and anyway that might have been purely coincidental, for the Young Pretender had been all over these Western Isles at that fateful time. More likely there was some connection between the various bays they had seen. Vaternish, Balephetrish on Tiree, and Ockle all had sandy beaches, which were not used as anchorages but could possibly act as landing points for flat-bottomed boats. And Petersport on Benbecula was never used as a port so it could serve the same function. The last mark was still to be visited. Maybe that would confirm this growing suspicion for him.

A black cormorant skimmed hurriedly across the water, heading for the furthest rocky outcrop of Ardnamurchan.

Sergeant Donald MacKenzie had had a busy day.

After Inspector Maggie Fraser had left him that morning, with her dubious message for Chief Inspector Gordon, he had spent some time ringing around the outlying police stations as she had asked. In fact, it had taken him a lot longer than he had expected, because some of the people he spoke to were old colleagues that he hadn't spoken to for some time. With Sergeant Bill Sutherland at Tarbert he had swapped tales about salmon-poaching and the death of the tweed-making on Harris. With Constable Jimmy Ferguson at Lochmaddy he had discussed the new ferry schedules and how they were affecting traffic on and off North Uist. With Sergeant Fraser Lawrie on Barra he had discussed the MacNeil clan gathering and the impact of so many American visitors to the island at one time. With Sergeant Craig Erskine at Mallaig the conversation had turned to the relative merits of Celtic and Rangers for the forthcoming premiership season.

None of his contacts had reported a sighting of *The Flodigarry* and certainly none had reported seeing Detective Chief Inspector Tallyforth or either of the MacPhersons in their patch. Clearly, whatever else the boat was doing, it wasn't stopping off at any of those places marked on the map. When the other stations had rung back to report their lack of news, he had told them to keep their eyes open and ring him if they sighted anything.

This had taken him the best part of the morning. At lunchtime he had left the young constable in charge and called in at the Community Centre to catch a glimpse of the piping competitions. As a founder member of the Isle of Skye Pipe Band, he was always keen to see the standards being set in the competitions. He knew how important piping was on the island, for it was the piping college of the MacCrimmons at Borreraig on the east of Skye that had been responsible for teaching the classical music of the pipes and handing on the tradition to successive generations until the defeat of Bonnie Prince Charlie's forces at Culloden, after which the wearing of the kilt and the playing of the pipes were banned.

When he had returned, it had been to find that Chief Inspector Gordon from Inverness, a man of generous girth and a ruddy complexion, wearing a dandruff-covered black blazer and grey flannels, and smoking a pipe, was waiting for him in Inspector Fraser's office.

'Well, MacKenzie, where's your superior officer? Your constable out there seems to have been struck dumb. Says he doesn't know. What's going on? I presume you know where she is? She was ordered to await my arrival and to do nothing further in this murder case,' he roared.

'She's been called away,' said Donald MacKenzie. 'Suddenly. This morning.'

As he looked at the bulky figure sitting opposite him, he thought about her last words to him and about the anatomical impossibility of what she had suggested he tell the chief inspector.

'Where the bloody hell to?' came a further roar.

'I don't know,' spluttered Donald MacKenzie. 'She doesn't always tell me what she's doing.'

'And can't you contact her on the bloody radio?' Chief Inspector Gordon bellowed, standing up from the chair he had been sitting on. The chair sighed its appreciation.

'It's not always possible in the hills,' said Donald MacKenzie. 'I think she's maybe gone up north.'

'Why d'you say that? You do know where she went, don't you? She's gone off chasing someone in connection with this murder, hasn't she? And she's told you to say nothing? I've heard of this Inspector Fraser. Bloody police college type. Keen to make a name for herself. Where the bloody hell is she, Sergeant? Tell me all you know.'

And Donald MacKenzie had told him all he knew. Well, almost all he knew. He had told him about the dead body, about the scarf, about the forensic report, about Chief Inspector Tallyforth, about Willie MacPherson, and about the map. And, when the map had been requested, he had shown it to Chief Inspector Gordon, only this time he had taken the trouble to point out that the likeliest route that *The Flodigarry* and its passengers would be taking would be clockwise, past Kyle and through the Sound of Sleat to Ockle then Tiree, Barra, and Benbecula, before returning to Skye at Uig. He had hazarded a guess that that was where his inspector might - he had taken care to stress it was only a possibility - might just have gone.

That had been enough.

Chief Inspector Gordon had needed no second invitation. Fastening his blazer tight across his large belly, he had left Portree police station and headed out over the hills towards Uig in his car.

That had left Donald MacKenzie with one remaining task, to interview the four Americans who were in Portree for the next day's Highland Games.

He had found them up, as he had expected, at The Lump, the natural amphitheatre above the harbour where the Games were held each year. They had been busy practising with the heavy weights - the light stone, the heavy stone, the hammer, the two iron weights which had to be thrown as far as they could from a standing position, and the fifty-six pound iron weight that had to be thrown over their shoulders and up over a bar. Their technique was better than he had anticipated.

The four Americans, two black and two white, had been only too pleased to tell him all they could. They were all at college at Utah in the States, they had told him, on athletic scholarships and had decided to spend some time in Europe on their summer vacation. To help pay their way, they had entered a number of the Highland Games competitions that were held throughout the north of Scotland in July and August. So far, they had had some success, but they were aware that technique was the most important factor and that was why they were now getting plenty of practice with the weights.

When asked about their movements the previous evening, they had told him that they had had a few drinks in the Royal Hotel earlier in the evening and then gone to the pier for fish and chips. Yes, they had seen four people going out in a dinghy to a boat anchored in the bay at about the time in question, when they had been sitting on the harbour wall eating their fish and chips. But they hadn't seen any other movement in the harbour while they were there, which had probably only been another twenty minutes or so, before they headed back to their camp site out on the road towards Staffin.

Donald MacKenzie had thanked them and wished them well in the following day's competition, though he had told them he hoped the Scots laddies beat them!

And that had seemed to be that. He had gone back to the police station, where there were no reports from the other police stations out in the isles, no messages from Inspector Fraser, and no sign of Chief Inspector Gordon, he was pleased to say.

'Georgie girl! It's Steve!'

She heard his voice crackling at the end of the telephone.

92

'Steve! Where are you? What are doing? Haven't heard from you for weeks! What are you doing?'

'Hey there, Georgie girl! How ya kicking? You were off to Ireland last time we spoke. So?'

Her voice sounded flatter now.

'Yeah, that's right. It was okay. I'm back at work now. Walking the mean streets of Birmingham, looking for criminals. But where are you calling from? I tried your London number but I was told you were working away and they wouldn't tell me where.'

'That's because I'm on a secret mission, baby! The James Bond of the Highlands and Islands. I've been seconded to the Scottish Office to help prepare for the devolution vote. My mission? To seek out and destroy any opposition to the government! No, but seriously, I've been told to tour the land sounding out opinion in a variety of places. I'm in Stornoway just now. That's why I'm ringing you. Don't come here if you ever have a weekend with nothing to do! You'd think Birmingham was bliss compared to this!'

'Stornoway!' he heard her squeal. 'That's hundreds of miles away, isn't it?'

'Too true, sweetheart! Too true! I could do with some action but there's nothing here but old men in raincoats and flat caps. Not my type, I think! But listen, I've got some news for you.'

'Go on,' came the reply.

'Saw your ex yesterday,' Steve Anthony said. 'Tallyho, or whatever his name is.'

There was a silence at the other end of the line.

'Go on, Steve,' said George Elliott, her voice modulated to a much colder pitch now.

'Well, sweetie, he's in Skye. Or he was, until last night. There's been a murder apparently and he's sailing around the islands looking for the murderer. *Plus ca change*! What's he doing up here? Don't you have enough murderers in Birmingham any longer to keep him occupied?'

'I heard he'd gone on holiday,' she replied, still coldly. 'Some bird-watching cruise.

'Well, seems he's caught some bird, and it's a dead one by the sound of it!'

93

'What d'you know about her?'

'Well, apparently, the murderee was supposed to be going on this cruise with him but was found dead in her bunk yesterday morning. Came from Tamworth, so they say. Godforsaken place! Weren't you there last year on some business? Name of Cassie Dillon. Though I ask you, what kind of name is that? Sounds like a new dish in an Indian restaurant!'

'Steve!'

'Sorry, sweetie! Blame Stornoway. It's driving me mad. Look. I'm going now. I'm starving and I'm sure there'll be some charming little Italian restaurant waiting to tempt me with something special. I'll call you tomorrow, when I'm back in Portree on Skye. It's the Highland Games and I wouldn't miss all those rippling muscles!'

'Steve, take care of yourself. If Tallyforth's in the area, you might bump into him and you know what he's like. He hates gays. Especially you, because you're a friend of mine.'

'It's alright, sweetie! I'll be careful. Call you tomorrow. *Ciao!*'

Tallyforth got the MacPhersons to drop anchor in the Sound of Sleat just out in Knock Bay, so that he could row the dinghy ashore himself on to the golden sands of the beach. As he rowed, his back to the shoreline, he could see the western coastline of Knoydart on the mainland and the grey-headed mountains behind reaching into the clouds of the early evening. The only sound was the plash of his oars and the distant call of a curlew. It was magnificent.

He rowed up to the sand and climbed out, pulling the small dinghy on to the beach and securing it with its painter around a rock. Then he set off along the now-deserted beach, scuffing sand and broken shells. There was a track at the northerly edge of the sands and he could see to his right above the cliffs the ruined outlines of Knock Castle, which Willie had told him had once been a major stronghold of the Clan MacDonald, one of the great clans of Skye.

He followed the short track past a couple of old houses, now also in ruins, and soon reached a main road. He looked down at the map he had brought with him. It would be maybe fifteen minutes from there to Armadale and the CalMac ferry that sailed to Mallaig in the summer months and maybe forty-five minutes to

Kyleakin and the new bridge.

He folded his map and turned to retrace his journey.

Even though Willie had told him about a further link with Bonnie Prince Charlie, in that it was to Armadale that Flora MacDonald had gone after saying her farewells to the Prince and from there that she had been arrested for plotting to support his escape, Tallyforth was beginning to dismiss the connections with the Young Pretender and the Forty-five uprising. The sites of the crosses did not collide precisely enough with the sites associated with the Prince, even though they were often close.

No, he had become much more interested in these sites as places where a flat-bottomed boat could land easily and without being watched, and places which were within striking distance of easy sea, road or air connections. From each of the sites they had visited, and he was fairly certain from Willie's description of that on Tiree that the Balephetrish beach had the same characteristics, it was possible to get to anywhere in the United Kingdom quickly.

But, if he was right, what was the connection to Cassie Dillon?

Involuntarily, the thought of her name brought back the memory of those cold nipples and he felt the anger returning. How little he really knew about her! Was she involved in some drug-smuggling scam? Some major scheme to bring drugs from across the Irish Sea illegally into Scotland and then, through easy air journeys, on to London and wherever?

Or did she have connections with terrorists? Was that what these secluded bays and landing-points were to be used for?

Or was there some simpler, some more innocent explanation?

The bar of the Royal Hotel was heaving with humanity. The pipers of that day's competitions were slaking their thirsts, as were the members of the Isle of Skye Pipe Band who had gathered that evening for the following day's Games, which they would parade in. Then there were some of the athletes, or at any rate some of those who would be in the throwing events, including the four Americans. Some of these athletes were drinking pints of orange juice but others were drinking the Cameron's bitter. Added to these were large numbers of tourists from all over Europe who had arrived in Portree especially for the Games.

In the cacophony of voices talking or shouting in French, Italian, German, Dutch, American or Scots, a small group of three men leaned across an old oak table the better to hear what each was saying.

'So who was this man, Hamish? Why didn't you tell us about him before now?' said Dugald MacLeod, who had taken on extra staff for the anticipated crush in the bar and, while it was still early and there was no likelihood yet of drunkenness and daftness, felt he could have a few moments to talk to his son and Iain McMillan, the solicitor. He brushed his long white hair back from his forehead.

Hamish had admitted to his meeting with the man he still thought of as John Smith. He couldn't keep it quiet any longer. Anyway he only meant to tell his father and his closest compatriot. And they wouldn't say anything!

'He said he worked for the Home Office and had been seconded to the Scottish Office to help prepare for the devolution,' Hamish replied, supping his whisky.

'Was he genuine?' Iain McMillan asked. He had changed out of his office suit after a session at the gym into a deep blue silk blouson over a grey tee-shirt and matching grey trousers. 'You're sure he wasn't just having you on?'

No!' Hamish was adamant. 'He knew too much about me. Knew I was in the S.N.P., knew I was involved in S.K.A.T., even knew I'd been a piper. Said that the government had records on lots of people. Said I was one of the 'movers and shakers'!

'Well, you are that, Hamish,' said his father, patting his son on the back. 'I have to give you that! You've surely made a mark for yourself in this island.'

'What else did he say?' demanded Iain McMillan, pulling at the gold chain around his neck.

'Well, that was the strange bit. When I told him that we weren't happy that the new government hadn't scrapped the toll like they'd promised, he said that the bridge was only a small issue compared to what was going to come.'

'Meaning?' asked Iain McMillan. He raised his gin and tonic to his lips.

'It's what I was telling you last night. The Atlantic Frontier. The oil exploration. He reckoned the islands could become very wealthy in the next few years, thanks to the oil. Look what's happened to Aberdeen!'

'Aye, well, that's all very well,' interrupted Dugald MacLeod. 'But I've been to Aberdeen and you should see the price of houses there since the oil. The young ones there cannot afford to buy them. If that happens on the isles, it could be worse than the Clearances. We have to be very canny about all this.'

'But, father, it could also buy us independence. Imagine it! Independence for the Western Isles! An independent Gaelic community! We could control housing then, couldn't we? And everything else we needed to control. That's why I want to raise the temperature at the S.K.A.T. meeting on Friday,' said Hamish, wiping froth from his moustache. 'We might be able to lobby for changes on the tolls if we could do a deal about the devolution issue.'

'Hamish is right,' said Iain McMillan. 'At least about trying to do a deal over the devolution issue. But I'm not convinced about this John Smith character. There's something that you both ought to know about. You know that woman that was found dead in Willie MacPherson's boat yesterday morning? Well, the police haven't said anything yet for some reason, but I happen to know that she was murdered. Just you wait, there'll be such a hue and cry when that gets out! And that will maybe take folks' attention more than the tolls for a while.'

'Murdered!' exclaimed Hamish. 'Here! In Portree! Never! Who by?'

'That is the mystery,' replied Iain McMillan. 'No one knows. A mysterious stranger perhaps?'

Hamish and Dugald exchanged glances of surprise at this information.

'And there's a senior detective from Birmingham here looking into the case,' Iain McMillan continued to astonish his compatriots. 'Although I understand that he has temporarily gone missing. A fact which our good Inspector Fraser is less than happy about. Though she too appears to have left the island for now. No doubt on some urgent business.'

'How d'you know all this, Iain?' asked Dugald, whose face betrayed the complete surprise he felt at hearing all this information.

'Little birds,' said Iain McMillan. 'I'm not the only one who has mysterious visitors, Hamish!'

He raised his glass to his lips again and smiled.

One further cross was made that Tuesday evening for, by one of those unusual coincidences, Inspector Maggie Fraser was driving across the Skye Bridge from Kyle of Lochalsh to Kyleakin after her trip to Oban to see James Orr at exactly the moment that *The Flodigarry*, with Detective Chief Inspector Tallyforth and the two MacPhersons aboard, was sailing under the bridge on the last leg of its journey back to Portree harbour.

Neither, of course, saw the other, as their paths traversed.

EIGHT

George Elliott had gone straight to the telephone directory after hearing Steve Anthony's news and found that there were four people with the surname Dillon living in the Tamworth area. It had taken four phone calls to establish that none of those knew anyone by the name of Cassie. So, she had concluded that the number must be ex-directory and had therefore used her police authority to get British Telecom to divulge the fact that there were three further Dillons in that area. Two of these also had no knowledge of a Cassie Dillon, while the third had an answering machine taking messages. She was fairly certain that this must be the one she wanted and so got the telephone people to give her the address.

On the Wednesday morning she had then driven from the Mercian Force's headquarters in Birmingham along the M42 towards Tamworth, where she soon found the housing estate where Cassie Dillon's house was. The house was a nondescript semi-detached one, whose only distinguishing mark from the outside was the purple wisteria that grew around the doorway. After knocking hard on the door for several minutes, George Elliott had forced it open by pushing a plastic card through the frame and raising the snib on the lock.

It was a typical single woman's house, she thought to herself. Rather like her own place in many ways. Two pairs of tights hanging over radiators to dry. A stray lipstick discarded on a shelf just inside the door. In the kitchen, jars of pasta and rice, a string of garlic bulbs hung up, racks of spices, and a cappuccino coffee machine.

She glanced quickly in each of the three bedrooms upstairs but there was nothing particularly noticeable there, just the usual collection of clothing and bedding. She went downstairs again into the main room which was clearly the room that Cassie Dillon spent most of her time in. She lifted the telephone and checked the answering device. There were several messages, so she listened to each in turn. The first was from a friend, inquiring about another friend, but it did confirm that this was Cassie Dillon's house. The second message was from someone with a Scots accent, asking her to call about the cruise. Presumably, she thought, this must be the skipper of the boat she was due to sail on. Must have called after she'd left. The third message was from someone who didn't leave a name but spoke to her in familiar terms, telling her that the parcel was on its way. There were two other messages but they were clearly from the same person who had left the first message, just checking that she had received it.

She then began systematically sifting through the room, beginning with the bookcase which was largely filled with paperback novels but did contain on its bottom shelf a number of hard-cover books. She lifted these in turn to examine and saw that they were all about endangered species of wild life. There were photographic journals about whales, about dolphins, about rare species of monkeys, about red kites in Wales, about ospreys in Scotland, and many others. Clearly Cassie Dillon had an interest in such topics.

She then noticed that the table at the far end of the room had some clutter on it and, when she looked, she found that the clutter consisted of a number of carelessly-folded maps and some typewritten papers. She opened up each of the maps in turn and saw that they were all Ordnance Survey Landranger maps of the Hebrides of Scotland or of the Orkneys and Shetlands. Some had pencil crosses on them at various points, but these markings meant nothing to George Elliott.

She picked up the sheaf of typewritten papers and, flicking through them, saw that they were all headed with the Greenpeace logo. She sat down in a stiff-backed chair to read more closely, in case these papers threw any light on Cassie Dillon, for it seemed odd to her that she should have gone on a cruise of the Hebrides without all these maps that she had obviously bought to look at the area in depth.

The first paper she looked at was headed 'Seismic Exploration'.

It was about the exploration by the oil companies of the Atlantic Frontier in their search for new reserves of oil. The exploration was done with underwater airguns which, claimed the Greenpeace notes, were affecting the marine environment of several species of whales. The second paper was concerned with St Kilda, the conservation site off the north west coast of Scotland, and the dangers to its protected wildlife from the increase in oil tanker traffic in that area. The third paper concerned something called the seventeenth licensing round, which appeared to be about the award of tranches of ocean to various oil companies for exploration, the tranches all being to the west of the Hebrides or to the north of the Shetlands. The fourth paper was a media briefing about the occupation of Rockall by Greenpeace activists in protest about this exploration.

There then followed copies of three letters - the first from Greenpeace to *The Guardian* about the dangers to island communities in the Hebrides of the oil exploration on the Atlantic Frontier. The second from Greenpeace to the Western Isles Council, reinforcing the same point but making clear that the whole eco-system of the area was under threat from the intended developments of the oil industry into the Atlantic Ocean. The third letter was from the Prime Minister in reply to an earlier letter from Greenpeace congratulating him on his victory in the General Election and seeking his support on the vexed question of oil exploration in the Atlantic. This last letter made it perfectly clear that Greenpeace was working alone and could not count on government support, since the Prime Minister stressed that, were the development of the Atlantic oilfields to be stopped, this would have a major impact on jobs and on the balance of payments.

There were two further papers, one a press cutting from *The Inverness Courier* which reported that a Scottish research group was claiming that the coral reefs of the west coast of Scotland could be damaged by the proposed oil exploration and production, and the other being an extended media briefing paper produced by Greenpeace about Atlantic Frontier oil, describing how the extraction of oil in much deeper levels of water required new technology from the oil companies and how the development of such new technology was taking place without a proper appraisal of the environmental impact of its usage.

George Elliott leaned back and pondered. The maps and all this Greenpeace stuff seemed unlikely preparations for someone merely going on a holiday. And yet there had to be some connection between all of this and the fact that this woman, this Cassie Dillon, had chosen to go to the very area where all this Greenpeace concern was focused. Or, at least, very close to it all.

She looked around her. There was a large framed photograph of a woman hung on the wall. Was that her? Was that Cassie Dillon?

George Elliott stood up and moved across to confront the picture. She noted the short dark hair, neatly cut behind the ears, the dark hazel eyes, the high cheekbones and the practised smile of someone who liked being photographed. Yes, she thought, just his sort. Bet she had him wrapped round her little finger!

But the woman was dead, she reminded herself, in mysterious circumstances and Tallyforth was sailing round the islands looking for her killer! She picked up all the maps and papers and headed for the door.

At precisely nine o'clock on that same morning, Inspector Maggie Fraser marched through the front doors of Portree police station, a look of grim determination on her face. Her uniform was freshly laundered, the white shirt pristine and the black trousers sharply creased. She nodded to Sergeant Donald MacKenzie, who stood as ever behind the main desk.

'Ma'am,' he called, trying to get her attention urgently.

'Not now, Sergeant,' she said briskly, heading directly towards her office.

'But, ma'am...'

'Not now, Sergeant!' she repeated, more firmly this time.

She gave him a fierce look and swung open the door of her office.

'Where the bloody hell do you think you've been, Inspector bloody Fraser?' bellowed Chief Inspector Gordon, who sat facing her in her chair behind her desk, his dandruff-flecked blazer straining around his massive shoulders and his face bright with apoplexy. 'You were told quite clearly yesterday bloody morning, for God's sake, to do nothing about this murder till I got here.

And what happens? You and your bloody girl-guide mentality think you can solve a murder case on your own, with no training and no back-up! Then you leave your sergeant here with some half-cocked story about a policeman from Birmingham going on a trip of the islands with a couple of locals. And I spend the whole of an afternoon and evening over in Uig waiting for this boat to return and what bloody happens? Nothing! Precisely zilch. No bloody boat. No bloody policeman from Birmingham. No bloody point me being there! And, by the time I get back here it's too late to find anywhere to stop the night because the town's full of bloody tourists here for the Highland Games, so I have to sleep in a cell in the station. Inspector, you have got some explaining to do, and it had better be good.'

She had been expecting this. She had heard of Chief Inspector Gordon's reputation. He was universally disliked throughout the Highlands region, because of his rudeness. No-one knew how he had managed to reach his present rank, because he had always shown the same patterns of behaviour even as a younger policeman. Then his size had helped him, particularly when he had served for several years on the streets in Glasgow. As he had got older and had been promoted to more sedentary work, his waist had expanded and the already-known temper had become steadily more choleric and intemperate. Now, in his last few years before retirement, he had lost even the vestiges of tolerance and forbearance.

Maggie Fraser looked him squarely in the eye.

'Sir, I had to interview a potential suspect in Oban,' she said unapologetically. 'It was important that this was done immediately. At the time I made the decision to go, I felt the suspect might go missing and there was no time to waste.'

Chief Inspector Gordon's face remained purple.

'Then why didn't you bloody well ring and ask my permission?' he bellowed. 'You were under orders, Fraser. My orders. And you disobeyed them. Didn't it occur to you that whoever this person was that you thought was a suspect could have been interviewed by Oban police? Did you think of that? Did you think to consult me? Did you tell your sergeant where you were going? Did you buggery! You just swanned off on your own. Who d'you think you are, woman? Miss bloody Marple? Hetty bloody Wainthrop?'

She let him rage on for a few minutes, saying nothing.

'And another thing, Fraser. This map business. What on earth made you think that it's got anything to do with the woman's death? And this Tallyforth character. I've spoken to the Chief Constable this morning and he tells me that he had a phone call from a Chief Superintendent Clarke of the Mercian Force insisting that this Tallyforth fellow was kept off the case. Didn't you tell him? We don't need bloody southerners up here telling us how to do our jobs, do we?'

'Yes, sir,' she replied tersely. 'I gave him that message. But he has chosen to ignore it. That was why I got Sergeant MacKenzie to contact all the stations on the isles to see if we could locate the boat he's on. We thought the marks on the map might be clues'

'And they were worse than bloody useless, weren't they, Fraser? The bloody boat's gone missing and this Chief Inspector bloody Tallyforth with it, hasn't it?'

'Sir.'

He took his pipe from his blazer pocket, placed it in the corner of his mouth and put a match to the bowl, sucking in the tobacco smoke.

'Anyway,' he continued, as his temper cooled slightly and his face returned gradually to its normal redness, 'what did this suspect in Oban tell you? Anything worth knowing?'

She coughed lightly and simultaneously pushed the door closed behind her.

'Sir, may I smoke?' she asked.

He nodded and she took out a packet from her trouser pocket and lit up.

'Sir, the man's name is James Orr. He was a friend of the deceased. She'd been staying with him prior to coming to Portree. He's innocent. I've checked out his alibi and it holds. He couldn't have been in Portree the night she died.'

'So,' he grunted. 'It was a bloody wild goose chase you were on.'

'Yes and no,' she replied, drawing on her cigarette. 'He did tell me something interesting. It seems that there was more to the situation between the dead woman and Chief Inspector Tallyforth, more than them simply being fellow-passengers on a bird-watching cruise.'

'Go on,' he grunted, but he was clearly interested now, against his own will.

'Apparently she had told Orr that she was attracted to Tallyforth and had been looking forward to getting to know him better on this cruise. The implication of what Orr told me was clear - she had been looking for a new partner and thought she might have found one. That would also explain why the Chief Inspector appeared so emotionally upset at her death.'

Chief Inspector Gordon picked up a pencil and doodled on a loose piece of paper on the desk in front of him.

'Are you suggesting that he killed her, Inspector?' he asked.

'I don't think he murdered her, no,' she said, choosing her words carefully. 'But I have thought very carefully about the boat they were on. They had cabins at opposite ends of the boat and the only way to each other's cabin was through the central cabin where the MacPhersons were sleeping. But there was a hatch in the ceiling of Tallyforth's cabin that he could have climbed through without disturbing the MacPhersons and then gone along the deck and down the stairway to the Dillon woman's cabin. And remember, she was found lying naked. And there were no signs of disturbance.'

He coughed as he caught a shaft of her smoke.

'What are you saying, Fraser? Come on. Out with it!'

She drew long and hard on her cigarette.

'I think it's possible that Chief Inspector Tallyforth may have inadvertently strangled her in the act of sex,' she said at last.

'You mean he wouldn't have bloody well known?' he expostulated, incredulously. 'Come on, Fraser!'

'Sir,' she insisted. 'I believe there are certain sexual practices where reducing the air flow to the brain is said to enhance the pleasure.'

'And you're saying that this Birmingham chappie was doing that? And he didn't notice she'd died? Where did you get all this from? Bloody police college? Or bloody personal experience?'

But, before she could answer, there was a sudden and insistent knock on the door.

'Come,' ordered Chief Inspector Gordon.

The door was pushed open and Donald MacKenzie's head

appeared around its edge.

'Sorry to interrupt, sir,' he apologised. He had heard the shouting and knew what had caused it. He had had his full share of the chief inspector's bile earlier. 'There's someone here who needs to see you both. He says it's very important. It's Hamish, ma'am, Hamish MacLeod from the post office.'

'The one who's involved in the bridge protests?' she queried, stubbing out her cigarette in the ash tray on the desk.

'Aye, but it's not about that. It's about something else, something that he thinks is very important. I know you're very busy just now but I think he's got something you ought to hear.'

'Show him in, Sergeant,' said Chief Inspector Gordon. 'Let's hear what he has to say. Over here, Inspector'

Maggie Fraser moved to stand beside him at the desk as Sergeant Donald MacKenzie ushered in the balding figure of Hamish MacLeod.

'My father says I have to tell you about this stranger,' he began. 'An Englishman. He came to see me in the post office on Monday morning and I had lunch with him in the Royal.'

'Why are you telling us this, Hamish?' she asked, glancing quickly at her superior officer to check that she wasn't forbidden from asking questions.

'Well, he knew an awful lot about me and told me some strange things,' Hamish continued hesitantly, then dried up.

'Go on, man,' said Chief Inspector Gordon, chewing on his pipe stem. 'There's plenty of strange Englishmen in the world. But why should we be concerned about this one?'

'Well, it's just that I heard last night that you think the dead woman you took from the boat the other day had been murdered.'

'Yes?'

'Well, I suddenly remembered that I'd seen this stranger before Monday morning.'

'Where?'

'He was in the Royal Hotel on Sunday evening,' Hamish said. 'He was on his own at a table behind us, that's Iain McMillan, my father and me. And the woman who's dead now was at another table, with Willie MacPherson and his wife Mary and another man I didn't recognise.'

'So you think he might have been involved in her death?' queried Maggie Fraser.

Hamish was clearly flustered. He pulled at his beard.

'I don't know about that,' he said. 'I just thought it was odd this stranger being there at the time and then turning up on the Monday morning and knowing so much about me and claiming to be from the Home Office and telling some strange tale about oil exploration out beyond the islands that would make us all wealthy.'

'You thought he was lying?' she asked.

'I just don't know,' he mumbled. 'Maybe it's nothing at all. I just thought you ought to know, that's all.'

'Thank you, Hamish,' boomed Chief Inspector Gordon, whose face had lit up. 'Just leave a full description with the sergeant at the desk, will you? We'll contact you if we need any more assistance. Goodbye.'

Donald MacKenzie showed him out and pulled the door closed behind them.

'There you are, Fraser,' chuckled a delighted Chief Inspector Gordon. 'I think you'll find we now know who our murderer is. Some English nutter on the island. Get his description circulated round the islands and on the mainland at once. The sooner we can catch this bastard, the quicker we'll solve this crime.'

'But, sir!' she protested.

'But me no buts, Inspector,' he said, holding up his palm to ward off her protests. 'Just remember what I said earlier. I'm in charge of this investigation now. And you will do exactly as I order. Clear?'

'Sir.'

She clicked her heels quietly together in mock salute.

Steve Anthony had ridden down through the Isle of Lewis from Stornoway and on to Tarbert on the Isle of Harris in the very early morning, when the sun was struggling to break through a hazy sky. He had been glad that his leather motorcycling gear afforded him some warmth but had enjoyed being able to drive at speed over the deserted early morning roads with their twists and turns. The Harley had, as ever, responded magnificently to every challenge he gave it, sliding smoothly into corners, accelerating away on straighter stretches with a throaty growl, always making him feel at one with the machine. As he had approached the port at Tarbert, the sun had begun to break through the haze and had glittered on the polished chrome of his bike. Ahead of him he had seen the day's first ferry arrive from Skye, disgorging its passengers past the old crofts and the piles of peat.

As he had sat astride his gently-purring bike in the compound for those waiting to board the Caledonian MacBrayne's *MV Loch Tarbert* with its black and white body and central red funnel, he had reflected on the views he had heard expressed in the bars he had visited on the previous evening and the people of note he had met in Stornoway. He had been a little surprised that the devolution issue had not been at the forefront of people's minds. The chief concerns of the people of this most north-westerly part of the British Isles had been to do with the economic depression being felt in the area as a whole, much of which they put down to the failure of the government to protect the fishing stocks in and around the Hebridean waters. These waters, they had claimed, were being dangerously overfished by trawlers from Spain, Iceland, Russia and Scandinavian countries, which was reducing the opportunities for Scottish trawlermen to maintain their traditional way of life and sustain their livelihoods. Many, it had been claimed, had already lost their jobs, many trawlers no longer went to sea, and unemployment was rising faster there than in other parts of the nation. The relative inaccessibility of the island made it difficult to develop a tourist industry, in the way that Skye, for instance, had and the tweed industry developed by the crofters over centuries and responsible for economic survival in many parts was now dying as the skills of weaving were being lost. There were serious social problems among the young people, who saw little prospect of employment in their own community and yet wanted all the lifestyles that television and magazines led them to expect should be theirs as of right.

Consequently, there had been very enthusiastic response to the opportunities opened up by the oil exploration of the Atlantic Frontier, and particularly to the possibility that there might be government money available to expand the quayside of the port at Stornoway, thus making it suitable to service the oil industry. Already, he had been told, the port was used for changing crews and for taking on board basic supplies while seismic surveys were being carried out but there was a need to develop it further so that it could act as a full supply base by the oil companies. It had also been argued that the airport needed similar expansion, since it too was likely to be used by the oil companies for changing crews.

That had been the formal view, expressed vehemently by local businessmen and politicians he had spoken to. The unofficial view, heard through casual conversations in local pubs, had been that little would make much difference. Life on the island had always been hard and would always be hard. Something would turn up. One enterprising youngster - a lad of eighteen with long wispy hair and several ear-rings - had insisted that the best hope for the island was the development of an indigenous music industry, taking the developments begun by such as Runrig and Big Country further down the line to create a genuine Gaelic rock music. A woman in late middle age with frizzed blonde hair, who had returned to the place of her birth from a lifetime working the streets of Glasgow, had suggested that the best hope for the women of the island, if the oil business took off, lay in legalising prostitution and she had hoped the new government would look at this seriously.

He had disembarked at Uig shortly after nine o'clock and set off through the small town past Captain Fraser's folly and out on the road to Portree, where he was keen to join the expected crowds at the Highland Games and, hopefully, to meet up again with Hamish MacLeod. But, just as he had been about to enter Portree itself, he was overtaken by a police car, which pulled in front of his Harley and motioned to him to stop.

Steve Anthony pulled into the side of the road, switched off his engine and removed his helmet. What on earth could these silly plods want? He hoped it would not delay him overmuch.

'Could I see your driving licence, sir?' said the uniformed constable who came up to him from the stationary car.

'I'm sorry, officer, I don't carry it with me,' Steve Anthony replied, giving a slight smile. 'Is there some problem?'

The policeman looked steadily at him.

'Would you mind telling me your name, sir?' he asked.

'Officer, would you mind telling me what all this is about?' Steve

Anthony said, beginning to feel rather angry at this unnecessary delay.

'Your name, sir?' the policeman repeated.

'John Smith!' Steve Anthony retorted. 'But why do you want to know? Why have you stopped me?'

'Just routine, sir,' said the policeman. 'Now, would you mind following me back to the police station. We'd like you to help us with our enquiries.'

Steve Anthony flinched. What was going on? He could not reveal his true identity, because he was supposed to be travelling incognito. On the other hand, he did not want to be getting into some sort of local difficulty under an assumed name. Still, a phone call back to the ministry should clear everything up.

'Would you mind telling me what all this is about?' he demanded. 'I haven't committed any crime. I don't believe there is anything illegal about my bike or about the way I was riding it. So what's this all about?'

The police officer continued to look him straight in the eye.

'I'm afraid I'm not at liberty to divulge that, sir,' he said, 'largely because I don't myself know. I was told this morning to keep an eye out for someone matching your description. The skipper of the *Loch Tarbert* was telling me about an Englishman on a Harley Davidson motorbike who came across from Harris on the morning boat. So I came out from Uig to look. Now, if you'd be good enough to follow me.'

'And am I the only Englishman to cross from Harris this morning?'

'You're the only one that matches the description, sir,' came the reply. 'Now, if you'll just follow me into the town, you can sort it out for yourself.'

'Sort what out, for God's sake!' said Steve Anthony. This really was insufferable! Still, he had supposed, it could soon be cleared up when he got to the police station.

So, reluctantly, he had followed the police car into Somerled Square, where he had switched off the engine on the Harley, parking it in the square, then followed the uniformed constable into the grey building.

He had been straightaway shown into the office belonging to

Inspector Maggie Fraser, where she stood beside her desk and at the side of the seated figure of Chief Inspector Gordon, who pointed the stem of his pipe at the newcomer.

'So, you are the John Smith we've been looking for,' he boomed, crinkling his brow. 'Been on Lewis, have you?'

'What is all this charade about?' sighed Steve Anthony. 'Why am I being put through all of this?'

'Just helping us with our enquiries, sir,' coughed Chief Inspector Gordon. 'Now, if you wouldn't mind, perhaps you'd give us a few details about yourself. What is your home address, sir?'

Steve Anthony looked at him contemptuously. If this was the calibre of person that was going to be running the country after devolution, then God help them! he thought. But he had to extricate himself from this as quickly as possible.

'Chief Inspector, there's obviously been some mistake. I am here on confidential government business. I am afraid that I am not at liberty to reveal my true identity but I can, if you will give me access to a telephone, get someone to vouch for me.'

Chief Inspector Gordon chuckled to himself and then lit his pipe.

'I suppose you'll be telling me your name's James Bond, not John Smith! Can I get you a vodka martini, Mr Smith?' he asked ironically.

'Chief Inspector, this is rather tiresome,' answered Steve Anthony, raising his eyebrows to the ceiling. 'May I use a telephone, please?'

But Chief Inspector Gordon was in no mood to allow this, at least not until he was ready.

'Mr Smith, I need to know where you were on Sunday night,' he shouted suddenly.

Steve Anthony was temporarily non-plussed.

'Why?' he asked, before he had regained enough composure to demand access to a telephone again.

'You were seen in the Royal Hotel here on Sunday evening and in the post office on Monday morning. At some point between those two events, a woman was murdered. Now, tell me what your movements were,' barked Gordon, pointing with his pipe stem again.

'Chief Inspector, this is no time for joking,' said Steve Anthony, who realised that this farce had gone on too long. 'And a difference of taste in jokes is a great strain on the affections. If you wish to retain your command, I suggest you allow me to make my phone call immediately. Otherwise you may find yourself in very serious trouble indeed!'

Maggie Fraser, who had stood in silence through this conversation and whose face had betrayed nothing of her feelings about what was going on, glanced sideways at her superior officer. He was clearly troubled. She wasn't herself sure whether the angelic-looking young man standing opposite them was bluffing or not. What she was sure of was that he was not the murderer, because she still felt that her own suspicions, of Tallyforth, were more than justified. And there was still the fact that Willie MacPherson, another of the boat's occupants at the time of the murder, had killed once before in his life.

She coughed discreetly.

'Shall I escort him to a phone, sir?' she asked tentatively.

Chief Inspector Gordon sucked on his pipe momentarily, then looked up at her, but before he could answer Steve Anthony interrupted.

'No, if I may, I will phone from here,' he said. 'Then you can find out for yourself what a terrible mistake you are making.'

Chief Inspector Gordon waved in the direction of the phone on the desk.

'Carry on,' he said, thinking to call the other man's bluff. 'Do your worst, Mr Smith.'

Steve Anthony moved across to the desk, lifted the receiver then pressed the required digits on the phone. When a voice came through at the other end of the line, he gave a coded number and then, when the minister in the Scottish Office came on, he merely gave a request that his identity be verified and handed the phone to Chief Inspector Gordon.

The latter listened impassively as the true identity of their guest was revealed. But, as he listened, the colour drained out of his cheeks, for he realised the terrible mistake he had been on the point of making.

NINE

It was almost eleven o'clock on the same Wednesday morning before *The Flodigarry* returned to Portree harbour. It was a warm morning and Tallyforth was wearing a grey tee-shirt over light blue canvas slacks and blue deck-shoes. He was sitting on the foredeck of the boat, for the MacPhersons had furled the sails while still a little way out at sea and had used the engine to chug slowly into the bay. He was listening again to the tape of Runrig's *Mara* album, with which he had now become very familiar, having played it through several times on their trip. The track *The Mighty Atlantic* in particular had stayed in his consciousness and its nostalgic lyric had replayed itself continuously in his head:

The roll of the wind
As we sail across the waters
The roll of the sea
As we're taken through the night
The dimming lamp of day
Leaves the crimson foam and spray
Across the face of the mighty Atlantic.

In the brief thirty-six hours since they had left Portree he had experienced enough of sailing to be able to appreciate those lyrics.

His original intention, which he'd pressed on the MacPhersons, had been to return to Portree the same day as they left Uig but his brief trip ashore in the dinghy to Knock Bay had delayed them and he himself had then felt no great need to rush back, for ideas were still formulating themselves in his head. So they had, at Mary MacPherson's suggestion, anchored for the night just to the south of Toscaig on the mainland. There, she had prepared for them all a supper of haddock and potatoes, followed by apple tartlets with

113

cream. They had sat on deck until quite late, Tallyforth and Mary drinking from a bottle of Talisker whisky, while Willie drank iced orange juice.

'What d'you think the inspector'll say when we turn up?' called Willie anxiously from the wheel, where he was steering them gently into the harbour. 'You've no better idea about how that lassie died than when we left, have you?'

Tallyforth turned his head in the direction of the cockpit and smiled. He transferred a small black film case from his left to his right hand.

'I have some idea what she was doing here in the Hebrides,' he replied, and then his voice turned unusually cold. 'And she wasn't here for a holiday, either, Willie. We were both fooled by that.'

Mary MacPherson, who was sitting in the cockpit beside her husband, broke in.

'What d'you know about her then, Mr Tallyforth? You've not said anything before now to us.'

Tallyforth's upper lip curled again.

'I was wondering all day about the connection between those places we visited out in the islands and the deceased.'

He accentuated the last word, for he needed, now more than ever, to think of her as no more than another dead body - another example of his trade.

'You know all that, because I was telling you yesterday that first of all I thought there was some connection with Bonnie Prince Charlie,' he continued. 'Then I thought the places marked on the map must have some other connection and, as I thought about it last night, I realised that the connection was more likely to do with possible landing places for flat-bottomed boats - landing places that were relatively unwatched and undetectable and within easy reach of transport to take someone out of the area very quickly. That's why I rowed the dinghy into Knock Bay beach yesterday evening, just to try out my theory. That's what I was thinking last night.'

'Aye, well you said as much,' said Mary.

Tallyforth glanced at her weather-beaten face. She seemed more than commonly interested in what he was thinking.

'Then I found this,' he said, holding up the film case in his left hand.

'What is it?' asked Willie.

'It's a film case, man,' snapped Mary MacPherson. 'Can you not see? Where's it from, Mr Tallyforth? What's that got to do with anything?'

'I had another hunt round the cabin that the deceased slept in,' Tallyforth replied, cupping the film case in his hand. 'And I found this on the floor.'

'Is there a film in it?' asked Willie. 'Will that tell you what you want to know?'

'Sadly, no, Willie,' said Tallyforth. 'The case is empty. But that's not the point.'

Mary MacPherson wrinkled her nose at him.

'You're talking riddles, man. What is the point?'

Tallyforth half-smiled again.

'The point is,' he replied, savouring his words, 'that not only was there no film, but there was also no camera.'

'So?' said Willie.

Mary MacPherson nudged her husband in the ribs.

'You mean, whoever killed the lassie took her camera?' she said.

'Exactly,' smirked Tallyforth. 'And it's my bet that the reason for that is that somebody wanted to know what was on the film in the camera and, rather than run the risk of exposing the film by taking it out of the camera, simply took the camera itself!'

'Well, Mr Tallyforth,' said Willie MacPherson, as he slowed the boat's engines right down and steered into a clear space of water. 'You've only to go into the chemist's in Portree to find out who's taken films in to be developed the last couple of days.'

'That should be awful easy,' teased Mary. 'I don't expect there'll be more than a few hundred with all the tourists here for the Games!'

Tallyforth turned and looked at her.

'Not necessarily, Mary. There may be other ways,' he said mysteriously.

Iain McMillan, junior partner in MacDonald and McMillan Solicitors, sat behind the piles of papers on his desk. Dapper as ever, he sported a white safari suit over a scarlet shirt, open at the neck to show his gold pendant. A matching scarlet handkerchief flopped out of his breast pocket. Being the day of the Highland Games, it was pointless keeping the office open all day since the whole local population would be up at The Lump, either competing, selling their services to tourists, or spectating. Besides he always looked forward to the spectacle himself, one of those colourful local traditions he hoped would never die. So he had dressed appropriately for the Games, calling in at the office merely to answer mail and complete a number of forms that needed his signature.

But now it was mid-morning and Iain McMillan had completed all the necessary chores of the office and had fortified himself with a cup of coffee brewed in his small glass cafetiére, for he was particular about what he drank and had no desire to sample the brew available in polystyrene beakers at the Games. There was just one more task to be attended to before he left and, in the quiet of an emptying Portree, this was an opportune moment to make that phone call.

He pulled the phone towards him, took out a thin pocket-book from the inside pocket of his jacket and, peering over his half-glasses, consulted it before dialling. It was not a number he frequently dialled.

Eventually, his call was answered.

'This is Iain McMillan,' he said quietly into the mouthpiece. 'You said I should ring when it was convenient.'

There was an audible pause at the other end of the line, then there was a lengthy reply which Iain McMillan listened carefully to.

'Yes,' he answered to a question at the end of the lengthy reply.

Another pause. Another lengthy response.

'Yes,' again he answered.

More words. Another question.

'No, I don't think so,' he said.

Yet more words. The voice at the other end, however, stayed modulated in tone.

'I'll have to find out,' said Iain McMillan, lightly tugging at his gold chain. 'It might be difficult.'

There came a sudden rap on the door to his office.

'I'll have to go. There's someone here,' said Iain McMillan, his voice sounding rather startled at the interruption. But he held on to the phone in order to hear the final words of the person at the other end of the line and, before he could put the receiver down, the door opened and Sergeant Donald MacKenzie's head appeared around the frame.

'Yes, I'll be in touch,' stammered Iain McMillan into the mouthpiece before finally replacing it. 'What can I do for you, Sergeant?'

Donald MacKenzie came into the room, taking off his cap and grinning apologetically.

'Sorry, sir, I didn't know you were on the phone. I couldn't hear you, so I let myself in. Sorry about that. I didn't mean to interrupt anything. I hope it wasn't important.'

'No, no, that's quite all right, Sergeant,' said the solicitor, quickly regaining his composure. 'Now, do you have time for a coffee?'

'That would be kind, yes,' said Donald MacKenzie. 'To tell you the truth, I'm fair famished. I've been directing traffic for the Games. I've only just come off duty. Thank you.'

Iain McMillan got up from his chair and emptied the coffee grains from his cafetiére into a sink in the corner of the room, at the same time switching on the electric kettle.

'Now then, Sergeant, tell me how I can help while we wait for the kettle to boil,' he said, turning to face Donald MacKenzie.

'Well, I'm here because I'm kind of puzzled about something,' the latter began. 'You see, I know all the arguments about the tolls on the new bridge and I hope you know that I sympathise with all you're doing in the S.K.A.T. business, Mr McMillan, even though I'm sometimes called to move your folk off the bridge. At least, since Inspector Fraser took over at the station in June. But I'm not so sure I understand about all this oil business.'

Iain McMillan looked sharply at him.

'What do you mean, Sergeant?' he said, and switched off the whistling kettle.

'Well, this business about the oil out in the Atlantic. Hamish was telling the inspector and Chief Inspector Gordon from Inverness about this man from the Home Office and what he's been saying about the oil in the Atlantic and how it's going to make everybody wealthy in the Isles. And I just didn't understand how it was all connected to the bridge business.'

'Here. Milk? Sugar?'

Sergeant Donald MacKenzie took the proffered cup, helped himself to milk and stirred it in.

'I mean, what's the connection?' he asked again.

'Sorry, Sergeant,' replied Iain McMillan. 'I can't tell you. I mean, I just don't know. Unless Hamish thinks that......but no, that would be impossible.'

'What's that?'

'Well, I was just thinking,' mused Iain McMillan. 'There was a rumour when the bridge was first being built that it was made so high so that the Royal Yacht could sail underneath her. Maybe Hamish has been thinking that oil tankers might find their way under it too.'

'Is that likely?' asked an incredulous Donald MacKenzie. 'Wouldn't that run the risk of spillage close to the shore? That could be terrible!'

'Yes, it would,' said Iain McMillan. 'But I don't think it's likely. Those oil tankers need a much greater space than that to manoeuvre in. I don't think that was it.'

'Aye, well, maybe not,' said Donald MacKenzie, draining his coffee. 'But I still don't understand it all. Still, never mind. Thanks for trying. You'll be up to the Games soon?'

'Yes,' came the reply. 'I was just about to go when you called. I'll follow you out.'

Although it was some time since the Isle of Skye Pipe Band had processed through the town, leading the march to the Games, crowds were still streaming along Bank Street. They slowed past the hospital, where a charity jog was taking place on treadmills, and then passed through the gate up to the playing field known as The Lump where the Highland Games were being held.

The weather was still warm, though not as hot as it had been the previous two days. The sky was blue with white cumulonimbus clouds. The air was filled with the sound of the wailing bagpipes and the smell of greasy hamburgers. Young pipers, in full regalia, puffed out their cheeks and tapped their right feet in time with

118

Piobareachd or the Strathspey they were practising for the under-eighteen piping competitions. They were carefully watched by their piping instructors, whose bleary eyes indicated the celebrations they had been sharing the previous evening at the end of the open piping competitions. To the left-hand side of the athletic track much younger children, all girls, all in their clan kilts and white blouses, were competing in the Highland Fling dancing competition, to the expert accompaniment of another piper.

In the middle of the natural arena local athletes were stretching themselves in the competitions. The young, lean and fit ran and jumped, while the older, beefier and more muscular threw the heavy weights. These were all local competitions in the morning, limited to residents of Skye and Lochalsh, but even beefier and stronger men could be seen on the fringes of the competition preparing for the afternoon's open competitions. Among these were the four Americans whom Donald MacKenzie had interviewed the previous day. Officials paced the arena in their kilts and green jackets, measuring throws or jumps, ensuring fairness, checking marks.

The crowds of spectators sat on the grassy banks around this natural bowl, munching sandwiches or hamburgers or crisps, licking ice-creams, drinking cans of coke or of lager. They compared the merits of various athletes with each other, cheered on their favourites, sighed when one failed to clear a height or tripped in a race round the tight circuit, applauded each tiny dancer as she smilingly curtseyed to the judge.

In one corner, beneath a Scots pine and leaning against its trunk, sat Hamish MacLeod and Steve Anthony. The latter had been allowed to leave the Portree police station and Chief Inspector Gordon's grilling immediately that his true identity had been established from Edinburgh. Chief Inspector Gordon had not liked it, indeed had not been convinced it was the right thing to do, since he still harboured suspicions, but had been left in no doubt that he must do what he was instructed.

Hamish was explaining the traditions of the Games to the man he still thought of as 'John Smith'.

'The Games has been held every year, except during the World Wars, for over a century. They've always consisted of heavy throwing events, athletics events, piping competitions and highland dancing. Highland games began as informal feats of strength and speed and stamina. They used to use big stones and tree trunks. You'll know about the piping? The MacCrimmons?'

'A little, Hamish,' said Steve Anthony, stretching out his legs in their stone-washed blue jeans. 'But do tell me more.'

Hamish MacLeod looked at his compatriot, this odd Englishman who knew so much about him and who had searched him out a short while earlier that day.

'Well, the MacCrimmons had their piping college at Borreraig on the west of the island. The MacCrimmons were the official pipers to the MacLeod Chiefs whose castle has stood at Dunvegan for over seven hundred years.'

'Would you be related, Hamish?' asked Steve Anthony, smiling lightly and pushing the collar of his blue cotton shirt away from his neck.

'Yes, but only distantly,' came the reply. 'Father tells me that he can trace the family back to the eighteen hundreds but no further. But all MacLeods are members of the clan. This is the MacLeod tartan. I always wear it.'

He briefly held his tie out for inspection.

'You were saying about the MacCrimmons?' Steve Anthony prompted him.

'Well, the story goes that the piping college lasted for two hundred years and that was where the MacCrimmons composed the classical music of the bagpipes, the Ceol Mor. Young men would go there for three years training in the pipes and to qualify as a piping master they had to memorise one hundred and ninety-five compositions of the Ceol Mor.'

'And did you have to know all of those when you were piping?' quizzed Steve Anthony.

'I still am a piper,' said Hamish proudly. 'You never stop being a piper. I just don't compete any longer, but I still play. No, a lot of the classical tunes were lost after Culloden. But a man called Donald MacDonald was responsible for preserving a great many of them. He collected them and published a book of them at the start of the last century. That's the ones that you hear today.'

Steve Anthony crossed his legs at the ankle and turned his head slightly.

'Now, Hamish, what do you have to tell me about local opinion on the devolution proposals?' he said, turning the conversation to where he had wanted it to go from the start. 'Wouldn't the MacCrimmons and the MacLeods have been in favour of what is being suggested?'

Hamish MacLeod felt his blood rising slightly. This young man had the ability to needle him and yet he couldn't tear himself away from him, for he held a strange fascination, not only because of whom he apparently represented but because of a personal magnetism which was hard to pin down.

'What the MacCrimmons and the MacLeods wanted is what Bonnie Prince Charlie wanted and that's independence for Scotland. And that's what all true Scots still want. An independent nation state. The Act of Union was the biggest disaster that's ever happened to this country. We've been under the yoke of the English for far too long and it's done us no good. Do you know who the present Lord of the Isles is? Prince Charles! That nincompoop with the big ears! Do you wonder that we are frustrated and angry? Do you wonder that we feel dispossessed?'

The few ginger hairs around his ears had begun to bristle as he spoke.

'Now, now, Hamish, I don't need the party political, thank you,' interrupted Steve Anthony. 'We all know what the S.N.P. stands for and maybe one day that's what you will get. But, for the nonce, we are talking *realpolitik* here, Hamish. What is being offered is a Scottish Parliament with tax-raising powers. Wouldn't that be a good start?'

'Yes, as long as it was genuine. But if, as we suspect, it will simply be a poodle of Westminster, then it will be nothing. It has to have real teeth. Scottish people need to run Scottish affairs. All of them, not just the ones that Westminster lets us have. All of them.'

Steve Anthony sighed. He had hoped to have a more reasoned discussion but he could see that Hamish MacLeod was too imbued with the party line, which ran through him like the name through a stick of rock. He could see that Hamish, like the rest of his party, would support the referendum but he could also see the naiveté of the new government in believing that granting a Scottish

121

Parliament to the people of Scotland was going to be sufficient. Ancient bitterness ran deep. The devolution proposals were raising that bitterness closer to the surface of the Scottish consciousness. It could be difficult to push it back down in the future.

Tallyforth had not been surprised to find that Inspector Maggie Fraser was as keen to see him as he was to see her. He had a theory about the real reason that Cassie Dillon had come to the Hebrides; she had a theory that Tallyforth was responsible for her death. He had also not been surprised to find Chief Inspector Gordon present at the Portree police station, since he was aware that a murder would draw in a superior officer to investigate.

He had persuaded the MacPhersons to accompany him to the police station, so that they could explain their reasons for acceding to his request for them to sail around the isles and he could then explain what he had discovered.

But it was himself that Chief Inspector Gordon wanted to speak to first, so he had followed Maggie Fraser, who had been sent to accompany him, into her office.

'Detective Chief Inspector Tallyforth,' boomed the large seated figure, puffing at his pipe, 'I've been looking forward to meeting you. I've heard a lot about you. Please, take a seat.'

Tallyforth looked round, saw a wooden chair and placed it at the desk facing his interrogator. Maggie Fraser took her place at the side of Chief Inspector Gordon.

'So, Tallyforth, you've been exploring the isles, I hear. Why was that now? Why didn't you stay in Portree where Fraser here could have found you? Why didn't you do what your chief superintendent told you to do and keep out of this murder investigation? Don't you have bloody discipline in the Mercian Force?' Gordon rattled off his questions, trying to intimidate Tallyforth from the outset.

'Have you found the murderer yet, Chief Inspector?' responded Tallyforth quietly. 'Have you arrested anyone? Have you even the slightest notion of why the lady was murdered?'

Maggie Fraser coughed discreetly but Gordon ignored her.

'And you have, I suppose?' he bellowed, pointing at Tallyforth with the stem of his pipe. 'Discovered the murderer's motive, I mean?'

Maggie Fraser could wait no longer.

'You slept with her, didn't you?' she interrupted, glaring angrily at him.

'Inspector, I told you to keep quiet,' shouted Gordon, before Tallyforth could even think of replying. 'This is my investigation. I will ask the questions. Got it?'

Tallyforth watched her as she pursed her lips and restrained herself.

'Perhaps it would be better if we talked alone?' he suggested, sensing the moment was right. 'Man to man?'

Maggie Fraser snorted, which only served to emphasise the point in Chief Inspector Gordon's mind.

'Yes, I think that would be a very good idea,' he said. 'Please leave us alone, Fraser. I'll call you when I need you.'

She started to speak but then thought better of it. She was not going to get anywhere with these two stubborn chauvinists. She walked stiffly around the desk and towards the door.

When she had left the room, Gordon sat back with some relief.

'I'd better tell you her suspicions,' he said, unbuttoning his blazer. 'Bloody woman! Should never have been given this station. Never had a woman in charge out here before. Or on any of the islands. No sense of bloody perspective. D'you smoke?'

Tallyforth shook his head.

'Don't mind if I do? No. Good.'

Chief Inspector Gordon relit his pipe and drew in the tobacco. His tone of voice had become noticeably friendlier and less loud. It was as if talking to someone of a similar rank to himself, and not that far removed in age, relieved him of the necessity to be overbearing.

'I tell you, Tallyforth, I don't know what it's like in the Birmingham area but we just can't get good men interested in taking on these outlying posts. They all want high-profile jobs in Edinburgh or Glasgow, somewhere to make their names. Fraser's got all the right qualifications, done the right courses, made a bit of a name for herself in Edinburgh, but she hasn't got the experience. Jumps to daft conclusions. Can't obey orders. Thinks she knows everything. Know what happened yesterday? Buggered off to Oban to interview somebody when she'd been ordered to wait for my arrival. Doesn't tell the desk sergeant where she's gone but he thinks she's gone looking for you up in Uig. So I spend all afternoon and evening waiting for your bloody boat to come in. Then, when I get back here, I have to spend the night sleeping in a bloody cell, because none of the hotels or boarding houses have got any room because of the bloody Games!'

He pushed the chair back to give himself more room, reached for his matches and lit his pipe again, sucking contentedly on it.

'So what's she been saying about me?' quizzed Tallyforth, who had listened patiently to this diatribe, realising that Gordon was obviously much more accommodating to him than Inspector Maggie Fraser had been.

'Now, don't be offended, Tallyforth,' Gordon began. 'I don't know where she's got the idea from. Probably tells you more about her than anything else. But she thinks that you and the dead woman were engaged in some unusual sexual practice, involving semi-asphyxiation, and that the woman died without you realising it.'

Tallyforth, who had heard some things in his life, whistled under his breath. His first reaction was one of numbness, which was quickly followed by one of burning anger.

'How the hell did she work that out?' he spluttered. 'The woman's barking mad!'

'Silly cow, didn't I tell you?' sad Gordon, shifting his weight in the seat once again. 'She thinks you were having an affair with the deceased. Bloke in Oban she went to see suggested that bit to her. Plus she clearly doesn't like you.'

Tallyforth was having difficulty keeping his anger in check.

'Look, I only met the woman once before and that was two weeks ago in Birmingham,' he explained, carefully slowing his speech down to ensure that it was lucid. 'We met up again on Sunday night, in the Royal Hotel, with Willie and Mary MacPherson, who own *The Flodigarry* which was to be our cruise-boat. We had a meal and a few drinks. We went back to the boat. We said goodnight. Next morning she's dead. End of story.'

'And start of inquiry,' added Chief Inspector Gordon. 'There were three of you on that boat with the deceased. And the three of you are covering for each other. Fair enough. The MacPhersons say you couldn't have got past to her cabin without disturbing them but Fraser says you could have climbed through a hatch.'

Tallyforth looked bemused.

'What hatch?' he asked. He was beginning to wonder whether this bluff and beefy policeman had been deliberately adopting this matey approach to try to trip him up. Maybe there was a delicacy of touch beneath that gross exterior.

'The one in the roof of your cabin apparently,' Gordon answered. 'Her theory is that you could have got through there and then along the deck and into the dead woman's cabin. Can't see it myself but that's what she thinks.'

Tallyforth realised he was right. This was a game of cat and mouse. But he knew how to play such games too.

'Just suppose for one minute that what Inspector Fraser suspects had any semblance of truth to it, what would have been my motive?' he queried.

'Sex,' said Gordon, puffing on his pipe and looking away from Tallyforth.

Tallyforth thought again of those cold nipples. For the first time in over twenty-four hours he was seeing Cassie Dillon as a woman again. If only, he thought.

'So, in the middle of sexual activity, I strangle her, is that it?' he asked.

'Accidentally,' said Gordon.

'Without noticing?' said Tallyforth incredulously.

'I told you it was bizarre,' said Gordon. 'But we'd better check the boat out just to see if it was at all possible. Course, I'm on your side, Tallyforth. But then there's the matter of MacPherson. His wife vouches that he never left her side all night but he is a convicted killer.'

'Was,' corrected Tallyforth. 'He told me that he was released from prison when they found out that the death was an accident.'

'Even so,' continued Chief Inspector Gordon. 'He once killed someone. And we don't have any other leads at present. I'll need to speak to him.'

Tallyforth watched him as he pulled a tobacco pouch from his pocket and, after emptying the black ash from the bowl of his pipe into an ash tray, proceeded to refill it with strands of some golden tobacco. Was this man subtle? Or was he just whistling in the dark?

he wondered. Could they work together? Or would he be better pursuing his own lines of inquiry?

'Chief Inspector Gordon,' he said, having made up his mind that he needed to try to work alongside rather than alone, 'let me tell you some of what I found on my travels yesterday, because I think it's important. It's my view, from long experience of murder cases, that it's necessary to discover a motive before you can hope to discover a murderer. To discover a motive, you have to find out as much as you can about the victim and the situation the victim was in. That means looking for evidence at the scene of the crime which tells you something about the victim's situation. Now that might be a weapon or the effects of a weapon, like gunshot or knife wounds, or it might be evidence left by the murderer - strands of hair, fingerprints, that sort of thing. Or it might be something more circumstantial, something that might at first appear perfectly normal but, when looked at coldly and objectively, might point to unconsidered directions.'

'You specialise in murder then, Tallyforth?' said Chief Inspector Gordon, looking across the room at him through the wisps of blue smoke. 'We don't get a lot up here in the Highlands, you know. But I recognise what you're saying. So how does all this fit in to the murder of this Dillon woman?'

'Well, I expect you've seen the map?'

'The one from her bedside? Yes.'

'And you'll have noticed the crosses?' continued Tallyforth, checking that he was being followed. 'That was where I went yesterday in the MacPhersons' boat, to look at some of the sites of those crosses. At first I thought it was something to do with Bonnie Prince Charlie but then I realised that each of those crosses marks a place where a flat-bottomed boat can land undetected and its occupants can quickly be on their way by road, ferry and plane to virtually anywhere in the country.'

'So?'

'So I reckon that the dead woman was involved in drug smuggling,' said Tallyforth conclusively, holding up the black film case. 'And this I think will prove it. I found it in her cabin this morning but there was no camera.'

'So?'

'So someone wanted the film that was in that camera and took the camera. That someone is your murderer, Chief Inspector,' concluded Tallyforth. 'Do you know of any drug runners on the island? On any of the islands? Because I suggest we start looking there.'

TEN

The Games had finished in the late afternoon, when the sun had reappeared in its strength to give a warm afterglow to the proceedings. Athletes and spectators had then wound their way slowly from the arena and back to their various places of residence in Portree. All that was left were the hamburger caravans, a few officials tidying up, the iron weights and two broken cabers, and the flattened grass.

Tallyforth and Gordon had watched the last few events together, enjoying the sight of the bedraggled figures returning from the hill race and the muscular exertions of the tug of war teams. It was Chief Inspector Gordon who had suggested it. Somehow in the course of the interrogation that had taken place earlier that day both men had come to respect the other's style and an unspoken alliance had formed between them in the pursuit of Cassie Dillon's murderer. The alliance was made all the stronger by each man's distaste for Inspector Maggie Fraser, whose ludicrous suspicions had angered Tallyforth and whose insubordination the previous day still rankled with Gordon.

So Tallyforth had happily agreed to Gordon's suggestion that they call in at the bar of the Royal Hotel for an early evening drink and then have dinner together, before Gordon had himself driven back by one of the young constables to Inverness later in the evening.

'Well, Tallyforth,' boomed Chief Inspector Gordon, taking the small glass of Talisker whisky and a pint of Cameron's from Tallyforth's hands and puffing on his pipe. 'You've been very quiet all afternoon. About the murder I mean. Any new thoughts?'

Tallyforth took a long sip of his beer, breathed deeply and wiped his lips before answering.

'I'm still convinced it's to do with those landing bays,' he replied. 'It has to be. She had a map with specific places marked on it. And all of those places are either sandy beaches or in one case a forgotten port where a flat-bottomed boat could easily land without drawing attention to itself. And every one of them is within easy reach of an airport or a road to an airport. Now why would she have such a map with such places marked on it? It has to be smuggling. It just has to be. But you're telling me that you don't get any smuggling around here?'

Chief Inspector Gordon slipped off his blazer and leaned sideways to hang it over his chair, revealing large patches of sweat on his shirt under his armpits.

'Yes, that's right, there's been none that we know of for many years. There used to be a bit of whisky smuggling out of the island but that's been stopped a long time now. And we don't have a drugs problem up here. If you wanted to bring drugs into the country, there's plenty of easier routes than bringing a little boat across from Ireland or wherever,' Gordon said, sucking at his pipe.

'What about landing people then?' continued Tallyforth, thinking aloud. 'Illegal immigrants? Terrorists? Anyone that might need to get into the country undetected?'

'Now just think about it, Tallyforth,' said Gordon. 'Illegal immigrants? You're not going to take folk with brown skin on the ferries or planes around here without being noticed, are you? And, if anybody wants to get their way into Glasgow illegally, then there's other easier routes. And it's the same with the terrorists. If they want to get into Britain, they come in on the main routes. You don't need a passport from Ireland remember.'

Tallyforth lifted his whisky to his lips and drained it in one swift gulp.

'So who else might want to come into the country undetected?' he mused.

'I'll get you another,' said Gordon, stretching across for Tallyforth's glass. 'Talisker again?'

Tallyforth nodded and looked around him. The bar was already filling up. He noticed several members of the Isle of Skye Pipe Band, still in their kilts, standing up at the counter, slaking their thirst after their busy day parading around the sports field in between events.

'Maybe you're looking at it the wrong way,' said Gordon, as he returned to their table with fresh glasses of Talisker. 'Maybe they're places for people who want to get *out* of the country undetected.'

'Such as?'

'No idea,' said Gordon. 'Just a thought. Or maybe places where folk want to hide.'

Tallyforth sighed. Things were getting murkier. He had hoped that the alliance with Gordon might prompt thoughts in him, the way that working with George Elliott had done. And for the first time in weeks he realised that he missed her.

'What about the camera then?' Chief Inspector Gordon reminded Tallyforth.

'I'm not sure about that yet,' came the reply. 'Maybe that would help, if we could find it. But where do we start?'

'Have you thought what the connection might be?' asked Gordon, rubbing the sweat from his brow with the sleeve of his shirt. 'I mean, between the map and the missing camera?'

'And the tape,' Tallyforth pointed out.

'Yes, and the tape,' sighed Gordon, 'though I don't know what you're listening to all that for.'

Tallyforth looked across at him before replying. He was disappointed in his companion. He had sensed in their earlier meeting that the man had a certain wiliness but clearly that was only in the way he conducted interrogations. He did not have the imagination, the verve, the spark, the creative instinct which the true detective had, he realised. That was what was so frustrating. All he was getting by way of response was a further set of questions or problems. He wasn't being driven forward in his thinking.

'There are always connections,' he said. 'Thin and ethereal though they may be at times, there are always connections. Everything, in the deepest sense, always hangs together. We collect the strands that float in the air and we put them together. It's probable that we put them together the wrong way at first. It's probable that there will be some strands that we haven't yet found. But when we have found them all and when we have them all connected accurately, then we have a solution. That's what detection is all about.'

'Very profound, Tallyforth,' said Gordon, shifting in his chair and taking another draught of his beer. 'But you're still no nearer finding who killed that woman in MacPherson's boat the other night.'

And Tallyforth knew, as he took another slug of whisky, that he was right.

In the Clansman Restaurant of the Portree Hotel another group of men were gathered after the Games. Hamish MacLeod had brought Steve Anthony, whom he still thought of as 'John Smith', to meet his friend and compatriot from S.K.A.T., local solicitor Iain McMillan.

'Iain, this is John Smith, the man I was telling you about,' Hamish MacLeod was saying. 'He's from the Scottish Office. He's the one who was telling me all about the oil exploration in the Atlantic just off the Hebrides.'

Iain McMillan reached out a hand to greet the new acquaintance, whose natty attire of blue cotton shirt and blue stone-washed jeans he admired, noting how much more stylish they were than Hamish's dull brown corduroy trousers and green shirt, with the ever-present MacLeod tartan tie.

'Though I did ask Hamish to keep my occupation secret,' smiled Steve Anthony, taking the proffered hand and noticing the whiff of eau de cologne. 'It really wouldn't do for everyone to know that the Scottish Office employs Englishmen to ride around Scotland on their motor-bikes communing with the natives. People might get suspicious of my motives.'

A waitress appeared at Hamish MacLeod's elbow.

'No, we're not ready to order yet,' he said, turning towards her. 'Oh no, just bring us some drinks, would you? G and T for you, Iain? What about you, John?'

'The same,' Steve Anthony smiled, then added wryly. 'With ice and a slice, if you please.'

'And a pint for me, thanks,' said Hamish. 'I'm sorry, John, I know you asked me to say nothing but, as I told you earlier, you can trust Iain. He's been a great strength to us since he came to Portree. We couldn't have fought the legal fight over the tolls without his knowledge and skill. He's been brilliant.'

Iain McMillan acknowledged the tribute smilingly, tucking his red handkerchief more securely into the breast pocket of his white jacket.

'Forgive me,' said Steve Anthony, 'I'm insatiably curious but is that delightful white suit from somewhere special?'

Iain McMillan smiled back.

'Nowhere exotic,' he said. 'Just Edinburgh. I have my suits made up for me there. I find it's worth the expense of the travel. There are certain dress standards expected of one in soliciting, even out here in the Isles.'

'Of course,' Steve Anthony replied. 'Oh, thank you so much.'

The latter remark was addressed to the waitress who brought them their drinks on a silver tray.

'Just give us five minutes, will you?' Hamish MacLeod asked her. 'Then we'll order dinner.'

She swivelled and moved away. Steve Anthony noticed, with some disappointment, how Iain McMillan's eyes followed her mincing walk.

'Now, John, I want you to tell Iain here about this oil business,' continued Hamish, tugging at his ginger beard. 'For I'm not sure I've understood it properly.'

'It's very straightforward in one way,' Steve Anthony replied, clasping his hands together over his crossed knees. 'And yet very complicated in another. Let me try to explain. You see, you will know that the discovery of oil off the north-east coast of Scotland in the nineteen-seventies was what allowed the previous government to change the political landscape of our times by declaring war on every entrenched interest group in the country from the trades unions to the public services, from miners to doctors, from paupers to politicians. That fortuitous discovery bankrolled the Thatcher governments through the eighties and allowed them to do more or less what they wished. Well, the oil companies of the world have known for some time that those oil reserves are running out and so they are constantly on the look out for new sources. That's why they have developed new fields at Foinaven and Schiehallion off the Shetland Isles. And that's why, at this very moment, there are ships out in the Atlantic off the coasts of Lewis and Harris conducting seismic exploration for oil reserves deep below the ocean bed.'

'So?' queried Iain McMillan, brushing a fly away from his blond hair.

'Patience, *mon ami*, patience!' Steve Anthony rebuked him mildly. 'I was coming to that. The point is that, just as the oil reserves off north-east Scotland were used to transform a whole economy and political stratosphere, so these new oil reserves in the Atlantic may be used to transform other areas, including the Western Isles. Now do you see at what I drive?'

Hamish MacLeod winced at this unusual verbal formulation, though he had been growing used to these oddnesses of phrasing from his new-found friend.

'Go on, John,' he said. 'Just spell out what that could mean for us.'

'Just think about it for yourselves,' continued Steve Anthony, sipping from his gin and tonic. 'And remember, I've seen the projections being done in the Scottish Office. First of all, there will be a need for a deep anchorage point for ships to dock at and maybe more than one. Then there will have to be good routes from the oilfields to all the major ports and easy transportation for getting people to and from the rigs. Then there will be a growing need for the crews on those rigs to have places for rest and recuperation, which means a big increase in hotel accommodation and all the associated leisure industries. And then the financial services that those crewmen will need. Do I need to continue?'

Hamish drank deeply from his beer.

'You see what I was saying, Iain?' he said. 'This could transform the islands.'

But Iain McMillan was less overwhelmed than Hamish had expected him to be. He stretched his arms out behind his head and flexed his elbows, as if doing some form of exercise.

'Nothing is so good as it seems beforehand. It could, of course, destroy the islands too,' continued Steve Anthony. 'Have you been to Aberdeen in recent years?'

'That's as may be,' Iain McMillan said. 'I hear what you are saying, John Smith or whoever you are, but I think we can deal with all that when we get to it. But we have to concentrate on the Skye

Bridge first of all. By the way, is it true the bridge was built so high so oil tankers could sail beneath it?'

Steve Anthony laughed.

'Hardly!' he laughed. 'That's a new one on me. Why would an oil tanker want to sail down there? They are far too big for such a narrow bit of ocean. Who on earth told you that?'

'That's what I said too,' replied Iain McMillan, laughing with him. 'It didn't seem very likely at all. But I still don't understand why you're so keen for us to hear all about this oil exploration. It's a long way into the future before we'll have to deal with it. And we have a problem right now with the Skye Bridge. That's where we have to focus our efforts.'

Steve Anthony shrugged his shoulders, as he unclasped his hands and reached again for his gin and tonic.

'Not so far into the future as you might think,' he said. 'There's quite a bit of fast-tracking going on. But, anyway, as you wish. I merely wished to alert you to the consequences. That's all.'

'Meaning?' pressed Iain McMillan.

'Simply that, in terms of *realpolitik*, it might be worth considering how best to ensure that government works alongside you in that future development rather than imposes something on you that you abhor.'

'We have the chance to change our governments,' interjected Hamish. 'In the ballot box. And the new Parliament will look after Scottish rights.'

Steve Anthony smiled condescendingly at him.

'My dear Hamish, don't be naive,' he said. 'Politicians don't decide things. They merely ride with the prevailing winds, steered there by their civil servants who have been planning the future for years ahead. It's capital that decides things, dear Hamish. And it's reading the movement of capital that so exercises us in the civil service.'

Iain McMillan shifted uncomfortably in his seat and reached for his gold chain. Hamish MacLeod reached for his beer and pondered the meaning of what had just been said.

She had been crossing the Scottish border when the radio news came on. As it did so, she had turned up the volume to hear it correctly:

"Seismic testing vessels attempting to survey two areas in the Atlantic Ocean off the Hebrides have lost many hours of testing after two Greenpeace activists climbed on to the air guns behind one of the testing ships. The guns emit explosions of up to two hundred and twenty-five decibels and the activists, a British man and a Canadian woman, sat on a gun each to prevent them being fired. This is the latest move in a four-day confrontation between the *MV Greenpeace* and the testing vessels which have been trying to test on behalf of oil companies."

She had slowed down in order to listen more carefully.

"The company operating the seismic vessels has alleged that Greenpeace's activities were potentially lethal actions and that they had notified the relevant authorities of the life-threatening behaviour. However, this is denied by the captain of the MV Greenpeace, who spoke to the newsroom earlier:

"The risk is entirely down to whether the seismic ships are irresponsible enough to fire the guns with activists so close. The main thing is that it is stopping them and every hour they lose is a gain for the climate."

"The encounter began on Sunday morning when Greenpeace swimmers entered the water five miles ahead of the testing vessels forcing them to divert. It brings Greenpeace actions against seismic vessels in the Atlantic Frontier into its sixth week with hundreds of hours of testing lost to disruption. The season for seismic testing will end in September when the weather becomes too bad for surveys to be carried out."

So, there was a connection!

Detective Sergeant George Elliott had leaned across to turn the volume down again and had then continued on her journey. She had left Tamworth just after nine thirty in the morning and reached the Scottish border by one o'clock and, after a very brief stop for a coffee and a tuna sandwich just north of Gretna Green, had carried on driving to Fort William, which she had driven through around five o'clock, and then on to Kyle of Lochalsh and the Skye Bridge. At seven thirty in the evening, almost exactly ten hours after she had first set off, she had entered the outskirts of Portree and spotted a sign for the police station.

The only person present in the police station was Inspector

Maggie Fraser, who looked up from her desk, where she was poring over her notes, to see the newcomer, dressed in blue denim jacket and jeans, framed in the open doorway.

'Yes?' she said. 'Can I help you?'

'I'm looking for Detective Chief Inspector Tallyforth,' came the reply. 'You wouldn't know where he is, would you? I believe he's in Skye.'

'And you are?'

'Detective Sergeant Georgina Elliott. Mercian Police Force. We work together,' said George Elliott, realising as she spoke that she had used the present tense when she had meant the past. 'Or, at least, we used to.'

She took her I.D. card out of her jacket pocket and waved it in front of Maggie Fraser's eyes.

Maggie Fraser's eyes grew wider. She had thought that, with Tallyforth's chief superintendent barring him from involvement in the murder inquiry, he wouldn't have been able to send for reinforcements to help him.

'Yes, he is in Skye,' she said, standing up and moving from behind her desk. 'Did you know there's been a murder here? Last Sunday night? A woman called Cassie Dillon was killed while she was asleep in her bunk on board a boat in the harbour. Your Chief Inspector Tallyforth was the only other passenger.'

George Elliott smiled grimly back at her.

'Yes, I know,' she said. 'And you've had to treat him as a suspect, for obvious reasons. And he's hated every minute of it. And 'Nobby' Clarke's banned him from getting involved. So he's taken it out on you and refused to help. And it wouldn't surprise me to learn that he's gone off and conducted his own enquiries, without telling you what he's doing, without consulting you, without considering you at all.'

Maggie Fraser's eyes opened even wider as she listened to all this.

'You know him very well,' she said, reaching for her cap on the peg behind the door. 'How you can work with him I do not know. But, since you're here and since you want to find him, I'd better take you to him. I've a pretty good idea where he'll be.'

And they had walked at a brisk pace through Somerled Square,

136

which was still busy with tourists taking the warm evening air, and up to the Royal Hotel. In the dining room of the Royal, Tallyforth and Gordon were enjoying venison steak in a juniper berry sauce, washed down by a bottle of Mouton Cadet. They did not at first notice the entrance of the two policewomen.

'Sir.'

Suddenly they were beside the table, their twin shadows falling over the plates of venison. Tallyforth and Gordon looked up simultaneously, the former with his glass half way to his mouth, the latter having just filled his mouth with food.

'Sir, you have a visitor,' said Maggie Fraser.

'Elliott!' spluttered Tallyforth, putting his glass down on the table. 'What the hell....!'

'Greenpeace,' George Elliott said, in a tone approaching deliberate mysteriousness.

'Who is this, Tallyforth?' asked Chief Inspector Gordon, scrutinising the new arrival in her denim outfit.

'What are you doing here?' asked Tallyforth again, still astonished to see her and ignoring Gordon.

'Greenpeace, sir,' she repeated, her face still revealing nothing of her feelings as she kept her eyes firmly on the window.

'Greenpeace?' said Tallyforth. 'Greenpeace? Those environmental idiots? Have you joined them, Elliott? Is that what you're saying? Why?'

'No, sir,' she said, careful not to rise to his bait. 'But the dead woman did. She was a Greenpeace member. And, if I'm not mistaken, a very active one. Have you heard today's news?'

Steve Anthony had left the island , catching the seven o-clock ferry from Armadale to Mallaig and then riding down the picturesque 'Road to the Isles' through Morar, Arisaig and Lochailort towards Fort William. He had left the sea behind him and was now enjoying the much more mountainous scenery that he rode through, with its white and purple heather patches, its grey stone outcrops and its misty peaks.

The Harley was behaving beautifully, as ever, and the joy of the wind against his face and the powerful throbbing engine beneath him had the effect of making him very relaxed. As so often, he felt as if man and machine were one, as the Harley responded to every variation in the road as if with a mind of its own, freeing him to reflect on his day.

He almost had to pinch himself to remember how long a day it had been, beginning early that morning with the ride down from Stornoway to Tarbert, followed by the gentle crossing of Little Minch and then the unfortunate scene with the fat policeman from Inverness, which had irritated him considerably. However, that had been smoothed over, after intervention from Edinburgh, and he had spent a pleasant enough time watching the Highland Games with Hamish MacLeod until mid-afternoon when Hamish had to go to help judge one of the junior piping competitions. So Steve Anthony had left the Games arena, collected his motorbike from Somerled Square and set off towards Armadale. He had stopped briefly at Broadford for a rather stale coronation chicken sandwich and a bottle of carbonated water but otherwise his journey had been uneventful.

It was clear, he thought to himself as he rode, that the chief preoccupation of the people of Skye was with the toll bridge and their ongoing campaign to get the tolls lifted. It was also clear that there would almost certainly be a huge vote in the referendum in support of the devolution proposals, because of the islanders' naive belief that they could better control their own destiny thus. He smiled to himself, remembering Hamish MacLeod's earnest face explaining how people wanted a Scotland freed from the yoke of the Englishman. The Scots lived too much in their history, he thought and remembered an axiom from his past - "The growing good of the world is partly dependent on unhistoric acts." How true, he thought, how true. The grand gestures may be necessary from time to time but it was the minute by minute decisions that shaped so much of the way people lived. That was why he enjoyed the work he did, for he knew that the careful wording of advice to ministers or of bills on their way through the parliamentary process made all the difference in the way that people could live their lives.

He glanced to his right and saw in the loch's water the sun's reflection as it began to set. The day was almost over. He would find somewhere to stay in Fort William, then head back to Edinburgh in the morning.

ELEVEN

'So what's he really like to work with?' asked Maggie Fraser, handing a steaming mug of Irish coffee to George Elliott who sat on the floor with her hands clasped around her knees.

It was approaching midnight. They were in the front room of the semi-detached house out beyond the Portree High School which Maggie Fraser had rented when she first arrived to take up her new post in charge of the Portree police station. She had been looking for somewhere more permanent but Cuillins View, as it was aptly named, suited her fine for the moment, since it was comfortably furnished and easily maintained.

She had invited George Elliott to stay with her, knowing the limitations on accommodation in the town because of the Games. So, after the confrontation with Tallyforth and Gordon and a certain amount of mutual clarification, they had left the two chief inspectors finishing their meal at the Royal, while they had returned to Maggie Fraser's house. There, after changing out of her uniform and into old jeans and a sweatshirt, she had prepared a quick risotto dish for the two of them.

Gratefully accepting the drink, George Elliott stretched out her legs and leaned back on one arm.

'Impetuous. Unpredictable. Irrational. Irritating. Unconventional. Conceited. And that's just the first few terms that come to mind,' she said.

'But you've worked with him for some years, haven't you? Didn't you say...?' Maggie Fraser asked, as she sat back in a brown moquette arm chair and lit a cigarette.

George Elliott sighed.

'That's just the problem,' she said. 'He's all those things but partly that's why he's so good to work with.'

'Explain.'

'Well, I was trained, probably like you were, to believe that the best police work relied on the careful and methodical gathering and sifting of evidence,' George Elliott began, sipping from her coffee. 'And that's what I believed too. Until I started working with Tallyforth. With him it's all intuition. So one minute you'll be interviewing some possible suspect or someone who might have useful evidence and the next minute you're driving off somewhere to look at some wild birds or you're being told to go and read some Dylan Thomas stories or to listen to the lyrics of a Van Morrison album!'

'Sounds bizarre to me!' interjected Maggie Fraser, blowing smoke through her nostrils.

'It is,' replied George Elliott, 'and that's why it's so enjoyable. When I first started working with him, I realised how much I had actually come to hate the boring mundane side of police work. With Tallyforth, life took on a new meaning. I found myself looking forward to going to work for the first time in ages. I really used to enjoy working with him.'

'Aren't you working together now then?' asked Maggie Fraser.

George Elliott felt her neck burning at the back, just below her short-cut blonde hair.

'No,' she said flatly. 'No, we're not.'

There was a silence between them as she pondered how much she should tell.

'Anyway.' George Elliott turned to face Maggie Fraser. 'How have you found him?'

It was Maggie Fraser's turn to feel slightly embarrassed now.

'Well,' she began, 'to start with, I didn't like him. He tried to pull rank on me and he couldn't or wouldn't see that he was a potential witness to the murder of the Dillon woman. I told him that I had to handle things properly, so he threatened to bring his chief superintendent in. And when that didn't work, he then gave me the slip and went off on his island-hopping with his new-found friends, the MacPhersons.'

'Yes, I heard all about that,' said George Elliott.

'Did you? How?'

'Look, you'd better keep this to yourself,' George Elliott replied, her voice dropping into a conspiratorial whisper as if she were afraid of eavesdroppers. 'If Tallyforth found out, he would hate it. You see, I've told him that it was 'Nobby' Clarke, our chief super, who dropped it out to me about the murdered woman but it wasn't. It was my friend Steve. He's a civil servant in the Home Office. We were at university together. He's been seconded to the Scottish Office for this devolution business and he was in Skye the other day and nearly bumped into Tallyforth. Anyway, he found out about the dead woman and rang me about it. That was why I knew she was from Tamworth. That was why I raided her home and found all that Greenpeace stuff. Plus her maps.'

A realisation was suddenly dawning for Maggie Fraser.

'He wouldn't be a rather good-looking guy with dark hair, tied back in a ponytail, would he? Your friend, I mean? Rides a Harley Davidson motorbike?'

'That's him!' cried George Elliott. 'Have you seen him?'

Maggie Fraser reran the embarrassing story of Chief Inspector Gordon's arrest of the man on the motorbike, who they had known as John Smith, and the humiliating orders they had been given from a government minister to release him at once.

George Elliott laughed.

'Steve! A murder suspect! Of a woman found naked! Hardly!' she said. 'He's gay. That's why Tallyforth hates him so much. He can't stand gay people. Thinks it's abhorrent and unnatural.'

'I thought he was rather angelic-looking,' said Maggie Fraser. 'Not that it means anything, of course. No, I wondered if it was your boss himself who'd done it. Accidentally, I mean.'

'You what!' George Elliott was startled by this revelation.

'Well, you see the dead woman had stayed in Oban with a teacher called James Orr just before she came up to Portree for this cruise. I went to see him and he told me that she and Tallyforth had been keen on each other and I wondered if, despite his denials, there had been some sort of relationship between them. I'd read somewhere that semi-asphyxiation can increase sexual pleasure and I wondered if he'd accidentally....'

'...strangled her? With her own silk scarf? No chance!' interrupted George Elliott fiercely, aware of a tightness in her chest now.

'It was just a thought,' said Maggie Fraser, her voice dropping. 'We didn't seem to have any clues. And he was on the boat at the time she died. Why d'you say that?'

'Because he doesn't do that sort of thing. It's not his style. And, believe me, I ought to know!'

She stopped, aware that she had said more than she had intended.

'Is that why...?' began Maggie Fraser.

'Yes,' came the terse reply. 'We were together for about twelve months. Then he broke it off. It caused difficulties, massive difficulties. I've had extended leave. And that's why he's here in Scotland.'

'And are you hoping to patch things up?'

'No! I'm here because Steve called me about the dead woman and I wanted to do something. I could have faxed everything through. I could have rung you or Chief Inspector Gordon and told you everything. But I didn't. I'm here, because, whatever else there is or isn't between us, we're a team. And a bloody good team. And we work better together than separate. So, Inspector Maggie Fraser, tomorrow we begin to make waves to solve this murder. Are you with us or agin us?'

Maggie Fraser smiled and sipped the remains of her Irish coffee. With Chief Inspector Gordon having had to return to Inverness and not likely to be coming back to the island for some time, she didn't seem to have much choice. Besides, though she had found Tallyforth difficult to like, she felt differently about his younger partner, this feisty woman who sat facing her.

'What do you think?' she asked, her ice-blue eyes smiling, and lit another cigarette.

Chief Inspector Gordon, having dined well with his opposite number Detective Chief Inspector Tallyforth, had walked rather unsteadily back to the Portree police station where he had summoned the young constable who was to drive him back to Inverness. He had an important meeting with the Chief Constable the following morning and, after his disturbed night in the police station the previous night, he needed to sleep in his own bed.

He had snoozed through the first part of the journey, the wine and whisky having its inevitable effect, and they had left Skye well behind them when he jolted awake suddenly as they were crossing the Shiel Bridge on the main Inverness road.

'Where are we, constable? How much farther?' he demanded of his driver.

'Shiel Bridge, sir,' came the reply. 'I would guess about another hour and a half.'

Chief Inspector Gordon, comfortable in the back of the police car, grunted and stretched one leg out along the back seat.

'How long have you been at Portree station, son?' he asked.

'Just a year, sir.'

'You from Portree?'

'No, sir. I'm from Broadford originally. My father was in the police.'

'Oh yes, what's your name then?'

'Robbie MacLean.'

'Would it be your father who was station officer at Portree before Inspector Fraser?'

'Aye, sir.'

'Must have been difficult for you, working under your father like that?'

'Not really, sir. I always admired my father. He was the reason I joined the police. We got on just fine. It was harder after he left.'

'You mean Inspector Fraser pushed you harder?'

'I didn't say that, sir.'

'Come on, son. I've seen the woman at work. She's a hard taskmaster, isn't she? Not easy to warm to.'

'I didn't join the police for an easy life, sir. You're always learning.'

Chief Inspector Gordon tried to catch his young constable's eyes in the driver's mirror but there was no trace of anything in the calm blue eyes.

'And what have you learned this week, constable, that you didn't know before?'

'Well, I've learned that experienced police are not necessarily the most observant police,' came the mysterious reply.

Gordon narrowed his eyes. Was there something this young man had seen which no one else had? And why hadn't he mentioned anything previously?

'Go on, constable.'

'Well, when the murder was first reported by the skipper of the boat, Willie MacPherson, I went to the boat with Inspector Fraser. And, after she went back to the police station, she left me with the dead body on the boat.'

'So?' Gordon scratched his belly.

'Chief Inspector Tallyforth and Willie MacPherson went ashore with Inspector Fraser, so the only folk left on the boat were me and the skipper's wife, Mary MacPherson.'

'What are you saying, constable?'

'I'm not saying anything, sir. Except it seems very queer to me that Inspector Fraser's been giving all her attention to Willie MacPherson and Chief Inspector Tallyforth and what they were doing in the night. Nobody's thought about the wife.'

'Was she doing something on the boat that made you suspicious?'

'No, sir. Nothing out of the ordinary. She was just tidying up the cabins.'

'Including the dead woman's cabin?'

'Aye.'

'Hadn't Inspector Fraser told you to keep it untouched until the forensic boys got there?'

'Yes, sir. That's what I told Mrs MacPherson when I heard her in there. I was just checking the other cabins. She wasn't in there more than about a minute.'

'Long enough to remove something she didn't want anyone to find, though, constable.'

'I don't think she did that, sir.'

'But you can't be sure?'

'Not completely, sir.'

Chief Inspector Gordon sat back and contemplated the impact of what he had just heard. It was true that no one had mentioned Mary MacPherson. Fraser had suspected Tallyforth or Willie MacPherson. Tallyforth, as far as he could gather from their earlier conversation, was more concerned to identify a motive before looking for a murderer. While he himself had made the mistake of trying to interrogate that person from the Scottish Office whom he had been warned away from. But the wife. That was a new possibility.

144

He sank back into the seat and pondered. Soon the lateness of the night and the still-lingering effects of alcohol overcame him again and he fell asleep before he could decide what to do about this new knowledge.

It was after midnight in the bar of the Royal Hotel before Dugald MacLeod was able to close the doors on the last of the revellers. The bar had been solidly packed all evening. A number of the athletes who had competed in the open throwing events during the afternoon's Games had taken over one corner of the bar and their initial quietness, brought on by exhaustion from their efforts, soon turned to rowdiness as they found other competitions to indulge in. First, there had been flicking growing piles of beer mats from the edge of the table and catching them mid-air. Then had been the fastest drinking of a pint of lager - a competition which had been repeated three times because of noisy but good-humoured disputes about who had actually won. Finally, there had been prolonged bouts of arm-wrestling, leading to a final match between one of the four Americans named Tom, a massive black athlete, and a Scot named Andy, who had won the caber-tossing event earlier that day. This final match had become the focus of the crowded bar's attention by now and all had turned to watch the two heroes of the hour pitting their strength against each other. As always in such situations, favourites had been chosen and alternate cheers and groans had risen through the smoky room as one or other seemed to be gaining an advantage. Eventually it was Tom that had managed to force Andy's arm down on to the table, which had occasioned a warm embrace and further drinks.

At that point one of the pipers from the Isle of Skye Pipe Band, many of whom, still in their kilts, had been drinking all evening at another corner of the bar, had donned his black bonnet, brought out his set of bagpipes and proceeded to entertain the laughing crowds with his own selection of well-known Scottish favourite melodies. His final tune had been, of course, the famous Skye Boat Song and one of his compatriots in the band, a man with a powerful tenor voice, led the massed singing of the Jacobite memorial to Bonnie Prince Charlie:

Speed bonnie boat like a bird on the wing
"Onward' the sailors cry;
Carry the lad that's born to be king,
Over the sea to Skye.

Loud the winds howl. loud the waves roar,
Thunderclaps rend the air;
Baffled our foes stand by the shore
Follow they will not dare.

Though the waves leap, soft shall you sleep,
Ocean's a royal bed.
Rocked in the deep Flora will keep
Watch by your weary head.

Many's a lad fought on that day
Well the claymore could wield
When the night came silently lay
Dead on Culloden's field.

Burned are our homes, exile and death
Scatter the loyal men;
Yet, ere the sword cool in the sheath,
Charlie will come again.

Speed bonnie boat like a bird on the wing
"Onward' the sailors cry;
Carry the lad that's born to be king,
Over the sea to Skye.

The crowds had then broken up into their own groups, where the noisy laughter and chatter filled the late evening air and spilled out on to the road outside. Leather-jacketed Dutch motorcyclists drank and joked with an American family who had come to Skye to research their family ancestry; sharp-suited Italians gesticulated wildly with ancient Scots who had come back from their homes in Glasgow on their annual pilgrimage to the place of their births; middle-aged English women from a coach tour giggled at the antics of a Scotsman of their own age, who was trying to demonstrate the Highland Fling to them; and a small group of young Englishmen, in their early twenties and with short-cut hair combed forward over their foreheads and wearing Manchester United football shirts, stood by the door watching proceedings over their bottles of Budweiser and hoping forlornly that someone would pick a fight with them.

At a quarter to twelve Sergeant Donald MacKenzie, who had been left on duty to oversee the night's revels, arrived at the Royal Hotel, knowing that this place would be at the heart of those revels and knowing that his uniformed presence would hasten its evacuation when the bar was finally closed at midnight.

So it was almost twelve thirty when the white-maned Dugald MacLeod, minus jacket and bow tie at last, brought three tumblers of Talisker whisky across to the table where Donald MacKenzie and Dugald's son Hamish sat.

'I hear you've been tangling with the Scottish Office's man,' laughed Dugald, as he sat down. 'That Chief Inspector Gordon needs to watch his back, for they'll be after his blood down in Auld Reekie. What was he like, this man you had brought in?'

Donald MacKenzie took a drink before answering.

'He was a rum cove,' he said, pressing his hair down. 'Spoke in a very strange way. Very high-falutin', you know? Not normal at all. I couldn't work him out. Had this very posh style of talking but rode this great old motorbike. Very odd. Mind, if it hadn't been for your Hamish here, Chief Inspector Gordon would never have known about him.'

'Oh, come on now, Donald,' interjected Hamish MacLeod, loosening his clan tie, 'I didn't know, did I? How was I to tell? Now I've got to know the man a bit better, I can see how wrong I was but remember I'd only met him briefly and he'd struck me as being a bit odd. Then, when Iain McMillan told me about the lassie being murdered on the Sunday night, I suddenly recalled that I'd seen him here before. He sat behind us on Sunday evening, don't you remember, father?'

'Was he a laddie with dark hair in a pony-tail? Very fresh-looking? Like he didn't need to shave?' asked Dugald.

'Aye, that's the one,' said Donald MacKenzie. 'Very fresh-faced. D'you know him?'

'Aye, he stayed here on Sunday and Monday nights,' said Dugald, smoothing his long white hair back over his head with his hand. 'Was very particular about where his motorbike was kept. Said it

147

was worth a lot of money. Harley Davidson, wasn't it? Beautiful old bike.'

'So what did he want with you anyway, Hamish?' asked Donald MacKenzie.

'Well, as far as I could make out, he was travelling the islands to get some idea about how people felt about the devolution referendum and the proposed Scottish Parliament. I told him that we wanted an independent Scotland, freed from the English yoke. He said that would never happen. He also said that we were too much bothered about the bridge tolls because the new oil fields in the Atlantic would bring a lot of wealth to the Western Isles.'

'Aye, you've told us all about that before,' said Dugald impatiently. 'But he had nothing to do with that lassie's death then?'

'No,' said Donald MacKenzie. 'Or, if he had, we've not to investigate him because the Scottish Office minister told Chief Inspector Gordon to lay off of him.'

'So, who did kill the lassie? And why?' asked Hamish, his ginger eyebrows raised.

'Aye, well, that's what's exercising better brains than mind, Hamish. I just do what they tell me,' replied Donald MacKenzie. 'One for the road, Dugald. Then I'd best be on my rounds.'

Dugald MacLeod rose from his seat to fetch another round of drinks from behind the bar.

Tallyforth was lying on his bed upstairs in the Royal Hotel, in that intoxicating state when he was not yet asleep so his thoughts were rational but not fully awake either, so those thoughts meandered loosely in his mind.

He was thinking about George Elliott. He had not thought about her for some weeks, he realised. He had, as if deliberately, shut thoughts of her out of his mind. But now, the surprise of her sudden appearance in the dining room of the Royal earlier that evening had reminded him of all that had happened during the previous twelve months - the time she had first taken his hand at the Van Morrison concert in Birmingham the previous June, the first time they had slept together, the romantic weekend in Paris that he had organised for the two of them, the holiday in Sardinia, the glorious meals she had cooked for him. And then the gradual growth of doubt in his heart, begun he knew not where, but a doubt that started to poison their relationship. He could not explain it, to her or even to himself. Maybe it had something to do with his awareness of his own obsessiveness with his work which had wrecked his marriage. Maybe it was because he felt they were not working together professionally as well as they had previously, because he could not argue with her in the same way, had to treat her as an equal instead of as a junior officer. Whatever it was and whatever its genesis, things had cooled between them, until he had made that fateful decision to end it.

And it had been the right thing to do. He was in no doubt about that. At the time it had been clearly the right thing to do. And, because he had trained his mind to keep elements of his life in separate boxes, he had packed that one away into a corner and forgotten about it. Or believed he had. But the sight of her tonight had brought all that emotional stuff diving out of the box and swimming to the front of his mind. She had looked good. She had looked very good. He remembered her body.

But George Elliott's body reminded him of another body, the naked body of Cassie Dillon that he had seen on the Monday morning, lying as if asleep on the bunk of *The Flodigarry's* aft cabin. As if asleep, but not asleep, he reminded himself. Dead. Dead. Dead. He could feel the word clutch at his throat. For almost two weeks now, he realised, ever since that first meeting in the Café Rouge on the canalside in Birmingham, he had been dreaming about this woman, imagining her body, thinking of it next to his own. He had fallen in love with those dark hazel eyes and their effervescent twinkle, that someone had snuffed out for ever. And they still were no nearer, nearly three days later, in finding her killer, let alone a motive for her murder. George Elliott had come up with all the Greenpeace materials and that had seemed to make some sense - presumably there was a connection between those crosses on the map, which he had identified as possible landing bays for flat-bottomed boats, and the Greenpeace action in the Atlantic. He could understand why Cassie Dillon had been listening to Runrig's *The Mighty Atlantic*. He would have to read all that Greenpeace material in the morning to work out the precise connection but it did seem they were on the right lines.

But that didn't get them any nearer to a solution. So, she had an ulterior motive in coming on the cruise but that didn't somehow make her a target for murder, did it? Who would want to murder a Greenpeace activist? It didn't make a lot of sense. Especially as, from what George Elliott had told him, Greenpeace activists were actually proceeding with their disruptive tactics out at sea at that very moment.

And what about the camera?

That reminded him that he had bought his daughter an expensive Canon camera before she had gone off to Zambia on her V.S.O. trip and she had promised to send photographs back, showing what life was like over there. But nothing had arrived. Maybe there was some difficulty getting the films processed. Maybe.....

But by this time he was finally drifting into sleep, letting his dreams be peopled with these women.

Willie and Mary MacPherson had stayed up late back in their cottage in Uig, where they had returned that afternoon, neither of them being particularly interested in the Highland Games. Willie had been preoccupied all evening and Mary, who knew his moods well, had left him to his own thoughts. She knew that he would talk when he was ready and there was no point trying to hurry him. So she had busied herself with making their supper, which had consisted of a broth with potatoes in it followed by tinned peaches, and then, when he still was disinclined to confide in her, she had spoken at length on the phone to her aunt who lived above the chandlery down by the port.

Eventually, Willie pushed back his shoulders and spoke.

'That Inspector Fraser's determined I killed the lassie,' he began. 'I can tell from the way she looks at me. She doesn't believe anything I say. What am I to do, Mary? You know I didn't do it. Even that Mr Tallyforth knows I didn't do it. But she thinks I did.'

'Whisht, man!' said Mary MacPherson. 'You're just reliving all that trouble you had earlier in your life, that's all. Just because they put you into prison then doesn't mean they're going to do it again. You had been in a fight then, remember? The man was dead, remember? But this time you've not been anywhere near the lassie. I can vouch for that, as I've told the inspector already. So stop your worrying, man. It'll be alright.'

But Willie was not so easily mollified.

'I feel it in my bones, Mary,' he said again. 'I hear what you're saying but I can feel it in my bones. It was like this before, you know. When that lad dropped down dead in Gallowgate, I knew that there was big trouble brewing, even though I knew I hadn't hit him hard enough to kill him. And I'm feeling the same now, Mary. You cannot stop that feeling.'

She looked at him and saw the pensive expression on his face, the worried frown on his brow, the way he kneaded his fingers together anxiously, the slope of his shoulders.

'Come to bed, Willie,' she urged, standing up and moving over to stroke his shoulder. 'You just need a good night's sleep.'

He looked up at her and reached up to take her hand.

'Aye, maybe you're right,' he said. 'It's been a long couple of days.'

And he followed her into the bedroom, switching off the lights behind him.

But at three o'clock in the morning, Willie MacPherson rose again from his bed, dressed himself in blue jeans and a warm jumper, and, without disturbing his sleeping wife, left the house.

TWELVE

Tallyforth had risen early. The dreams of the night had been disturbing and he had woken several times, on each occasion drifting back into a light doze where he thought himself to be awake and yet the occurrences that fluttered through his mind were unreal and were from the realm of dreams. Eventually, and still feeling quite tired, he became impatient and decided to take an early morning walk in the hope that this would simultaneously calm and bring clarity to his fevered brain.

So, at six-thirty in the morning, having followed a brackeny footpath around the shoreline beyond the Cuillin Hills Hotel as far as it would take him and then, after returning via the same route, having revisited The Lump where the Highland Games had been held the previous day, Tallyforth now found himself once again at the end of the pier. It was already warm and his blue polo-shirt was sticking to him under his linen jacket after his walk. The harbour was full of pleasure yachts, moored up for the night, and several small fishing ketches were setting out of the bay about their day's business. The usual squawking of gulls filled the air but there was no other sound in the early morning town.

Tallyforth was still very puzzled, not only about the murder of Cassie Dillon which remained intractably difficult to understand but also about his own reactions to George Elliott's appearance in Portree. He would be seeing her later in the morning and he was not sure how they were going to manage things. Was she intending to stay in Portree indefinitely? Did 'Nobby' Clarke know she was here? If not, should they tell him? Did she think they could just resume their old professional relationship as if nothing had ever happened?. Or was she hoping that their recent intimacy could be rekindled?

He hadn't had chance to talk to her about such matters the previous evening, because of the presence of Fraser and Gordon, and it had seemed difficult to try to find time to talk to her on her own. And she hadn't been, apparently, looking for such an opportunity either.

Just then the quiet of the early morning was disturbed by the phut-phut of a two-stroke motorbike engine. Tallyforth looked around to see a helmeted figure in a yellow cagoule coming along Quay Street in his direction on a small Honda motorbike. The bike came to a halt beside him and its rider pulled off the black helmet.

'Mr Tallyforth,' said Mary MacPherson, pushing hair away from her mouth and switching off the motorbike engine. 'Is he here? My Willie?'

Tallyforth looked at her with surprise.

'The boat's not here, if that's what you mean,' he answered. 'Why? What's happened?'

'When I woke this morning, Willie was gone,' she said rather breathlessly. 'We stayed up talking till late last night. Willie was very worried about that Inspector Fraser, for he thinks she suspects him of the murder of the lassie. I thought I'd calmed him down when we went to bed. I was tired from the long day and I must have slept very deep, for I didn't hear him get out of bed. I don't know what time it was even. All I know is that, when I woke, he wasn't there.'

'And *The Flodigarry*?' queried Tallyforth.

'That's gone too,' came the reply from a clearly-worried Mary MacPherson. 'That's the first thing I checked when I couldn't find him in the house. But it's gone too. I don't know how long he's been gone but I just thought he maybe had come back round to Portree. Though I don't know why. But I didn't know where else to start looking. What d'you think, Mr Tallyforth?'

Tallyforth looked at the forlorn figure in the bright yellow cagoule in front of him.

'Did you have a fight?' he asked.

'No! Nothing of the sort!' she exclaimed.

'Sure?' he pressed.

'Aye! Absolutely.'

He wasn't sure if he believed her. He had spent enough time in their company to know who wore the trousers, as the saying went. And it was just possible that what she thought of as 'calming him down' had actually been her telling him, in no uncertain terms, not to be so daft.

'Is that your bike?' he asked.

'Aye,' she answered. 'It's very handy for nipping about on. You know, if you haven't much to carry with you. Why?'

'Nothing. Just wondered,' said Tallyforth, sucking the inside of his cheeks. 'I suppose he wouldn't have gone to stay with someone, would he? A relative? Friends?'

'Mr Tallyforth, we're not very social folk. I told you that Willie's family didn't want anything to do with him after that incident in his younger days. He hasn't spoken to his mother or father for nigh on twenty years,' she told him.

'No other possible places he might have gone?'

She paused, scratched her face, and rested the motorbike against her stomach, while she thought.

'No, not really, Mr Tallyforth. All I know is that he took the boat. I don't know what time he went but he's a good sailor so it wouldn't matter how dark it was. He's used to night sailing.'

Tallyforth decided it was time for a positive step.

'Look, Mary,' he began, taking the motorbike from her and wheeling it round so that it faced back towards the town, 'I think the best thing is to report Willie missing at the police station. With any luck it'll be Sergeant MacKenzie, and he can be very discreet. It's my guess that Willie just needed some time to himself to think about things. He'll probably just turn up in his own time. But we'll ask the police to keep an eye open for him. But first of all, I think you could do with something to eat. Come and join me for breakfast.'

And Tallyforth set off back down the cobbled street towards the Royal Hotel, pushing the motorbike and with Mary MacPherson in her yellow cagoule in train.

Two hours later, having sent Mary MacPherson up to the police station to report Willie's disappearance, Tallyforth sat at a round table in the huge and splendid Ceilidh Room, the Royal Hotel's banqueting suite where the piping competitions had been held two days previously. He had toyed with inviting her to his room but decided that was too risky, in view of the recent past. Naturally, there was no way they could use the police station, since Inspector Maggie Fraser had made it very clear to him that he was not welcome there. So he had negotiated with old Dugald MacLeod, the manager, for another room that he might use and the only one available was the Ceilidh Room, because the bar and the dining room were still untidied from the previous day's celebrations.

He had ordered a pot of coffee, which the young waitress Annie had deposited on the table in front of him, together with two cups and saucers. But he did not pour any. He had breakfasted earlier, with Mary MacPherson, then sent a message with her to the police station, requesting George Elliott to join him as soon as she could.

At nine-fifteen the door of the Ceilidh Room opened and George Elliott stood briefly framed in it, the sun shining fiercely through the windows of the dining room behind her. She wore an orange halter top and a short black skirt.

Tallyforth was surprised at her choice of clothing.

'I need to talk to you,' she said determinedly, for she had been mentally rehearsing this scene for some time.

'Likewise,' he replied. 'That's why I asked you to come here. Away from the police station. On our own. Coffee?'

He held up the silver pot by way of invitation. She nodded and, closing the door behind her, moved across to join him at the table as he poured two cups of strong coffee.

'Look,' she said, 'this is strictly professional. I heard about the murder and about the fact that the woman was from Tamworth.'

'Bit of a coincidence, eh, George?' he cut in, smiling wryly. 'And you don't believe in that sort of fate, do you?'

She pulled her skirt towards her knees.

'It seemed that you might need someone to check out Tamworth,' she continued. 'It didn't take long to identify the deceased's address. So I took it on myself to explore a little. Thought it might help.'

'Tut, tut, George,' he said patronisingly. 'Not like you to go off on your own. Didn't you consult Clarke? Or is someone else in charge now?'

She could take it no longer.

'Sir', she said, sitting straight-backed, 'I'd prefer 'Elliott' or 'Sergeant'. I'm here to help with this case. That's all. I was in a position to help, so I did.'

He watched her closely. Was that really what she meant? Was she saying this but meaning the opposite? He couldn't tell. For all his expertise at reading the criminal mind, he had never been any good at reading the feminine mind. Unless, of course, it was a criminal feminine!

'Very well, Geor.....Sergeant,' he said at last. 'Then you'd better tell me all you found in Tamworth.'

She repeated for him all she had read in the file of Greenpeace papers relating to the current oil exploration in the North Atlantic. She told him of the maps with their pencil crosses. She told him about the wildlife books.

'What do you make of this Greenpeace business then?' he asked.

'I get the impression that Greenpeace are seriously concerned about the threats to the marine environment and to global warming from the possible expansion of oil extraction down into the bed of the Atlantic. I know the papers only give one point of view but they are remarkably well informed papers. Greenpeace clearly has some very capable people working for them, people who have a background in environmental issues and know what they're talking about. Which is just as well since they're taking on the oil barons who are some of the wealthiest bastards on earth.'

'You taking sides, Sergeant?' he queried, raising an eyebrow and half-smiling.

'The arguments have a lot to commend them,' she said, bristling slightly. 'The planet's future is the concern of all of us. They tell me your daughter's doing V.S.O. in Zambia, is that right?'

He sat back at this unexpected remark.

'So?' he said.

'Saving the planet in her way,' George Elliott replied. 'Your generation just doesn't get it, sir. Mine hasn't been much better but at least we have some awareness. It's your daughter's age-group who are taking the direct action for change.'

'You know all this,' he said, with heavy sarcasm.

•

'I know that the dead woman was almost certainly a Greenpeace activist. It's too much of a coincidence that this action is taking place out in the Atlantic at the same time as she was killed.'

'You mean the action is in response to her death?' Tallyforth whistled. 'I hadn't thought of that! Good stuff, Elliott.'

'No, I didn't mean that,' she said, pleased to be ahead of him for once. 'The action in the Atlantic has been going on since last Sunday morning. The *MV Greenpeace* moved down from Rockall, after the end of the occupation there at the end of July, in order to harass the exploration vessels which were trying to conduct seismic testing. Their tactics were to send swimmers into the water in front of the vessels, so they wouldn't explode their air-guns, and to disconnect some of the navigational equipment the ships were using. The action began early on Sunday morning. When was the deceased....was Ms. Dillon found dead?'

'Monday morning, though she was almost certainly killed some hours before that,' he answered. 'Where did you get all this from?'

It was her turn to smile at him.

'Maggie Fraser's computer is hooked up to the Internet,' she replied. 'She showed me how to log on. I downloaded some Greenpeace press releases last night.'

He took a sharp intake of breath, then leaned forward to reach for the coffee pot.

'More?'

She pushed her cup in his direction.

'So, it wasn't retaliation for her death,' he mused, almost to himself, as he poured the coffee. 'So what's the connection?'

'Sir, have you got the map you were using yesterday?'

'Sure,' he said, reaching into his jacket pocket for it and producing it. 'Bit crinkled now, I'm afraid. But here you are.'

He smoothed it on the table with the flat of his hand.

'There, you see!' George Elliott pointed at the crosses against Petersport on Benbecula and Vatersay south of Barra. 'Perfect spots for hiding a boat. And there, look!'

She pointed at Balephetrish on Tiree.

'Yes, and I guess you'll say the same for the other two spots at Ockle and Knock Bay,' he interrupted. 'I'd already worked that out, Sergeant. They are all isolated places where you could land a flat-bottomed boat without detection, if you wanted.'

'Or set sail in a flat-bottomed boat,' she said, pushing the map to the centre of the table.

'Yes, of course,' he snapped. 'I meant that.'

She smiled to herself.

'And they are all within easy access of ferries, airstrips or roads, so it's quite easy to get to or from any of them in a hurry,' he said. 'That's why I wondered if it was drug-smuggling.'

'The drug barons wouldn't take risks like that,' she said, looking at him in surprise. 'They use much more conventional routes.'

'So I'm told, Elliott,' he said dryly. 'So, okay, all these sites could be used or may already have been used by Greenpeace as landing bays for their flat-bottomed boats. And Cassie Dillon presumably knew all that. But that leaves us with two huge unanswered questions - why was she coming on this cruise and why was she murdered?'

'What else is there, sir?' George Elliott asked.

'There's the missing camera,' he told her. 'And, just possibly there's Willie MacPherson, who is also currently missing. Oh, and there's the Skye Bridge protest and some civil servant from the Scottish Office riding round on a Harley Davidson causing confusion.'

She blushed at the reference to her friend Steve Anthony but, looking across at Tallyforth, saw that he had not realised who it was.

'I know about him, sir,' she said. 'Maggie Fraser told me all about that. I don't think he's involved.'

He cocked a quizzical look at her.

'Getting pally, are you?' he asked, with an edge to his voice.

'Sir, there is very little point conducting this murder investigation when we can't co-operate with the local police force. Inspector Fraser is a good person. She had to treat you the way she did because of the circumstances. You know that. What would you have done if you had been in her shoes?'

'Huh!' he grunted.

'We've got an opportunity today to start working together,' she continued. 'Chief Inspector Gordon, as you know, is back in Inverness and won't return till later. What's the point of continuing to work against each other?'

'I suppose you've already talked to her about this?' Tallyforth said.

'Yes. She's willing.'

'But we still have no answers to those two questions.'

'But maybe with three of us working together we might come up with some possibilities. What have we got to lose?'

Tallyforth gave in gracefully and gratefully. It was what he had missed the previous day when he had caught himself wishing that Gordon was George Elliott. They worked well together. Things moved forward.

Willie MacPherson had in fact sailed beyond Portree and gone further round the coast until he reached Loch Sligachan. He knew there was anchorage to be found off the Sconser pier from where the ferry crossed to Raasay so he sailed into the loch and anchored. He had then walked along the main road up to the Sligachan Hotel, where he had left the road and set off up towards the Cuillin Hills, following the course of the stream.

As he walked past the waterfalls and fords and at times heard the stream going through deep chasms with a roar like an aeroplane, Willie was deep in thought. He barely noticed the purple heather and the yellow tormentil that carpeted the ground all along his route, nor the many pied wagtails dipping in and out of heather around him, nor the dragonflies droning above the stream in the morning heat. He did see two young buzzards which appeared suddenly in his vision, cavorting through the air, once high up and heading for the Cuillin heights, once just beside the hillside over towards Sligachan. But the glorious changing views of the Red and Black Cuillins which constantly surrounded him as he walked were of little significance to him.

As he walked ever higher up the path of peaty and springy turf, his thoughts became ever more concerned and confused. He had left his wife because he wanted space - space to clear his mind of all the mess he felt he was in. But instead of clearing his mind, the walk was having the opposite effect and actually clouding matters.

Ever since the interview with Inspector Maggie Fraser, he had been reliving that time in his youth which had led to his six months' imprisonment. He remembered how he had left his family at the age of seventeen to go looking for work in the Clyde shipyards. The youngest of five, he knew there was little prospect of work on Skye for him. His two older brothers had both been taken on as shepherds, following on from their father, who had been one of the fastest shearers in Skye. His two sisters were only interested in getting married and settling down to be full-time housewives. So he had got his father to pay for a train ticket to Glasgow and, once there, had had no difficulty finding work. He was, even at seventeen, a big lad and there were plenty of opportunities for lads with muscle to find work in the shipyards on the Clyde. He had found cheap lodgings in the centre of Glasgow and was soon earning good money, prepared as he was to work as much overtime as there was available. The highlight of the week was, however, always Saturday night, when a group of the lads from the shipyard would meet up in the city centre for the night's drinking. Sometimes they stayed in one bar all night - Murphy's Irish Bar, for instance, was one of their favourites - and at other times they would tour several bars, having a drink in each one. It was not uncommon, indeed it was normal, for at least twelve pints of beer to be drunk on such a night out, plus several whiskies towards the end of the evening. Then they would stagger back to their lodgings, knowing that the following day was Sunday and a day when they could sleep in as long as they wanted.

On the night of the incident, it was exactly this pattern that they had followed. Willie MacPherson and his two closest work-mates, Jimmy Beaton from Motherwell and Jock McKinlay like himself an islander, from Mull, together with a crowd of other lads from the shipyards, had spent the whole night drinking in Murphy's, where there had been a country and western band playing that night. And that was where the trouble had begun. The band's lead singer, a Scot from Renfrew dressed in white spangly shirt and a black cowboy hat, had been introducing a number when Willie MacPherson, then on about his eighth pint, had shouted out loudly at him, calling him a Scottish wanker. The singer, used to such jibes from years of playing Glasgow bars on Saturday nights, had retaliated with some sarcastic put-down which Willie didn't hear but which everyone else seemed to. The crowd in the bar cheered the put-down, the singer smiled his thanks, and launched into a Jim Reeves number. But afterwards, as they left the bar, Willie and his mates had come across the country and western singer loading his gear into the band's old van.

'If you ever call me a Scottish wanker again, I'll slit your throat,' said the singer, as he stood upright in front of Willie, pointing a warning finger at him and spitting furiously.

'Oh aye,' said Willie. 'What with? Your plectrum?'

And he had turned laughing to Jimmy and Jock who stood beside him.

It was at that moment that the singer swung a punch at Willie who, warned too late by his companions, staggered backwards, then, after shaking himself to clear his head, swung a huge uppercut at his attacker. The punch caught the singer right on the point of the chin and he fell backwards, catching his head on a lamppost as he fell. And he didn't get up.

The next part of the night was much more hazy in Willie's memory. He could remember the police van arriving, the handcuffs being placed on him. He could remember the ambulance arriving and two men in uniform placing the singer's body on a stretcher and loading it into the ambulance. But the next thing he clearly remembered was appearing in court the next day and learning that the singer was on a life-support machine. Then two weeks later the man died and Willie was charged with murder.

The rest was a nightmare. The trial. The sentence for culpable homicide. The prison at Barlinnie. And then, miraculously, his release when new evidence came to light.

Then his return to Skye and the rejection by his family. Then the wandering around the island, looking for work of any sort, before eventually turning up at the chandlery in Uig where Mary was and her uncle agreeing to take him on.

He stopped walking. He had reached the highest point on the Glenbrittle pass. Behind him as he looked back he could see the stream rushing down towards Sligachan and beyond that lay Raasay and beyond that, visible through the heat haze, was the mainland. Ahead of him was the path which led down through the forest towards Glenbrittle. To his left was the steep path that led up to the rocky heights of the Black Cuillins. He had scaled those heights

161

often as a young man and was sure that he could do so again, so he took that path rather than heading down to the Glenbrittle Road.

He looked up to the craggy tops. High in the sky above them a golden eagle soared, its wings outstretched as it surveyed its land. It seemed to be a signal.

He was soon panting as he began to scramble through the rocks. The exercise was beginning to clear his mind.

His thoughts turned to Mary, his wife.

When he had turned up at the chandlery all those years ago, it was her he had first seen, standing behind the counter. She was already a big woman, broad-shouldered and broad-hipped. She wore no make-up and her fresh face was reddened by exposure to the sun.

'What d'you want?' she had asked, no trace of fear in her voice at this large stranger who had suddenly appeared in the shop.

'I'm looking for work,' he had said humbly. 'And a cup of tea wouldn't go amiss either.'

She was twenty-five and he was just nineteen but immediately they had taken a liking to each other.

'You'll take it without sugar then,' she had said defiantly but already half-accepting him.

She had made him tea, had listened to his sad tale, had taken pity on him and told him to come back the next day when she'd had chance to talk to her uncle who owned the chandlery. He had spent the night huddled in the corner of a derelict bothy out of the town and returned the next day, unshaven and clearly starving. She had made him breakfast and told him that her uncle had agreed to start him on.

And from then it had all got better. Mary had arranged for him to lodge with her uncle and aunt until he had enough money to find somewhere for himself. He had worked hard in the shop, for hard labour was something he was not afraid of. And by the time he had the money to pay the initial rent on a little cottage, Mary was ready to come with him, with the blessings of her aunt and uncle, who had seen how happy she had become, this girl whom they had taken on into the chandlery after her father was lost at sea and her mother remarried and whom they had expected never to find a man.

They had scrimped and saved, they had worked hard, and eventually had bought their own boat and Willie had made a small living out of the fishing. But, as the waters became overfished and he was forced to sail to ever-deeper waters for his fishing, with all the attendant risks, Mary had begun to plan an alternative way of life. She had enrolled on a course organised by the Highlands and Islands Council to train local people in new careers related to the burgeoning travel and tourism industries. And, when Willie had finally realised himself that there was no longer a livelihood to be had from the fishing, she it had been who organised for him to sell his fishing boat and buy a small sailing boat to take tourists on short trips. They had begun in Uig with trips up the coast for visits to Flora MacDonald's memorial at Kilmuir. Later, with a better boat, they had based it at Portree, since that was where so many of the island's tourists went, and offered similar trips up the coast. These had gradually extended first to whole-day trips and then to three-day cruises around the islands, until eventually they had come to the point where the specialist Hebridean bird-watching cruise had become their main activity.

What would she be thinking now, with him going off in the middle of the night?

Willie paused to catch his breath. He had been climbing hard for the past twenty minutes and, strong as he was, he needed to get some air into his lungs. He sat down on a large rock and unfastened the top three buttons on his tartan shirt. His red chest heaved as he sucked in air.

That Inspector Fraser, he told himself, she doesn't know any of this, she doesn't understand the hardship there has been, she doesn't have any idea how hard it's been for Mary and me. Just because I was once involved in a man's death doesn't mean I've had something to do with the death of that lassie in the boat.

And him disappearing would only have confirmed her suspicions.

And gradually Willie MacPherson came to see that he needed to explain all of this to Inspector Fraser and that the reason he hadn't done was because he had an instinctive, long-held mistrust of the police, stemming from those earlier times - a mistrust that was understandable perhaps in its origin but one that was causing him to show fear, to be hesitant, to seem guilty. The only way he could clear this air of suspicion was to confront it. He had actually made things worse by disappearing, not better. He had been very stupid.

He stood, looked up at the Cuillin heights he had intended to climb where the golden eagle was again soaring, then turned and began to descend the mountain slope.

At exactly eleven thirty that Thursday morning, Chief Inspector Gordon of the Highlands Force left the office of his Chief Constable in Inverness, closing the door behind him with a satisfied smile. The Chief Constable had agreed that he could retire at the end of the following month, which freed him to take the part-time job as messenger-at-arms for the Inverness sheriff. He was very pleased with the way the interview with the Chief Constable had gone. There had been no recriminations over the sometimes fractious relationships he had with many of his fellow officers, no mention of the ongoing problems over the Skye Bridge protesters and whether they would or would not have to pay their fines, no reference to the outstanding cases that had never been resolved. He had merely been asked to ensure that he completed as much work as possible before he left and to leave any unfinished work in a state where his successor could easily take over.

After leaving the Chief Constable's office, he had marched straight out of the building and across to the nearest hotel, where he had rewarded himself with a double scotch. From there he had rung his wife Jean to tell her the good news. And then he returned to the police station to look for the young constable, Robbie MacLean, who had driven him from Portree late the previous evening.

He found him in the canteen.

'Now then, Constable,' began Chief Inspector Gordon, 'I expect you'll be wanting to get back home.'

Constable Robbie MacLean dropped his knife and fork on the table and stood up quickly. He had not noticed Gordon's entry.

'I'm waiting for your orders, sir,' he said.

'Well, I've no plans to return today,' came the reply. 'I've things to do here in Inverness. I'm expecting to go back to Skye tomorrow. I'll telephone Inspector Fraser and tell her to expect us then. Can you keep yourself occupied until the morning?'

'Yes, sir.'

'Good. Report to my office at nine o'clock in the morning then. We've no need to get there too early. I'll make sure Inspector Fraser knows what to do. After all, she's got Detective Chief Inspector Tallyforth to help her.'

Gordon smiled smugly to himself. He would phone Fraser, then go and visit the court office straightaway to sort out his future work.

The three of them were in Maggie Fraser's office in Portree police station.

'This is Inspector Fraser speaking, yes,' Maggie Fraser said into the telephone mouthpiece.

'Fraser, this is Chief Superintendent Clarke. Mercian Force. You have one of my officers in Skye, I believe. Detective Chief Inspector Tallyforth.'

'That is correct, sir. He's in my office with me now.'

'Let me speak to him.'

Maggie Fraser handed the phone to Tallyforth.

'Tallyforth, is that you? What are you doing? Have you solved this murder yet?'

'Yes, sir, it is me. And I am co-operating with the local police as you requested. And no, we haven't solved this murder yet. Though it's no thanks to what you told the Chief Constable of Highlands about me.'

'Never mind about that, Tallyforth. I knew it wouldn't stop you getting involved. You never were very good at taking orders. Now, that's not why I'm ringing. I've lost Elliott. Took off yesterday morning without a word to anyone and hasn't been seen since. Any idea where she might have gone? You haven't heard from her, have you?'

Tallyforth smiled and looked over to where George Elliott was poring over the map again with Maggie Fraser.

'Haven't the faintest idea, sir. No use asking me. Haven't been in touch for weeks. Wasn't she going to Ireland?'

'Yes, but that was weeks ago. She's been on special duties for the past three weeks, liaising with the Home Office. Started back in

Birmingham on Monday.'

'Convenient, sir.'

'Never mind that, Tallyforth. Where the hell would she have gone?'

'Mysterious mission, sir. Maybe the Home Office have recruited her. Or maybe the I.R.A. turned her when she was in Ireland.'

'Don't be facetious, Tallyforth. Look, if you hear from her, ring me at once. Clear?'

Tallyforth put the phone down and smiled to himself but no sooner was it back in its cradle than the telephone rang again. He picked up the receiver.

'Yes?'

'Is that you, Tallyforth? Chief Inspector Gordon here. Is Fraser with you? No, never mind that. I'll tell you.'

'What?'

'I had a thought last night. About the murder, you know. Has anyone thought to question the skipper's wife, Mary MacPherson?'

'I don't think so. What's made you think of her?'

'Well, apparently she was in the dead woman's cabin for a few minutes on her own after Fraser had gone back to the station with Willie MacPherson and you.'

'So?'

'The camera. Remember? Could have been her that took it.'

'How do you know she was on her own there?'

'The constable who drove me back to Inverness last night, MacLean, he mentioned it. He was left to guard the boat, if you remember.'

'Well, well, that's a new one. When are you getting back here?'

'Tomorrow, Tallyforth, not until tomorrow. Work, you know. You can look after things. Get Fraser to talk to the wife. Could produce something. See you the morrow.'

And the line went dead.

THIRTEEN

It was time for some positive action, Tallyforth had decided. He had taken George Elliott's advice and made his peace with Maggie Fraser. From now on, the three of them were working together and she had accepted that he was the senior officer while Gordon was not there. So they had refreshed their memories of all they had so far, reading the Greenpeace materials, scrutinising Cassie Dillon's map, reminding themselves of the forensic reports on the manner of death, checking all the notes they had so far collected from the conversations with Willie and Mary MacPherson together, from Tallyforth himself, and from elsewhere. This had taken time but Tallyforth had insisted it was time they needed to take, since four days after the murder they were still no nearer identifying a suspect, let alone arresting someone. Finally, he had ordered fresh coffee and sandwiches, duly delivered by Sergeant Donald MacKenzie who was the only other policeman on duty at the time, and summoned his two female companions to join him.

'Right, let's just review what we have,' he began. 'Cassie Dillon was found dead in the aft cabin of *The Flodigarry* on Monday morning at around six o'clock by Mary MacPherson. The other people on the boat were the skipper, Willie MacPherson, and yours truly. The last time she was seen alive was at around midnight of the night before on the deck of *The Flodigarry* by me.'

'As far as we know,' interjected George Elliott. 'Presumably, if it wasn't one of you three, she was seen alive later than that by whoever killed her.'

'Obviously, Elliott,' sighed Tallyforth. 'You know what I meant. Let's return to the body. Remind us what forensic had to say, Inspector Fraser.'

She gave him a quick glance, realising that he was retaining a formality with her that he was not extending to George Elliott.

'They say that death was due to asphyxiation, caused by the tightening of a silk scarf around the neck. There was no other bruising and no evidence of any sexual interference, such as might have been expected if she had put up a struggle.'

'Stomach contents?' asked George Elliott, making notes.

'Only alcohol. No traces of any other drugs. She'd had quite a lot to drink, it seems.'

'We all had,' snapped Tallyforth. 'This was supposed to be a holiday, remember? Nothing wrong with a few drinks to launch it, was there?'

'Didn't you say at some point that Willie MacPherson didn't drink alcohol? Wasn't he drinking orange juice and water all evening?' asked Maggie Fraser, lighting a cigarette.

'Yes, that's right,' said Tallyforth, allowing himself to be corrected. 'So, you want to focus on Willie MacPherson. Okay, let's do that. What do we have about him?'

George Elliott turned back several pages in her notebook and read from them.

'Owner of *The Flodigarry* with his wife Mary. Aged thirty-nine. Did three months in Barlinnie prison over twenty years ago, convicted of killing another man in a street fight in Glasgow. Released after three months when medical evidence showed the dead man had had heart problems. Returned to Skye, met and married Mary, set up in business running pleasure cruises for tourists. No other information.'

'Do we know Mary's maiden name?'

'No.'

'And do we have a full police record of this incident he was involved in?'

'No, just the summary.'

'See if you can find those, will you, Elliott? Glasgow police should have some notes on the case and there must be someone on the island who knows the wife's maiden name. How about your sergeant, Fraser?'

She winced slightly. She was down in the ranks again. She tapped the ash from the end of her cigarette into an ash-tray.

'Now, you still suspect him, don't you?' he continued, looking in her direction. 'Why?'

'Because it seems to me that if a man can kill once he can kill again.'

'Even if the first time was not a deliberate killing? Even though the situations are completely different? Even though this looks like a carefully premeditated murder, whereas the Glasgow business was clearly a spur of the moment thing, brought on by too much drink, which he now doesn't touch?'

'I still think...' she began, realising that he was deliberately stacking the odds against her suspicion being correct.

'Do you not believe that a man should be able to pay for his mistakes, without having to fear that he'll constantly be under suspicion?'

'Something to do with leopards and spots, sir,' cut in George Elliott, thinking that he was being too harsh on Maggie Fraser. 'It's not unknown, is it?'

'Not saying that, Sergeant,' he responded, turning his attention away from Maggie Fraser and on to George Elliott. 'But it's too easy. And there are just too many dissimilarities here. And what would have been the motive?'

George Elliott consulted her notes again.

'Didn't Mary MacPherson say that Willie couldn't have gone to the Dillon woman's cabin in the night because she would have noticed his absence, him being a heavy snorer?' she asked.

'Yes, that's right,' said Maggie Fraser.

'So how did he get out of their house last night without disturbing her?' she asked, triumphant at exposing a flaw in the evidence they had collected before she arrived.

Tallyforth looked at Maggie Fraser, who stared straight back.

'Let's look at it another way,' he tried again after a moment's pause. 'Maybe she's been lying. What do we have on her?'

'All we know is that she's married to Willie, that they are partners in the boat business and that they live in Uig. Oh, and she's six years older than him and has an aunt who keeps the chandler's in Uig,' answered George Elliott, reading again from her notes.

'Nothing else?'

'No. Why?' said Maggie Fraser.

'Chief Inspector Gordon thinks she may have greater involvement than we have so far considered. Apparently she was in the aft cabin of *The Flodigarry* cleaning up after you had left for the police station and I had gone to the Royal Hotel to ring 'Nobby' Clarke. That constable you left on board, MacLean, saw her. Gordon thinks she may have the camera. And remember also that it was her who first found the body,' Tallyforth said.

'You think she did it?' asked George Elliott. 'What was her motive?'

'I don't know that,' he said, 'but I think we need to talk to her. Is she still in town?'

Maggie Fraser nodded, stubbing out her cigarette.

'Right, you interview her, Inspector. Now, what else do we have? Run that Greenpeace stuff in front of us again, Elliott.'

George Elliott did so, summarising the Greenpeace papers about the Atlantic Frontier and the press releases about the current action being mounted out in the Atlantic. She also showed how the sites marked in pencil crosses on the map from the dead woman's cabin were likely to represent possible places for Greenpeace boats to land or set out without drawing great attention to themselves and how people could get in and out of those sites very quickly using mainstream transport systems, which would also protect their anonymity.

'So, we're fairly sure there is a connection between her visit to the Hebrides and this recent Greenpeace action, though we don't know what,' Tallyforth mused aloud. 'And again we have a problem of motive. Who would have a motive to kill a Greenpeace activist? What would be gained? I still think the film in that missing camera might hold a clue. Have we tried local shops where films can be developed? I know it's just an off-chance but it may be worth it. Can you organise that, Inspector Fraser?'

She nodded, noting the formality this time.

'Now who else haven't we considered? Has anyone else been at all thought about in this case?'

'There was the man from the Scottish Office,' said Maggie Fraser, rather uncertainly glancing at George Elliott, who kept her eyes fixed on her notebook, though her neck reddened slightly.

'Go on. Remind us.'

Maggie Fraser then repeated the story of how Chief Inspector Gordon had decided that this English stranger should be arrested, how he had been apprehended on his Harley Davidson motorbike just outside Portree and brought to the police station, how Gordon had begun to question him, and how the young Englishman had insisted on making one phone call, which turned out to be to the Scottish Office in Edinburgh where the minister had warned them off any further enquiries and they had had to release him.

'That pal of yours has a Harley Davidson, doesn't he?' asked Tallyforth, swivelling to face George Elliott. 'Him from the Home Office? Do they get them with the job in the civil service nowadays?'

George Elliott decided against responding. She had found in the past that was the best way to handle his cranky attitude to Steve Anthony. And besides, he clearly still hadn't made the connection.

There was a lengthy silence. Tallyforth knew he had needled her and was beginning to regret it. Professional relationship or not, this was no way of re-establishing contact with George.

'Just remind me again how Chief Inspector Gordon heard about this Scottish Office person,' Tallyforth eventually resumed the discussion.

'It was Hamish MacLeod who told us,' Maggie Fraser told him, lighting another cigarette and inhaling deeply. 'From the post office. Apparently this John Smith character had sought him out to discuss feelings in the Western Isles about devolution.'

'And what do we know about this Hamish MacLeod?' he asked.

George Elliott looked through her notes again, then gave a shrug to indicate there was no mention of him.

'He's a leading light in the S.K.A.T. campaign,' explained Maggie Fraser. 'That's the Skye and Lochalsh Against Tolls group. They oppose the tolls on the new road bridge you crossed over when you came here at the weekend. We've had one or two run-ins with the protesters when we've had to pull them off the bridge.'

'Anything else about him?'

'He's quite big in the Scottish Nationalists on Skye.'

'Has he been asked about his movements on Sunday night?'

'No. There was no reason to,' Maggie Fraser answered defensively.

171

'Doesn't it strike you as odd that a person should be seeking to implicate someone else in a murder case? If you'd been involved in as many murder cases as I had, Fraser, you'd soon realise that the person who finds the dead body and the person who seeks to blame someone else are very frequently the ones who know more than they're letting on,' Tallyforth said, trying to sound profound. 'I think we need to talk to this Hamish MacLeod. We'll do that, Elliott. Can you arrange it, Inspector Fraser?'

Maggie Fraser's ice-blue eyes glared at him. She was beginning to wonder if it was deliberate, this alternating of address to her.

'Yes,' she replied tersely.

'Now, what have we missed? Anything else, Elliott?' Tallyforth asked, tugging at his jacket collar.

She reread her earliest notes, where she had summarised the Greenpeace papers.

'No, there's nothing,' she said, still reading. 'Oh, wait a minute, there were the voices on the answerphone. Cassie Dillon's. In Tamworth. There were some messages - one woman who rang three times, who sounded like a friend from where she worked, someone with a Scottish accent ringing about a cruise, whom I took to be Willie MacPherson, and another man saying something about a parcel.'

'That might be important,' said Tallyforth. 'We've got no other personal links to the deceased. Can we get somebody to send us the tape? Without 'Nobby' Clarke finding out?'

She nodded.

'And there was James Orr,' Maggie Fraser reminded him. 'The teacher she stayed with in Oban before coming to Skye.'

'But you interviewed him, didn't you? And checked his alibi?' he queried.

'Yes,' she agreed.

'And did he know Donald McMillan?'

She glanced quizzically at him.

'Who he?' she asked.

'Brother of the local solicitor here,' Tallyforth said. 'Mary MacPherson thought that Orr might know him. Presumably they teach at the same school in Oban. Cassie Dillon didn't know. It's probably nothing, but just get Oban police to check out whether these two people do actually teach together.'

Maggie Fraser nodded again.

Tallyforth stood up and clapped his hands.

'Right, girls,' he said, with a broad grin, knowing how much they would hate the term. 'Sandwiches. Then to work. Let's catch our murderer.'

Maggie Fraser glanced sideways at George Elliott, who grimaced but shrugged her shoulders.

It was Sergeant Donald MacKenzie, half way round his calls to the town's chemists to check on film processing done in the previous four days, who had told Hamish MacLeod that he was wanted at the police station. Hamish, busy as ever behind the counter of the post office, had retorted that he had missed enough time in the shop this week and he didn't see why the police couldn't wait. Donald MacKenzie had explained that, as far as he knew, it was just routine enquiries related to the murder of the woman in the boat the previous Monday. Hamish had said that he knew nothing about that apart from what he had already told them about the man who said he was from the Scottish Office. Donald had said that Inspector Fraser probably wanted to ask him some more questions about that. Hamish had snorted, hearing the name of the woman who had given the order for him to be pulled off the Skye Bridge during the last protest. Donald had insisted that it was best to co-operate and Hamish had eventually conceded.

As he entered the police station, Hamish MacLeod, wearing his inevitable green shirt and yellow MacLeod tartan tie, almost collided with Inspector Maggie Fraser, who was just leaving to go looking for Mary MacPherson.

'I hope this isn't going to waste too much of my time, Inspector,' growled Hamish, tugging at his ginger beard. 'The post office doesn't run itself, you know. And it's a very busy day today.'

She looked down at the bald head of the squat figure in front of her. The wisps of ginger hair around his ears made him look strangely elfin.

'Detective Chief Inspector Tallyforth and Detective Sergeant Elliott want to talk to you, Hamish,' she said. 'They think you might be able to help them with their murder enquiries.'

'Who?' he squawked. 'Aren't you handling this any longer? Who're they?'

'We're working together on this case, Hamish,' she said magisterially.

He looked up at her ice-blue eyes, with a quiver of apprehension. 'Why me?' he asked.

'They just want to talk to you, Hamish,' she answered. 'Remember it was you who came to us about that John Smith character the other day.'

He blushed slightly. He had heard the outcome of that inquiry.

'They're in my office,' she continued. 'Just go on in. Now, I have to get going. Excuse me.'

Hamish's ginger eyebrows raised slightly as she brushed past him. He moved forward and knocked on the office door with her name on the outside.

'Hamish MacLeod?' asked George Elliott, opening the door to him. 'Come in. We've been expecting you. Good of you to come. I expect you're busy but we won't keep you long hopefully. Come in and sit down.'

As he entered the room he took in the short blonde hair, the orange halter top and the short skirt of the woman who had greeted him. He had not seen her before but he had seen the other person in the room - the man in the linen jacket who sat behind the desk twiddling a pencil. He had been the MacPhersons' other passenger for the cruise and had been in the dining room of the Royal Hotel the previous Sunday evening, the night before the woman was found murdered.

'Hamish MacLeod,' mused Tallyforth, putting the pencil down on the desk. 'Are you one of the MacLeods of Skye?'

'We're not directly related to the clan chiefs,' Hamish said, wondering where this line of questioning was leading. 'We can trace the family back quite a way and I expect we are related somewhere. I always wear the tartan, as you see.'

And Hamish held forward his tie.

'Yes, so I see,' said Tallyforth, glancing quickly across at George Elliott who had now seated herself next to him and was opening up her notebook. 'Now, Hamish, would you begin by telling us about this mysterious stranger who visited you this week.'

As Hamish described John Smith, George Elliott scribbled furiously in her notebook, aware that the back of her neck was burning. Surely Tallyforth would realise now that it was Steve! She heard Hamish describe the dark hair, tied back in a ponytail, and the fresh face. She heard him tell of the unusual way with words. She heard him describe the Harley Davidson. But still there was no reaction from Tallyforth, though she did not dare look at him.

'And what did this person have to tell you, Hamish?' pressed Tallyforth. 'What was he doing here?'

'Well, at first I couldn't make that out,' came the reply. 'But then, when he knew so much about me, I realised that he must be who he said he was.'

'And what was that?' asked Tallyforth.

'He said he was a civil servant from the Home Office who had been seconded to the Scottish Office to help prepare for devolution and that he'd been told to travel around the Highlands area to ascertain the views of the people. I asked him why he'd chosen me and he said it was because of my involvement with S.K.A.T. and because I was in the S.N.P.'

There was a noticeable lull in the proceedings. George Elliott knew that Tallyforth had finally realised who John Smith was. But she dared not look up. He wouldn't raise the matter until Hamish MacLeod had gone, she knew that. But then! She was not looking forward to the explosion!

'Very well, Hamish, I can accept all of that but I don't understand why you decided to come to the police with suspicions about this stranger, this John Smith character.' Tallyforth stressed the John Smith heavily.

'I saw him in the Royal on Sunday evening,' began Hamish, tugging at his beard again. 'I was having a meal with my father, who's the manager there, and Iain McMillan, who's a solicitor here and helps us on the S.K.A.T. campaign. You wouldn't remember us but I saw you come into the room with Willie and Mary MacPherson and the woman that's died. We spoke briefly to the MacPhersons, remember now?'

Tallyforth nodded. He could visualise the dining room now. At the time, as Hamish had pointed out, he hadn't particularly taken in its occupants, so preoccupied had he been with meeting up again with Cassie Dillon and the prospects of getting to know her really well on the forthcoming cruise.

'Well, sitting right behind us, out of sight from you, was this John Smith character,' continued Hamish. 'I'd forgotten until Iain McMillan told me about the murder. Then he came to see me on the Monday morning and told me to meet him for lunch. Well, it just seemed an odd coincidence, him being here in Portree at the very time when the woman was murdered and I just thought someone ought to know.'

Tallyforth scratched his right earlobe.

'But you've talked to him subsequently?' queried Tallyforth. 'After Chief Inspector Gordon and Inspector Fraser took him in? Did he tell you about that?'

'Yes, he said it had been a terrible mistake and that he'd had to get the minister in Edinburgh to square things,' Hamish answered, then added sheepishly, 'Of course, I didn't tell him it was me that was responsible.'

'So what was he really here for, do you think, Hamish?' mused Tallyforth, staring at the ceiling. 'It surely wasn't just about this devolution business?'

Hamish shifted in his chair and adjusted his tie.

'Well, I thought that too,' he answered. 'I thought he'd come to maybe nobble me over the S.K.A.T. business. You'll maybe not know that the Secretary of State has said he'll reduce the cost of the toll but the Labour party promised to abolish it completely before the election. So I thought he was maybe sent to soften us up on that. But he wasn't really interested in all that. He was more interested in telling me about the new oil fields out in the Atlantic and how they could bring new wealth to the Western Isles.'

Both George Elliott and Tallyforth pricked up their ears at this.

'Go on,' said Tallyforth.

'That was it really,' finished Hamish rather lamely. 'He just said that the bridge business was a minor thing compared to what was going to come with the oil.'

There was another lengthy pause. George Elliott decided to risk looking at Tallyforth but he was lost in thought and didn't return her look.

'You don't have much of a Scottish accent, Hamish,' said Tallyforth at length. 'Why's that?'

'I was at Glasgow University,' Hamish replied, tugging again at his beard. 'I did a degree in political science but I decided I wanted to come back to Skye. So I took up work with the post office. My accent went in Glasgow. I was mixing with a lot of overseas students.'

He shrugged his shoulders.

'Can you account for your movements on Sunday night and early Monday, Hamish?' asked Tallyforth, suddenly raising the temperature.

Hamish MacLeod sat up straight. The wisps of ginger air above his ears seemed to follow suit.

'Why? Oh, well,' he stuttered. 'After I'd eaten with Iain and my father, I went home. I was there all night. Then I was at the post office at ten to nine on the Monday to open up.'

'You married?'

'Yes. Two children. They were at home with me.'

'Thanks, Hamish. Just procedures, you understand. Thank you for your time,' said Tallyforth, turning in the direction of George Elliott with a look which betokened trouble.

'Mr McMillan? It's Willie. Willie MacPherson. Can I talk to you?'

Iain McMillan adjusted his half-glasses on the ridge of his nose and pushed a strand of blond hair away from his eye, as he heard the voice at the end of the phone.

'Of course! Where are you? Why don't you just come into my office?'

'I cannot do that, Mr McMillan. You see, I think I may have done something very daft. Has Mary been to see you? My wife?'

'No, why? Were you expecting her to?'

'Well, I didn't know, Mr McMillan. You see, I left home at three this morning without saying anything to her. She'll be fair worried. And I've rung home but there's no answer, so I wondered if she might have come to you.'

'Willie, what were you doing at three in the morning, for God's sake? Is this something to do with that business you were telling me about the other day?'

'Aye, it is, Mr McMillan. I've been worried stiff about it all. Ever since I spoke to that Inspector Fraser. It was the way she looked at me. I could tell she thought I'd murdered the lassie. I think she knows about what happened in Glasgow all those years ago. But I didn't, Mr McMillan! On my oath, I didn't!'

'Where are you, Willie?'

'I'm at the Sligachan Hotel, Mr McMillan. I've been walking up the Cuillins and it's cleared my head. I can't keep running away. I've to face up to things and talk to Inspector Fraser about it all.'

'Yes, that may be a good idea but I think it would be best if we talked first. Remember, you asked me to represent you. Why don't you come in?'

'That's just it, Mr McMillan, I cannot at the moment. I've left the boat by the pier at Sconser and I don't have any way of getting to you quickly. You couldn't come and fetch me, could you?'

Iain McMillan looked at the pile of papers on his desk, then looked up at the clock and saw it was nearly two in the afternoon. He picked up his silver pen and fastened it in the inside pocket of his pin-striped jacket.

'Stay where you are, Willie. I'll be with you in twenty minutes.'

Sergeant Donald MacKenzie returned to the police station from his tour of the town's photograph processing shops. There were only three shops that handled the processing of films and all three had promised to check their records for films that had been given in on the Monday and Tuesday for developing. It was like looking for a needle in a haystack, he thought, for goodness knows how many films had been handed across the counter on those days. He didn't really know what Inspector Fraser wanted with the information anyway. He supposed it was something connected with the murder but he didn't know what. On her instructions, however, he had asked the shopkeepers to put their clients into two lists - one of Portree residents and one of tourists.

There was a fax waiting for him on his return. It was from police records in Glasgow. He picked it up and read it:

Re. WILLIAM MACPHERSON

William MacPherson, at the time an employee of Clyde Shipyards, was convicted on 10th May 1976 of the culpable homicide of one Donald Allen Cruikshank, a part-time singer with a country and western band. The aforesaid Cruikshank and MacPherson were involved in a fight outside the now-closed Murphy's Bar in the centre of Glasgow late on the evening of 10th April 1976, as a result of which Cruikshank suffered a severe blow to the head, was taken to hospital and put on a life-support machine. He never recovered consciousness and died on 24th April 1976. MacPherson was given a life sentence and sent to Barlinnie maximum security prison. On 30th July 1976 new evidence was produced by MacPherson's solicitor which showed there had been a miscarriage of justice. Cruikshank had a history of heart trouble and had been only given three months to live. This evidence was not presented at the original trial. The sentence was quashed and MacPherson was released. The judge ruled that it had been accidental death as a result of a criminal affray and that MacPherson had served sufficient time in prison. MacPherson was released from prison on 12th August 1976.

There are no further records relating to this person.

Donald MacKenzie put the fax down. He could hear loud voices in Inspector Fraser's office, where Tallyforth and George Elliott were. They sounded angry about something or other.

He made himself a cup of tea and reached for the phone. He had to ring Oban police about this James Orr character and someone called Donald McMillan to see if they both worked at the Oban Academy.

He would take the fax through when the voices died down a little.

He was still on the phone when George Elliott stamped out of the inspector's office, slamming the door behind her.

'Hurry up, Sergeant,' she said to him, her face flushed, 'I need to use that phone.'

Donald MacKenzie pushed the fax across the counter towards her, as he wound down his conversation, which had ascertained that both the men mentioned did teach at Oban Academy.

'Here you are,' he said, as he finished talking and passed the phone over to her. 'You're in a rush.'

'That man!' George Elliott screeched. 'That man has only had the nerve to tell me off for speaking to someone for whom he has no time and then, mark this, Sergeant, then he's told me I should phone this same person for some help! Would you credit it? The man's impossible!'

Donald MacKenzie smiled.

'Would you be liking a cup of tea?' he asked.

'No!' she shouted, then realised she was taking her anger out on the wrong person. 'Sorry. Yes, I will. Thanks.'

While Donald MacKenzie brewed a fresh pot of tea, she dialled a number, scribbled down what she was told, rang off then dialled again

'Steve? It's George. Look, sorry to bother you. I'm in Portree. Yes, I know. But look, I need a big favour. Can you do a telephone tap on an answerphone?'

And she explained about the messages on Cassie Dillon's answerphone and how Tallyforth thought they might hold some clue to her murder. And Steve Anthony had replied that anything was possible but it might take a few hours.

Then, and only then, she took the cup of tea that Donald MacKenzie proffered.

FOURTEEN

Inspector Maggie Fraser had found Mary MacPherson out along the pierhead. It was almost as if Mary had made her mind up that her husband was bound to sail into Portree harbour in *The Flodigarry* at some point and she wanted to be there to greet him. Because of the heat of the day, now as hot as it had been earlier in the week with a strong sun beating down out of a clear blue sky, she had removed the yellow cagoule she had been wearing earlier in the morning and now wore a short-sleeved blue cotton blouse and denim jeans. She had spent most of the day wondering around Portree, looking in each bar, just in case Willie in his anxiety had broken all his vows and returned to the drink, but she had not found him. She had asked everyone working in the harbour and everyone who sailed into the harbour if they had seen the white hull of *The Flodigarry* but no one had. In the end, she had bought herself some fish and chips and sat on the low wall at the end of the pier, eating mindlessly and staring out to sea.

'I wondered where you'd got to,' said Maggie Fraser, coming up behind the sitting figure.

Mary MacPherson looked round startled, then saw who it was.

'Have you found him? Our Willie? Have you found him?' she asked, shielding the sun from her eyes as she looked up.

'No, we haven't, Mary. Not yet,' came the reply. 'But the chief inspector would like to talk to you. Would you come up to the station with me?'

And, thinking that by doing so, she might help towards finding her missing husband, Mary MacPherson agreed to do so and accompanied Maggie Fraser back to the police station in Somerled Square.

But it was not Tallyforth who wanted to speak to her. It was someone she had not seen before, a woman in fashionable clothes who invited them into the inspector's office.

'Now then, Mrs MacPherson,' said George Elliott, sitting herself down on the chair recently occupied by Tallyforth, while Maggie Fraser sat beside her. 'Let's start at the beginning, shall we? I'm Detective Sergeant Elliott from the Mercian Force in England. I work with Detective Chief Inspector Tallyforth. Just assume that I know nothing, will you?'

Mary MacPherson nodded her agreement.

'Good. Now, let's start with the formalities,' continued George Elliott. 'Your full name is?'

'Mary Elizabeth MacPherson.'

'And you are married to Willie MacPherson, is that correct?'

'Yes.'

'And your maiden name?'

Mary MacPherson shifted uncomfortably.

'My given name was Carmichael,' she answered. 'But I became a MacLeod when my mother remarried after father was lost at sea.'

'You wouldn't be related to Hamish MacLeod at the post office, would you, Mary?' asked Maggie Fraser, surprised at this new information.

'Aye, technically Hamish is my step-brother,' Mary MacPherson replied, 'though we didn't stay together long. I was fifteen when mother married Dugald MacLeod and Hamish was only nine. I didn't much like it with the MacLeods and, when I left school the next year, I went to work for my uncle in the chandler's in Uig. I bided there too. Till I married Willie.'

George Elliott made a note before looking up again.

'So, Mary, take us back to this last Monday morning on the boat,' continued George Elliott. '*The Flodigarry*, isn't that what you call it?'

'Aye, it's named for Flora MacDonald's house up in the north of the island.'

'And you were the first to find the dead woman, I believe?'

'Aye, I was that. I took the lassie a cup of tea, like I always do on the cruises, and that's when I found her like she was,' said Mary, whose eyes began to water at the memory.

'So what time would that have been?' asked George Elliott, all the time making notes.

'It was about six o'clock. I had the alarm set for five thirty, like I always do,' came the reply.

'And was the cabin door open?' asked George Elliott. 'The one where Ms. Dillon was?'

'No, I don't think so,' stuttered Mary, trying to recall exactly the sequence of events. 'No, wait a minute, it was ajar, I remember now. I knocked and she didn't reply, so I pushed the door open with my foot and that's when I saw her.'

'And what did you think?'

'I was a wee bit surprised to see her with no clothes on but I just thought maybe she was still fast asleep.'

'Then what did you do?' asked George Elliott, leaning forward. 'Did you touch her? Shake her or something?'

'Aye, I walked across to her and shook her shoulder but her arm just flopped down to the floor. That's when I thought there was something wrong, so I felt her wrist for her pulse but there was nothing.'

'And then?' insisted George Elliott.

'Then I shouted to Willie to come. He was up on deck.'

George Elliott sat back in the chair and looked at her notepad.

'We have Willie MacPherson's description of what happened when he came into the cabin,' interrupted Maggie Fraser.

'Yes,' said George Elliott. 'Yes, that's fine.'

She looked again at her notes, flicking back through several pages till she reached the one she was looking for.

'Now when Inspector Fraser here left the boat with your husband and my chief to go back to the police station, she left a young constable on board with you, is that right?' she asked.

'Didn't I tell you to leave the dead woman's cabin alone?' cut in Maggie Fraser. 'Constable MacLean says you went in there. Why?'

Mary MacPherson looked anxiously from Maggie Fraser to George Elliott.

'I thought you had something to tell me about Willie. Have you not found him yet?' she said.

'No,' said Maggie Fraser abruptly. 'Just answer Sergeant Elliott's questions.'

'Go on, Mary,' said George Elliott gently. 'It's best we know.'

Mary MacPherson sighed deeply. This was not what she had been expecting. She searched again in her memory.

'I only went in to clean up a bit. I wasn't thinking. I always clean up the cabins first thing in the morning. I suppose I must have been in shock after you'd gone. I just set about my normal chores. Then I found myself in the dead woman's cabin and remembered. How could I have forgotten? She was still lying there!'

'So you didn't take anything from there?' asked Maggie Fraser.

'Cross my heart and hope to die, I didn't touch a thing, Inspector.'

'You sure, Mary?' pressed George Elliott in the same gentle voice she had been using earlier. 'You didn't see a camera there, for instance?'

'No! I didn't,' Mary MacPherson shouted, as she suddenly realised what was behind their questions. She remembered Tallyforth finding the film case and speculating on a missing camera. And they thought she had taken it! 'Definitely not! I'm not a thief!'

Maggie Fraser and George Elliott watched her as she shouted. It did not seem a put-on display of anger. The woman certainly seemed genuinely upset at the allegation they had implied.

'Okay, Mary,' said George Elliott at length, speaking quietly and calmly. 'Now, I want you to tell us why you think your Willie has disappeared.'

And Mary MacPherson bit back her anger to tell them of what she was afraid about her husband's disappearance and about the emotional state he had been in the previous evening when they had stayed up late talking.

'And you never heard him going?' asked Maggie Fraser, as Mary finished her description of events. 'You told me that Willie's a very heavy snorer and that you'd have heard him if he'd got up in the night. That was his alibi on the night of the murder. How come you didn't hear him getting up last night?'

'I can't explain it,' Mary MacPherson said, her eyes moistening. 'I know I was awful tired. I know he was very restless. I must have just fallen into a deep sleep, I don't remember a thing until I woke at five thirty this morning to find him gone from my side. And that's the honest truth!'

'Alright, Mary, that's all for now,' said Maggie Fraser, sensing that George Elliott was no longer interested but was scanning through her notes again.

'What about Willie?' asked Mary MacPherson. 'Will you find him?'

'He'll turn up, don't you worry,' said George Elliott over the top of her notebook. 'Men always do. Unfortunately.'

'So she's related to Hamish MacLeod,' said Tallyforth, as he listened to George Elliott's account of the interview with Mary MacPherson shortly afterwards.

Mary MacPherson had left the police station and gone back to the end of the pier. Tallyforth had now rejoined the two female police officers in Maggie Fraser's office.

'Yes, but they're not close,' explained George Elliott. 'She only lived with the MacLeods for twelve months before she left to work in Uig.'

'What about the father? Isn't he the manager at the Royal?' asked Tallyforth.

'Yes,' replied Maggie Fraser, drawing on a cigarette. 'Dugald MacLeod. You must have met him. You're staying there, aren't you? Big man with long white hair. Always wears a black suit and bow tie.'

'I've seen him, yes,' said Tallyforth.

'But what's the point of dragging him in?' interrupted George Elliott. 'Mary MacPherson's not your murderer. You can tell by looking at her. She's in shock, wondering what's happened to her husband.'

'Could be acting, Elliott,' said Tallyforth. 'Did you ask her about the camera?'

'After a fashion,' replied Maggie Fraser, inhaling. 'She said she'd gone into the dead woman's cabin out of habit.'

'You believed her?'

'Yes,' Maggie Fraser and George Elliott chorused together.

Tallyforth looked to the ceiling.

'Women's intuition?' he said. 'Are you sure?'

'Yes,' they chorused together again.

'So, where next?' he asked, spreading his hands out before him on the desk. 'Any ideas?'

The three police officers looked at each other, almost daring one another to speak.

'We've had confirmation about Willie MacPherson's imprisonment and release,' said George Elliott at last. 'From Glasgow. The story's the same as the one he's told you. God knows why he's gone walkabout. He's nothing to fear, in my opinion. The death in Glasgow was an accident. He was drunk out of his skull and got into a fight. We've seen enough young men do the same as that. He was unlucky because of the medical history of the other man. But that doesn't make him a serial killer. Besides, didn't you say he was off the drink now?'

Tallyforth nodded to confirm this last point.

'So any theories where we might find him?' he asked. 'If only to clear him from the inquiry? Some bar perhaps?'

'Mary said she'd been in every bar in Portree,' replied Maggie Fraser. 'That was her first thought, that he'd broken his vow to stay off the drink. He promised her that when they first married, so she told me.'

'And you believed her?' he asked.

'Sir, I think we're barking up the wrong tree,' said George Elliott, who had been consulting her notebook again. 'I think the clues we're looking for are on the answerphone at the dead woman's house and in that missing film. Sergeant MacKenzie's doing a trawl for the film and Steve's said he'll get hold of a copy of the tape from the answerphone.'

'Your creepy friend!' said Tallyforth, not disguising the dislike he felt. 'Mr Smith! The phantom motorcyclist!'

George Elliott looked at him, pityingly, then glanced at Maggie Fraser as if to say, 'See what I mean?'

'And what about this James Orr character?' Tallyforth continued, ignoring the looks between the two women. 'Anything further on that front?'

'I'll just go and check, sir,' said George Elliott, getting up to leave the room.

'Inspector Fraser,' he said, as he saw George Elliott heading for the door. 'Can you get your sergeant to rustle up some tea? I'm feeling rather parched.'

Maggie Fraser was about to reply, something to the effect that she wasn't used to being treated as a servant, but decided to ignore him and followed George Elliott out.

At four o'clock in the afternoon, while drinking the cup of tea that Sergeant Donald MacKenzie had dutifully made for him, at his own request, and while staring out of the window of the police station at the crowds of tourists in Somerled Square flopping on to benches, squatting on the hot tarmac, catching buses, disgorging from buses, parking cars, or simply standing and talking to each other with hats fanning their faces from the sweltering heat, Tallyforth became aware of two figures who were moving across the square more determinedly than the rest. He leaned forward and confirmed his initial suspicion that one of the two figures was definitely Willie MacPherson, dressed in blue denim jeans and an open-necked tartan shirt. His companion Tallyforth did not recognise. He was a dapper man of medium height, in a dark pin-stripe suit with a blue handkerchief dangling out of his breast pocket and wearing his blond hair sharply parted in the middle. He carried a black leather document case under his right arm. He looked to be in his early thirties, Tallyforth guessed. The pair were clearly heading for the police station.

Minutes later, Sergeant MacKenzie showed them into the office where he sat.

'Mr McMillan, the solicitor, would like to see you with his client Willie MacPherson,' explained Donald MacKenzie, as he held the door open for the two newcomers.

So, thought Tallyforth, the plot thickens. First, Willie goes missing, then he turns up with his solicitor. What next? A signed confession?

'Of course, please come in and sit down,' he said, standing up to greet them. 'It's good to see you again, Willie. How are you?'

He reached forward to shake Willie MacPherson's hand. Willie took it somewhat reluctantly and looked down at his feet.

'Aye, aye, Mr Tallyforth,' he mumbled. 'Not so bad.'

'I don't believe I've had the pleasure,' said Tallyforth, turning towards Iain McMillan and holding out his hand.

They exchanged a firm handshake and then all sat down.

Tallyforth eyed the solicitor, who was dressed for his trade but must have been feeling uncomfortable in the heat.

'Mind if I switch this fan on?' Tallyforth asked, leaning across to a table behind him to do so without waiting for an answer. 'Now, what can I do for you, gentlemen?'

Iain McMillan took his half-glasses from behind the handkerchief in his breast pocket and put them on. Then he unzipped his document case and pulled out a thin sheaf of papers. He glanced quickly at them to check they were the correct ones, then cleared his throat to speak.

'My client wishes to make a statement, Chief Inspector,' he began, tossing his hair away from his eyes. 'My client feels that he has been unduly harassed by one of your police officers.'

Tallyforth's eyebrows rose but he said nothing.

'My client considers that the questioning of him by Inspector Fraser of the Portree police station was designed to implicate him in the murder of the woman, Cassandra Dillon, whose body was found on his sailing boat, *The Flodigarry*, on Monday morning of this week,' continued Iain McMillan, speaking firmly and addressing his remarks directly at Tallyforth.

He paused to weigh the impact of his words. Willie MacPherson stared down at his feet. Tallyforth still said nothing but held the solicitor's gaze.

'My client wishes it to be known that the incident in Glasgow for which he was arrested and imprisoned when he was a young man and whose tragic outcome was the death of another man was long ago in his past and he was released from prison after completing only three months of his sentence because of new evidence which showed the dead man had a medical condition that caused his death. The charge against my client was reduced from one of culpable homicide to one of criminal affray.'

Iain McMillan adjusted the glasses on the bridge of his nose.

'Yes, we know all that,' said Tallyforth, responding at last. 'When Inspector Fraser was talking to Willie the other day, it was standard procedure.'

'I don't think it's standard procedure to accuse someone of murder without any evidence, Mr Tallyforth,' growled Willie MacPherson, looking up.

'Did Inspector Fraser say that?' asked Tallyforth.

'Not in so many words, Mr Tallyforth, but I knew that was what she was getting at,' said Willie MacPherson. And he looked back at his feet.

'My client wishes to read a statement he has prepared,' cut in the solicitor and he took one of the papers from his sheaf and handed it over to Willie MacPherson. 'I would be grateful if this could be witnessed.'

Tallyforth's eyes opened a fraction wider at this request but he decided to go along with it, so he went across to the door and summoned Sergeant Donald MacKenzie.

'Go on then, Willie,' urged Tallyforth when Donald MacKenzie was ensconced at his side with a notebook and pen. 'We're ready now.'

Willie MacPherson looked sheepishly across at Donald MacKenzie, then at Iain McMillan, who nodded for him to proceed.

'I, William MacPherson, of Uig,' he started to read from the piece of paper given him by the solicitor, 'wish it to be known that I was not involved in the death of Cassandra Dillon on Monday 4th August 1997. Furthermore, I have no knowledge of how she died or when she died or of any person who might have been involved in her unlawful killing. As far as I was concerned, the last time I saw the aforesaid Cassandra Dillon alive was at eleven thirty on the evening of Sunday 3rd August 1997, when I and my wife Mary retired to our cabin on *The Flodigarry* for the night. The aforesaid Cassandra Dillon was found dead by my wife Mary at six o'clock the following morning when she took her a cup of tea. I ascertained that the aforesaid Cassandra Dillon was dead by checking her pulse and by trying to give her mouth-to-mouth resuscitation but this was to no effect.

'I, William MacPherson, of Uig, also wish it to be known that I have paid for the incident in which I was involved as a young man. I served three months of a sentence for a crime I did not commit. I was subsequently rejected by my family for going to prison. Since that day when the man Cruikshank died I have not touched a drop of alcohol and have never been involved in a fight with another man or woman nor engaged in any unlawful activity of any kind.

189

'I, William MacPherson, of Uig, have signed this sworn testimony in the presence of my solicitor, Mr Iain McMillan of Portree, and hereto swear that it is true.'

Tallyforth looked at him, trying had not to smile in some sympathy for this man who had spent all his adult years repairing the damage of one foolish incident in his youth, only to have that same incident come back to haunt him just at the point when he had established a decent living for himself and his wife.

'Right, Willie, thank you,' he said. 'Sergeant MacKenzie has made a note and no doubt you will be leaving us a copy of what you have written. Now, was there anything else, Mr McMillan?'

Iain McMillan re-adjusted his glasses.

'Chief Inspector,' he replied, 'I have advised my client that for the moment this is sufficient action. He does not wish to take the matter any further. However, I do have to state that, should he be harassed any further in this matter, I may have to advise him about alternative courses that are open to him.'

'That sounds like a threat, Mr McMillan,' said Tallyforth, who was used to such legal bluster and usually disregarded it.

'Not a threat, Chief Inspector,' said Iain McMillan, teasing his handkerchief further out of his breast pocket and checking that the knot of his tie was sufficiently central. 'But I think it is best that we know where we stand, don't you? We wouldn't want any unfavourable press coverage, would we?'

He smiled fulsomely across at Tallyforth, who returned the smile grimly.

'Thank you, Mr McMillan,' said Tallyforth. 'I'll bear what you have to say in mind. Good day to you. Cheerio, Willie. Oh, your Mary's been looking for you all day by the way. You'll probably find her down by the pierhead. She seems to think you'll sail into the harbour out of the sunset.'

Willie MacPherson looked startled at this last piece of information and almost ran through the door to go to find her. Iain McMillan swiftly replaced his sheaf of papers in his leather case, removed and pocketed his glasses, and, pushing his shoulders back into his jacket and with head held high, marched after him.

It was very late in the afternoon when Sergeant Donald MacKenzie received a message from one of the Portree photo-processing shops that he had called on earlier in the day. They had found an uncollected film which had been handed in on the Tuesday morning. The film had only seven photographic images on it, which suggested that it had been unloaded before it had been fully used. It was the only film among those that had been given in for developing that week which wasn't complete and they had no recall of any other similar films being given in and collected on the previous couple of days. It was also unusual in that all seven photographs had been successfully developed, whereas it was normal when a film was removed from a camera before it had been fully utilised for that film to be exposed to sunlight and therefore ruined. Only a few expensive cameras had the facility for films to be removed before completion without damage being done.

When he told Tallyforth about this, Donald MacKenzie was told to get down to the shop and pick up the photographs and to find out the name and address of the person who had left the film to be developed. So he had quickly gone to the shop in Wentworth Street and collected the package containing the seven photographs.

'But there was something very odd about it, sir,' he explained to Tallyforth on his return as he handed the package over.

'What's that?' asked Tallyforth, sliding his finger into the yellow envelope to reach for the photographs.

'There wasn't an address given,' replied Donald MacKenzie. 'Just a name. So it must have been someone who lives in Portree or someone who was staying here for a while. Or maybe someone they knew.'

Tallyforth looked up at him, pausing with his fingers over the corner of the first photograph.

'What about the person who took the film in on Tuesday? Can they remember nothing?' he asked.

'The lassie who was working on Tuesday has her day off today so we couldn't ask,' answered Donald MacKenzie. 'And she's apparently gone to the mainland for the day, shopping. So we'll not be able to speak to her until the morrow.'

'So what was the name on this package?'

'Well, that's the funny thing, sir,' explained Donald MacKenzie.

191

'The name was J. Smith.'

Tallyforth's hand froze as he was about to extract the first photograph from the package.

'And it was given in on Tuesday, you say? They're sure about that?'

'Aye, you only have to look at the stamp on the packet,' Donald MacKenzie pointed. 'It says ten o'clock on Tuesday morning.'

Tallyforth turned the packet over to check, then took out the first photograph.

'This is the bridge, isn't it?' he asked, holding it out for Donald MacKenzie's inspection.

'Aye,' was the reply. 'That's the new Skye Bridge that all the fuss has been about.'

'And this? And this?' Tallyforth held out two further photographs.

'Aye, that's it from Kyleakin. And that one's from Lochalsh.'

Tallyforth flicked quickly through the remaining four photographs.

'Sergeant, they're all of the Skye Bridge. Look!'

Donald MacKenzie moved beside Tallyforth to see the whole set of photographs as they lay on the desk.

'That one looks as if it's from back down the road to Kirkton. That's from the toll. That's from the toll on Skye side. And that's from Kyleakin too. That's very queer. That Mr Smith must have a fancy for the bridge.'

'You're assuming that the J. Smith who gave this film in and the John Smith from the Scottish Office are one and the same person, Sergeant?' queried Tallyforth. 'I think that's extremely unlikely. I know who John Smith is in reality and I can assure you that he wouldn't be seen dead near a naked woman. Sorry! Unfortunate choice of words. No, Sergeant, the J. Smith who gave that partly-used film in to be developed is someone else entirely and someone who probably knows we are looking for them. Otherwise, why didn't he or she simply collect the film? It must have been ready for at least the last twenty-four hours?'

'I don't know, sir,' replied Donald MacKenzie, who had moved back to the other side of the desk and was clearly anxious to get to answer the phone that was ringing just outside the office door.

'Unless it's someone deliberately laying a false trail,' mused

Tallyforth, before looking up. 'Okay, Sergeant. Go and answer that.'

Maggie Fraser had taken George Elliott on a quick familiarisation tour of Portree during the afternoon, pointing out the various landmarks and points of interest. She had recounted as much as she could of the village's history, which she had picked up from guidebooks to prepare herself when she had first heard about her appointment. So she could quite confidently talk about the original Gaelic term for the village Port-an-Righ, which meant Port of the King - the king in question being James the Fifth who had sailed there to assert his rule over the Highland chiefs. And she was able to tell briefly of the exploits of Bonnie Prince Charlie, who was known as such because he was reputedly gay, Maggie Fraser had said, and his links with the Royal Hotel and Flora MacDonald. She had also told of some of the town's other famous visitors, such as Dr Samuel Johnson and his amanuensis James Boswell, Alfred Lord Tennyson and various modern royals. Then she had taken George Elliott down to the pier, built by Thomas Telford, she had explained, where they were just in time to witness the tearful reunion of Willie and Mary MacPherson.

After their brisk walk around the town and its environs, George Elliott and Maggie Fraser returned to the police station in Somerled Square. By now it was approaching six o'clock and there was no sound within. The station seemed deserted, though it seemed likely that Tallyforth at least, if no one else, would be somewhere about. Seeing that he wasn't in the office they had been using earlier, George Elliott set off to hunt him down elsewhere in the building, leaving Maggie Fraser by the main desk.

She walked behind it to read the papers left on the top, in case there was anything that affected her. She scanned them quickly but then paused on a handwritten note, in Donald MacKenzie's unmistakable hand. It looked like a note of a phone call. She picked it up and read it carefully.

James Orr - teacher of music at Oban Academy
Home address- 13 Balmoral Crescent Oban
Donald McMillan - teacher of history at Oban Academy
Home address - 34 Lochside Road Oban

Then she read it again. Just to be absolutely sure. Then she reached into her blouse pocket for her notepad. But there was no mistake. The address of the married woman who had vouched for James Orr's whereabouts on the night of Sunday 3rd August was 34 Lochside Road, Oban. And the woman's name was Lindsay McMillan! And her brother-in-law was Iain McMillan, the solicitor!

FIFTEEN

Tallyforth was listening to them. They were like two excited schoolgirls. George Elliott was sitting on his desk, her legs crossed and her skirt riding up on her thighs, nodding agreement and occasionally saying 'Yes!' Maggie Fraser, in her summer uniform as ever, was telling him about the discovery.

'This could be the link we're looking for,' she said, excitedly, waving an unlit cigarette at him. 'James Orr is having an affair with the wife of his colleague at the Oban Academy, Donald McMillan, who just happens to be the brother of the solicitor, Iain McMillan, here in Portree! And the dead woman was staying with Orr for a week before she arrived in Skye! There has to be a connection!'

'Absolutely,' agreed George Elliott, stretching her long legs out. 'Hasn't there?'

Tallyforth gave them a disdainful smile.

'Just tell me what it is, then, will you, Inspector?' he said.

Maggie Fraser was almost hopping on the spot.

'I don't know yet,' she said, lighting her cigarette. 'But there has to be one! It's the first bit of luck we've had and you know that.'

'I don't get it,' he said, trying to calm them down. 'According to your report, Orr was with this McMillan woman on the night in question and they will vouch for each other, so that appears to rule them out. Are you saying that the woman's husband knew about the affair and got his brother, a respectable solicitor here on Skye, to kill Cassie Dillon? But why? I've never heard anything so preposterous! What's he like anyway, this Orr fellow?'

'Not much to look at,' Maggie Fraser explained. 'Looks like a middle-aged schoolteacher and dresses that way. Tries to disguise

195

his baldness by having long strands of hair across his forehead.'

'Like Bobby Charlton?' he asked.

'Who's he?'

Tallyforth sighed.

'So he's not exactly God's gift to women,' he continued. 'Was he having an affair with Cassie Dillon as well?'

He blanched at the thought, as the memory of her naked body floated briefly into his consciousness.

'He said not and I believed him,' Maggie Fraser answered. 'Especially when I met Lindsay McMillan. Small, big-busted woman and not very attractive at all. Wore very dowdy clothes and looked as if she had brushed her hair with a garden rake. If that was his type, then I somehow doubt that the Dillon woman was as well.'

'So what was their relationship?'

'Like I said in my report, they were friends at university and they shared an interest in environmental issues,' Maggie Fraser replied, drawing again on her cigarette. 'She got back in touch with him after she returned to Britain following her divorce. That's all it was, according to him. And I believed him. Still do. Didn't she tell you anything?'

'Not about Orr,' Tallyforth said. 'At least, no more than you've just mentioned. So you're still not making sense. And, even if there is some connection, which I somehow doubt very much, then how does all this involve Greenpeace? And what's it got to do with these photographs of the Skye Bridge? We're fairly sure they're from the film in Cassie Dillon's camera when she was murdered and we believe the murderer took off with the camera. Can you explain all that?'

Maggie Fraser looked crestfallen. George Elliott swung herself off the desk and faced Tallyforth.

'I think the photographs are important,' she began. 'But I also think that Maggie's touched on something important. Let's hold on to this connection that Maggie's established but let's also think harder about this bridge business. We know that Hamish MacLeod is one of the leaders of S.K.A.T. but we don't, or at least I don't, know precisely what all the fuss is about and how this S.K.A.T. crew operate. Can we get some clarity on that now?'

Tallyforth reached into his jacket pocket and took out a packet of mints, from which he carefully extracted one and popped it into his mouth.

'Okay,' he said. 'But I'm curious about these photographs. We haven't really considered the bridge since you established the Greenpeace connection. I'd thought that was the major factor. Though it now seems there's suggestions of a link to the bridge, and maybe the protests about it, and of a link to these people in Oban. Are we agreed that those are the three strands with possibility?'

George Elliott looked at Maggie Fraser who had recovered her composure somewhat after Tallyforth's put-down and who gave a curt nod.

'We're with you, skipper,' said George Elliott. 'So what next?'

He kept his reaction to this cheeky familiarity to himself.

'I want to see exactly where these photographs were taken from and maybe that'll help us work out why,' Tallyforth replied, standing up. 'How far to Kyle, Maggie? Can we get there in daylight?'

She looked up at him in surprise at the familiarity.

They took his Range Rover and he placed the tape of Runrig's *Mara* in the cassette player as they swung out of the town and followed the coast road before heading inland towards the Cuillin Hills and Sligachan. Though it was early evening, the sun was still strong and he needed his sun glasses to drive in.

'Right then,' said Tallyforth, once they were under way. 'Tell us about S.K.A.T.'

Maggie Fraser was sitting in the back of the car, so she leaned forward between them to speak.

'Remember that I've only been here since June,' she began. 'So I wasn't here when the whole thing started. I can only give you a potted version. You need to talk to Hamish MacLeod if you want the full story.'

'Okay,' said Tallyforth. 'Just give us your version. I don't want to join them, for God's sake!'

'Well, as I understand it, it began when the government decided that there was to be a bridge from Kyle on to Skye to replace the ferry that's been operating for ever,' she started. 'Now, it wasn't the bridge itself that people were unhappy about but the fact that it was to be privately-financed, privately-owned and privately-run. That's the crux of their complaints. Ever since the government made that decision, there's been protests here on Skye. I remember seeing some of them on television and in the newspapers when I was in Edinburgh.'

'So they basically object to paying a toll at all?' asked George Elliott.

'They say that it's a public road and that they have already paid for it through their taxes. And they've produced a lot of literature which shows that the government gave loads of money, fifteen million pounds according to S.K.A.T., to the bridge company to support them and they also got European grants. Another argument they use is that they have no alternative means of getting off the island by car, except when the ferry runs from Armadale to Mallaig in the summer.'

'So how are they protesting?' asked George Elliott. 'What sort of things do they do?

'One tactic is to use legal trickery. One of them will drive up to the toll booth and say they're quite willing to pay the toll but only when they're shown satisfactory documentary evidence that the company who runs the bridge has the right to take money from motorists. They usually do this with drivers from both sides of the bridge simultaneously. Then, while they're arguing with the people in the booths, other drivers from S.K.A.T. will block both lanes and stop other traffic from driving on. Then their kiddies get out of the cars and they have picnics on the bridge.'

'And what do the police do?' asked George Elliott.

'I understand that the police were very slow to react initially. Since I've been at Portree, we have responded more promptly, I'm pleased to say. Once we get a call that there's trouble, we get down to Kyle as quickly as possible and do whatever we have to do, which can include physically moving cars into the wide load lane, in order to clear the public highway.'

'Which isn't actually a public highway,' interjected George Elliott, 'if it's privately-owned and privately-run, like you said.'

'That's not what the Chief Constable thinks!' replied Maggie Fraser.

They were coming downhill into Sligachan, where the road swings dramatically east along the shores of the loch. Tallyforth engaged third gear. They were silent for a while, listening to the strong rhythms of the Runrig album. George Elliott looked up at the steep slopes of Glamaig, while Maggie Fraser watched a grey heron rise slowly from the shoreline. Tallyforth concentrated on the road as it swept round the mountain and then down to the coastline again along the edge of Loch Ainort.

'So it's just organised protests, is it?' he asked, as the road straightened out again opposite the island of Scalpay.

'No, they tell people to refuse to pay and they've issued instructions so people know how to do it,' Maggie Fraser explained further.

'Go on,' said George Elliott. 'What sort of things do they say?'

'Oh, they're very specific. Drivers are told to drive up to the barrier and say they are unable to pay. When the toll staff ask them to pull over on to the wide load lane, they are to ask them to call the police before they obey. They even suggest that drivers should ask the staff to come out and guide them back if there is traffic behind and even to ask them to push the car back. If we don't get there within half an hour, they are told to go up to the toll booth and tell the staff that, if the police don't arrive soon, the car will be brought back and will block the barrier.'

'And what do you do when you get there?' asked George Elliott.

'We'll take the name and address of the driver and of any passengers and then inform them that their details will be passed to the Procurator Fiscal.'

'Then what?' asked Tallyforth.

'That's where the trouble lies,' replied Maggie Fraser. 'They have some very clever lawyers in S.K.A.T., including our friend Iain McMillan, who have disrupted all the courts' attempts to deal with the matter. So some people have been fined, some have been let off, and others have heard nothing at all. It's a real pain in the butt.'

He looked sharply at her.

'Clear now, Sergeant?' he said, turning to George Elliott. 'Now, if I remember rightly, we've just come past that big garage in Broadford and the bridge isn't far now. I want us to find the places where those photographs were taken, presumably by Cassie Dillon on her way here. Do you recognise it?'

'You're right,' cut in Maggie Fraser before George Elliott could answer. 'It's not very far now.'

'Maggie,' Tallyforth announced, 'I'm going to drop you off on this side of the bridge. Here's the three photographs taken this side, two from Kyleakin and one from by the toll booth.'

He took the photographs from the inside pocket of his jacket and passed them over.

'We need to know if there was anything significant about where she stood to take these photographs. Just find the spots then look around you. It's still just about light enough. Anything you notice, anything at all, make a mental note of it. We've got to get this lot sorted. Clear?'

'Yes,' she said, puzzled by the way Tallyforth moved from the familiar to the authoritarian. 'How long will you be on the other side?'

'Depends how far down the main road we have to go to get the right angle,' he replied. 'I would say about twenty minutes at the most. But allow half an hour. You have to get down towards Kyleakin anyway. Let's say, after I drop you off, we'll meet up again at the same point on your side of the bridge in thirty minutes.'

'Fine,' she said and placed her cap on her head.

'Of course,' Tallyforth grinned at her, 'I'm assuming you can fix the toll people so we don't need to pay. I don't really want to have to cause an obstruction!'

'It's good to be working with you again,' Tallyforth said, smiling at George Elliott, as they drove out of Kyle of Lochalsh, having dropped off Maggie Fraser, and headed in the direction of the hamlet of Kirkton.

George Elliott looked at him and returned a half-smile. She had hoped for more.

He glanced at her when she said nothing.

'What's up?' he asked. 'Have I said something?'

She shrugged her shoulders but still said nothing.

'Well?' he tried again. 'What is it?'

'I thought that you might just, now we're on our own, have said something more,' she said, staring straight ahead. 'Something a little less to do with working together and a bit more to do with being together.'

So that was it!

'But you said this morning,' he spluttered, 'that you wanted to get things back on a professional basis, didn't you? You told me not to call you by your first name, didn't you? You said you'd come up here because you'd heard about the murder and because of Tamworth being close, so you raided her house, didn't you? Or was I imagining things?'

'I might have said those things but you should have realised I didn't mean them,' she said, staring straight ahead through the Range Rover's windscreen. 'You don't think I came all the way up here just to be reminded of your brilliant detecting methods, do you?'

What was going on in her head? he wondered. He'd never understood women.

'Look, George, I told you in June that it was over between us and you didn't disagree. It hadn't been working for some time and you know it. And it was affecting our work in the force, and you know that too,' Tallyforth tried to explain. 'So, if you've driven all the way up here in the hope of reviving something that's over, I'm sorry, but I never asked you to. Anyway I'm surprised 'Nobby' Clarke hasn't guessed where you are. It was him that told you about Cassie Dillon's murder, wasn't it?'

'No, it wasn't.'

'Oh! Who was it then?' He sounded genuinely surprised.

'If you must know, it was Steve Anthony,' she said, with a stagy sigh. 'He saw you in Portree on Monday and then found out about the murder the next day when he was in Uig. He rang me that night to tell me.'

'So it was that little creep who got you up here!' Tallyforth said grimly. 'I expect he told you I was pining for you, didn't he?'

She said nothing and they drove for some minutes in silence.

'I think here looks about right,' Tallyforth said, bringing the Range Rover to a halt at the side of the road where the coastline jutted out into Loch Alsh. 'I've been watching in the mirror and this looks fairly close to the view in one of those photographs of

Cassie Dillon's.'

They got out and looked back at the Skye Bridge, behind which the sun was beginning to set on the horizon, giving the bridge an eerie silhouette in its red glow.

'Did you sleep with her?' asked George Elliott suddenly, turning to face him with her arms folded across her chest.

He was startled by her directness.

'No!' he said abruptly. 'Not that it's any business of yours anyway! But I didn't. I only met her once before the cruise, and that was in Birmingham nearly a fortnight ago. At lunchtime. We had a meal and talked. That was all. And, when we got on board the MacPhersons' boat, they put us in separate cabins at opposite ends of the boat, with their cabin between us.'

'You wanted to, though, didn't you? I saw a picture of her in her house in Tamworth. She was attractive, wasn't she? You fancied her, didn't you?'

He looked at her as she stood facing him, her legs slightly ajar, arms folded and eyes blazing. She was very angry.

'Yes,' he answered at length. 'Yes, I fancied her. Yes. I wanted to go to bed with her. Yes, all of that. But I didn't. And that's all there is to it. And I never will now. So let's forget it, shall we? We're here to catch her murderer, in case you'd forgotten.'

She turned and walked a few paces away from him, kicking at a loose stone.

'I thought so,' she said. 'And you fancy Maggie now, don't you?'

He had been about to get back into the car but was stopped in his tracks by this question.

'Maggie?' he said incredulously.

'Maggie Fraser. You like those ice-blue eyes of hers, don't you?' she said, turning to face him again. Tears were beginning to fall down her cheeks. 'I've been watching you staring at her. And it's 'Maggie' now, isn't it? And I'm still 'Elliott' or 'Sergeant', aren't I?'

He watched her cry for several seconds, then stepped to her and put his arm around her bare shoulders.

'George, don't be silly,' he said. 'You know that's not true. Inspector Fraser is definitely not my type at all. She's tall and thin and she smokes too much. You know I can't stand smoking.'

George Elliott sniffed, at the same time adjusting her position slightly so that her shoulder nestled warmly under his arm.

'You sure?' she asked.

'Yes,' he said. 'Here. Use this.'

He took a white handkerchief from his jacket pocket and passed it to her. She wiped her face and blew her nose loudly.

'I'll get this washed for you,' she said, pushing the handkerchief into the pocket of her skirt. 'I'm sorry. I didn't mean to get into this state. It's just that I've been very lonely these last few weeks. I thought I was handling it, until I saw her picture in that house and then I felt the jealousy creeping into me and I had to come here. I wanted to try to get back to the professional bit, like it was, you know, and I have tried all day. But when you started saying 'Maggie this' and 'Maggie that', I just couldn't take it any more. I'm sorry.'

'George, I was teasing her,' Tallyforth said, taking his arm from around her shoulders. 'Come on now, get back in the car. You'll be getting cold soon.'

She climbed into the Range Rover, still dabbing at her eyes with the handkerchief. Tallyforth reversed the car and headed back towards Kyle of Lochalsh. There he stopped the car once again, this time above the pier from which the CalMac ferry used to cross to Kyleakin. At that very moment Inspector Maggie Fraser was just turning away from the grey Kyleakin pier to walk back uphill towards the new bridge. So far neither had found any particular significance to these photographs - they were simply, it seemed from their joint perspectives, pictures of the bridge from different angles.

'Why would anyone take so many photos of the same thing from different positions?' he asked George Elliott as he climbed back into the car after strolling down the slope of the pier to view the bridge from the position where Cassie Dillon must have taken one of her pictures.

'She must have had a particular interest in it,' she answered. She had stayed in the car to fix her face and was just checking her lipstick in the vanity mirror. 'Maybe she was a member of S.K.A.T.'

'No,' Tallyforth said, shaking his head and at the same time checking that she was composed again. 'Not the right sort of issue. No, if she was heavily into this Greenpeace business, she wouldn't have had any truck with the bridge protesters. Where's the connection? S.K.A.T. are just the islanders with a grievance about having to pay too much to cross the bridge, while Greenpeace is involved in much bigger matters. I was going to say 'has bigger fish to fry' but it somehow didn't seem appropriate!'

He saw her smile.

'Look, George,' he said, turning round in his seat, so that his left arm rested along the head-restraint behind her, 'I know it's difficult but we have to try. You're the best partner I've ever had. To work with, I mean. You know we complement each other. I'd love us to be working together again. That's why I was so glad when you said this morning that was what you wanted too. And I'd thought, today, that we were managing brilliantly. I'm sorry.'

'You're blocking again, aren't you?' she said, looking squarely at him, more in control now. 'You're just freezing up your emotions. I know you. You hate it when you get exposed. You can't stand it when someone gets underneath that skin of yours and sees what's really there, can you? Especially when that someone finds that there isn't very much there at all, except for pretence. You're a fraud, that's what you are, a bloody total fraud.'

'George,' he pleaded, 'don't take it like that! You're angry with me. I understand that but I'm not a fraud. What I told you about how I felt when we were together was true. It's just that things change, feelings change. Don't they?'

'For some people they do,' she answered bitterly, looking down at her lap.

'Come on,' he said, turning away from her to restart the engine. 'Inspector Fraser will be waiting for us. We'd better get going.'

But before he could engage the gears, George Elliott stretched across in front of him, put her arm around his head and pulled it towards her, and kissed his mouth fiercely.

At first, he was stunned but then his arms folded around her and he pulled her into his embrace.

By the time that Maggie Fraser, who had been standing chatting to the woman in the toll booth on the Skye side of the bridge, climbed into the back seat of the Range Rover, both George Elliott and Tallyforth looked rather rapt, she noticed.

In the lounge bar of the Royal Hotel that evening were gathered Hamish MacLeod, his father Dugald MacLeod, Sergeant Donald MacKenzie, whose evening off it was, and the two MacPhersons, Willie and Mary. The bar was quieter this evening after the crowds who had come for the Highland Games had dispersed, so Dugald felt no compunction about leaving his staff to look after everything. There was important business to discuss.

'So you're saying that the police know that you're my step-daughter?' asked Dugald, frowning. 'Why did you need to tell them? They'll be thinking all kind of things now.'

Mary MacPherson sat up straight.

'I had to tell them,' she said. 'They asked my maiden name. I had to explain why my given name was different from my maiden name. I don't know what records they have on folk but I thought I'd better tell them the truth. Just in case. That Inspector Fraser's spent enough time suspicious of our Willie here because of you know what. I wished you'd never adopted me, then I wouldn't have had the problem.'

'It was what your mother wanted, God rest her soul,' said Dugald, his eyes moistening at the thought of his second wife who had died two years previously. 'At the time, with your father drowned, it seemed the best way to be sure you were looked after if anything else happened.'

'But it was a waste of time, wasn't it?' she countered.

'Father wanted to treat you like his own,' interjected Hamish. 'It wasn't his fault that you didn't like the way things turned out, you know.'

Hamish had always felt some anger towards his stepsister because her leaving the new family home in Portree and going to live and work with her aunt and uncle in Uig had been the cause of frequent arguments between his father and stepmother. He lifted his glass of beer to his mouth and supped deeply, leaving a trail of froth around his ginger moustache and beard.

'No, I know that now,' said Mary MacPherson. 'But at the time I didn't. I thought you were trying to wheedle yourself into my mother's affections in place of me. You were a bonny wee lad at the time, Hamish, all ginger curls and freckles. And she really loved you, my mother did.'

'Aye, she did that, Hamish,' confirmed Dugald, shaking his head in memory. 'She knew you'd not had much fuss made of you since your own mother died and she really gave you a lot. I can see now why Mary here felt she was being pushed out.'

'But what's all this got to do with the murder inquiry?' asked Hamish. 'The police don't have some notion that, just because you and I are related and didn't happen to mention that to them before today, we're co-conspirators involved in murder, do they? Is that what's going on, Donald?'

Donald MacKenzie, dressed in an old green cardigan, plaid shirt and navy flannels, put his beer glass down on the small table.

'No,' he said. 'They've dismissed that idea now. It's that Tallyforth. He seems to think that, if they're some connection between things, that will lead him to the result of his inquiries. Very queer, if you ask me. Which no one ever does, of course.'

'So where is he now, this great detective?' asked Hamish MacLeod.

'Him and his Sergeant Elliott and Inspector Fraser have gone down to Kyle to look at the bridge,' Donald MacKenzie answered and explained about the photographs.

'That's odd,' said Hamish, whose attention had been roused by the mention of the bridge. 'Why would she have taken seven different shots of the bridge?'

'Aye, that's what the inspector wanted to find out too,' replied Donald MacKenzie.

At that moment Iain McMillan entered the lounge bar, dressed in a grey track suit and with a face that was red from exertion.

'Here's another one that's under suspicion,' continued Donald MacKenzie. 'Just because his sister-in-law is having a wee bit of slap and tickle with another teacher in Oban, and because the dead woman stayed with that other teacher last week before coming to Portree, they think he may be involved.'

'I see you've been out running again, Iain,' laughed Dugald. 'You'll maybe need to be running soon, for the police are out looking for you.'

Iain McMillan smiled at Dugald's comment.

'Well, I hope they have something rather more substantial to challenge me with than they had for poor Willie here,' he said.

'Now, who's empty? My shout!'

'Is that Mr Smith? Mr John Smith? Please hold. I have a message.'

George Elliott blew a raspberry into the phone and giggled. She was in the bedroom of Maggie Fraser's house in Portree, lying on the floral-patterned duvet and holding the cordless phone to her face. After their journey to the bridge and back, all three had felt tired and had gone their separate ways, Tallyforth to the Royal Hotel and Maggie Fraser and her guest back to her house. Maggie Fraser had gone to take a bath.

'Sorry, Steve, but I've been hearing so much about this John Smith character today and I've had to keep my lip buttoned most of the time. Until Tallyforth finally made the connection.'

'What did he say, sweetie?' came Steve Anthony's voice.

'The usual. I won't bore you with the precise terms. You can imagine but, hey, guess what?'

'Go on,' he sighed audibly. 'You and he are getting married!'

'No,' she laughed. 'But I think it's back on again.'

'So where is he now, the great lover?' asked Steve Anthony. 'Why aren't you with him? Or maybe you are?'

'No,' she laughed. 'Keeping him dangling a little longer. I'm at Maggie Fraser's. Inspector Fraser to you. You met her in Portree police station. Yes, the tall thin one with the ice-blue eyes. Any news on the tapes?'

'Honeybunch, I'm doing my best. I've managed to get some super-sleuth from MI5 to crack the code and he is, *ce moment*, arranging for a special delivery of a copy of the tape to be with you first thing tomorrow.'

'That's brilliant, Steve,' she said, genuinely pleased at this news.

'Please, it's John Smith. I have to protect my invisibility.'

'Bit of a tacky choice of name though, wasn't it? Couldn't you have thought of something better?'

'It is memorable, you have to admit,' he replied. 'They didn't forget me, none of them.'

'True,' she said. 'More's the pity, in one particular case. Guess what else I found out today?'

'Go on, intrigue me.'

'Did you know that Bonnie Prince Charlie was known as such

because he was gay?'

'I always thought he looked a little over-rouged for my liking,' came the reply. 'Still, *chacun à son gout*, as we say in Portugal!'

'But he didn't have a Harley Davidson to ride around the islands on, did he?'

'It might have been better for him if he had,' Steve Anthony said. 'Look, sweetie, I have to go now. Pasta's boiling over. *Ciao*!'

SIXTEEN

Friday morning began grey and overcast. There was even some light drizzle, leaving cloud-drops on the cars parked outside the Royal Hotel, but it was still very warm. Tallyforth was taking a light breakfast of boiled eggs and toast inside the hotel dining room. He had had another restless night, wondering how to manage his feelings towards George Elliott after what had happened the previous evening at Kyle of Lochalsh. Just as worrying was the fact that they seemed no nearer discovering who had murdered Cassie Dillon.

His right hand, holding a slice of toast, paused half-way to his mouth. Hard to remember that it was only four days ago that Cassie Dillon's dead body had been discovered. Hard to remember what he had been hoping might happen between them. Hard to remember now the reasons that had brought them together in the first place in response to the MacPhersons' advertisement in *The Sunday Times*. Hard to remember even that he had been supposed to be on holiday, away from police work, recuperating, clearing his mind. But not hard to remember the sight of her naked body or the coldness of her nipples.

He sensed a figure behind him and looked around. Standing discreetly behind his left shoulder was the white-haired Dugald MacLeod, the manager of the Royal Hotel, dressed formally as ever in black suit, white shirt and bow tie.

'Mr Tallyforth,' he began apologetically, as if he had not wanted to interrupt his guest's thoughts. 'Is it possible to have a word with you? I know you're a busy man but I wouldn't need more than a few minutes of your time.'

Tallyforth looked up at him ruminatively, chewing on a piece of toast. This was the man who was father of Hamish MacLeod in the post office, the ringleader of the S.K.A.T. business, and stepfather, it now turned out, of Mary MacPherson on whose boat he had recently sailed around the Hebrides.

'Of course,' he said, pulling a chair half-out from his table. 'Come and sit down, Dugald. I expect you've had breakfast. Coffee?'

Dugald MacLeod sat down stiffly, taking the proffered cup of coffee.

'Thanks, Mr Tallyforth,' he said hesitantly. 'I'm not so sure I ought to come and talk to you but there's been one or two things been bothering me about this lassie's murder.'

Tallyforth looked at him keenly. Was this the breakthrough they had been waiting for? Was this going to be the significant piece of information that moved them forward? Was Dugald MacLeod about to provide him with the missing piece of the jigsaw?

'No, no,' he said. 'That's quite alright. You just tell me whatever you want. Anything at all. You never know in these cases what may prove to be significant, however tiny it seems at the time.'

Dugald sipped from his coffee, then leaned his elbows on the table and lowered his voice.

'Mr Tallyforth,' he tried again, 'I've to tell you about my family. I know you've met Hamish, from the post office. He's my only son and I'm very proud of him. I brought him up myself from when he was two, after his mother died, till he was nine, when I wed again. My second wife had a daughter that I took in but things didn't work out and she left us to live with her aunt and uncle in Uig. That was Mary. Willie MacPherson's wife, Mary. You were going on their boat trip.'

'Yes, I know all that,' said Tallyforth impatiently.

'Aye, well,' continued Dugald MacLeod, 'and you'll no doubt be aware that Willie had a wee bit of trouble earlier in his life?'

'Yes, we know all about that too.'

'I have to tell you, Mr Tallyforth, that Willie has been a good husband to Mary,' Dugald said. 'He's never given her an ounce of bother since they got wedded and he's stayed off the drink all these years. He's a good man, Mr Tallyforth. I know you had to investigate him because of what's happened but I swear to God you've the wrong man if you still think that Willie killed that lassie.'

Tallyforth sucked in his breath and toyed with piece of toast on his plate.

'So who do you think did it, Dugald?' he asked.

Dugald MacLeod sat back in his chair and let his arms fall down by his sides.

'I don't know, Mr Tallyforth,' he said quietly. 'I'm not a detective. I used to know old Inspector MacLean before he retired this year and he wasn't a detective either but he had a theory that dogs always return to their own vomit afterwards.'

'Hm?' Tallyforth looked at him.

'He thought that real criminals who thought they'd got away with a crime couldn't resist coming back to watch what was happening,' Dugald explained. 'He said he'd known many cases where he'd found it useful to remember that. Maybe that's what you need to do, Mr Tallyforth.'

A look of understanding passed across Tallyforth's face. Maybe Dugald MacLeod was right. Maybe they needed to stage a reconstruction of the murder and see who turned up. He sat back in his chair, musing thus.

Dugald MacLeod stood up.

'Aye, well, Mr Tallyforth, I just thought you ought to know about Willie and Mary,' he said. 'Now I've work to do. You'll maybe like a look at the *Free Press*?'

He handed Tallyforth a copy of that week's edition of the *West Highland Free Press*, published that Friday, then left the dining room.

Tallyforth opened the newspaper and flicked quickly through the pages. Much of what he saw related to local issues he knew nothing about, inevitably, though he read with interest that the expectation regarding the reduced rate for islanders using the Skye Bridge was that this would not come into force until the return of parliament after the summer recess. He also read of the Secretary of State's talks with leaders of the Western Isles Council, in which he reassured them that the devolution proposals would secure the unique characteristics of the culture of the Hebrides and give the islanders greater say is such issues as fishing rights, forestry control, Gaelic broadcasting, and the redevelopment of crofting.

He had almost finished skimming through the newspaper, when his eye was taken by an article on the back page which startled him.

Skye lawyer under investigation over land purchase

A Skye solicitor is currently under investigation by the Law Society of Scotland because of allegations made by a former client that he defrauded her in the matter of a land purchase undertaken in her name some five years ago.

The woman, Mrs Eileen Farquharson of Stirling, alleges that the solicitor, Mr Iain McMillan of Portree, was engaged by her to effect the purchase of farming land and buildings in the Kirriemuir area in 1991. She alleges that delays in the purchase of these lands and properties were responsible for the value of the said lands and properties falling, so that when she came to inhabit them late in 1992, there was a need to spend large sums of money on raising them to acceptable standards.

Mrs Farquharson alleges that the cost to her of the delays in the purchase amounted to £300,000 and that she holds Mr Iain McMillan personally responsible. She states in her allegation that the delays were caused by an unacceptable slowness in responding to telephone calls from the vendor and the purchaser. She further states that Mr McMillan made verbal promises to her at the beginning of the transaction which he was subsequently unable to keep.

Mrs Farquharson further states that she is unable to sell the property in question until the Law Society has concluded its investigations. Mr Iain McMillan was unavailable for comment.

Tallyforth folded the newspaper and read the article again, then put the paper down on the table and emitted a long slow whistle.

Inspector Fraser's office at the Portree police station had only one early morning occupant and that was George Elliott, who had come in early to see if Steve Anthony's promise of a copy of the tape from Cassie Dillon's answerphone had been met. She had expected it to be so, for he rarely let her down, and sure enough a package delivered by special courier from London awaited her.

The early morning drizzle had forced her back into her blue denim jeans and jacket, although she now realised that the drizzle had been deceptive and it was a sultry warm day. She shed her jacket once in the office and searched for the tape recorder which Maggie Fraser had told her was kept in a cupboard. Once she had located it, she inserted the cassette and listened:

"Hi, Cassie, this is Rose. I'm just ringing to ask if you still have Angela's number. I've lost it somewhere. Call me, please."

A woman's voice, George Elliott noted, reminding herself. Sounded like a friend. No apparent mystery. She clicked the 'on' button again:

"Miss Dillon, I'm just ringing to check what you're doing about travelling up to Portree for the cruise and what time you'll be arriving. We've arranged for a room at the Royal Hotel by the harbour for you to change before dinner. Ring if you've any problems."

Definitely Willie MacPherson, she thought, even though she still hadn't met him. But now she knew all about the intended cruise, *The Flodigarry*, and its owners, it could only have been Willie MacPherson. So, again, nothing odd or mysterious about that message. She listened again:

"Cassie, you know who. Hope all is well. Be nice to see you again soon. I've put the parcel in the post. You should get it in plenty of time. Take care."

Male voice, deep and throaty. Vaguely American. Could, just possibly, be disguised. It was not a voice familiar to her, but she had not yet met everyone concerned. But someone who was expecting to see the dead woman soon and yet had put a parcel in the post to her. That didn't sound like someone who knew of her trip, for surely anyone close would have known that she was going to be away from home for three weeks, what with the week in Oban followed by the two-week cruise of the Hebrides. So why say that she would get the parcel in plenty of time? Plenty of time for what?

Of course, there was a simpler explanation, one less mysterious. The caller might have been hoping to see her again soon, rather than expecting to. And the parcel that she would get in plenty of time might be nothing more than what it sounded like - a gift, perhaps, or a returned loan that she had wanted for some future activity. It wasn't difficult to think of possibilities - an item of clothing wanted for a special event, a birthday present, a book or C.D., anything.

And then there was the possibility that the message had been deliberately left after Cassie Dillon had set off to go to Scotland, for she could access those messages at any time. And maybe the parcel, whatever it contained, was not on the way to Tamworth but to somewhere else, Oban maybe or even Portree itself, for her to collect.

George Elliott decided to play the other two messages, and then return to this one, which had been the most intriguing when she had first listened to the tape and was even more so now, as she considered the possibilities:

"Cassie, it's me again. Did you get my message? I'm still trying to get Angela's number. Have you got it?"

"Cassie, it's me again. It's Tuesday. I guess you must be away. I knew you were having a holiday soon but I didn't know when. Sorry. Ring me when you get back."

Definitely the same female voice as on the first message. That was Rose someone or other. There didn't seem to be any more to those three messages. And Willie MacPherson's call seemed straightforward enough. That left only the parcel-sender. She rewound the tape to find the third message again and re-played it:

"Cassie, you know who. Hope all is well. Be nice to see you again soon. I've put the parcel in the post. You should get it in plenty of time. Take care."

Now, George Elliott thought, just supposing that the parcel might have been going to Cassie Dillon somewhere during her trip - Oban or Portree seemed the likeliest. What might it have contained?

Might it, for example, have contained the camera with which they believed Cassie Dillon had taken those seven photographs of the Skye Bridge? If so, then it must have gone to Oban for the photographs had certainly been taken before she arrived in Portree. And if so, then that again implicated James Orr, since that was with whom she had been staying and presumably to whom the parcel had been addressed.

Or might it have contained something to do with Greenpeace? Might the unknown caller with the hoarse voice have been telling her of something she was to deliver to the Greenpeace activists at that moment harrying the seismic explorer vessels? Maybe that was what those crosses on the map were about? Maybe Cassie Dillon had to meet the activists from the *MV Greenpeace* to hand over something they needed for their campaign? But then, why so many crosses? How would she have known which one to get to? And how could she have got there from the cruise in *The Flodigarry*? And wouldn't the contents of this parcel have been discovered in the cabin she died in?

Or maybe there was a simpler explanation. Maybe it was all

perfectly explicable, perfectly innocent, perfectly insignificant. Maybe it was just a gift from a friend.

George Elliott had begun to dismiss the wilder of her conjectures, as she realised that they sounded like scenes from a Hollywood blockbuster. But she also remembered what Tallyforth had taught her, about hanging on to the threads that hovered in the air around any murder and which, of themselves, meant little but, when connected up in the correct way, led to a solution. The parcel-sender, the parcel-sender's voice and the parcel itself constituted such threads.

She removed the tape and switched off the tape recorder.

Tallyforth was walking determinedly, with the *West Highland Free Press* newspaper tucked under his arm, from the Royal Hotel along Wentworth Street when he almost bumped into Maggie Fraser as she came out of one of the small shops.

'Chief Inspector,' she said breathlessly, 'I didn't expect to see you!'

He stepped back a pace and looked sternly at her. She was dressed in a clean white shirt, black trousers and her peaked cap.

'What are you doing, Fraser?' he asked. 'I thought we'd arranged to meet at the station at nine this morning. There's work to be done.'

'Yes, I know that,' she said, composing herself now and taking his stern look. 'That's why I came here early. You remember that, when Sergeant MacKenzie collected the film with the seven photos of the bridge, the girl who had taken the film from the 'J. Smith' character was on her day off? Well, I thought, if I came down to the shop early, I'd catch her before they opened.'

'So?'

'So, Chief Inspector, I have just finished speaking to her.'

'And?' he asked in exasperation. 'Come on, woman, what have you found?'

She allowed herself a half-smile, for she had succeeded in needling him and, now she knew so much more about him from her conversations with George Elliott, she realised that this was not something to be anxious about but something to be triumphant about.

'Sir, the girl has described the person who signed 'J. Smith' on the back of the order form.'

'Go on! Go on!'

'The person concerned was a white male, aged about forty, and with only a slight Scots accent,' she said.

'That only eliminates fifty per cent of the population of Skye then!' Tallyforth said.

'That's not all, sir,' Maggie Fraser continued. 'The man concerned had a rather unusual hair style. He had a very low parting on the left with a long wave of lank blond hair over his forehead.'

'Like Bobby Charlton?'

'As you have said before, sir,' she answered then waited for him to make the connection.

'Orr?' he quizzed, cocking one eyebrow at her. 'Orr? Here in Portree? On Tuesday of this week?'

'Sounds like it, sir,' she replied, feeling quite pleased with herself for what she had discovered. 'What now?'

Tallyforth put both his hands into his jacket pockets and pondered briefly.

'We need to get Orr back here straightaway,' he said, setting off in the direction of Somerled Square and the police station. 'Can you spare someone to fetch him?'

Maggie Fraser strode alongside him.

'There's only Constable MacLean, sir,' she said, 'and he's still in Inverness waiting to bring Chief Inspector Gordon back here.'

'Call him,' ordered Tallyforth briskly. 'Call MacLean. Get him to go to Oban first and pick up this Orr character. Oh, and while he's at it, he'd better bring the woman with him. What was her name again, Inspector?'

'McMillan, sir,' she reminded him. 'Lindsay McMillan. Sister-in-law of the solicitor here in Portree.'

'Oh, yes!' said Tallyforth, holding the back page of the newspaper out to her. 'Have you read this?'

The three police officers were assembled in Maggie Fraser's office. Donald MacKenzie had brought them cups of coffee as requested. Tallyforth was pacing ferociously around the room, while George Elliott and Maggie Fraser sat behind the latter's desk, waiting for him to speak.

'Right!' he said at last, coming to a halt in front of them and slipping his jacket off his shoulders. 'I want to stage a reconstruction of last Sunday night. I want the MacPhersons and their boat. And I want it in the exact spot in the harbour it was in last Sunday night. Sergeant, I want you to take the deceased's place in the aft cabin. Inspector Fraser, I want you to take my place. The MacPhersons can play themselves.'

Maggie Fraser and George Elliott exchanged looks.

'Sir,' said George Elliott, who knew his moods from several years of working with him, 'what's the exact purpose of this? With what Maggie found out about Orr giving in the film to be developed, surely we've got our chief suspect. So what's the point of all this re-enactment?'

Tallyforth reacted sharply, pointing his index finger at her.

'Sergeant, you may have solved this case in your mind but there's still too many loose ends,' he said. 'Did you read that article about McMillan the solicitor?'

'Yes.'

'Curious coincidence, don't you think?' he asked.

Maggie Fraser nodded.

'But we already have him linked to Orr,' she said. 'It's his sister-in-law that Orr has as his alibi for last Sunday night, remember?'

He turned sharply in irritation.

'Of course I remember!' he said loudly. 'I can see all the connections. Of course I can. But what I can't see is why they connect and how they connect. If Orr is having an affair with McMillan's brother's wife, why should McMillan be in cahoots with Orr? You'd expect him to be agin him, wouldn't you? Isn't Scottish logic the same as English logic?'

Maggie Fraser looked slightly abashed at the ferocity of this attack.

'And, what's more, none of it makes any sense as regards the dead woman,' he continued. 'Inspector, you may well be right but we have to know more. I'm staging this re-enactment in order to flush out whoever is behind all this, so we understand what has happened and why. Got it?'

Maggie Fraser nodded.

'I think so,' she said.

217

'Good! Now, did you manage to get hold of that constable of yours?'

'Yes, Constable MacLean was just about to leave Inverness,' she answered. 'Apparently Chief Inspector Gordon had told him that he had no intention of returning to Skye today. So I've instructed him to come back via Oban. And I've got the Oban police to bring Orr and the McMillan woman in for him to pick up. They're not happy about taking orders from an English policeman but they are co-operating.'

'Good! How long will he be?' asked Tallyforth.

'It's a long journey, sir,' she replied. 'They won't be here till late afternoon.'

'So we have plenty time to stage this re-enactment,' he said. 'Inspector, I want you to get hold of the MacPhersons and organise them. Get *The Flodigarry* in position for eleven o'clock and we'll do it then. Sergeant, I want you to see if you can find someone fit, strong and nimble. You'll maybe find one of those athletes from the Games the other day.'

'What to do?' queried George Elliott, surprised at this latest twist.

'I need to see how possible it is for someone to row from the pier to the yacht, climb aboard, get into the aft cabin and leave the boat without disturbing anyone on board.'

'Oh,' she said. 'And where will you be?'

He looked sharply at her.

'I shall be on the pier,' he replied. 'Watching the re-enactment.'

'Is that all?' George Elliott asked, still thinking this exercise was a waste of time.

Tallyforth allowed himself a brief smile.

'Ever heard about dogs returning to their own vomit?' he asked mysteriously.

George Elliott looked at Maggie Fraser, who glanced towards the ceiling by way of response.

'Sir?' she asked.

'I shall be very interested in who else will be watching our little play-acting,' he said. 'Very interested indeed. Now, let's get to it.'

While Maggie Fraser had gone off down to the harbour to find the MacPhersons, George Elliott had asked Donald MacKenzie to find

218

someone to row the dinghy and climb aboard *The Flodigarry*. She had reasoned that the desk sergeant knew the people of the town far better than she did and he had been happy to accede to her request.

Meanwhile she had been puzzling more about the third message on Cassie Dillon's answerphone, the one from the parcel-sender. It wasn't so much the contents of the message that had been bothering her now but the accent of the speaker. She had suddenly realised that it was an accent with which she was familiar. When she had been at university in Swansea, one of her lecturers had been from Vancouver and he had had that same North American drawl. And then she had remembered that in the notes on the case she had been reading the day before there was a reference to the fact that Cassie Dillon had lived for some years in Canada.

Something was niggling her, so she had gone back to Maggie Fraser's house and logged on to the Internet on the computer, as she had been shown, and typed in 'Greenpeace Canada'. What she found was:

"Greenpeace was born in September 1971 when a group of concerned citizens sailed from Vancouver for the Aleutian Islands (off the west coast of Alaska) in protest against American nuclear testing. The group of activists never made it to the islands but their intention was so widely covered by the media, that one year later nuclear testing in Alaska was halted and the area was declared a bird sanctuary."

This was too much of a coincidence! Greenpeace! Vancouver! Cassie Dillon! And possibly the parcel-sender!

There was only one thing for it, whatever Tallyforth thought, and that was to get some help from Steve Anthony.

'Steve, it's George. I need some help. It's urgent,' she said into the phone, when she was finally put through to him in Edinburgh.

'Georgie girl, I'm in a meeting. Can't it wait?' he pleaded.

'No,' she said.

'Can't the great Sherlock solve it on his own?' he tried again.

'No, Steve, this is important. I know you're busy but I think I've hit on something very important. Can you get access to information on Canadian citizens?'

'Of course,' came the reply. 'Might take a little longer but can do. We still have our sources in the colonies, you know, sweetie. Thatcher used to use them for some of her social experiments. Who d'you want to know about?'

'It's that Dillon woman, the one who was murdered here in Skye. I think I've found a Canadian connection. Specifically Vancouver. Remember that lecturer at Swansea?'

'You mean Rowan Buck? I used to love his suede trousers.'

'Yes, that's the one. Well, all I've got is a voice with an accent like his. But the Dillon woman lived in Canada for some years. Can you do a trace on her there? Definitely a Greenpeace connection. See if there's any particular male associates.'

'Okay, sweetie. I'll do my best. Have to go now. Devolution blues. *Ciao!*'

SEVENTEEN

By eleven o'clock the sultriness of the early morning had been replaced by the heat of a summer's day much like those earlier in the week. Overnight puddles had dried, raindrops on cars had turned to streaks, and the sun shone from high in a blue sky.

The participants in the re-enactment of the murder scene had been gathered by Tallyforth at the end of the pier - George Elliott in white blouse and denim jeans, Maggie Fraser in her summer uniform, Willie MacPherson still in his denim jeans and tartan shirt, Mary MacPherson still in her short-sleeved blue cotton blouse and denim jeans, and two of the American students who had participated in the Highland Games earlier in the week. One of these was Tom, the black athlete who had won the arm-wrestling competition in the Royal Hotel the evening after the Games; he was six feet four, fifteen stone and powerfully built. The other was a man called Jake, who was only about five feet ten and twelve stone but was almost as powerfully built. Both of these wore black leotards only, at Tallyforth's request, for he wanted their movements to be as free as possible. The other two athletes stood in track suits near to them, though they were not to be used in the re-enactment. *The Flodigarry* lay alongside the end of the pier, ready for them to board.

Standing next to Tallyforth was Sergeant Donald MacKenzie who had been kitted out with a whistle to start and a stop-watch to time the various parts of the proceedings as detailed by Tallyforth.

'Right,' said Tallyforth, facing the others and addressing them as if they were a film set and he the director, 'we're going to try this out three ways, okay? I want Sergeant Elliott, Inspector Fraser and you, Willie and Mary, to get aboard *The Flodigarry* in a moment, take it out to the anchorage where it was on Sunday night and go into the cabins as I've explained. Then I want Tom here to row the dinghy out to *The Flodigarry*, climb aboard, go down the steps into the aft cabin, wait two minutes, then climb back out and return to the pier. Sergeant MacKenzie, I want you to time him out and time him back. Then we'll do the whole thing again with Jake here, okay? Then, I want you, Inspector Fraser, when you hear the whistle, to push open the hatch in the roof of your cabin, climb out and along the deck, go down the steps into the aft cabin and then back again. And those of you on board I want you to make a note of anything you hear at any time between the start and end whistles blown by Sergeant MacKenzie. Any questions?'

They looked round at each other. Mary and Willie MacPherson looked noticeably less comfortable than the other participants, for the obvious reason that the events of the previous Monday were still fresh in their minds and this exercise was bringing them vividly back alive, as, of course, was the intention. The two Americans grinned at each other and slapped hands in high five manner, for they had a private bet on as to which would complete the two trips out and back the fastest. George Elliott looked vaguely amused, for she had already decided that the exercise was futile and had forearmed herself with the copy of the *West Highland Free Press* discarded by Tallyforth in the station office earlier. At least that way she would have something to do while she sat around waiting for his silly games to end. Maggie Fraser rattled some loose change in her pocket. This was all new territory to her and, even though she shared many of George Elliott's misgivings, a part of her was fascinated to see how it all happened and with what result.

'Right then, ladies and gentlemen,' Tallyforth said, striding briskly over to the steps leading down the side of the pierhead to where *The Flodigarry* was fastened. 'Let's get this show on the road!'

Mary MacPherson led the way down the steps, followed by her husband Willie and Maggie Fraser, with George Elliott bringing up the rear. Once aboard, Willie started the engine and *The Flodigarry* slowly chugged out into the bay. When it had reached the spot where it had been moored the previous Sunday, Mary threw the anchor overboard and Willie turned off the engine.

Although it was mid-morning and the town was still busy with tourists, some of whom had stayed on after the Highland Games and others of whom were just arriving for the following day's Agricultural Show, at that moment an eerie silence seemed to fall across the bay.

Tallyforth looked up. High above him a sea eagle, wings outstretched in seemingly effortless flight, glided at speed across from one side of the surrounding hills to the other. It was all over in less than a second.

'Okay, Tom, are you ready?' shouted Tallyforth, then, seeing the large black athlete poised as if about to start a race, added, 'over to you then, Donald.'

Donald MacKenzie held his stop-watch out in front of him and blew his whistle, whereupon Tom sprinted to the steps, jumped down them in three strides, landed still upright in the dinghy and, scarcely breaking motion, rapidly rowed it out to *The Flodigarry* as if he were in a canoe. As he reached the yacht, he placed his paddle in the dinghy's hull, tied a mooring rope around his wrist and quietly pulled himself up on to the deck where he fastened the rope to a stanchion. He then crept stealthily along the deck to the steps for the aft cabin and descended to where George Elliott sat reading the *West Highland Free Press*. As his head disappeared, Sergeant Donald MacKenzie clicked his stop-watch. This first stage had taken two minutes and twenty seconds.

In the aft cabin, Tom grinned at George Elliott, who raised a finger to her lips to remind him of the need for silence. He was an extremely good-looking man, she noticed, as she watched the beads of perspiration forming on his broad shoulders.

Two minutes later and Tom was gone. As soon as his head re-appeared, Donald MacKenzie clicked the stop-watch and held it until the American athlete had completed the return journey. Then Donald MacKenzie blew his whistle again, to indicate that the first exercise was over.

'Any problems?' asked Tallyforth, handing a towel to Tom as he stood breathing heavily at the top of the pier steps.

Tom shook his head and grinned.

'Okay, then, Jake,' said Donald MacKenzie, turning to the smaller of the two athletes. 'Your turn. Same again.'

And Jake repeated the exercise undertaken by his compatriot, taking ten seconds longer on the outward journey but returning in ten seconds less, so that honour was even between the two of them.

Tallyforth had pulled away from the group on the pier and was standing a few yards further down Quay Street and looking back towards the town. He noticed that several people had appeared, as if from nowhere, to watch the proceedings, attracted no doubt by the whistle-sounds and then the sight of Donald MacKenzie in his uniform. As his eyes scanned these scattered people, Tallyforth noted that Dugald MacLeod stood with his son Hamish from the post office at the bottom of Quay Brae, and that the girl Annie, who had lent him the headset when he first listened to the Runrig album, was also there, standing just in front of them. He didn't recognise any of the other inquisitive watchers.

Donald MacKenzie watched the four Americans as they laughed gently with each other, then he stood upright and held out his stop-watch again as he remembered that there was one more activity that he had to time. He blew his whistle shrilly, bringing Tallyforth's attention back to *The Flodigarry*.

But nothing was happening. All was still on the boat and there was no sign of Maggie Fraser, who was supposed to have climbed through the hatch on to the deck, for at least two minutes. When she did appear, it was in the cockpit, where she stood waving at those gathered on the pierhead.

Something had clearly gone wrong, Tallyforth realised, as he saw Donald MacKenzie motioning to him to come back to the steps. He took one last look back towards the town, just long enough to notice the blond-headed figure of the solicitor Iain McMillan lean briefly towards Hamish and Dugald MacLeod to say something before turning away from them and disappearing up Quay Brae.

'Okay, Sergeant,' he called as he marched back to join Donald MacKenzie and the four Americans. 'Somebody had better take the dinghy out and bring them back, so we can find out what's happened. Let me have those timings, will you?'

Donald MacKenzie passed over his notebook and prepared to descend the steps himself, but was overtaken by the black athlete Tom who, quickly recovered from his first trip, was happy to take the dinghy out to *The Flodigarry* again.

'Well?' demanded Tallyforth of Maggie Fraser, the first to ascend the steps after Tom had rowed the five of them back to the pier. 'What happened?'

'I couldn't shift the hatch,' she said, shaking her head. 'It's stuck solid. Mary says it's not been opened for over a year, as far as she knows. My guess is that the wood's swollen.'

Tallyforth smiled grimly.

'So that clears one line of inquiry, yes, Inspector?' he asked, gazing pointedly at Maggie Fraser.

She looked away.

'Yes,' she said. 'Of course, though..... But I did hear something in the first try.'

'What?' Tallyforth asked.

'Yes, I heard something too,' chipped in George Elliott who had also now appeared.

'And we did,' added Mary MacPherson, while her husband nodded firmly beside her.

'What?' repeated Tallyforth in exasperation. 'What did you hear?'

'I heard Tom when he climbed out of the dinghy and on to the yacht,' said George Elliott. 'And I felt the boat move.'

'Aye, that's right,' said Mary MacPherson. 'I nearly fell backwards on my seat when he pulled himself up on the boat.'

Tallyforth mused on this information for a moment.

'But nothing when Jake came on board? You heard nothing? Felt nothing? Is that what you're saying?' he asked, scratching his earlobe.

All four shook their heads.

'How long did they take, Sergeant?' Tallyforth turned to Donald MacKenzie who held up the notebook that had been returned to him.

'Outward trip was between two minutes twenty and two minutes thirty. Return trip between two minutes forty and two minutes fifty,' he read out.

'So,' said Tallyforth, 'at most our mysterious assailant would have needed about five minutes, if he was as fit as these lads, to get to and from the boat. What about the cabin, Sergeant? Any observations?'

George Elliott looked at him from under arched eyebrows.

'The door opens very easily,' she said. 'Someone could have got in without making a noise. I certainly didn't hear Jake come on board, and I was wide awake, remember. And alcohol-free. Mind you, I did keep my clothes on!'

Tallyforth narrowed his eyes and looked back at the defiance in her eyes. Tom nudged Jake and they exchanged grins.

Tallyforth turned his back on the assembly and took a couple of paces before facing towards them.

'So,' he began, 'we know that someone of about twelve stone or less could have got to *The Flodigarry* from the pier and back in about five minutes without disturbing the sleeping inhabitants of the boat. Presumably he, or she, would not have needed more than a couple of minutes to strangle the victim and steal the camera.'

'There was maybe something else stolen,' interrupted George Elliott, holding up the copy of the *West Highland Free Press* which she had folded to show a particular item. 'You obviously didn't notice this in the Personal column, did you? Look! It says "Parcel ready for collection. JS." Curious, eh, sir.'

She stressed the 'sir' as heavily and sarcastically as she could, to remind him.

He took the newspaper and read where she pointed.

'So?'

'I had the tape this morning, if you recall. From the Dillon woman's answerphone. There was an odd message about a parcel being delivered. Remember? I did tell you but you were full of this reconstruction business,' George Elliott said witheringly. 'And Maggie thinks the J. Smith who gave the film in for development is Orr. Odd that this message is about a parcel and has the initials JS, don't you think, sir?'

There was a lengthy pause as Tallyforth took in this new information.

'Okay,' he said at last. 'So, you seem to know all the answers, Sergeant. Why don't you go and arrest someone?'

Tallyforth had left the others on the way back from the pier in order to call in at the post office in Quay Brae to speak to Hamish MacLeod, who came from behind the post office counter to the opposite end of the shop where it was less busy.

'Hamish, I'm sorry to bother you again,' began Tallyforth, 'but I wonder if you'd have a look at these photos and tell me if there is anything significant about them.'

As Tallyforth took the packet of photographs out of his pocket and prepared to spread them out on top of a shelf of stationery, Hamish fingered his yellow tartan tie nervously. He had thought that his involvement in this murder case had been over and was unsure why he was being dragged back into it. Presumably, he thought to himself, the police were still following a number of leads, since apparently no one had been arrested. Presumably that business down at the end of the pier a short while beforehand, with people rowing boats back and forth in the harbour, had been connected in some way. But why was the chief inspector wanting to talk to him? Was he trying to implicate him in some way?

'Now, Hamish,' said Tallyforth, after he had finally got all seven photographs precariously balanced, 'as you can see, these are all photographs of the infamous Skye Bridge. Does anything strike you about them?'

Hamish leaned his head forward to peer carefully at each of the photographs. He could see exactly where each had been taken from.

'That's the view from the pier in Kyleakin, that's from outside the post office in Kyleakin, that's from the toll on the Skye side and that's it from the other side. That one looks as if it's from back down the road towards Kirkton. And those two are from Lochalsh, one from the old pier and one from Kyle Hotel behind it, I would say,' he answered, pointing at each in turn.

'So does anything strike you as unusual about them?' repeated Tallyforth.

Hamish's ginger eyebrows lifted towards him, then he looked back at the photographs.

'Not really,' he answered after studying them again.

'You can't think of any reason why somebody should want to take seven photographs from different angles of the same object?'

Hamish scratched his bald head.

'Chief Inspector,' he said, 'we don't need photographs of the bridge from every possible angle in S.K.A.T. We have to live daily with the injustice of that monstrosity and the charges that are being

227

levied against us by the Anglo-Canadian bank that owns it. We don't need photographs because we carry the image of it in our heads all the time.'

Tallyforth sighed. He really didn't want to hear the political stuff again.

'So you wouldn't expect somebody who was a member of S.K.A.T. to be taking photographs like this?' he tried again.

'No! I can see no reason why,' said Hamish, shaking his head. 'As I said just now, we're all very familiar with the bridge. It looks to me like some tourist took them. But I've no notion of why someone would want so many from different angles. Sorry, Chief Inspector. Is that all you were wanting? I've work to do.'

Tallyforth looked around. He could see that the shop had filled up since his arrival and that Hamish MacLeod did certainly have work to do.

'Yes, that's fine, Hamish,' he said, collecting the photographs together and placing the them back into his jacket pocket. 'Sorry to have troubled you. If anything comes to mind, let me know, will you?'

Hamish nodded agreement, then held the door open for Tallyforth to leave the shop.

By the middle of the day the sun was blazing fully as it had earlier in the week and the heat had returned to the air. The town of Portree had also returned to the busyness of previous days, as the organisers of the Skye Agricultural Show began preparations for the following day's event out on the King George the Fifth playing field past the Community Centre. Lorries with metal pens for sheep, cattle, goats and horses were arriving from other parts of the island, as were vans with trade equipment and displays. The main traffic would, of course, not appear until the following morning when the livestock wagons arrived and their charges were dispersed into the various pens out on the playing field.

In the bar of the Royal Hotel, a group of young farmers from the mainland, who had come for the sheep-shearing competition on the following day, were demonstrating their technique on invisible sheep to the four American athletes who had been helping Tallyforth a short time earlier in the reconstruction.

In the Camanachd Bar in Somerled Square, solicitor Iain McMillan sat alone, dressed in a dark blue single-breasted suit, pale blue shirt and red tie. On the table in front of him was a glass containing gin and tonic and a copy of the *West Highland Free Press*, folded so the back page was uppermost. He was deep in thought, scarcely moving in his seat but his eyes looked heavy and there was a permanent frown on his brow.

In the post office Hamish MacLeod was taking a few minutes break from serving in order to enjoy a cup of coffee. He was sitting on a wooden chair, out of sight of the grille, drinking his coffee and reading from some handwritten papers. Tonight was to be a full meeting of the S.K.A.T. organisation and he had prepared a detailed speech for it. As he read, he occasionally made a minor change with a pencil. It was important for him to get this right.

In the police station Sergeant Donald MacKenzie was completing the weekly time sheets and ensuring that all the other paperwork was up to date. In the scurry of events that week, a lot of normal routines had been forgotten and, as he had explained to Inspector Fraser, the regular work didn't stop just because of this extraordinary case. Maggie Fraser too was becoming anxious to get back to ordinary routine. The excitement of the past few days had made her tired and she realised that part of the reason for this was that she had ceded control to Tallyforth and no longer felt in charge of the Portree police station. She sat in her office, smoking and pondering.

Out in the harbour, aboard *The Flodigarry*, Mary and Willie MacPherson sat in the cockpit and gazed out to the gently-lapping sea, saying little to each other. Privately each was wishing that they could go back to the previous Sunday night and start again, without Chief Inspector Tallyforth and without Cassie Dillon, but with two respectable and ordinary customers instead. They knew that this was impossible now, but there was no harm in remembering the trouble-free cruises of the past years and in hoping that future years would bring many more such. The business they had so carefully built had been threatened by the week's events, as had the stability of their relationship.

Tallyforth was leaning on the railings on Bank Street above the post office and also gazing out to sea. But his thoughts were not on any of these matters. His thoughts were clearly focused on the murder and what they now could surmise about the murderer and the murderer's motives. The forthcoming interview with this James Orr character and his woman would be, to say the least, interesting. He didn't expect it to produce the solution but he did anticipate that it would put them well on the way to such a solution. There were still too many loose ends floating about, too many threads that were unconnected and yet had to link somewhere.

He watched a couple of gulls diving into the harbour.

'So, who done it, sir?' asked George Elliott, coming up behind him and catching him off guard. Her voice was heavy with sarcasm. 'Haven't you found who murdered your girl-friend yet, sir?'

He turned on her furiously, almost feeling his hand rise to strike her, but then caught himself in time and leaned back on the rails, staring out to sea as he spoke to her and avoiding her eyes.

'Not yet, not yet,' he answered. 'But I will. And soon. And she wasn't my girl-friend, Sergeant. I've told you.'

'Oh, so it's 'Sergeant' again is it, sir?' she mocked him. 'What's happened to 'George'? Have you forgotten my real name again? So soon? It wasn't 'Sergeant' last night, was it?'

Tallyforth continued staring out to sea, even though George Elliott had now placed herself beside him leaning on the railings.

'George, can we leave this now?' he said quietly. 'This isn't the time or the place. And you know it. We've got a very nasty murder case to solve and we haven't been making a lot of headway.'

'So, aren't you glad to see me?' she persisted.

'Look,' he said, half-turning towards her, 'I've told you I'm glad you're here because we work well together. Though I have to admit I don't think we're being very together on this case so far. You seem keener to be talking to Inspector Fraser or that queer friend of yours.'

He had done it deliberately and she knew he had. Even so, it was difficult to hold her anger back.

'And why is that?' she mused aloud. 'Why is it, do you think, that we are not working as well together? Could it just be that the great detective isn't sharing things as well as he might? Or is there something else that's troubling him?'

'For God's sake, George!' he said loudly, turning now to face her.

'You know what the problem is. It should never have happened. I should never have let it happen. But it did happen and now it's over. I've told you. There's nothing more to talk about, as far as I'm concerned. It's over. Last night was a mistake too. I'm sorry. Really sorry. I'd hoped we could get back to working together because we work well together. You know that. Even 'Nobby' Clarke knows that. Everybody in the Mercian Police Force knows that. But, if you can't manage it, if you can't bury your personal feelings, if you can't hack it, then it would be better if you went back to Birmingham now.'

George Elliott listened to this outburst with a mixture of emotions - anger that he should be behaving this way, when the previous evening she thought she had shown him that he still had an emotional attachment to her, fear that he meant what he was saying, and simultaneously love for this curious mixture of boyishness and manliness that he showed. She knew she had got under that tough outer skin and knew that he needed to shed that skin at times, even though he thought that he needed to toughen that skin so that it became permanent.

'I'm staying,' she said at last, in a quiet voice. 'I'm staying here with you till this case has been resolved. But, remember, we still need to talk properly. This is only temporary. Okay?'

Tallyforth grunted and resumed his gaze out to sea.

'We'll see,' he said, non-committally. 'We'll see.'

EIGHTEEN

Maggie Fraser quickly sat up and stubbed out her cigarette as Tallyforth entered her office. Although he made no comment, his movements indicated that he was not in a good humour. He pushed the door closed behind him; he wafted smoke from her cigarette away from his face, wrinkling his nose in mock disgust; he opened the office window more widely and switched on the fan.

Maggie Fraser watched him as he did all this, at the same time straightening her blouse and tie and standing up.

'Anything new to report, sir?' she asked tentatively, hoping to engage him in conversation without having her head bitten off.

He grunted, sat down behind the desk in the seat she had occupied a few seconds earlier, moved some papers on the desk, but said nothing.

'Constable MacLean should be here soon,' she tried again, having moved to the other side of the desk.

Again Tallyforth grunted but said nothing.

'Can I get you anything?' she asked. 'Tea? Coffee? Anything to eat? I've not had any lunch yet. Shall I organise some sandwiches?'

He looked up at her and spoke for the first time.

'Inspector Fraser,' he said, in a voice that was tightly controlled, 'I may have misjudged you. I apologise. I can see now that you were doing your job and doing it well. When you tried to exclude me from this murder inquiry at the start of this week, I was rude to you and I tried to countermand you. I see now that was wrong of me. If I had been in your situation, I would have done exactly as you did.'

Maggie Fraser had frozen in her stance, as she heard what he was saying. What had made him change his view towards her?

True, since George Elliott had arrived, he had been much more co-operative and she had been happy to accept Chief Inspector Gordon's instruction that she let Tallyforth take command of the case. But she had not expected him to start apologising! What had caused this abrupt change of behaviour?

'So,' he continued, in the same tone of voice, 'I apologise. I was wrong. I was wrong to try to get my chief superintendent to support me against you; I was wrong to go behind your back to persuade Sergeant MacKenzie out there to show me that map; I was wrong to drag the MacPhersons off on that jaunt around the islands, when I knew that you would be wanting to interview Willie. And, now that we have been working together over the past couple of days, I can see that even more clearly.'

'That's alright,' she stammered, still taken aback by this odd behaviour. 'It doesn't matter now anyway.'

'So, Inspector Fraser, may I ask you something personal?' Tallyforth said, arching his right eyebrow in her direction.

'Y-yes,' she stammered again. What was he going to come out with?

'How old are you, Inspector?' he asked.

'Thirty two, sir,' she replied.

'Are you married?'

'No, sir.'

'Ever been?'

'No, sir.'

What was all this about? she wondered.

'Any intentions?' he continued.

'Sir?'

'Of getting married? Or of having children?'

'Not at present, sir,' she answered, colouring slightly.

'Not conscious of the old biological clock then?' he queried. 'Unlike someone I might mention.'

'Sir?'

'You know who I mean,' he sighed. 'Sergeant Elliott. I expect she's told you everything. We've just had another little incident, about an hour ago. Opposite the Royal Hotel.'

Maggie Fraser shuffled on her feet. She was beginning to feel uncomfortable.

'I'm sorry, sir,' she said, not knowing what else to say.

'Oh, for Christ's sake, Maggie,' Tallyforth suddenly cried out. 'Let's cut all this formal stuff, can we? I'm trying to tell you something. I've been a copper for over thirty years and a good one at that. But, maybe because I was a good one and wouldn't take short cuts, it cost me my marriage. I spent too much time working. Once you become a detective, normal hours just disappear. And I wanted to be good. No, I wanted to be the best. And the only way I could be the best was to go that extra mile. And that has a cost.'

'What are you telling me, sir?' Maggie Fraser asked, still not comfortable enough to drop the formalities, despite what he had said.

'I'm telling you, Inspector Maggie Fraser,' he continued with an exasperated sigh, 'that there is more to life than being a copper. It's too late for me. This is my life. I don't expect, and now I don't even want, anything other. This is what I do. This is what I am. But you are young enough not to get trapped into this. What I'm telling you is that at present you think you're doing so well - rapid promotion through the ranks, in charge of your own station at thirty-two. But one day you're going to ask yourself what else there is in life and, if you leave it too late, you'll find there is nothing else.'

She looked at him and noted that his eyes were cast down now, as if he were contemplating his own life more than advising her about hers.

'What has all this to do with Sergeant Elliott, sir?' she ventured.

Tallyforth took a long breath and exhaled slowly before replying.

'That's what George's problem is,' he said. 'Or rather Sergeant Elliott's problem. She's worked with me too long and she thinks it's all wonderful. She's come to love the pursuit, the investigation, the digging, the solving of the mystery. She's learned to get her kicks from this work, as I do, but she's young enough to still feel the biological clock ticking. And she thinks - and I don't say this is conscious, because I suspect it probably isn't - that she can satisfy both urges simultaneously. That's why what happened between us did happen. And that's why she can't let go. And that's why, really, she's here on Skye.'

'And what about you, sir?' Maggie Fraser asked, realising that he was reaching into territory which was difficult for him as well as for her.

'Mm?' he asked, looking up at her, as if he had forgotten she was there.

'Just supposing that you're right about Sergeant Elliott,' she said, aware that she was running the risk of arousing his anger, 'how do you explain your motives?'

'Sorry?' he said, still not catching on.

Maggie Fraser pulled up a chair and sat opposite him.

'If George is being driven by unconscious urges, as you say she is,' she said, leaning towards him and looking directly into his eyes, 'what are you being driven by?'

'What do you mean?' he asked. 'The male sexual urge doesn't have a time-limit. You know that!'

'That's not what I meant,' she continued, sitting back now and smiling thinly at him. 'I mean, what are you afraid of?'

Tallyforth looked startled.

'Me? Afraid?' he cried out. 'Don't be stupid, Inspector! I don't know what you mean.'

Maggie Fraser decided not to elaborate but she knew that what she had said had hit home. She stood up from her chair and smoothed her blouse.

'Now, sir,' she said, 'can I get you a drink and something to eat?'

Tallyforth's eyes flitted around the room, as if looking for somewhere to rest, before at length they settled on a gently-rising sheaf of papers blown by the fan.

'Yes, I'll have a coffee, thank you. Nothing to eat,' he said, sinking back contemplatively into his chair.

Constable MacLean had made rapid progress and brought James Orr and Lindsay McMillan to the Portree police station by three thirty that afternoon. They had been ushered, at Tallyforth's insistence, into Maggie Fraser's office, where they had been told to wait, watched over by Constable MacLean.

James Orr was dressed in the same brown tweed jacket with leather elbow patches and green canvas trousers that he had been wearing when Maggie Fraser had visited him earlier in the week and the long wave of lank blond hair that swept across his forehead was at that moment firmly in place. His companion, Lindsay McMillan, the wife of his colleague at the Oban Academy, Donald McMillan, was dressed in a knee-length pleated navy skirt and a high-necked green cotton blouse. She was a small, big-busted woman with tousled hair, aged thirty-four but appearing older, and was clearly still very distressed at having been brought in a police car from Oban to Portree to be interviewed without knowing what she was to be interviewed about.

Fortunately, the evening before her husband had rung to say that he and the children planned to stay until the weekend at his friends' house, so she hadn't had any difficult explaining to do but, throughout the journey in the back of the police car driven by Constable MacLean, she had been either close to or in tears, comforted by James Orr who had kept hold of her hand throughout the trip and who continued to hold her hand now.

Constable Robert MacLean, who had observed this behaviour through his driving mirror as they had travelled up the coast from Oban, watched them carefully now, though his face gave away no clue as to his own feelings.

After being left thus for about ten minutes, the trio's quietness was broken when the door was suddenly flung open and Tallyforth marched in, followed by Maggie Fraser and George Elliott. They sat down behind the desk facing James Orr and Lindsay McMillan, with Tallyforth seated between the two female police officers.

'Thank you, Constable, that will be all for now,' said Tallyforth, dismissing Constable MacLean from the room peremptorily before turning to the newcomers. 'Good of you to come, Mr Orr, Mrs McMillan. We appreciate your help. You've met Inspector Fraser, I think. This is Detective Sergeant Elliott of the Mercian Police Force. I'm Detective Chief Inspector Tallyforth, also of the Mercian Police Force. I expect you want to know why we've brought you here.'

'Chief Inspector,' began James Orr falteringly, 'we have come here willingly, despite the distress that you can see it has already caused Lindsay. We were told it was something to do with poor Cassie's death and anything we can do to help, we want to do it. Do you have some new information?'

'Just a minute, sir,' interrupted Tallyforth, 'I'm aware that you have come here voluntarily but there are a number of things we need to satisfy ourselves about. First of all, you were somewhat conservative with the truth when Inspector Fraser here spoke to you earlier this week, weren't you?'

'What do you mean?' asked James Orr, flicking his hair back out of his eyes.

'I think you know what I mean, Mr Orr,' said Tallyforth, 'but let me remind you. You told Inspector Fraser that you were with Mrs McMillan here throughout Sunday night, is that right?'

'Yes,' Orr answered, looking at Lindsay McMillan for support. She nodded her head.

Tallyforth turned his gaze on her.

'I understand, Mrs McMillan, that your husband's brother is a solicitor here in Portree, is that correct?' he asked her.

'Yes,' she almost whispered, unable to look him in the eye.

'Mrs McMillan,' Tallyforth tried again, 'we're not here to pass judgement on your private life. We just need to get to the truth of what happened to Cassie Dillon. Do you see much of your husband's brother? Are they close?'

'No,' she whispered again. 'No, Donald and Iain are not particularly close, even though there's only two years between them. Iain was always very ambitious, while Donald only ever wanted to be..........'

She stopped, choking on her words, as her emotions got the better of her.

'Go on,' urged Tallyforth. 'Take your time, there's no rush.'

Lindsay McMillan sniffed, blew her nose loudly into a paper tissue taken from her handbag, then sat up in her seat.

'When we married ten years ago, Iain was our best man and James was an usher. Donald was already teaching in Oban by then but Iain was still finishing his articles in Glasgow and we used to see him quite often on a weekend,' she explained. 'But, after he qualified and went to work in Stirling, we saw less of him. And that coincided with the birth of our two children.'

'So it was just a natural drifting apart?' suggested Tallyforth.

'At first, yes,' she replied. 'But Iain started to change then as well. He became very ambitious, he wanted to be rich and Donald couldn't understand that. Schoolteachers never get wealthy, as I'm sure you know, and Donald has no personal ambition. He just loves teaching youngsters.'

'You sound as if you admire him for that,' interrupted George Elliott, half-smiling at Lindsay McMillan as she looked up from her notes.

'Yes, I did...I do admire him,' came the reply.

James Orr looked sharply at her and she squeezed his hand.

'Chief Inspector, may I ask where this questioning is leading? What has all this got to do with poor Cassie's death?' he asked peevishly.

'Just a moment, sir,' replied Tallyforth. 'We'll come to you in a minute. Now, if you don't mind. Go on, Mrs McMillan.'

Lindsay McMillan blew her nose again but it was more of a nervous gesture this time.

'Chief Inspector, there are many people who would consider my husband to be the perfect man,' she said, her eyes watering as she spoke. 'He is a brilliant teacher and his pupils worship him, he is a wonderful father to our two children, and he cooks, does the washing and ironing, hoovers and dusts, cleans the toilet, mows the lawn, repairs anything that gets broken. And he finds time to be on the P.T.A., be in the choir at church, and run our local Neighbourhood Watch scheme.'

Maggie Fraser and George Elliott exchanged meaningful glances, which Lindsay McMillan noticed.

'You'll be wondering why I'm having a fling with someone else when I've got this paragon for a husband? Well, I'll tell you,' she said, sniffing and leaning forward towards the three police officers. 'He's a bore. James here has more excitement in his little finger than my husband has in the whole of his being.'

Maggie Fraser and George Elliott both turned to look at James Orr, wondering where this excitement was hidden, for it was not a quality they would have anticipated finding in the shabbily-dressed, middle-aged figure in front of them. Orr looked down at his knees in embarrassment as he sensed their curiosity.

'Mrs McMillan, did you know the deceased?' asked Tallyforth suddenly.

'I had met Cassie Dillon a couple of times, I think,' Lindsay

McMillan replied.

'And it didn't bother you that she was staying with your friend Orr last week?'

'No! Why should it? She was a friend of James. It wasn't a problem.'

'You weren't jealous of her at all, were you, Mrs McMillan?' probed Tallyforth, scratching his ear-lobe.

'No! Not at all,' she said, staring straight back at him. 'They were at university together. She was an old friend. That's all it was. I know James well enough to know when he's telling the truth.'

'And you are quite sure that you spent the whole of the night on Sunday last with Mr Orr?' asked Tallyforth.

'Yes,' she said, looking down at the floor.

'At his house?'

'Yes.'

'And what time did you leave there on the Monday?'

'I didn't,' she replied, looking in embarrassment at James Orr for confirmation. 'We stayed in all that day. We went into town the next day to do some shopping and had some lunch there, then we went for a walk down along the front. James wanted to take the boat across to Mull for the afternoon but I didn't think it was worth it, even though the weather was fine.'

'So you were together on Monday night as well?' asked Maggie Fraser. 'You didn't tell me that when I spoke to you the other day.'

'You didn't ask,' replied Lindsay McMillan.

'So how do you explain the fact that Mr Orr was seen giving in a film to be developed at a shop in Portree here on Tuesday morning?' asked Tallyforth.

James Orr and Lindsay McMillan both sat bolt upright in their chairs and looked first at each other and then at Tallyforth.

'What?' said Orr in a strangled voice.

'You were seen handing in a film to be developed here on Tuesday morning,' repeated Tallyforth. 'And we have reason to believe that that film was taken from a camera which had been in the possession of Cassie Dillon when she was murdered.'

'But that's impossible!' said Lindsay McMillan, her voice rising as she sought to defend her lover. 'We were in Oban. Together. I've just told you that.'

'He was seen, Mrs McMillan,' repeated Maggie Fraser. 'Here in Portree. You're just covering up for him.'

'That's not true,' Lindsay McMillan said, defending herself. 'We were in Oban all the time.'

'Yes, that's right,' said James Orr firmly. 'It wasn't me, Chief Inspector. I was with Lindsay.'

'Sir, you won't mind me saying but you have a rather unique hairstyle and the shop assistant's description clearly fits you. Can you explain that?' asked Tallyforth.

'No, I can't, Chief Inspector,' said James Orr angrily. 'But I know it wasn't me. I was with Lindsay. In Oban. All that time. It couldn't have been me.'

'So you keep telling us, sir,' observed Tallyforth dryly.

'James's hair style may be unusual, Chief Inspector,' said Lindsay McMillan, 'but it's not unique. He's not the only man who uses that hairstyle to cover his hair loss, is he?'

'Can you prove that you were in Oban?' asked George Elliott, looking up from her notes. 'Any witnesses who saw you? Any tickets or bills?'

'Yes, wait a moment!' said Lindsay McMillan and she reached into her handbag, where she ferreted around until she found what she was looking for. 'There! That's our shopping bill from Tesco's.'

She held the bill out towards the police officers. George Elliott took it and examined it.

'Yes, it has the date and time on it,' she said. 'But that only places one of you in Oban on Tuesday. It doesn't prove that both of you were there.'

Lindsay McMillan's face fell.

'You didn't keep the bill from that café we had lunch in, did you, Lindsay?' said James Orr, suddenly remembering.

She again reached into her handbag and eventually found another bill, which she passed over.

'This tells us that two people ate at this café,' said Maggie Fraser. 'At lunch time. It doesn't prove it was you two.'

'They'd remember us, I'm sure,' said James Orr. 'I knocked a glass off the table and it broke. You could check.'

'Okay, let's all relax,' said Tallyforth, who had been watching the two of them carefully during this exchange. 'We will check. Now let's suppose you're right. Then who was it who handed in that film to be developed? And why did that person resemble you so closely?'

George Elliott had been called out of the interview with James Orr and Lindsay McMillan by Sergeant Donald MacKenzie, who informed her that there had been a telephone call for her from the Scottish Office in Edinburgh and gave her a number to call back.

She thanked him and went to an empty room to phone Steve Anthony.

'Steve? News?'

'Hi, Georgie girl! How's criminality? Still giving you a hard time?'

'Come on, Steve! Have you found anything? They told me you'd called but you hadn't left a message. You must have something!'

'Alright, sweetheart, I've traced the good ship Cassandra. You were right. She did live in Vancouver. Was there for nearly twelve years. Emigrated in nineteen seventy-nine after Thatcher got in. Married a man called Benedict Dillon.'

'So?' she interrupted impatiently. 'What's the significance of all that?'

'Hold on, sweetie,' came Steve Anthony's reply. 'Just coming to the juicy part.'

'Go on!' she insisted.

'Okey dokey. Well, this Benedict Dillon is one of the big cheeses in Greenpeace. He's a few years older than she was. He was one of the original group that sailed from Vancouver in nineteen seventy-one to the Aleutian Islands off Alaska to protest against American nuclear testing.'

'I know about that,' she said. 'That's how Greenpeace started.'

'Correct, sweetheart! That was like being on *The Mayflower* for Greenpeace,' he answered. 'Now, hear this! Benedict Dillon is one of the senior executives responsible for co-ordinating world-wide policy for Greenpeace. He would certainly have known about and probably been involved in the outline planning for that spat in Rockall recently and the current activity in the Atlantic.'

'But she was divorced from him, wasn't she?' asked George Elliott.

'There is no record of a divorce,' replied Steve Anthony. 'Sweetie, whatever story she told the great Sherlock was not the whole truth. At the time of her death she was still married to the aforesaid Benedict.'

'But I don't get it,' said George Elliott. 'What was she doing in England then? She's supposed to have been here for the past six years, working in Tamworth.'

'She probably has been,' he said. 'For part of the time at least. To establish some sort of cover for herself.'

'But why?'

'I don't know but listen, there's something else you ought to know.'

'Go on.'

'When I was talking to my friend Hamish MacLeod, whom I assume you have met, I got interested in this Skye Bridge business and I've been doing a little bit of digging of my own.'

'Go on, Steve! Tell me!'

'The Anglo-Canadian Bank, which is the actual owner of the Skye Bridge, is also known as OilCan.'

'OilCan! Who are they?'

'They're the oil company that has recently acquired the largest dollop of the Atlantic Ocean off the west coast of Scotland for oil exploration.'

He paused to allow her time to take this in.

'Say that again,' she said.

'Okay, sweetie, listen carefully. The people who own the Skye Bridge are the same people who are searching for oil in the Atlantic. And that's the people your Greenpeace protesters are currently trying to stop. Got it?'

'I have to tell Tallyforth,' she said suddenly. 'This has to be all connected. Steve, you're wonderful. Speak to you soon.'

She hung up and dashed back into Maggie Fraser's office.

Tallyforth, sensing that she was not overacting but had something really important to tell him, had left Maggie Fraser with James Orr and Lindsay McMillan and followed his sergeant out of the room.

'The dead woman wasn't divorced,' she blurted out. 'She was still married. Her husband's a very big noise in Greenpeace, based in Canada. He would have planned the action in the Atlantic.'

'You sure?' Tallyforth quizzed. 'I don't need to ask where you got this from!'

'It was that voice on the tape,' she said. 'Once I'd realised it sounded just like one of our lecturers from university who was from Vancouver, I had to involve Steve. He was at Swansea with me, remember.'

'So you think the message about the parcel was from her husband?' he asked.

'I'm sure of it,' she replied. 'Steve reckons she's been creating an identity here in England for several years but in reality has been involved in Greenpeace activities and was preparing for a major Greenpeace mission here in the Hebrides. The parcel must have been the camera!'

'A bit far-fetched all this, isn't it?' he asked, scratching his head.

'That's not all,' she said. 'Ever heard of OilCan?'

He shook his head.

'Stands for Oil Canada apparently, though it's a totally private outfit. They're one of the groups investing in the seismic exploration of the Atlantic. You know they're predicting that there could be two hundred years of oil under the Atlantic, don't you? And, just remember, we've virtually used up the whole of the North Sea oil reserves in thirty years.'

'So?' he pressed.

'OilCan is also the Anglo-Canadian Bank,' she explained. 'They own the Skye Bridge.'

He whistled softly to himself. There was a lengthy pause as he took all this in and weighed it with what they already knew.

'I think we can let those people in there go home,' he said at last. 'It's all making sense now. And it has nothing to do with James Orr and his lady friend. Tell Inspector Fraser for me, will you?'

NINETEEN

When Constable MacLean and Sergeant MacKenzie had entered his office in Wentworth Street late that Friday afternoon, Iain McMillan had been shredding papers. He had stopped as the two police officers had come through the door and he had put up no resistance when Donald MacKenzie had asked him to accompany him to the police station where Chief Inspector Tallyforth wanted to interview him. Nor had he protested when told that Constable MacLean was to remain in his office to guard the premises.

When Donald MacKenzie ushered him into the room where Tallyforth, Maggie Fraser and George Elliott sat awaiting him, it was noticeable that Iain McMillan's normally assured manner had disappeared. His appearance was as immaculate as ever - he wore the same dark blue suit, pale blue shirt and red tie he had been wearing all of that Friday. His blond hair was as neatly parted in the middle as ever and fell down equally on either side of his forehead. But the pallor of his skin was not the healthy hue that it normally was and he had developed a noticeable tic in his right eye.

'Thank you for coming to see us, Mr McMillan,' Tallyforth began, as the solicitor sat down opposite them and Donald MacKenzie left the room. 'I think you know what this is all about?'

Iain McMillan sought to compose himself, taking his gold-rimmed half-glasses from his breast pocket and balancing them carefully on the bridge of his nose.

'Sergeant MacKenzie said you wanted to talk to me,' he replied, his voice gradually gaining strength as he sought to recapture his confidence. 'In connection with the death of the woman, Ms.

Dillon.'

'That's correct,' said Tallyforth. 'Would you like to tell us all you know?'

'Only what everyone else knows, I imagine,' blustered the solicitor.

'No, I think you know a lot more than everyone else knows, Mr McMillan,' said Tallyforth, gazing steadfastly at him.

'What do you mean?' asked Iain McMillan, still attempting to bluster.

'Alright, Mr McMillan,' said Tallyforth, 'I can see that you are not going to do this the easy way, so let me take you through what I understand.'

Iain McMillan crossed his legs and looked at Tallyforth over the top of his glasses.

'Let's begin at the beginning, shall we?' continued Tallyforth, as he reached for the copy of the *West Highland Free Press* from the desk in front of him. 'No doubt you saw this article?'

Iain McMillan nodded as Tallyforth held up the back page of the newspaper in front of him.

'And I take it that substantially the article is true? And you are being sued for three hundred thousand pounds?'

'Yes,' answered Iain McMillan.

'And would I be correct in surmising that this Mrs Farquharson has a strong case against you?'

The solicitor nodded.

'And you are already substantially in debt because of what you had to pay to buy yourself into this partnership here in Portree? Is that a reasonable surmise too?'

Iain McMillan's face had become totally drained of colour and the tic in his right eye had increased in frequency.

'I don't see what my financial circumstances have to do with the death of Ms. Dillon!' he protested, forcing himself to maintain his bluster as long as possible.

'I was coming to that,' said Tallyforth. 'Sergeant Elliott, just remind us of the information you discovered today, would you?'

The solicitor's gaze moved to George Elliott.

'It would appear, sir, that the Anglo-Canadian Bank, which is the company that owns the Skye Bridge, is also known as OilCan, or Oil Canada, which is one of the major companies exploring the Atlantic sea off north-west Scotland for oil,' she said.

'What has all this to do with me?' asked Iain McMillan.

'I think you know very well what all this has to do with you, sir,' argued Tallyforth. 'I shall be very surprised if the search of your office currently being conducted by Sergeant MacKenzie and Constable MacLean - and don't worry, they have a search warrant - doesn't find that you are in considerable debt to the Anglo-Canadian Bank. Did they ask you to do some work on their behalf in order to defray some of that debt, Mr McMillan?'

'What do you mean?' asked Iain McMillan, though his pale features and the still-increasing tic told that he knew exactly what was coming next.

'You were asked to infiltrate S.K.A.T., weren't you, Mr McMillan?' said Tallyforth. 'You were asked to keep an eye on the activities of the anti-toll protesters here on Skye and to keep the bank informed of those activities. At the same time you were to ensure that their protests continued for as long as possible and that the islanders paid little or no attention to the oil exploration that was beginning out in the Atlantic and which will have a profound impact on these islands in years to come. At no time were the islanders to make any connection between the building of the Skye Bridge and this oil exploration. Am I right?'

Maggie Fraser had turned towards Tallyforth as she heard this and her mouth had dropped slightly open in amazement. How had Tallyforth worked all this out? She looked over towards George Elliott, who smiled smugly back.

Iain McMillan's head had fallen forward and he stared down at his knees, no longer able to face his accuser.

'I see you don't contradict me, Mr McMillan,' continued Tallyforth. 'So let me change tack slightly. You knew that your brother's wife, Lindsay McMillan, was having an affair with James Orr, didn't you?'

It was George Elliott's turn to show surprise now. She dropped her pen on the floor as she heard Tallyforth ask this question of the hapless solicitor.

'Yes,' came the rather faint reply from Iain McMillan, who had realised now that Tallyforth knew all. 'Donald phoned me last week to say that he had discovered about Lindsay's affair with Orr. He hadn't challenged her about it at that stage. He told me he was planning to take the children to stay with friends for a period to give himself time to think about what he was going to do. I hadn't heard from him for quite some time before that call. We weren't that close, so for him to ring me showed how desperate he was.'

'He rang you from Oban?'

'Yes.'

'And that wasn't the only phone call you had from Oban last week, was it, Mr McMillan?' pressed Tallyforth, his eyes ablaze now as he moved in for the kill.

Iain McMillan could only shake his head to signify that Tallyforth was correct.

'You also had a phone call from Cassie Dillon, didn't you, Mr McMillan?'

The solicitor nodded, his face now ashen and the tic in his right eye regular and fast.

'And she told you that she was from Greenpeace and that she had proof that you were in the pay of the Anglo-Canadian bank and were being used by them to infiltrate S.K.A.T. and to distract attention in the Hebrides from the activities of their OilCan ships conducting seismic explorations out in the Atlantic Ocean. Correct?' asked Tallyforth.

The solicitor nodded again.

'And she also told you that she was on her way to Portree and would show you the proof she had. Correct?'

A further nod confirmed Tallyforth's suspicions.

'And that was when you had the most amazing stroke of luck, wasn't it?' insisted Tallyforth. 'You dialled to find out the number she was ringing from then phoned that number and James Orr answered, giving his name. What a piece of fortune! You must have thought God was truly on your side. Here was this man, this James Orr, who was having an affair with your brother's wife and at the same time, or so you imagined, having an affair with this woman from Greenpeace, this Cassie Dillon, who was threatening to blow your cover.'

George Elliott sat back in her chair and tapped her pen on her notebook. She looked across at Maggie Fraser and shrugged her

247

shoulders, as if to show that she had never heard any of this before either.

'So, there you were last Sunday, believing that a woman was due to arrive in Portree who was sleeping with the man responsible for ruining your brother's life and who was also about to ruin your life,' continued Tallyforth. 'You had only one way to act. You had to get rid of her to protect yourself, and hope that Orr would get the message. But you didn't know what this Cassie Dillon looked like or precisely when she was intending to arrive in Portree. And that was when you had your second piece of enormous fortune, wasn't it?'

Maggie Fraser's mouth was half-open again as she listened. She was intrigued by this story that Tallyforth was concocting and yet which Iain McMillan was constantly corroborating.

'The MacPhersons had booked a room for Cassie Dillon and a room for me at the Royal Hotel on Sunday evening for us to change before our cruise in *The Flodigarry*. You knew nothing about this, of course, but you did know you were dining in the Royal that same evening, with Dugald and Hamish MacLeod. You saw the MacPhersons eating dinner with a man and a woman you didn't know. The man was me, of course, as you subsequently discovered, and I suspect if you had known then precisely who I was you might have acted differently. But anyway, be that as it may, you had no way of knowing. But you did discover our names, by the simple expedient of looking in the hotel's guest book as you left that evening. I noticed you go before the others and stop at the reception desk.'

He paused for effect, letting his words sink in. Iain McMillan's body had slumped in his chair and his chin rested on his chest as he waited for what was to come next.

'So you found that the woman who had threatened to expose you was in Portree, was about to go on a cruise in the MacPhersons' boat, *The Flodigarry*, and would be sleeping there that night, and had not, of course, recognised you,' explained Tallyforth. 'Do you work out, Mr McMillan?'

The solicitor nodded.

'Think of yourself as fairly fit, do you?'

Another nod.

'What weight would you be, approximately? Twelve stone?'

'Eleven and a half,' came the faint reply.

'I think you noted our little reconstruction this morning, Mr McMillan. I saw you talking to the MacLeods,' continued Tallyforth, his voice becoming more angry now, though it was still controlled. 'Dugald MacLeod was right - a dog always returns to its own vomit. You just couldn't resist it, could you? We established how easily a fit person of twelve stone or less could have rowed out to *The Flodigarry*, strangled Cassie Dillon, and rowed back to shore in a short space of time and without disturbing any of the others on board the yacht. It would have been a matter of less than ten minutes. And that was what you did, wasn't it?'

There was no response from the solicitor, who sat totally still in front of them, gazing blankly at the floor.

Tallyforth glared ferociously at his slumped figure.

'You killed her, didn't you, McMillan? You got into her cabin, you held your hand over her mouth and you strangled her with her own silk scarf. She never even woke up to see you, did she?'

The solicitor still didn't move.

'Didn't you, you bastard?' shouted Tallyforth, standing up from his chair. 'You killed her, didn't you? Didn't you?'

George Elliott and Maggie Fraser each reached out a hand to touch either arm of Tallyforth, frightened that he was losing control in his anger. He brushed them both off and leaned forward menacingly towards Iain McMillan. He could see the naked body of Cassie Dillon, could sense the coldness of her nipples still.

'Then you unzipped her sleeping bag to make it look as if there had been some sexual link to her murder. You were trying to implicate me, weren't you, McMillan? You wanted people to think that this other man on board the boat had done her in, didn't you?'

There was a lengthy pause as Tallyforth glared at his victim, then gradually his anger got under control again and he sat back in his chair.

'And then you stole her camera, because you thought it might have the evidence against you that she'd spoken of, didn't you?' persisted Tallyforth in a voice that was tight with emotion. 'And two days later you gave the film in to be developed but you gave a false name and you weren't recognised because you wore your hair in an unusual style, didn't you? You had found out by now who I was and you'd decided to try to implicate James Orr in Cassie Dillon's murder, so you brushed your hair in a way that replicated Orr's hair-style, am I right?'

Iain McMillan gave a perfunctory nod.

'Inspector Fraser, he's ready to give a statement,' said Tallyforth, standing up and moving around the desk. 'You know what to do. Read him his rights, though if anyone should know them it should be a solicitor. Then charge him. I've seen enough of the bastard.'

Tallyforth momentarily stood over Iain McMillan's slumped figure and for a second it looked as if he might strike him. George Elliott was even half out of her seat to restrain him. But the second passed and Tallyforth turned away from the solicitor with a look of complete disgust on his face, then reached for the door handle.

Aitreabh An Eilein, the Portree Community Centre, was already filling up at seven fifteen that Friday night. The general meeting of the Skye and Lochalsh Against the Tolls organisation had been well advertised and there was a sense among the community that this evening's meeting was especially important, partly because people believed that further action was to be proposed and partly because rumour had it that there had been a significant development. And once rumour gets hold of a people, they will not rest until they have ascertained the truth of it.

The rhythmic sounds of Runrig's *Long Distance* album boomed out of the loudspeakers in the hall of the Community Centre. In the entrance lobby stood Dugald MacLeod, greeting all arrivals as they came through the doors. He was dressed for once not in his formal hotelier's outfit but in his clan tartan kilt and a black jacket. Dugald was one of the oldest members of S.K.A.T. and, because of the status of the Royal Hotel which attracted varying groups from business and commerce for meetings and conferences, he knew large numbers of people on Skye.

Behind him stood Mary and Willie MacPherson, attending their first S.K.A.T. gathering, for, as the previous few days had unwound, they had come to realise more and more that their business interests coincided very closely with the interests of the community at large.

A new political awareness had grown in them and they were eagerly looking forward to what they would discover about S.K.A.T.

Beside them but turned away from them, his back to the incoming people, stood Hamish MacLeod, nervously clutching a sheaf of papers. He was wearing his usual green corduroy trousers, tweed jacket and bright green shirt with the yellow tartan tie. But tonight was to be Hamish's night and the nervous energy he was expending as he waited for the meeting to commence would be well worth it. Tonight he was to address the gathering about the future and the news recently passed on to him by Sergeant Donald MacKenzie had only succeeded in making him more enthusiastic to speak publicly to his fellows.

As half past seven approached, Dugald MacKenzie ushered Willie and Mary MacPherson into the hall along with the last few arrivals. Then he turned towards his son Hamish.

'Are you feeling fine then, son?' he asked. 'You've a good turn-out to hear what you have to say. I've no doubt you'll have them eating out of the palm of your hand. Are you ready then? Time to get started.'

'Yes, father, I'm ready,' replied Hamish, gritting his teeth and turning towards the doorway leading into the hall.

And then he swept through the doorway and marched up the aisle between the rows of chairs up to the platform at the end, his jacket flying behind him. As he climbed on to the platform, his audience quietened.

'Friends,' he began, 'this is a very important night for us all. Tonight we celebrate the success of our campaign, which has become a symbol of everything that every Scot has ever wanted. Freedom! Freedom from the English yoke! Freedom to control our own lives and our own destiny! I believe that the fight begun by Bonnie Prince Charlie and the clan chiefs in seventeen forty-five and those brave ancestors of ours, who were so cruelly murdered by the English at Culloden, is about to be won at last. And history will show that we were at the forefront of that fight; we, the people of Skye, are in the vanguard of that fight. I am proud to stand here in front of you tonight, as your representative, the representative of a people who will be free!

There was a short burst of applause.

'Tonight I have some very important news for you about S.K.A.T. and I have proposals to put to you about what action we should take next in our campaign. For, remember, our campaign does not end until those tolls are ended for ever!

'Let's just remind ourselves what S.K.A.T. has achieved before we look to the future.

'Firstly, we showed that the whole tendering process for the bridge was a stitch-up. Some of the prospective bidders, including the Skye Bridge Corporation which was a front organisation for the Anglo-Canadian Bank, had information about the project specifications almost a year before the others. And the way the specifications were drawn up was unduly favourable to this Skye Bridge Corporation, because of its friends in the Scottish Office. And I know now of some reasons why that was so but I'll save those for later.

'Then there was the intention that the bridge would be privately financed, which meant that the Skye Bridge Corporation could legitimately levy tolls in order to recoup its outlay. We showed that the Tory government gave fifteen million pounds to the project and another twelve and a half million came from Europe. We still don't know how much money the Anglo-Canadian Bank put in, but we do know their profits have soared since the tolls have been in operation.

'Then there was that business at the public enquiry about the subsidy paid to CalMac to maintain the Kyle to Kyleakin ferry. We showed that the ferry had produced profits regularly over the years and we also showed that the cost of collecting the fares on the ferry was a third of what they were to be on the toll bridge.

'Then we showed, through our direct action in the courts, that the legislation permitting the collection of the tolls had been shabbily drawn up and it isn't clear now, in law, if the Skye Bridge Corporation has any right to collect tolls from motorists or not. That's what's causing so much confusion in the courts when one of us has been arrested for non-payment. Some sheriffs are dismissing cases, others are fining us. The whole thing's a complete load of blether!

'Now we've got the Labour party in power and, whereas before the general election they were marching alongside us and promising to cancel the tolls if they got elected, what have they done? Nothing! Only some mealy-mouthed promises from the Secretary of State about giving islanders a reduced toll. And what will happen to that promise after the devolution referendum? The same as happens to all Labour promises.'

There was a burst of applause at this last comment, for the majority of Hamish MacLeod's audience, like himself, gave their allegiance to the Scottish National Party.

'Friends,' Hamish began again, raising his ginger eyebrows, 'I have some very important news to give you tonight, news that I wish I didn't have to but news that I must give you. Friends, we have been infiltrated these past two years by someone who was in the pay of the Anglo-Canadian Bank, someone whom I, like many of you, believed to be not only a full supporter of our cause but also a friend. But he never was. He was a traitor and we have harboured him in our midst. We have trusted him and told him our secrets and he has betrayed us. Every move we made, every scheme we planned, every idea we explored was passed straight back to the Anglo-Canadian Bank. That's why our progress has seemed so slow at times. That's why the authorities always seemed to know what we were doing.

'That traitor is now in a cell, friends. He was charged late this afternoon with the murder of that young woman, Cassie Dillon, whose body was found in Willie and Mary MacPherson's boat, *The Flodigarry*, last Monday morning. She had found out that he was in the pay of the Anglo-Canadian Bank and she paid for that knowledge with her life. The man charged with her murder, the man who befriended us and then betrayed us, is the solicitor Iain McMillan.'

There was a commotion in the audience as this information was revealed. They all knew Iain McMillan, or thought they did. He had spoken eloquently at previous meetings. He had advised many of them individually over their charges for non-payment of tolls and many had subsequently taken their other legal concerns to the firm of MacDonald and McMillan in Portree.

'Friends,' said Hamish, raising his voice over the commotion and trying to still the noise, 'this is as big a shock to me as it is to you. But it can only strengthen our resolve. Now the traitor is no longer in our midst, we can redouble our efforts. And from now on we will have the element of surprise on or side.'

At the back of the hall, two people, who were not members of S.K.A.T. and had arrived late but heard the bulk of what Hamish MacLeod had said, looked at one another. Detective Chief Inspector Tallyforth motioned to Inspector Maggie Fraser that they should leave.

'What did you make of that then?' asked Tallyforth, turning up the collar of his jacket against the cool evening air, as they stood on the tarmac outside the Community Centre.

'Brave words,' replied Maggie Fraser. 'There's a bit of me that wants to believe him, even though I have to uphold the law here in Skye. He's a different person is Hamish when he's on a platform. I've never heard him in that sort of environment. Impressive.'

Tallyforth thrust his hands deep into his jacket pockets.

'Yes, he's a good rabble rouser,' he said. 'Though I don't quite see some of those middle-aged folk waving their claymores and charging into battle to the skirl of the bagpipes, do you?'

'No,' she smiled. 'But he is impressive.'

'But he hasn't really got the whole message still, has he?' said Tallyforth, as he set off back towards the centre of the town.

'What d'you mean?' she asked, keeping pace beside him.

'Didn't you notice?' he added. 'No mention of OilCan. No mention of the fact that the Anglo-Canadian Bank owns both the Skye Bridge and Oil Canada.'

'Does he know that?' she queried.

'Oh yes, I made sure that Sergeant MacKenzie gave him the full story. I knew he was speaking to S.K.A.T. tonight. He knew alright. But he still hasn't realised the impact of all that. He's still reliving the old Bonnie Prince Charlie stuff.'

They walked on in silence for a while.

'Sir?' Maggie Fraser asked as they entered Somerled Square, now almost deserted. 'May I ask you something?'

'What?' he asked.

'There's a couple of things still puzzling me,' she said. 'How did McMillan know to use the name John Smith when he gave that film in to be developed?'

'Very clever,' he answered. 'He obviously didn't want to use his own name. And, remember, he was wearing his hair to make himself look like Orr. He'd met Hamish on the Monday night and heard about this John Smith character. It's my guess he intended to collect those photos but wanted to divert our attention on to Orr, if anyone did inquire. And it did work for a while.'

'And what about the message in the Personal column of the *West Highland Free Press*?' she continued. 'The one about the parcel being ready for collection. That had JS on it, didn't it?'

'True,' he replied. 'But I think that was McMillan too. Riding his luck. Diverting our attention again. Remember, he'd already used that John Smith persona.'

'One last thing,' she asked. 'Why did Cassie Dillon take all those photos of the Skye Bridge?'

'I guess we'll never know that,' he replied. 'My personal suspicion is that she collected the camera somewhere in Lochalsh and she was supposed to use it to photograph all those places that were marked on her map. Presumably she had been planning to persuade Willie MacPherson to call in at all of them during the cruise. Maybe she just took the photos to try the camera out. Who knows?'

She nodded and they walked on to the police station in silence.

TWENTY

It was Saturday morning in the Royal Hotel and staff were busy cleaning the lounge bar. It had been another busy night as those arriving for the Agricultural Show - sheep-shearers, stonewallers, log sawyers, the Isle of Skye Pipe Band - had been joined by the S.K.A.T. supporters from the Community Centre gathering, still agog at the news about the solicitor Iain McMillan. The bar had been full in the latter part of the evening and there had been much fevered debate about the events of the past week.

Tallyforth had packed his belongings and had been settling his bill when Dugald MacLeod, the hotel manager, had asked him to come through into the empty dining room for a cup of coffee before he left.

He was surprised to find, sitting around a table in the dining room, Hamish MacLeod, and Willie and Mary MacPherson. They smiled a welcome at him.

'Sit yourself down, Mr Tallyforth,' said Dugald, calling the young waitress over to pour coffee for the assembled group and at the same time taking a seat next to his son Hamish. 'We couldn't let you leave Portree without thanking you for what you've done this week.'

Tallyforth smiled grimly back at Dugald.

'It's my job,' he said by way of explanation. 'That's what I do. It's not what I came here to do but it's what I've ended up doing as usual. Murder has a way of finding me wherever I am.'

'Mr Tallyforth,' said Hamish MacLeod, 'I need you to know how very appreciative we are in S.K.A.T. for what you've done. It's been a terrible shock to everybody that somebody we trusted completely and whom we thought of as a friend should have been responsible for this awful murder. It's still very hard to believe. It's only a few days ago that I was here talking with him about our future plans and now....!'

Tallyforth nodded. It was interesting, he thought, that Hamish's chief concern was with the betrayal of S.K.A.T. by Iain McMillan and not with the dead woman.

'Well, Hamish,' he said, after a moment's pause in which he sipped from his coffee. 'No doubt you'll be able to fight the government and the Anglo-Canadian Bank with renewed vigour after this.'

'Won't the bank be implicated in the murder?' asked Dugald, running his fingers through his long white hair.

'Oh, they'll deny everything,' answered Tallyforth. 'They can't deny that McMillan was in considerable debt to them but they will say that he was working entirely on his own.'

'But what about all the information about S.K.A.T. that he was passing on to them?' insisted Hamish. 'Surely they can't deny that.'

'Hamish, you can rest assured that any documentary evidence linking McMillan to the Anglo-Canadian Bank or the Skye Bridge Corporation will have been shredded by now. McMillan will know that too. The success of his cover was in the fact that there were no formal links. We've found papers which show he owed the bank a great deal of money but nothing other than that. No, I'm afraid that you'll have to keep on fighting them. And good luck to you!'

He half-smiled in Hamish's direction before taking another sip of coffee.

'Mr Tallyforth,' cut in Willie MacPherson, 'I know you have to leave the island now and I know that you haven't had the holiday you were planning but Mary and me would like to invite you to come with us again. Some other time maybe. When you feel you're needing a wee break. Just give us a ring and we'll make the arrangements. We're very sorry you've not had the holiday you were wanting.'

'Willie,' said Tallyforth, turning sideways in his seat to face the two MacPhersons. 'You've nothing to reproach yourselves for. What happened wasn't in any way your fault. I'd love to do the cruise as we intended but you know my chief superintendent is insisting I get back to Birmingham.'

'Could you not come later in the summer?' persisted Mary MacPherson. 'We'll cancel other folk if you say you can. Maybe you could bring that sergeant of yours. She'd maybe enjoy a cruise as well.'

Tallyforth coughed lightly and tried not to show his feelings at this latter suggestion.

'I don't think it's very likely, Mary,' he said. 'But thanks anyway. Maybe next year. Now, if you'll excuse me, I have to be on my way. It's a long journey but I want to be back home by this evening.'

He drained his coffee cup and stood, shaking hands with all four of them.

'You'll be travelling back together with Sergeant Elliott?' queried Dugald.

'We're travelling in convoy, if that's what you mean, Dugald,' Tallyforth answered. 'Remember, we have two cars here. So, good luck to you all. We'll maybe meet again some time.'

He was followed by Dugald MacLeod to the hotel lobby where he collected his bags before shaking hands once more with the hotelier and then heading for his Range Rover in the car park.

George Elliott in her blue Renault Clio was following Tallyforth's Range Rover. They had met up at the Portree police station where they had said their farewells to Donald MacKenzie and Maggie Fraser, who had told them that Chief Inspector Gordon had rung from Inverness to congratulate her on the successful conclusion of the murder inquiry and to say that he had always had complete confidence in her ability as a police officer. Tallyforth had insisted on leading the convoy on the first part of the journey and she hadn't demurred. If it got him into a pleasanter mood, so much the better, she thought.

She turned up the volume on her car stereo system as the last of Portree's houses disappeared from her rear-view mirror and she settled in for the journey. She was playing an album which was a compilation of Van Morrison songs sung by other singers and the track on was Brian Kennedy singing *Queen of the Slipstream* - an appropriate title for herself, she thought, as she followed Tallyforth's Range Rover into a sharp bend.

She had still not forgiven him for his behaviour towards her and, although she had successfully kept her emotions under control in the concluding hours of the murder inquiry, she still, as she had confided in Maggie Fraser late the previous evening, was intending to have it out with Tallyforth.

Tallyforth, up ahead of George Elliott, was enjoying being back behind the wheel of the Range Rover again, even though the weather was sultry and the sky quite overcast, so that the tops of the Cuillins were shrouded in mist. The stereo system was playing in his car too but his choice was Runrig's *Mara* again, but the track he had been replaying again and again for the past twenty minutes was the Gaelic *Meadhan Oidche Air An Acairseid* and its insistent chorus:

> *Gealach air an acairseid*
> *Ceatharnach 'na fheileadh*
> *"Te bhan, te bhuidhe bhan"*
> *Mu meadhan oidche.*

He had forgotten what the words actually meant, except that the title translated as *Midnight on the Anchorage* and that made him think of Cassie Dillon on the deck of *The Flodigarry* the previous Sunday night, as she had leant towards him to kiss him goodnight. The rhythmic beat of the drums behind the singers was echoed by the blood beating in his heart as he thought of her. Even though he knew now that she had been not what she had claimed, that she had been in Skye on a mission for Greenpeace; even though he now realised that she had merely been flirting with him and that in reality she had still been married; even though he knew all this, he could still recall the lightness of her fingers in his, the smell of her perfume as she had leant against him. And, worse still, he could still see before him her naked body and still sense the coldness of her nipples in his mouth.

He licked his lips, as if to cleanse them of the memory, and pressed the button on his stereo system to replay *Meadhan Oidche Air An Acairseid* . His eyes were beginning to mist over with the recollections.

So, what was she to do? George Elliott asked herself. She had come all the way to Scotland on a whim, a flight of fancy, an intuitive sense that it was the right thing to do. It wasn't like her at all. She was normally deliberate, meticulous, foresightful. That was what made her such a good police officer and what made her the perfect foil to Tallyforth. So what had made her abandon all her normal behaviour?

She knew what it was. She loved him. Impossible, irritating, compulsive, bossy, as he was. And more. But she loved him. Those twelve months with him had shown her something she had never known before.

She had spent six years living with Andy, the games teacher she had met in Coventry in her first posting after she had joined the Mercian Police Force straight from Swansea University. But their relationship had foundered when he moved away for another job. Then there had been the passionate eighteen months with her colleague in the force, Roger Miles - the ambitious, hard-edged, dangerous Roger Miles, who had threatened her with a knife. It was only at that point that she had realised what he was really like.

But with Tallyforth it had been different. He was warm, he was caring, he was mature. He had made her feel wanted for herself and confident in herself as a human being not just as a copper. She knew he carried guilt for his children around with him but she had been prepared to cope with that. In one way that made him a better person, even though at times it meant she lost him as his mind was absorbed with thoughts of them.

She switched up the volume control again as the words of Van Morrison's *Crazy Love*, sung by Cassandra Wilson, echoed her thoughts:

> *Yes, he makes me righteous, he makes me whole*
> *Yes, he makes me mellow right down to my soul.*

He had let the tape run on and the number playing was *The Dancing Floor*, whose more lyrical rhythms were lightening his mood. As he listened and tapped his fingers in time to the music, his thoughts turned away from Cassie Dillon to George Elliott, whose face he could just see in the car behind through his rear-view mirror.

Had he been too hard on her? he wondered.

True, he had found it more difficult to work together with her the longer their relationship had lasted. She perhaps hadn't felt this in the same way, he mused, but he had found it almost impossible. He was constantly aware of not having the space to develop his own thoughts. She was always there, at work and at home. They were never apart and he needed that space to think. He hadn't explained it very well, he knew that, but he had had to end it all. It was driving him to distraction.

But now he could see that he had been wrong to believe that simply ending their affair was sufficient to return them to the professional relationship they had enjoyed beforehand. It was impossible to go back, he realised now. In truth, he had always known it, though he had tried to pretend otherwise during the past few days, since she had arrived in Portree to help him with his inquiries. And her help had been invaluable, even though he regretted the fact that they had had to rely, once again, on information from that gay friend of hers, Steve Anthony.

As they passed through Broadford on the way to the Skye Bridge, he thought again of the ferocity with which she had kissed him two nights ago. He could feel the flesh of her lips glued to his, her teeth grinding slightly against his, her tongue flickering in the roof of his mouth. And he wondered why he had reciprocated and why he hadn't pushed her away. Was there still some feeling there? Was there something he was denying?

No. It was impossible. It would never work.

Friday's child can't stop now
Friday's child can't stop now.

She was singing along to Lisa Stansfield's version of Van Morrison's *Friday's Child*, realising that she had made her mind up. Whatever the cost, whatever his resistance, whatever she had to do, she wanted him back. As a lover. As her lover.

And if he had some problem, as he had protested, about how this affected their professional relationship, then they would just have to work on that. She really didn't mind being subordinate to him at work. She really didn't care that he called her 'Elliott' or 'Sergeant'. She had been fooling herself to think that was important. It wasn't. What mattered was something much deeper, something much more substantial, something called love.

They could work it out.

He pulled up just before they reached the toll-booth on the Skye Bridge and waited for her to draw in behind the Range Rover in her Clio before he climbed out and walked back to her.

The sun was breaking through from the white mist overhead, just as it had done the previous day, and its warm rays were sparkling on the waves beneath the bridge. A half-torn S.K.A.T. poster blew gently from a metal post.

She wound her window down and looked up at him as he leaned over the car to speak to her, but before he could speak she turned up the volume on her stereo even louder. The Hothouse Flowers blasted out the lyric of *Bright Side of the Road*:

> *Let's enjoy it while we can*
> *Help me share my load*
> *From the dark end of the street*
> *To the bright side of the road.*

'George,' he said, 'we need to talk.'

Also by

Bob Bibby

Be a Falling Leaf

The first of the Tallyforth crime fictions is set in Tamworth, Staffordshire, the legendary home of Offa, King of Mercia. It opens with the discovery of the school inspector's dead body in the middle of a school inspection.

"A school inspector found dead on the first page! Naturally I couldn't put it down till I had found out whodunnit."

Chris Lowe, Headteacher

"… sharp insights into the sometimes painful processes of a range of late century educational initiatives."

Trevor Dickinson, School inspector

"It made me wonder why more murders aren't committed during OFSTED inspections."

Anne Barnes, Chief Examiner

"If anything can send shivers down the spines of teachers, it's when the inspector calls."

Shropshire Star

"… a journey through the tangled web of staffroom jealousies and emotional liaisons."

Raw Edge Magazine

"I enjoyed it immensely."

Pulp Publications

"Tallyforth and George are, clearly, intended to have a continuing life, and it will be interesting to see how they measure up in a different setting."

Times Educational Supplement

ISBN 0 9533196 0 1
From Pierrepoint Press,
2 Southwell, Riverside, Bridgnorth, WV16 4AS
£5.99 + £1 p&p